Year One

By Sasha DeVore

Year One
Book Three – The Genesis Key Trilogy

Summary: The City of Fire and Underground City's governments are at
odds, but even more pressing than that – the Ancient Ones have decided to
accelerate their plans. In the final installment of The Genesis Key Trilogy,
the Dissenters prepare for their final stand against the Ancient Ones. But
with civil war on the horizon in the underground, and a disturbing
prediction from the Intergalactic Council, will anyone be able to survive
Year One?

ISBN 9798773291664

[1. Fiction – Science Fiction, General. 2. Fiction – Action and
Adventure]

❧❧❧

This story is dedicated to the FACES of
Texas State University – past, present and future.

❧❧❧

Prologue:
The Beginning of the End

The Uninhabitable Zone was a very dry and dusty place. An unnatural desert that was swallowing the planet. Its miry, poisonous heat crept sleepily into the holographic jungle that surrounded Capital City, rendering whole sections of greenery gone as its projectors flickered and failed. The city started to look a bit bare because of this, having no buffer between itself and the surrounding wasteland. And along with the sick fog, a blanket of unease loomed over its citizens.

The people who lived in the housing units on the outer rungs of the city were evacuated first as their homes stared down this wall of murky gloom. Yet they clung to hope, because the Ancient Ones had anticipated this problem, and had quickly relocated to the Uninhabitable Zone to contrive a solution.

At least that's what the Council reported several days after Agrigore and his court made their hasty and unannounced procession from the District of Operations and straight into the desert. Naturally, people gathered along the street when they saw this spectacle – forty-six Convoys and twelve Nomads silently speeding their way out of the city. This was all very confusing as word of the Dissenters' protest at the District wall quickly spread. A large number of people even claimed to see drones zipping around in the thick of it all.

It was the Dissenters who had sabotaged the city's protective containment field, according to the Council. They did this, in conjunction with attacking the District of Operations, in order to carry out their most sinister of plans – to halt the celebrations at Year One. But the Ancient Ones assured the populace that they'd soon have things in their proper order. And the citizens were happy to leave the matter to the Ancient Ones, because there were just certain things they'd never be able to handle for themselves. As the Ancient Ones said, they never really knew how to manage their own disagreements, so they would have to rely on their extraterrestrial overseers' expertise in peacekeeping.

There was actually quite a lot that the citizens of Capital City never really knew – especially about the Uninhabitable Zone. Like why it had grown so uncharacteristically noxious over the years, or why the Council never bothered to rehabilitate it before. They especially didn't know that it was, in fact, the ideal conditions for the Ancient Ones, and that it was actually very much *inhabited*.

Sixty-two miles to the south, there was a canyon deep enough to hide a whole city – complete with hundreds of communal nest-homes surrounding a shiny, spired fortress. This is where the Ancient Ones now operated from, having been pushed from the District of Operations when its portal was closed.

The transition was one they would have soon made anyway. Their facilities and homes were completely functional, thanks to the hybrids who constructed them. It was only a matter of surreptitiously transporting their equipment into the new environment over the next few months. But in light of recent events, the transition had come earlier than expected. This caused them to accelerate certain plans.

And to abandon others.

Year One

Good Grief

Hanu's wooden fold-out chair protested under his weight as he slumped further into it, struggling fruitlessly against the wrath of the midmorning sun. His eyes swept the cemetery plot behind him, finding that hundreds of people had filed in since the last time he checked. A mixture of pride and sorrow and helpless apprehension filled him as he watched them find their seats. They were all similarly dressed in black garments – collared dresses, crisp robes, uniforms, slacks and buttoned-up jumpers.

Some of them wore sunglasses, which were popular among the City of Fire's citizens. Having lived in the dull glow of the caverns all their lives, they weren't used to being immersed in a sharp blanket of constant sunlight. Others wore wide-brimmed hats or visors. But the smartest of the group came early enough to pull their chairs close to the shady base of the only tree that occupied this plot of the cemetery. These people looked significantly less cooked by the sun than Hanu felt at the moment. He had chosen to wear his EAG, it being the most formal thing he had, and he was thoroughly regretting it.

He pressed his stinging eyes into the back of his sleeve, but it offered very little help. A crisp drum cadence started up from somewhere in the rear, breaking up the murmurs of hushed conversation. Vanessa, who was sitting to Hanu's left, elbowed him in an effort to get him to sit up straight, but only hurt herself in the process. She rubbed her elbow and scowled at him as if he intentionally made the suit harden on impact. Akesh, who was sitting in the row behind them, snickered louder than he probably should have, because several old women were now scowling at them.

Hanu straightened up in his seat just in time to see a number of guards marching up the narrow path that divided the sea of onlookers. These men and women wore black EAGs similar to Hanu's, except they had pins and sashes hanging around their upper parts and their collars were exaggerated. He wondered if these were the City of Fire's formal uniform.

Hanu had never been to a funeral before and, despite the incredible heaviness in his chest he was trying to ignore, he was intrigued by the procession. The guard carried very long guns with both hands, stepping purposefully in rhythm with the tune. Right behind them were four drummers – the ones responsible for the music – and behind the drummers were more soldiers, bearing an enormous casket with a black cloth draped over it. They wore no facial expression as they marched dutifully up the path, making their way to the front of the assembly where a stone dais marked their destination. Several people in the crowd had begun crying, as if the music had given them permission to do so.

It had been over a month since the attack on the City of Fire, and it was time to pay their respects to the people who were either dead or missing.

Hanu shifted uncomfortably as the place behind his eyes began to burn. Sadie, who was sitting at the end of the row, rocked back and forth, allowing silent, heavy tears to splash into her lap.

She had been very quiet over the last month, actually. Hanu could think of a number of missing people she was mourning, like Sam and Andy. And there were the dozens of people she had formed friendships with during her training and in her dormitory. Hanu never thought about what Sadie's life was like in the City of Fire, and he didn't realize until now that what had become her home – one more fitting than the Flush had ever been – was now completely gone.

The procession stopped abruptly, having made their way to the dais, and turned with a brisk pivot to face the crowd. The ones who were carrying the casket lowered it gently as a rather tall man from the front row stood to address the assembly. He waited a few uncomfortable moments, allowing the bulk of the groaning and nose-blowing to dwindle, which made it harder for Hanu to control the squeezing sensation in his chest.

He wanted to mourn for their friends, too, but doing so would mean that they were actually dead. And Hanu refused to accept that until someone had actually confirmed it with hard evidence.

The man walked around the casket, his covering trailing behind him. Hanu didn't know him, but he recognized the style of garment her was wearing. The man was an intuit – a member of the Underground City's Intelligence Division.

"We gather here, as one body, today," he said firmly, removing the cloth. Hanu could see now that it was actually a flag, bearing a golden, sideways eight; the symbol for the Resistance. The sun reflected off the casket's brilliantly silver surface. "To remember and honor our fallen loved ones in the Last Stand of the City of Fire."

A fresh wave of moans and sniffles and deep whooping wails shivered through the crowd, but he continued. "We honor the lives of the civilians who were taken before their time, and those soldiers who fell while protecting them. We remember their hearts and their deeds, which -"

Hanu forced himself to stop listening. He squeezed his eyes shut, pushing away the deep, heavy sob that had been sneaking up on him. If he crumbled now, there would be no coming back from it. He shifted uncomfortably in his seat, searching for anything that might distract him. His eyes caught a glimpse of the casket, and his stomach dropped. Etched along the silver parts of it, there were names – thousands, covering every inch of the monument.

Hanu straightened himself up in his seat, blinking hard. His heart raced. Had someone carved Tui Feng, La Feng, Anderson Nanton, or Samuel Gains into it? He tore his eyes away, unwilling to find out. Then he tried doubly to think of anything else besides his friends' memories etched into that casket.

The intuit continued his speech. "As the sun sets in the natural world, so does the sun set on this chapter in our journey toward freedom. But in it, we will find new beginnings -"

Hanu had already set himself to thinking about other things again. Like Kabo. He'd been able to trade a pair of sunglasses for a ball, and merely had to find a couple of hilts before he and Akesh could play. Then, painfully, the memory of the Kabo field being scorched intruded on his thoughts. He whimpered, then sucked in a deep breath, pushing the memory away. But it pressed in harder. The field was burning. And there was shooting. Crafts falling out of the air, with thick smokey plumes tailing them. He could recall the deep, booming sounds of the explosions that rocked Donna's hull as they retreated from the City of Fire. Hanu's gut churned. He sucked in another breath. Then his eyes popped wide open. There was a memory of another sensation. A shock of something he couldn't quite name. It came in a flash of painful cold. Icy blades peeling away his flesh. Just for a moment. Then it was gone.

Hanu hugged himself, blinking tears from his eyes. For a moment it was all he could do. Then, when he was confident the memory wouldn't be coming back, he took a deep breath and forced himself to sit up properly. His heart rate had slowed to a normal pace; he was much calmer. But he dared not probe whatever it was that snuck up on him. He scanned the row and found Ester. She offered him a sympathetic smile, but her face was so pale it would hardly be considered comforting. Dark circles lined the underside of her eyes, making her look rather skinny. What happened in the City of Fire had taken a great toll on her as well.

Hanu committed to staring off into the city, far beyond the dais. That would be all the crying he would do today. Then a silent bolt of lightning streaked across the sky, drawing his gaze. He watched its path until it disappeared behind the woods just off the cemetery plot, then waited for the sound of thunder.

It didn't come.

Hanu cocked his head, curious. Then, out of his periphery, he saw something else. Someone was making their way toward the back of the congregation rather quickly, trudging through the thicket just alongside the clearing. A double-take revealed that it was Mavis. Her baggy old face and tight lips sent a hot wave of annoyance deep into his gut. Clearly, she'd know better than to haunt the funeral service of those she worked so hard to publicly condemn these last few weeks.

From what Hanu heard, as soon as she secured Garion in prison, Mavis ordered for Arrangement to round up all of the refugees who came through the barrier after the City of Fire was destroyed. But the task proved to be near impossible, given the amount of people they would have to secure and having no facilities or training necessary to detain them.

If they did manage to round everyone up, though, what did they plan on doing with them? Hanu was disturbed at the question. He remembered when he accidentally overheard Mavis telling the highest ranks of Arrangement that she would be happy to let them be killed by the Ancient Ones as long as Underground City was safe. It filled him with a deep sense of unease to think that she probably would have ordered the refugees back outside of the barrier, if she could.

It was from that same overheard conversation that Hanu truly learned about Year One, which was nothing more than a mass extermination, disguised as a grand celebration of a *new humanity*. Which, eerily enough, wasn't a lie at all, because Hanu saw first-hand that they'd actually been quite successful in creating a new human – a human and alien hybrid – to serve them. The Ancient Ones, who had no further need for the old humanity, planned to restart time for themselves. This event also coincided with the arrival of Command. There had been much speculation on exactly who Command was, but he was absolutely certain that, whoever they were, they weren't invited to Earth.

Since the emergency migration into Underground City, war had been declared – or acknowledged, rather – by the City of Fire's Hierarchy. The Ancient Ones now knew exactly where they were located, and a number of attacks on the barriers were already confirmed. Arrangement, on the other hand, was content with ignoring this fact, and therefore made no such declarations. There was simply no reason to alarm the general population when their barrier technology would be keeping them safe.

As a result of this, Arrangement had been pretty vicious about hushing the Hierarchy's attempts to inform the public, even to the point of publicly condemning its leaders and imposing curfews and other restrictions on its citizens.

The man stopped talking now, and Hanu realized he had

opened the casket. It now looked twice as large, propped open as it was, and Hanu could see that more names were written on the inside of the heavy looking lid. Droves of people were making their way to the front, placing pictures, figurines and other small mementos into its empty compartment. Some stayed at the casket for a while, searching for the names of their loved ones through tired, puffy eyes or whispering quiet goodbyes. One woman laid at the base of the casket, wailing desperately into the cold stone, and had to be helped back to her seat by a gangly teenaged boy. Others returned to their seats quickly and quietly, and when there was an opening in the foot traffic, Sadie shuffled her way to the front.

She found a space at the head, or perhaps the foot, of the casket and grabbed on tight as if she were going to be sick. And for a moment, Hanu believed she would. Her nostrils flared as he took several deep breaths. She bit a lip, allowing her eyes to lull as they swept the monument.

Hanu prepared to run to the casket; to catch her if she passed out. He would only have to shuffle past Ester, who was the only one left in the row, crying quietly into a sleeve. But he didn't have to. Sadie suddenly started blubbering like a baby, which was even more alarming.

Under normal circumstances, she would never allow herself to be seen so indisposed. Hanu looked away, knowing she'd pummel him if she ever found out he watched, and it was lucky he couldn't hear her crying over someone behind him who was talking loudly. Their voice cut sharply through the moans of the sweaty, weary mourners, almost angrily, but Hanu couldn't exactly hear what they were saying.

Two minutes later, when he checked back in on Sadie, she had gotten herself together considerably. She was no longer bawling, and had resigned to staring pitifully into the casket. But after an appropriate amount of time had passed, Hanu realized she wasn't budging. Mostly everyone else had already sat, waiting for whatever comes next in a funeral, but she stood there, feet planted firmly in the ground, staring angrily into the casket. Hanu forced his feet toward where she was standing.

"Come on Sadie, we gotta move on." He tugged at her elbow, but found himself rooted to the spot as she suddenly clasped her arms around his neck, sobbing into his shoulder.

For a few moments he allowed her to cry, patting her head gently. He didn't know how to get her back to her seat without flat-out dragging her away from the casket, but then he had an idea. He grabbed at his waist, but quickly remembered that they weren't allowed to wear their utility belts in public. One of his tools would have been a good offering to any one of her friends. Next, his leg pocket. He struggled to get the awkward little box out, scraping his knuckles against the hard fabric of the suit. Then he shut it in her hand.

"What's this?" Sadie asked weakly.

"You know, an offering." And it seemed to be a fitting one for the occasion, being a small spoil from their battle with the Ancient Ones. Hanu gestured for her to put it in the casket.

"But what is it?" She turned it in her hand curiously. The

broken chain dangled between her fingers.

"It was a holographic cloak," Hanu explained. "Reggie and Andy invented it, but the Ancient Ones got hold of the technology and started using it for themselves. That day we closed the portal, I took it from a hybrid who tried to kill me."

"Oh," Sadie sniffed. "Are you sure you wanna..."

"I'm sure."

Then, sweeping fresh tears from her chin, she slipped the charm into the casket and allowed Hanu to steer her toward the perimeter where people were standing. They would've had to shuffle sideways toward their seats, but someone had already taken them, so they continued to the open area in the back.

This gave Hanu an opportunity to see who it was that was talking so loudly behind the congregation. Adam Lilley was standing with Mavis, overlooking the ceremony. And though he was wearing a crisp formal uniform, he looked like a disaster. Red rings tinged his eyes and his sandy hair looked to be balding at the top. This last month must have been especially terrible for him, having to represent the City of Fire in negotiations with Arrangement, on top of losing his home and people. The tactical coordinator looked as though he was trying to say very little to Mavis; he looked straight ahead as he spoke, spitting out his words as precisely as he could.

"You personally gave us consent," he said with a shaking voice.

"For the standard funeral," Mavis retorted, matching his gaze toward the casket.

Then the man who was conducting the ceremony stood up again, bringing Hanu's attention back toward the service. He could see now that Ester was sneaking her way toward where they were standing, perhaps coming to make sure Sadie was okay.

"And now as we pay tribute to those who fell," the intuit said loudly. This cued the armed guards to step forward and aim their weapons toward the sky. But Mavis rudely continued, drowning out whatever it was he was saying.

"We gave you the space and accommodations," she said, not even bothering to keep her voice down. "We even provided the casket! Do you know how long it took to create a casket this fine?"

The mourners that were within earshot craned their necks to scowl at her now, and somebody mumbled something about how itemizing was unbefitting of a leader. But she didn't seem to hear it. She didn't even notice when Adam closed his eyes as if saying a little prayer before he turned his head toward her. "And we're thankful for that," he said through pursed lips. Then his eyes popped open. "But this is *our* standard funeral."

Then, with a deafening crack, the guard fired their weapons. The blast caused several members of the congregation to jump simultaneously. A flock of birds fled a nearby tree indignantly, then there was more sobbing. Mavis scoffed, rounding on Adam. "This is barbaric!" she exclaimed.

"And may their eternal souls go to a place of peace," the intuit said, still louder, competing for the crowd's attention. He closed the lid on the casket dramatically, running a hand down the length of it before latching the locking mechanism. Then another crack of weapons fire.

Sadie was also glaring at Mavis now, who of course wasn't finished harassing Adam. "Stop this!" she yelled at him. But Adam had now placed a hand to his temple in a salute and the frustration in his face had turned to reverence. Most of the assembly followed suit. "You cease this nonsense right now. This isn't a training ground!"

"This is our way," said a dark-haired woman who had suddenly appeared from nowhere. Her fierce eyes warned Mavis.

"I think we should get out of here," Ester's voice warned in Hanu's ear. "She'll be nothing but trouble."

Then another shot came, and for a moment, it seemed that Mavis was afraid of it. She shook her head as if trying to get the sound out of her ears. Then she rounded on Adam. "You will turn these weapons in to Arrangement immediately, Mr. Lilley," she breathed. "*Your* way died when your city fell."

And just as the last word slipped out of her lips, several people were rounding on her. It took the combined efforts of Ester and Hanu to keep Sadie from jumping in on it. They each clasped desperately to an arm as she yelled profanities. A chair crashed into the aisle as its occupant jumped his way over three full rows of people, and two of Adam's comrades half-heartedly fended off a young lady who was also yelling unintelligibly.

"Let's calm down," said Adam, raising his arms in a desperate attempt to soothe the frenzied crowd. But it didn't work. Half of the funeral had now become an angry mob and the other half was crying inconsolably. Several people rushed away from the clearing to finish mourning in peace.

"You hag!" Sadie screamed into Mavis' face. Hanu tried to pull her away from the scene. The last thing they needed was for her to be put on some sort of watch list. "You ruined everything. You shouldn't even be here!"

"She just doesn't understand," Ester tried to reason with her. "You have to ignore all of this."

"Oh, I understand all right," Mavis sneered at Ester. "I understand that traitors and sympathizers have no place in Underground City."

"We've protected your precious city for *years,* Mavis," a man yelled from somewhere behind Hanu. Then a rock hurtled toward them, and thankfully he was able to duck just in time to avoid it.

"I dare you to touch me," Mavis screamed over yet another blast from the guards' weapons. Then she dusted off her jacket indignantly, searching the crowd. "These outdated customs aren't welcomed in Underground City."

"You're offending a lot of people here," Ester warned.

"Good," Mavis said. "I mean to offend."

Then all of a sudden Ester let go of Sadie's arm. And this gave Sadie the perfect opportunity to rip the sleeve straight off of Mavis' jacket. Hanu played with the idea of letting her other arm go, but the way Mavis was screeching, she was probably already looking at jail time.

"My apologies," said Adam, rushing Mavis just out of reach of several other people who also wanted a piece of her. The last bit of color in his face had gone. "These citizens will be reprimanded to the fullest extent of our laws."

"Now that just won't do," said Mavis, glowering at their angry faces. Then she stalked away, smoothing out what was left of her outfit as the last of the ceremonial shots echoed through the trees.

Agrigore's Plight

Agrigore made his way toward the innermost parts of the desert city, shuffling his taloned feet reluctantly over the bone-littered path. A dry wind flurried through the smaller feathers on his face and neck and, though it proved to be much easier to breathe in their native environment, the breeze only eased his apprehensions a little. He could not take pleasure in such things just yet, for it would still require all of his concentration – and what was left of his dignity – in order to achieve today's goal.

As he trudged through the city, trying his best to keep his back erect and proud, he noticed that his subordinates mostly left him alone. They offered no greetings or questions or attempted conversation as he passed, which he appreciated. Even the guards at the fortress, decorated in their woven kilts, made no eye contact as they removed their locks from the gateway and opened the barricade for him to enter.

Inside the fortress there were many rooms – the first of which was meant to instill humility upon the entrant. Agrigore allowed himself to be closed into the bright, sunlit hall. He turned. A silent guide, whom he made no effort to greet, waited for him on the opposite end by a slightly smaller door. Agrigore peeled off his tunic and allowed it to fall to the floor. He puffed himself up and gave his feathers a good shake. Then he crossed the room and waited at the door.

The guide studied Agrigore through dark amber eyes, clicking his beak several times. Agrigore never understood what they looked for, or how they knew it was time to continue into the next room, but he did know that there was no point in rushing it. So he conceded to reading and re-reading the inscription on the golden frame of the door. It was in the old language, and it loosely translated to: To gain the future, one must lose the self.

After a time, Agrigore's guide took a large gurgling breath and opened the door, revealing a slightly darker room. He allowed Agrigore to enter, and quietly followed.

In the center of this room was a very tall pulpit that held an open book. Light shone onto this display from an unknown source high above, and a single, high-pitched frequency permeated the room. This one was meant to renew one's loyalty and obedience to the regime. Agrigore approached it immediately and began to read. Then, having read the necessary oaths and laws in the traditional language, he was quietly admitted into the next room.

It was in this small chamber that Agrigore was to bathe, which he did quickly. His talons clacked against the smooth floor as he crossed the room to a lone porcelain basin. It was already filled with a small amount of slightly brown liquid – water and something else; perhaps mud, by the smell of it. Agrigore dipped large, clawed hands into the basin and scooped it up, then splashed it onto his face and neck. He did this several times until his attendant was satisfied. He was allowed to dry himself with a small towel before the guide robed him in a crisp, white covering. This meant that he was now worthy to enter the throne room and approach the Luminous Great.

Upon entering the dark chamber, Agrigore lowered his head, careful not to make eye contact with his superior. He stepped further in, bowing so low by the time he got to the foot of the throne he was practically looking at his own kneecaps. It was a good thing. He had a few moments more to hide the disgust and shame and regret that littered his face. It would've been Agrigore sitting on the throne had he not panicked and chosen to summon Saleel. He scanned the room from his limited vantage. Several guards – tall, majestic and alert, all wearing deep yellow tunics – were strategically placed around the throne room, each a deadly assassin if the need for protection arose.

"My Lord," Agrigore said formally.

Saleel quietly studied the back of Agrigore's neck through uncommonly green eyes. He could easily plunge his claws through the creature's exposed flesh or destroy him by a number of other satisfactory means. The Luminous Great had the power to kill almost anyone for almost any reason; this was a privilege that he foremost enjoyed. But, though he despised Agrigore's weakness, he would not be able to justify killing someone of his title. Command would not favor him if he did so.

Seconds seemed to turn into minutes as Agrigore anxiously waited for Saleel's permission to speak.

Then Saleel conceded. "Go on," he waved lazily.

Agrigore erected himself and beheld the Luminous Great. Saleel sat comfortably in a large, opulent throne atop three golden steps. His flesh was less feathered and more scaled than the average ranks, which was more evident around his stark white face. A pale yellowish light emanated from his bare chest and shoulders – a sign of his irrefutable right to rule. Agrigore had emulated this figure in his public addresses; he even went as far as forging a copy of this very throne, but its magnificence paled in comparison to the original.

"With your permission," Agrigore began carefully. "I would like to propose a few changes to your current plan, which will correct the deviations from our previous timeline."

"I shall consider," said Saleel, straightening up in his seat. "Let's hear them."

Agrigore stepped closer, slightly aggravated. He wasn't used to being the one who had to choose his words wisely. "First, we must restore the containment fields, or at least the one around Capital City," he said firmly. Saleel blinked. "Then we could set the human Council to assist with some of the more time-consuming tasks. Restoring the underground silos requires too many resources. With proper training, I believe they will be able to maintain the collider in the District while we dedicate our time to ensuring the hybrids' reproduction. This way, we will be prepared to welcome Command on schedule – or even earlier, if we desire."

Saleel clicked short, gray talons against the arm of his throne, studying Agrigore with unpredictably calm eyes. The bird-giant was, undoubtedly, considering every possible outcome. "And we are to trust these humans to build the very thing that would erase their own existence?"

Agrigore shifted uncomfortably. "A simple crisis would convince them the technology was necessary," he explained. "They will obey."

Saleel sighed deeply. "Do you hear this?" he asked one of his guards. The sentinel remained quiet, offering the Luminous Great an acknowledging blink, then returned his gaze to Agrigore. After a moment's pause, Saleel descended the throne's steps and almost walked straight through his subordinate. "There's the error in your thinking," he said, striding toward a barely visible shadow on the wall. "You're so willing to give power to these creatures... you give them a place in your plans, and therefore your priorities will always be out of order."

"My Lord, I only wish to use our current resources wisely," said Agrigore, taking a few uncertain steps. He wasn't sure if he was supposed to follow or not. But Saleel disappeared into the wall, forcing Agrigore to trail him. It was a tunnel which led to various hallways and staircases; an intricate maze. "We are able to bring about Year One only if we act precisely," he called into the hallway.

Agrigore caught up to Saleel, who was waiting just inside one of the larger rooms. It was well lit, and equipped with a number of tables, each littered with tools and bulky machinery. Three large cells lined the furthest wall, one of which contained a lone prisoner. A glass console jutted from the adjacent wall.

"Therein lies the fallacy," Saleel continued. A baleful grin pulled at the corners of his beak as he studied the terrified woman. "A functional collider and well-established settlement will mean absolutely nothing if a single underground city remains intact."

"But the hostile Dissenters have been eliminated, My Lord. Twelve cities fell in a matter of – "

"Twelve, not all." Saleel sneered, narrowing his eyes at Agrigore. "As long as a single human is alive down there, he will learn to *become* hostile. And that is where your priority should have lied."

"I dedicated more than enough resources to finding those cities," Agrigore snapped. Then he forced himself to add, "*My Lord.*" He averted his eyes and made a halfhearted effort to bow his head. "I only mean to say that our plans have been made stagnant long enough. The last of their strongholds show no signs of aggression or desire to move upon us, and besides, we cannot breach their protective shielding. We should let them live down there in fear while we dominate up here."

Saleel glared threateningly at Agrigore, his eyes flashing a hint of revulsion. "Your weaknesses have stagnated your own plans," he said, moving toward the glass console. He opened the lid and began tuning a small dial. "Bowl parties, celebrations, parades... *entertainment* programming. These creatures have become your pets, Agrigore."

"They were kept docile, compliant, through these means," Agrigore defended.

"And they will now be kept docile by the atmospheric shift. There is no need to bring any of the containment fields online – any of them." The prisoner began to whimper, hugging her knees to her chest, but neither of them paid attention. "Your focus should have been on isolating them from higher dimensional frequencies."

"You have seen the extent to which I've accomplished this," said Agrigore. "And manipulating the human genome – "

"Is ineffective," said Saleel. He finished tuning the dial on the console before speaking again. "You should have known by now that you cannot sever their subconscious ability to access those frequencies, not even with their conscious permission. You can only isolate them from the beings who counsel them in their subconscious state." Saleel watched the woman with a satisfied smirk. "You should have focused on killing each member of the Faedon."

Agrigore was at the console within three large strides. "You mustn't," he warned. "We cannot interfere with *any* branch of the Intergalactic Council; that would be considered an act of war against them."

"The Intergalactic Council are, in no way, a police force, despite their foolish ideals." Saleel sneered angrily. "We made the changes to our portal technology thousands of years ago, as they demanded. Therefore, they have no right to interfere here anymore."

"And you do not fear bringing their wrath to this planet, as Safthon did?"

Saleel seethed, glaring at Agrigore through narrowed eyes again. "My father's reign was a short one, thanks to the Intergalactic Council. I am within my own rights to retaliate, am I not?"

Agrigore wanted to protest this, but was afraid he had already overstepped his boundary. And besides, he would not change Saleel's mind. "But they do not interfere with the planet in this dimension," he said gently. "And since we cannot reach their dimensional space, we cannot touch them."

"Wrong again," Saleel said flatly. "I've studied your research. Two years ago you successfully captured three members of the Intergalactic Council – albeit, it was an accidental abduction, but you captured them in third dimensional form, nonetheless."

Agrigore blinked several times at Saleel, embarrassed at his own oversight. Then he looked away, embarrassed further still. Saleel must've also read that those beings were rescued by the Dissenters, along with dozens of other prisoners.

"I've recreated those conditions here," Saleel gestured toward the bawling woman. "And I must say, the results have exceeded my expectations."

With that, Saleel gently swiped his hand over the far end of the console, and the woman immediately began screaming. Electric filaments licked her body as she writhed on the floor in pain. As Agrigore watched, a peculiar sense of unease tugged gently at his gut. He prepared himself for the supposed arrival of a fifth dimensional being.

Then, in a confusing instant, a large, greyish something slammed against the bars from the inside of the woman's cell. Then a creature fell to the ground in a mass of singed robes and smoke. Saleel deactivated the electrical charge and allowed the creature to pull the woman to her feet.

"What is this?" The creature coughed, studying the woman's charred body. His tall form towered over hers, but his long ivory face was gentle and concerned. He shook the bars of the cell, realizing what had happened. "You cannot pull me here," he told the Ancient Ones. "You are violating the – "

Saleel didn't allow him to finish, though. He had already activated a series of controls, which forced a thick, sticky gas into the cell. The woman grabbed helplessly at the gentle being's robes as he choked to death, then she collapsed into a tired, sobbing heap.

Saleel spoke louder, boorishly drowning out the sound of her whimpering. "We will recover our original timeline after we've exterminated every one of them."

"But I don't understand how this would help us to capture the last of the cities," Agrigore said urgently.

"It would serve to cut off their help from all outside sources," Saleel said triumphantly. "The Faedon would no longer be able to help these humans to maintain the higher dimensional frequency, which powers their barrier technology, and with that, they will become vulnerable to infiltration."

Agrigore clicked his beak irritably and straightened himself as much as he safely could. He was annoyed at himself for not thinking of this before calling for help, but he would not give the Luminous Great the satisfaction of knowing this. "I understand," he said simply.

"I knew you would," Saleel smiled. Then he suddenly emitted a low guttural clicking noise. He was giving telepathic instructions to a nearby hybrid. "You will assist me this time, and then you will train the sixth division to complete the work," he said. "The ninth division will be continuing their attempts on Underground City's barriers."

Just then, two large humans wearing identical green jumpers entered the room. They wore the same malicious expression as they escorted a third, smaller person by the arms. He struggled fruitlessly against them, spitting and cursing all the while, as they systematically moved him toward the cell on the far end of the wall.

He croaked out scathing threats. "You're all going to die, even if it's the last thing I do!" he said. "The Council will hear about this. They'll expose you!"

Agrigore chuckled amusedly. Saleel swept across the room and held the cell door, preparing to slam it once they dumped the disgruntled man in. But then another voice came from somewhere within the room.

"You couldn't possibly believe that would work."

The Ancient Ones whipped around, looking for the source. The man, who had suddenly stopped struggling, saw him first – a small, oddly catfish-like creature perched atop a cluttered table on the far side of the room. He'd seen this creature before in his dreams; it was a Nergal. He wore an amiable smile behind his silvery beard as he studied one of the larger pieces of equipment.

"You trespass here," Saleel said simply.

"Funny, I was about to say the same to you."

"Yaar..." The man hung limply in the hybrids' grasp as he tried to make sense of everything. "You're real."

But Yaar ignored the man. Instead, he advanced toward Saleel, gazing pointedly into the bird-giant's eyes with a round and short finger. "Your actions will cause your swift and permanent end."

"Is this a declaration of war?" Saleel faltered slightly, stealing a glance at Agrigore.

"No."

"Then you've wasted your time coming here." Saleel recovered his composure as he moved to meet the Nergal, clicking covert instructions to his servants. Then, on cue, one of the hybrids snatched a slender tool from a nearby table top and sent a blast of bright light just behind Yaar. Saleel rushed the creature at the same time, grabbing him by the robes and flinging him toward the open cell.

Yaar slammed against the metal bars and fell to the floor. In an instant, the hybrid swept him up and attempted to secure him inside, but Yaar put up a fight. The man struggled against his hybrid captor and the woman yelled profusely as she shook the bars of her cell. Agrigore watched intently, awaiting Saleel's orders.

Yaar overturned one of the tables, distracting the hybrid just long enough to get to the woman's cell. With the flick of his wrist, the door flung open and the woman spilled out onto the floor. Saleel intervened at this point, charging the Nergal in a pale yellow flash, but Yaar disappeared into thin air.

He instantly reappeared right behind the hybrid who was holding the man captive, and placed a glowing hand at the base of his skull. The hybrid immediately fell unconscious, toppling onto the man and pinning him to the floor.

Saleel's feathers quivered as he sucked in a large breath. The pale light emanating from his chest intensified slightly, then subsided as he ejected an energy blast through his arm and out of his open palm. The blast he created smashed into the wall behind where Yaar was just standing, sending clay bits and metal shards raining down on the unconscious hybrid. The man, still pinned underneath him, screamed wildly.

Yaar hurtled toward the woman, who was now trying to escape into the empty hallway, and grabbed her by the wrist. They disappeared just in time to avoid a second blast from Saleel, and reappeared where the man was. He'd managed to pull himself free and was charging Saleel, who was preparing to fling another blast at him straight on. Agrigore was ready to intervene, moving to ambush Yaar from behind, but he was too slow. Yaar had already grabbed the man with his free hand, and a brown, spheric vessel instantly materialized around them.

Saleel slammed a claw down onto the craft, talons ready to pierce it if they could, but he quickly retracted it as if he was burned. The craft hovered for just a moment, then abruptly shot a series of brilliant green blasts straight into Agrigore's chest. This gave Saleel just enough time to regenerate his power. He aimed the largest orb of energy he could muster at the vessel, sending it crashing toward the far wall. It fizzled into quiet nothingness, leaving the Ancient Ones collapsed among the rubble.

Garion's Hold

The next several days passed uneventfully enough for everyone in Underground City. Adam detained the citizens involved in the incident just long enough after the funeral to jot down their testimonies, which he scribbled by hand on a spare bit of paper from his backpack. Then, after everyone had had their say – using very colorful language, mind you – he gathered them into a huddle and set the piece of paper on fire. "Consider this your formal reprimand," he said flatly. "Go home and lay low."

Which is exactly what Hanu did. And as far as he could tell, Mavis made no efforts to make the City of Fire's citizens pay for their behavior. Or at least, nobody had come door to door looking for them, and he didn't see any members of Arrangement out patrolling the streets. Maybe because she realized she was the one who started the whole thing, Hanu reasoned. And happy to accept his own explanation, he laced up his sneakers and balled up his bedding just well enough to stuff it into his duffel bag. Then he slipped out of the west wing bathroom at the recreation annex.

Hanu learned that this particular bathroom happened to be the least frequented place in the building, and therefore, a perfect place to sleep. The sudden arrival of thousands of refugees from the City of Fire had left Underground City with a serious shortage of just about everything, including space. Arrangement wasn't too keen on giving Hanu his old apartment back, either – not with so many families who needed to be grouped together. So he, along with many of the other refugees, resorted to just camping out wherever they could.

The recreation annex was also pretty close to Arrangement, which came in handy this brisk morning. It seemed safe enough to be seen around the government building, so he would take his chance. Today, he would visit Garion again. And no matter what, he would ask the question that had been a weight on his tongue, too heavy for him to lift from it.

He shoved his hands as far into his pockets as he could and pushed quickly through the rear exit doors of the annex. The dewy grass licked at his pant legs, soaking them little by little. But despite having a chill from the cool morning air, Hanu made no attempt to minimize the damage. He knew he would need the help once the afternoon approached and the sun was at its hottest.

The sun in Underground City didn't rise or fall, so it was a bit of a mystery to Hanu as to how these changes occurred, but he'd given up on thinking about this quite some time ago. Right now it glowed a soft orange, radiating pink and purple streaks in some places over the city, and sending a lazy reflection off the two enormous pyramids that towered in the distance.

Hanu stole one last view of the cityscape before descending

into it. It had changed so much since the last time he was here; thousands of aircraft were now grounded – stored atop buildings and alongside rooftop gardens, or fitted between houses. With this new look, the city no longer held its innocent quirkiness.

"Trading toothbrushes for cloth!" A woman yelled at Hanu as he made his way through the main road. He smiled in return, shaking his head to indicate he wasn't interested. But she persisted. "What about sunglasses?"

"Nothing today," he said over his shoulder as he squeezed past a group of people who were figuring out how best to divide a large sack of beans seven equal ways.

The main road had become somewhat of a shanty town, complete with its own market – which was just as busy as any Hanu had ever been to. Except the people who were trading here didn't laugh so much or wander about lazily, stopping for small talk or to admire a nice bit of art. The people here smiled just enough to hide the desperation in their voices when they offered you a trade.

Several people had fashioned themselves up a table, which helped organize the chaos just well enough to keep the foot traffic mostly flowing. Hanu slipped between two of these tables to cross onto an intersecting dirt road that led toward the courtyard in front of Arrangement.

Moments later, a gust of cool air greeted him as he snuck into the building. Hanu nodded politely at the receptionist and made his way toward the staircase. He cautiously climbed toward the third floor. Then, as he was about to round a corner to get to the security station, he heard an angry voice. It belonged to River. He knew it was wrong to do so, but he hung back anyway, straining to hear the argument she was having.

"The event can't be ignored," she said in an urgent tone.

Then a familiar voice came. "It can, and it will," he said. "The committee agrees, River. We won't document the Last Stand in the Living Library – "

"But it's part of our *history*," she urged. "The sacrifices those people made – "

"Shouldn't be immortalized," said the man angrily. "They were reckless, and it got them murdered. And besides, with those malcontents sucking up all of our energy to reinforce the barriers, it's a wonder our generators haven't failed already."

Hanu fought down a sudden jolt of anger. He squeezed his lips shut, allowing his anger to settle into sharp concern. Could the generators actually fail? What would it mean for Underground City? There was a pause that made Hanu draw in closer, but he dared not peek around the corner.

Then he jumped as the man continued, defeat lining his voice. "We don't have the power to finalize the disc, anyway. It'll end up being shelved soon."

Hanu squinted, trying to recognize whose voice it was. Then he remembered. It was Mr. Abbott, who was at his admission meeting when he first arrived at Underground City. He leaned in, ready to hear more, but was taken aback when River suddenly rounded the corner, almost running straight into him.

He tried to act natural, offering a smile as if he were surprised to see her. For a moment, she looked stricken, but she quickly recovered, giving Hanu a curt nod before walking off.

Hanu moved quietly toward the security station, but his mind was hard at work, digesting what he'd just overheard. He was so distracted that he didn't think to prepare the clerk as she searched his duffle bag. She had the misfortune of pulling out a large wad of Hanu's dirty underwear in the process, leaving them both smiling sheepishly at one another by the end of it. By the time she escorted him to the waiting area at the end of the hall, he could do nothing more than reassure himself that if nobody else could fix the energy problem, Salcedo would. The clerk waved faintly before leaving him in the quiet room.

Hanu had come to visit Garion exactly three times, with each visit being subjected to tighter and more stringent security. This didn't surprise him very much, though, being as Arrangement had no jails or prisoners before Garion. Therefore, it would stand to reason that they had to make things up as they went. Hanu was just glad they granted Garion visitors at all.

Moments later, a guard, distinguishable by the collared shirt he wore with a small emblem fixed to the chest, came to collect him. "Let's go," he grunted through the door, skipping the pleasantries.

Hanu shuffled his feet down the dim, quiet hall. His stomach grew heavy as he did so. It seemed like nothing good was ever at the end of a long hallway. Today, it would be a hard conversation.

Garion's cell, which was nothing more than a large metal box, was placed squarely in the center of the room, which allowed the guards three hundred-sixty degree access around him. Thick cables sprawled across the back of the box, connecting it to an energy source in the room. It looked rather eerie, as if it were made to contain a monster. And maybe it was.

He stepped into the room, hiding trepidation behind a smile. He knocked at the corner of the cell. "How're you holding up?"

Garion, who was barely distinguishable from a large pile of clothes, raised his head curiously from the floor. "Hey," he said. His voice was gritty and feeble. He smiled. "Not too bad, all things considered."

Hanu glanced over his shoulder at the guard, who was leaning into a wall, inspecting a fingernail he had just chewed down. "I've got something for you," he whispered, digging into one of the side pockets of his duffel bag. Hanu pulled out a handful of blueberry granola bars and slid them toward Garion.

"Way to go," he breathed, perking up considerably. He scooped them up and shoved one into his mouth whole before the guard could protest. "So what's new in the outside world?" he asked thickly, tearing the wrapper off a second one with his teeth.

"Oh, you know... the usual chaos."

Hanu sighed, finding a comfortable spot on the floor to sit. He leaned against the bars, recounting many of the events and rumors he'd heard in the last week, including what had happened at the funeral.

Garion, who was good and cheered up, having finished off his sixth granola bar, giggled hysterically at the part where Mavis got her jacket torn. And Hanu, who hadn't seen him this happy in a very long time, spared no detail.

"So Adam let everyone go?" Garion's eyes glimmered with scandal behind the thick bars. "He didn't do *anything?*"

"I'm sure he actually wanted to thank us," Hanu laughed. "You should've heard the stuff she was saying."

Then Garion sighed soberly. "Yeah, stress doesn't do Mavis any favors," he said. "She nearly ordered for me to be tortured last time she came to visit, even though I gave her all the information I had."

Hanu shot up on his haunches. "Do you think she would've done it?" he asked seriously. He was familiar with torture, at the hands of the Ancient Ones, and couldn't imagine that Mavis would do anything of the sort to a citizen of the Underground. But Garion wasn't a typical citizen and everyone knew it.

"I think she would have," Garion said confidently, almost in adoration. "She's intense all right, but her heart's in the right place – or at least, she has the right intentions."

"She's insane," Hanu protested in a huff, but Garion raised a finger to silence him.

"She's been protecting Underground City for forty-two years," he said. "And she's done a good job of it. But now that it's all about to blow up in her face, she doesn't know how to handle it."

Hanu played with the buttons on his jacket for a bit. The

guard had made himself comfortable in a chair that he pulled right up to the door, and was now staring at the ceiling. "So do you think it is?" Hanu whispered. "Gonna blow up in her face, I mean?"

"I think it already has," Garion laughed. "Just look at you for example – you somehow managed to leave Underground City without permission, then convince the City of Fire to go and tick off the Ancient Ones, only to come back into Underground City without permission."

"With a couple thousand friends and the Ancient Ones hot on our trail," Hanu added uncomfortably. He was starting to think he should have been the one in jail, not Garion. It was actually Garion who had wanted to be involved as little as possible, but Hanu somehow found a way to drag him right into the thick of it.

"Well," Garion said thoughtfully. "All of that from just one rogue Dissenter. Now she has to somehow keep everyone else in line, or risk more security breaches."

For a while the two of them were silent, which was perfectly fine for Garion, who naturally preferred to be alone. He spent most of his days by himself, anyway, unless you counted Donna. But Hanu was trying to figure out how he would ask what he really wanted to know.

"So, Garion..."

"Yeah, Hanu?"

"Remember that guy that was impersonating Raoul... in the District?"

"I do. What about him?"

Hanu took a rattling breath. "Well, he wasn't human... at least not all the way," he began. But then he quickly added, "And it's okay to not be all the way human, cause you can't help how you were born." He could feel Garion become rigid, and regretted not saving a few of the granola bars for this moment.

"Well, what about him?" Garion said.

And Hanu knew he would be finished with this conversation very soon, so he blurted. "He said you were a hybrid, too."

Garion scoffed coolly. "I'm sure he said a lot of crazy things."

"Yeah he did," Hanu agreed feebly. But he knew that he would have to press the issue if he really wanted to hear it for himself. And he'd have to do it fast because Garion was getting up now. Hanu stood up too, his gut churning anxiously. "Well it's true, isn't it? I saw what happened in the Uninhabitable Zone. You were just like them."

Garion focused very hard on smoothing out the sheets on his bed. He rubbed both hands over it, then pretended to be interested in a small rip on one of the edges. Hanu walked around the box to confront him from the other side of his bed. It was lucky Garion was confined to a cell, he thought. There was no way he could run away this time.

Then, after an uncomfortably long minute, Garion sighed. It was deep and pained and resigned. "Have you ever thought about how it would feel to jump into the ocean?"

"What?"

"The oceans used to be pristine, Hanu. You could jump right

in." Garion smiled into the distance, dropping down onto the cot. "You could swim with the fish. There used to be fish in those waters, you know." He chuckled to himself. "Or what about climbing an ice-cold mountain? That's a real thrill."

Hanu began shaking his head; he didn't understand. He tried to clarify. "But in the desert last month – "

Garion pulled at the ripped fabric. "I got to enjoy those parts of Earth, Hanu," he said. His face twisted. "But they were never really for me."

Hanu squeezed his face closer to the bars. His heart thumped unevenly in his chest, understanding now. He licked his lips. "You've been alive a long time, haven't you?"

"Oh, yeah," he breathed. He smiled timidly, not quite meeting Hanu's gaze. Then his face melted into a somber frown. "And now I'm the last one."

"No, you're not," Hanu said more forcefully than he meant to. But his mind was reeling with images of the hundreds of hybrids he'd seen in the Uninhabitable Zone. He knew for a fact that Garion was not the last of his kind.

"I haven't seen any other Deh around here," Garion said. He tilted his head to study Hanu. "Have you?"

"Any other *who*?"

Garion popped up from his cot, crossing the room to where Hanu was sticking his face nearly all the way through the bars. "Remember the other half of the race I told you about when we were heading to the City of Fire?" He raised a brow. "They left hybrids behind, knowing the Anuh would return."

Hanu gasped. "And you're one of those!" Then he felt a violent pang of guilt as he remembered the rude comment he made about those hybrids being nothing more than dead help. He sputtered, mortified at what he'd done. "I'm sorry... So, sorry... about all of that..."

"So am I," Garion said simply. He sighed, allowing a blanket of silence to fall over the room again.

This provided Hanu with the opportunity to think of all of the implications of it. "Then, if that's the case," Hanu said slowly. "You're meant to help us get rid of the Ancient Ones."

"And I've been such a huge help, too," Garion said sarcastically, rolling his eyes away from Hanu. He threw himself back onto his cot with a loud crunch and the guard, who had dozed off in the corner, bolted straight up in his seat. Then he grunted that they had ten minutes left and went back to staring at the ceiling.

"So why haven't you just bent the bars and escaped?" Hanu whispered, crouching lower as if that would help prevent the guard from hearing it. In all the ways Hanu planned on breaking Garion out – in case peaceful negotiations didn't work, of course – that one seemed to be the most plausible. Hanu recalled how Garion had fought off one of the Ancient Ones and came out with nothing more than a scratch. Surely he was strong enough to bend the bars and slip through. "And why didn't you stay in the City of Fire?" Hanu pressed. "They could've used your help a long time ago."

"I've tried," Garion groaned from his pillow. "Everything.

I've tried everything."

Hanu paused, eyeballing the guard cautiously. But he just might have fallen back to sleep, because his chest was rising and falling evenly again. "What do you mean?"

"I mean I've tried everything," repeated Garion. "If I try to bend the bars I get a nice shock, and besides, this cage is made from intelligent metal. It adapts every time I think of a different plan of attack." Then he sat up again and faced Hanu, who had taken a step back from the bars to avoid being shocked. "And as far as the City of Fire goes, I've tried to help them, too. I managed to screw it up every time, so I learned to stop trying."

"Someone got killed," Hanu remembered.

"It's more than that," Garion explained. "You're not the first one to learn about the portals, obviously. I found out they were keeping them open maybe fifteen years ago now."

It was easy for Hanu to forget that Garion was so old, given his boyish features, and Hanu almost started wondering what his real age was. He took note to ask about that later.

"Some kid from the City of Fire used to come out to the field with me," Garion continued. "He wanted to be a scientist, so I let him come along on some of my missions. We went to the District of Operations a few times, and he had a lot of great research ideas. But one day, he wanted to actually leave the ship to collect DNA samples from the Ancient Ones."

Garion paused to draw in a ragged breath. His eyes had grown heavy, ringed red and forlorn. Hanu leaned closer into the bars, the hairs on the back of his neck pricked ominously.

He cut his eyes toward the guard. He continued to lightly snore in the corner. Hanu nodded, urging Garion to go on.

"Of course, as soon as we got off the ship they detected us. We managed to steal a bunch of files from their database – including a partial blueprint of the technology that kept the portals open – just before they knocked me out and captured him." Garion's hand moved to the back of his head automatically, rubbing a spot behind his right ear.

"But you managed to get out alive," Hanu said.

"Donna saved me," he said. "I was already back in the City of Fire when I came to. And they weren't happy with me at all. Rumors got started, and I was eventually pushed out."

"Because they killed the boy?"

Garion swiped thick tears from his cheeks. Then he cleared his throat, but even still he could only muster a thin whisper. "Yeah," he said. Then he grimaced. "Not before they tortured him. I went back at least a dozen times, with anyone who would help – even after Arrangement ordered me not to – which is how I managed to get Beatrice Price killed – "

"Beatrice Price?" Hanu racked his brain, trying to remember where he'd heard the name before.

Garion scowled. "That would be Cherry's sister," he sighed, squeezing the bridge of his nose regretfully. "Since then, it just got worse and worse."

"So is that why people, you know..." Hanu was unsure of how to politely ask. He tried again. "That's why they treat you like they do?"

Chapter Three

"You got it," Garion said bitterly. He sniffled. "They hadn't wanted much to do with me or my research before, and they especially didn't want anything to do with me since then."

"But they have to listen to facts," Hanu argued, standing up now with a sense of urgency. "We proved you were right, Garion. And besides – with the Ancient Ones on our doorstep, we'll need your help now more than ever."

"Well, I've been getting the feeling I'm not gonna be much help from here on out," Garion sighed. "I'm tired."

"Well, you can get plenty of rest while you're here," Hanu said. But he knew that wasn't at all what Garion was talking about. He tried anyway. "Adam submitted his appeal to Arrangement last week, so you still have plenty of time to think up a new plan while we wait."

Garion forced a smile, but his face looked more drawn than it ever had. It would have to be the end of their conversation, though, because the guard jerked from his slumber and, without even looking at his watch, announced that their time was up. He dragged his chair back into the corner with a loud scrape, which gave Hanu the opportunity to lean in close.

"We'll get you out of here either way," he said. "I promise."

The Northern Woods

Hanu pushed through the double doors of Arrangement and reluctantly stepped into the brightness of the afternoon. After his time in Garion's dim, gloomy prison room, he had to give himself a little shake to alert his body that it wasn't bedtime. Then, not having anywhere in particular to be, he allowed his feet to wander up a cobbled road toward the game fields.

He did a lot of wandering lately, not only because he had no home, but because many of his usual hangouts had been overrun by other homeless people. Moira's house had become a textile mill and the wildlife preserve had to be partitioned off to provide room for crops. Even their secret swimming holes were overcrowded by people who were either doing laundry or offering to do other people's laundry for a trade.

Walking provided Hanu a chance to think about his talk with Garion, too. He quickly generated a slew of new and obvious questions, along with a healthy amount of regret for having not asked them. For instance, was Donna made of intelligent metal, too? And what were Garion's parents like? Were they like him? Or were they drones; only focused on the mission to save humanity?

These questions gave him a break from his recent obsessions.

He'd become rather preoccupied with trying to identify that strange, cold pain that seemed to randomly immobilize him. It had happened two more times since the funeral – once when he was showering, and the other as he was jogging to the market – each time whipping in sharply, then fading just as quickly, leaving him feeling horribly sick with dread. He considered maybe it wasn't a memory at all. Perhaps a side effect from interacting with the portal. The stabbing sensation along the underside of his skin felt similar to what the Lemon felt like, though. He asked Ester if there could be lasting effects from the version they gave him at Intelligence, but she assured him it wasn't the case. For now he'd settled with the theory that he'd been traumatized so many times that his body was just providing him with additional disturbances to lament.

Beyond this new and disturbing sensation, he struggled to find any kind of satisfaction for his situation as a whole. After all, he'd accomplished the thing he set out to do – he closed the portal, just like Yaar told him to – but the victory was a hollow one. In the process, they lost the City of Fire and scores of its citizens.

As a result, the Hierarchy was reduced to half its original force, which Mavis decreed was officially dismantled. And on top of it, they were no more closer to getting rid of the Ancient Ones than they were when he started.

Since then, he'd been preoccupied by a nagging restlessness. Hanu vowed to be a Dissenter; he would get rid of the Ancient Ones, no matter what. But that seemed to mean very little as

Year One drew closer each day.

The Northern Woods were becoming more distinct now. Hanu could see where the last of the tidy little cottages had given way to the tree line. Several newer dwellings had been erected there, complete with mud brick fences and ornaments decorating their barely tamed lawns. Along the row, he could see smoke rising from decently constructed chimneys. Hanu slowed to admire an elaborate etching on one of the mailboxes, but before he could get a good look, a bone chilling screech ripped through the air.

He hiked his bag higher onto his shoulder and sprinted toward the source of the sound. A quick glance overhead told him that they probably weren't being attacked by the Ancient Ones, but someone was definitely in trouble. He crossed the cobbled street and rounded a larger building, following a second scream. This one sounded clipped, as though the victim's mouth had been covered halfway through.

A moment later he found himself in a small field where a gang of raucous children gathered to watch a sword fight. Hanu sighed with relief at the sight. The older one dramatically raised his weapon, which was nothing more than a thin hilt, then brought it down in front of the younger one's face. "There, I chopped off your head," he declared. The younger boy dropped his hilt and grabbed his neck, letting out another gut-wrenching shriek.

"Your head is chopped off, Jayden," one of the onlookers protested. "You can't scream with no head!"

"Alright, who's next?" The older boy asked.

A lanky girl, who couldn't be more than ten or eleven years old, grabbed the hilt from the grass and took a firm stance. Then someone counted down from three and they began their match.

It was very entertaining. The children swung wildly at each other, crossing imaginary blades, with occasional grunts and groans to let the crowd know who was winning and who was losing.

Then Hanu moved in closer to where they were playing, having recognized the hilts they were using. He fumbled hastily through the large compartment of his duffel bag, scraping aside food wrappers that he'd forgotten to recycle, and pulled out a small mechanical ball.

"Hey where'd you get those?" he asked after the challenger pulled her sword out of the boy's chest.

"They're mine," said one of the older kids. "And you can't have them." He was probably about thirteen, and by the look of him, he was the leader. Though his shirt was terribly faded, he stuck his chest out with pride. A fancy pair of sunglasses covered half his face. He marched up to meet Hanu, stone-faced, and several of the others followed right behind him.

"Oh, I don't want them," Hanu reassured the group. "I have something *you* might want, though." He opened his hand, letting the ball rest in his open palm.

As quick as a flash, one of the younger children grabbed it. "Oh cool, can we play with it?" he squealed.

"Me first!" cried yet another, snatching the hilt from the little girl.

"That's mine, Ziggy. Let *go*!"

But then the leader grabbed the ball from the little boy, who jumped frantically to try and reclaim it. But the leader held it just out of reach. "It's rude to snatch, Ray," he said. And with a very harsh look at Ray, he offered the ball back to Hanu. "Sorry, we haven't been able to get hold of one of these yet," he explained.

Hanu waved away the apology. "Well, you have one now. Let's play."

And with that, the children scattered into confusion. The leader introduced himself as Glenn, and referred to everyone else as 'the crew,' before helping Ziggy tie his shoe.

"Go get your hilt, Sebastian," one of them yelled. "Where's the extra glove?"

"What do I do?" whined a little girl in an orange dress.

Then there was a bit of shoving as two kids fought over a hilt while a second one lay two feet away in the grass. The boy named Jayden ran across the street to see if his cousin had any extras.

"What do I *do*?" The little girl in the orange dress stomped her feet this time.

"Find a position, Camille." Glenn shoved a hilt into her hand, but the little girl just continued staring at him with a look of perplexity on her face.

"You never played Kabo before?" asked the lanky girl.

Camille shook her head.

Then there was another eruption of confusion as several children tried to explain it all at once. Ziggy was attempting to describe how the hilt used a series of magnets to affect the speed of the ball, and the lanky girl, whose name happened to be Rachael, said that the only thing that mattered was having good aim. Sebastian offered the best help, by showing her the proper form for a couple of basic moves, but then Ray wrenched the ball from Glenn's hand and threw it at her. The ball hit Camille squarely on the shoulder with a solid smack.

"Why would you do that?" Camille yelled, clasping where the ball hit. Tears were welling in her eyes as she scowled at Ray.

"We haven't calibrated the ball yet," said Glenn. Hanu rushed to help, but the leader was shooing everyone away already. "Alright everyone back off," he said. "Give her some space."

"Is she hurt?" someone asked.

Ray dropped his hilt, and with a quivering lip asked, "Is she gonna die?"

This made several of the children laugh. Jayden, who had just arrived back with two hilts, dropped them to the ground and wheezed slightly as he caught his breath.

"You don't die unless you go to war," said Rachael.

"That's not true!" said Ziggy. "My uncle died when he got real old."

Glenn laughed at this heartily, slapping Sebastian on the back.

"Okay, war and old age, obviously," Rachael agreed.

By this time, Camille had already wiped her eyes with the bottom of her dress and was swinging the hilt. "Wars don't even happen anymore," she said distractedly.

"Of course they do," Hanu said pointedly. "There's a huge war going on now."

"Yeah, right," Camille laughed. "Between who?"

"Hello?" Glenn gawked at her disbelievingly. "Between us and the Ancient Ones."

"My sister says they could infiltrate Underground City at any minute," Rachael said matter-of-factly, pulling open a small panel on the ball. Then she double checked the numbers on her hilt, making sure they matched the frequency of the ball.

"But my dad would destroy them first," Jayden bragged. "He already figured out how to destroy their war blimps."

A look of horror slowly crept over Camille's face as she drank in the information. But the other kids didn't seem to notice.

"So are your parents in the Resistance?" Hanu asked Jayden.

"Yeah, my dad is," he said, sticking his chest out. "And both of Rachael's parents, too."

Rachael nodded proudly at this. "They work together in Munitions."

"Mine are, too," said Ray.

"My big sister's gonna get me in soon," said Sebastian.

"What about you?" Glenn asked. "Are your parents part of the Resistance?"

"No," Hanu smiled sheepishly. He grabbed the ball from Rachael next, and programmed his hilt to match its frequency.

"But I guess you can say I'm part of the Resistance, myself."

"No way," said Ray, whose eyes had grown to be twice as large. His mouth hung open in awe.

Hanu blushed. "Yeah," he said coolly. "I've even gone on a couple of missions to the District of Operations."

Then the children gathered around Hanu, shoving at one another as if only the closest of them would hear the details. But Camille had the most pressing questions. "Who are the Ancient Ones?" she asked. "Are they trying to hurt us?"

"Well, yes, but we won't let them," said Hanu. He smiled reassuringly at her. He hadn't run into very many children since his return to Underground City, and he especially hadn't run into any that weren't from the City of Fire. He realized too late that she had no clue that there were suddenly so many refugees here because the Ancient Ones were destroying whole cities. "When I went into the District the first time, we rescued a lot of people that they were doing bad things to. Now those people are safe, and we'll be safe, too."

"Awesome," said Sebastian. "Rescue missions, huh? What else did you do?"

But Camille, who was quite alarmed by now, had more questions. "Are they gonna come here next?" she demanded, her voice quivering violently.

Hanu started to grow uneasy. He decided he didn't want to be the one to tell her all of this and, luckily, he didn't have to. Just then, a middle-aged woman grabbed her by the arm and swung her around.

"I've been looking all over for you, Camille," she said. Her face was morphing from fear to relief to anger. Then she dragged Camille by the arm toward their home, but Camille protested the whole time, yelling something about getting ready for an attack on Underground City. And before they were just out of earshot they could hear the mom say, "Don't go playing with those City of Fire kids again."

The whole thing didn't seem to put a damper on anyone's day, though, because as soon as they had disappeared around the corner, the children went right back to questioning Hanu about his experience in the District. Forty minutes had passed before they were able to get the game started, and by that time Hanu had become somewhat of a hero.

Glenn imitated Hanu's moves as often as he could, making sure his form was exactly the same. This was very entertaining to Hanu since he had never had actual training in this and, therefore, was making up most of it. Sebastian asked for tips on what the Resistance was looking for in a cadet, and Ray and Ziggy kept offering to hit the ball toward Hanu if he wanted it.

Rachael insisted that she was unable to pronounce his name correctly, and had to call him *Hunny* instead, which she did frequently. Then, when the sun's light began to wane, parents trickled in to collect their children until only Glenn and Hanu were left.

"You sure you don't wanna come with us to the eight o' clock market?" asked Glenn. He zipped a couple of hilts into his backpack and threw it over his shoulder.

Hanu groaned, tossing the ball into the air and catching it again. "I'm all out of rations for the next couple of days."

"That's rough, man," said Glenn.

"I'll think of something," Hanu said, grinning at Glenn. Then they parted ways, agreeing to meet there as often as they could at three o' clock.

Hanu crossed to the west side of the field lazily, deciding who he would try and convince to share food with him. Akesh was always starving as it was, and Sadie had already given him two of her rations in the last week. And last time he asked Ester, she flatly refused to help him anymore and told him to ask Vanessa.

And that would've been a good idea, except his brain went fuzzy and nonsense spewed from his mouth every time he had to talk directly to her. Then Hanu realized he was leaving without his duffel bag, so he doubled back.

The bag was right where he left it, slightly agape, with his underwear spilling out haphazardly. He shoved them deep into the bag and placed the ball on top. Then he zipped it up and slung it over his shoulder. But when he began to walk away, he got a sharp buzzing feeling; static had begun prickling at the back of his neck. Someone was watching him.

The first thing Hanu thought was that Camille's mother had come back to reprimand the children for scaring her so badly, or perhaps to clear them out. But a glance around the field told him he was alone. The row of houses that lined the cobbled road was quiet, too. Nobody was out watering their flowers or collecting their children's toys from the front yard. And the woods on the opposite end of the field were also quite still. A dull flash of lightning stretched silently across the sky to the west. Hanu rubbed his eyes, thinking maybe he was more tired than he realized.

Then there was the slightest movement in his periphery, somewhere to his left. He turned his head sharply to see that under one of the trees just ahead, a woman with short hair and rather large eyes was sitting; watching him. There was nothing extraordinary about her at first glance, except that she was wearing a very thick-looking cloak, which was never necessary in Underground City.

He offered a quick smile and continued walking back across the field, but the chill continued crackling into his back. The closer he got, the more he started to notice that she didn't seem quite human. Her skin was slightly iridescent as the sun reflected off of it, and her eyes were thin slits of a deep and luminous yellow.

Hanu's first instinct was to run, but thought better of it. The woman didn't seem to want to harm him, but might have given chase if he made sudden movements – that was what Vanessa had told him about the bears at the wildlife preserve, at least. So he continued walking as if he hadn't noticed her strangeness, all the while his skin prickled ominously. The buzz of static electricity danced through the hairs on his back as he fought the urge to look over his shoulder. He climbed the stairs out of the field.

Then, when he was what felt like a safe distance away, Hanu

stole a glance over his shoulder. And, thankfully, the woman was nowhere to be seen. He sprinted as fast as he could away from the Northern woods.

The Apprentice

Agrigore's home was a neat and orderly temple only twenty minutes ago – with smooth marble walls etched with elaborate markings, and tall openings on several sides where windows might normally be. But now, bits of statue and roughly splintered wood decorated the floor, and the silken drapes – reduced to shreds – stirred feebly in the wind like ghosts.

He shrank into the rubble, gasping for air, as the first light of day fought through the noxious desert and found its way into the open side of the shrine. It crept over the piles of what used to be furniture and remnants of days old food, then – much to his aggravation – found a piece of glass and reflected straight into his eyes. He snatched up the shard, ready to crumple it to dust, but hesitated. It was a piece of the mirror he'd commissioned over eighty years ago.

With a pained breath, he turned it in his hands, studying its ornate markings. It was a trophy that he'd rewarded himself with, to commemorate their stabilizing the portal that fed the Ancient Ones their life-giving energy. It was thus far his most celebrated achievement.

A moment later he hurled the glass at the far wall, shrieking as a fresh wave of fire crawled and prickled and radiated through his bare chest. The glass exploded into pieces and rained down over an altar; the last of his possessions that wasn't completely devastated by his tantrum. Agrigore scratched at the place on his torso where feathers used to be, sucking in air as best he could through his thin beak. The golf-ball sized hole in his chest oozed fetid puss, and though it wasn't very deep, it only managed to grow a very thin membrane across the top of it. Normally a wound like this would've healed by now; it should have been nothing more than a patch of soft new feathers. But it seemed like the more he treated himself, the worse it got.

He would have called for a medic by now, to figure out what was happening to him, but the only one who survived the closing of the portal – the only one who wasn't too old or weak to survive the atmospheric shift – had made his allegiance to Saleel very clear. And he would not allow news of his illness to be delivered so easily to his superior, lest he decided Agrigore was no longer fit for his position as second in command.

When he was able to stand again, he barreled toward the altar and proceeded to destroy it next. He spent quite some time doing this, allowing the activity to distract his body from the pain in his chest. It was only when he heard the quiet call that he stopped, mid-throw, holding what was left of a wooden frame over his head. He listened for a moment, jerking his head in all directions to hear where it was coming from – a low screech. Someone was at the property gate.

He pulled a tunic from the rubble and was down the footpath in a flash. "What do you want?" he bellowed as he snatched open the heavy door.

It was Jinora.

"My Lord, forgive the intrusion," she said, bowing her head slightly. "The transport has been waiting for you and we weren't sure if you were still – "

"No, I'm coming," Agrigore said, straightening out his tunic. "I had something to attend to, but it is now taken care of."

Then he latched the door shut behind himself and strode swiftly toward the fortress with his apprentice on his heels. In all that had been happening over the last few weeks, starting with the attack where he proved himself completely useless to Saleel, he forgot about today's assignment. And being late would only earn more ostracism from the Luminous Great.

To his dismay, a whole procession had been waiting on him in the courtyard of the desert fortress. The entire sixth division lined the walkway on both sides, and by now had begun either shifting their weight restlessly or preening their feathers. He wasted no more time, stalking down the path irritably, with the eager ranks following suit. He gave no speech or reminders, as everyone's role had already been explained. He simply boarded the first Convoy in the lineup, rubbing his chest and grumbling something about land vehicles being an embarrassment to the race.

"Make haste," he snapped at the blank-faced chauffeur, slamming the door behind himself. And when the rest of the division were loaded in and all of the doors were secured, they sped into the void, toward Capital City.

Chapter Five

Agrigore settled himself as best he could into his seat, hoping he would be able to withstand another of the fits. He was grateful to have the next few minutes alone, at least. He forced himself to calm, to summon the grace and quiet confidence that was befitting a strong leader. The bird-giant focused his attention through the window. He admired the warm, lazy desert that was their new home. It was peaceful – nowhere near the chaotic space he was born into – and quiet and lonely though it was, those were the qualities the Ancient Ones enjoyed; a sign of total domination over their habitat. He had accomplished a great thing.

Capital City appeared seemingly out of nowhere. A series of clicks told Agrigore that the hybrid was converting the propulsion system to interface with the magnetic strip. This would lead them through the winding streets and directly into the tunnel at the entrance to the District of Operations.

Breathing proved to be just a bit harder than it was only ten minutes ago. They had now left the thick, nutritious environment of the Uninhabitable Zone and everyone in his procession would labor to breathe, move and even speak. But Agrigore knew he was especially disadvantaged. He would have to use all of his strength and cunning to keep up appearances, though he wasn't sure it would be enough.

When the vehicle was parked inside the District of Operations, he pushed open the door and was immediately rushed by the eager staff, whom he ignored as diplomatically as he could.

"Agrigore, sir, I'm so happy you're back," said a gaunt faced administrator. "I'll need your approval for the last two food safety inspections – "

"Lord, we need your feedback on that proposed screening process right away – "

"How much longer will it take to re-establish – "

It was easier to navigate through the frenzied welcoming party than Agrigore anticipated, being as he was almost twice their size. He lumbered straight through them, forcing the desperate humans to redirect their questions to the subsequent members of his escort.

When he reached the main hall of the palace, he stopped just along the foot of the grand staircase that led to the upper levels of the tower. His ranks filed in cleanly behind him, according to their division, and prompt awaited orders. The humans hung back, their questions waning as they realized the Ancient Ones would not be helping at the moment. Agrigore turned on his heels, climbing the staircase, and began doling out instructions to the division. "Xananda, you will oversee the decompilation of the cyclotron, and Tameus will ensure the fissile materials are properly stored for transport."

His obliging counterparts filed onto the appropriate floors, taking their necessary teams with them. Then the remaining ranks climbed further into the tower in resolute silence. This was Agrigore's team, who would be extracting the collider from its position in the belfry at the very top of the tower.

Halfway up the winding staircase, though, he faltered. For

one panic-stricken moment Agrigore paused, clutching the doorframe leading to the old nursery. A spike of hot, prickly flames jabbed his chest just enough to remind him of his secret, but not enough to incapacitate him. Not yet, at least.

"Is something wrong, Lord?" asked Jinora in her now wispy voice.

"Absolutely not," Agrigore breathed, quickly recovering his composure. He feigned a squint through the glass of the door and into the abandoned corridor, hoping to divert everyone's attention from him. "Are we sure no humans have invaded this space?"

"They were given strict orders to continue to abstain from this section of the palace," Jinora replied.

"But were those orders enforced?"

Several of the Ancient Ones stepped cautiously into the hall, taking the bait. They surveyed the darkness for signs of intrusion. And this was all Agrigore needed.

"You four will survey the tower for intruders or any evidence of the sort," he ordered. "Jinora, Hikoru and Magorium – you will go and interrogate the Council."

"But Lord, we have our assignment – "

"I will complete the assignment," Agrigore said, concealing the slightest wince. "It is a simple task."

Jinora inspected her mentor dubiously. "Are you feeling ill, My Lord?"

Agrigore suppressed an urge to lash out at her. "I am well, thank you," he growled, quite in control of his body now. "But

I would be a great deal better if my subordinates obeyed my orders the first time."

At this, the ranks turned on their heels and hastily proceeded to their new missions. But Agrigore grabbed Jinora by the arm, just a little harder than he meant to, and pulled her back. "You will interrogate the Council covertly; without their knowing," he added. "And concede to their political needs. You will give the approvals they seek in my stead."

"We no longer have to maintain this facade," Jinora protested. "Why waste the time?"

Agrigore matched her gaze. He could sense that she was concerned, and maybe confused by his actions. And he could hardly be angry with her, because he immediately regretted the order, himself, as soon as he gave it. He had no idea why he would tell her to do that; he wouldn't normally bother with diplomacy if he didn't have to. But he couldn't retract it now. That would only further prove that he was losing his ability to command.

"It will preserve our ability to come and go as we please," he reasoned. "In case we need further cooperation, materials or labor from them."

Jinora bowed swiftly and proceeded back down the stairs, seemingly satisfied with his answer.

For a moment Agrigore rested against the wall, relieved to have survived the interchange relatively unexposed. Softer flames licked at his chest, an aftershock that threatened him. He allowed himself a stifled groan, pulling at his tunic to expose his own flesh. It was so hot he could almost see the warmth radiating into the darkness of the stairwell. He pressed himself faster now. He knew the next wave was coming, and that he wouldn't do well to be stricken on the staircase.

Moments later, he threw himself onto the floor of the belfry. He was certain he couldn't be heard, but he knew he would have to keep his wits about him. He would risk more than exposure if he went tumbling off of the platform, or worse, if he accidentally destroyed the collider. He sucked in as much of the thin air as he could, and found that it was slightly helpful.

Then he willed himself to control his own pain, channeling the worst of it as best he could by squeezing the large copper bell that was mounted to the ceiling with both hands. He was able to stabilize himself rather well by doing this. The wave came, just as he expected. It tore through his chest, blazing a tender, burning trail through his arms and down his lower back, forcing him to draw his hips in tightly. He clawed silently at the hard surface of the bell, then squeezed until the pain of his arms out-protested the pain of the rest of him. And when the wave of pain subsided, he straightened out his tunic, gasping and coughing and clicking his beak. Then he shook his feathers back into place and examined the bell. It was only slightly dented on either side. He had survived the encounter, and left very little evidence of it.

Agrigore found the collider placed surreptitiously at the edge of the platform, looking innocently over Capital City. This was the detonation point where, once complete, the nuclear bomb would create a spatial fissure large enough to allow their mothership and her fleet passage into this dimensional space. Agrigore turned his attention to the device now, inspecting its intricate design. The front panel lay on the ground, right where they'd left it, and a series of chambers within chambers were exposed.

He collected the myriad of stray parts, then dumped them unceremoniously into the compartment. After this was complete, he grabbed it by the handle on top and carried it down the steps and back through the main hall to where the vehicles were parked. His chauffeur dutifully opened the trunk on his arrival, allowing Agrigore to slip the thing into the back of the Convoy just as inconspicuously as he intended to. He thought about returning to the Uninhabitable Zone, having completed his portion of the mission, but was interrupted before he could properly consider the option.

"My Lord, are you leaving so soon?"

Agrigore turned on the spot to see Aric. The councilman bowed deeply, then crossed his arms behind his back and sauntered down the staircase that led from the entryway of the palace to the street. Clearly the absence of the Ancient Ones had no ill effects on his pompous demeanor.

"We will remain for a short while," Agrigore said, crossing the road to meet him at the landing. He led the councilman back up the stairs and into the main hall of the palace, just in case they started loading in the other parts of the laboratory that he preferred to be kept secret. "Have you spoken with Jinora yet?"

"I have, sir. She was quite pleased to find that we kept things running smoothly in your absence."

Agrigore could see that Tameus' team was now descending the stairs, carrying large briefcases. This is where they housed the small canisters of volatile materials. "Excellent, he said, pulling Aric's attention away from the staircase. "Three months is a long time. Have there been any more Dissenters making trouble in the streets?"

"Not a one," Aric reported proudly. A dimple danced at one of his cheeks. "Sir, I believe we've actually gotten a leg up on that issue. Listen to this – "

The councilman paused at Jinora's voice. She approached from the main hall with several other council members in tow. "I will report your findings to Lord Agrigore," she said firmly. It was apparent that she had finished her interrogations, but the council members weren't finished with theirs. They buzzed around her in a frenzy of questions.

"We'll need signatures for the twelve patients awaiting override," said a flustered woman, rifling through a briefcase full of documents. Her browband swayed dangerously as she dipped her head further into the bag.

"After that, I'll need to inform you of the recent malfunction in the detection networks in the northern region," chimed another of the councilmen. "Could be a flaw in the automation sequencer, perhaps."

Jinora ignored them, though. She simply strode up to Agrigore and gave him a small curtsy. "I trust our work here is done," she said meaningfully.

"It is."

"Then we must get back to work in the Uninhabitable Zone, My Lord."

Then Aric piped in cheerfully. "Yes, Agrigore, Jinora has explained to me that you will now be rehabilitating the entire Uninhabitable Zone in time for Year One!"

"Absolutely," said Agrigore. "In as little as three months, it'll be populated again."

Aric clapped his hands together. "Now that's something to celebrate."

"But, Lords," said the woman. "Is there something we can do in the meantime to stop the radiation from seeping any further into the city? It's completely crippled the Residential District."

"Unfortunately, there is no solution yet," said Jinora, who had begun to walk toward the exit.

But she stopped when Agrigore didn't follow. He hesitated, watching the expectant faces of the human Council members. Their wholehearted trust in the Ancient Ones was rather sickening to witness. But not because he despised them or had any other kind of ill hearted feelings, but because he realized Saleel was right. These people had become pets – patiently awaiting the return of their masters, and desperately seeking their approval and guidance. But somehow, he couldn't bring himself to abandon them, at least not so rudely.

He took a small stride closer to the woman. "You will find

three hundred and twenty-six emitters surrounding the city," he instructed. "They are similar to the holographic projectors, but these will be small and round. Find them, and manually reboot the internal systems. From there, it's a matter of manipulating the particle density of the field. That may knock the atmospheric resonance slightly out of phase and create a force field that will separate the atmospheres of the city and the Uninhabitable Zone."

When the Council had all finished scribbling their notes, they quickly thanked Agrigore and fled to their different departments, racing to implement the new plan, undoubtedly. Jinora turned around sharply and stalked toward the door.

Agrigore adjusted his tunic, running a taloned hand gingerly over his chest. He had nothing to do now but figure out how he would justify what he'd just done when Saleel came asking. Any action could be explained away, after all, as long as the justification was decently sound and delivered with conviction. Agrigore made his way toward the exit and let himself into his Convoy.

But the vehicle wasn't empty. Jinora was waiting in one of the seats, arms folded crisply in her lap and solemn-faced. Agrigore chose the seat right across from her, setting himself gracefully into the seat with a steeled composure. He fixed a relaxed gaze straight into Jinora's eyes. He had nothing to explain to his subordinate, and would not be made to feel shame.

"Take us home," he ordered the hybrid. He immediately

obliged, pulling the vehicle onto the magnetic strip. For a while they rode in a silent impasse. Until Jinora broke the silence.

"May I speak candidly?" she asked.

"You may," said Agrigore. He silently reaffirmed that he owed nothing to her, but would merely entertain whatever she had to say. He was careful not to withdraw his gaze first. To do so would be a sign of weakness, or even guilt.

Jinora drew a contrived breath, as if buying herself additional time to decide how to proceed. "I am increasingly concerned about your actions lately," she said. "I would not know how to report if Saleel were to question me –"

"Are you planning to make a report?"

"Absolutely not, My Lord. But I cannot force others to abstain from doing so." At this Jinora bowed slightly, breaking her gaze to look at her own feet.

Agrigore rattled the feathers on his neck slightly as he made himself more comfortable in his seat. "And what might Saleel have need to investigate?" he asked.

"Understand first, Lord, that I have been by your side for seventy-six years and my allegiance is to you," Jinora began. "You have taught me a great deal about rulership, conquest... logical and objective reasoning. I would not be a reliable apprentice if I failed to address my concerns about your recent judgments."

"And your qualms are what?" Agrigore forced himself to suck in air slowly and evenly; he hadn't realized he was holding his breath.

"For one, you've holed yourself up in your compound for weeks," she said. "Nobody has access to you anymore."

"I am no longer the sole ruler of the regime," Agrigore said coolly. "I can afford to take time to myself."

"But, My Lord, surely you know this sudden absence could be misinterpreted."

"I'm sure it could," Agrigore said simply. He watched through his window as a man changed the marquee outside of his casino in the Entertainment District. "For two...?"

"For two," said Jinora cautiously. "You defied the wishes of the Luminous Great just now when you told the humans how to fix the containment field."

"I defied his wishes, yes. But he never gave a direct order to withhold the information."

"I understand, My Lord, but why are you going to such great lengths to comfort them?"

"What is the harm in conceding to their meaningless desires?" Agrigore hoped to wave away the grievance, but she pressed it.

"Sir, I'm afraid your decisions aren't as logical as they used to be," she explained. "Think about it – these humans will no longer exist in a couple of months. What's the difference if they suffer before their extinction? Why risk Saleel's wrath?"

Agrigore made it a point to ignore her question. Instead, he looked out of the window, watching the transition back into the desert. Neat streets turned into cracked, rocky soil and thirsty weeds clustered together for protection against the sun.

"Remind me, Jinora. Why have we come here?"

"What do you mean, Lord? We've collected the collider and now – "

"No, why have we come to Earth – to this planet of all the others?"

"Earth?" said Jinora uncertainly. "Well, because it was an easy candidate for requisition. The humans are docile, trusting, easy to manipulate." She gave a small nod toward the window. "The environment is suitable enough for terraforming."

"Has it been all that easy, though?" Agrigore asked pensively. "Could we not simply find a world in our own dimensional space to transform?"

"We should never have fallen into that dimensional sphere," she said. "We deserve to reclaim our former glory, which we can only achieve with decisive action, by taking our destiny into our own hands."

"Oh?" Agrigore tore his eyes from the window and fixed them on his apprentice. "Will we achieve that glory by acting as thieves, liars and murderers?"

Jinora adjusted in her seat, the muscles in her jaw bunched and her eyes narrowed. "With all due respect, My Lord, those are *human* morals. You couldn't possibly – "

"Couldn't possibly believe that nonsense?" Agrigore laughed, forcing an exaggerated grin. Then he snorted a short breath, straightening himself up and clicking his beak seriously. "No, of course not," he said coldly. "But I wonder if you think I've begun to."

"Absolutely not," said Jinora, offering a tepid laugh. "I only wanted to express my concern of what others might think."

For an impossibly uncomfortable minute, Agrigore watched his apprentice. The air in the cabin grew thick with the desert air. He considered helping her to forget her worries. It would only take the subtlest intrusion on her mind, just like he and his command had been doing to the humans for so long. It would be easy to do with the help of the neural network that thrived in their atmosphere. He focused intently on the thought – *Agrigore is well, and his judgement is sound and resolute.* He breathed evenly, growing the thought in his mind until it was almost heavy enough to press down on his eyelids. But he couldn't blink; it was best to maintain eye contact.

The hard part, though, would be hiding the distinct shimmer that would emit from his forehead at the moment he implanted the thought. Humans could not perceive it due to their biological makeup, but his kind knew very well of this technique, and the ranks of his command were especially well practiced in blocking this type of intrusion. But just then, another thought flashed in his mind, making him stop his plan short.

"The truth is, I have an ulterior motive, myself," Agrigore said, opting to restore his apprentice's faith through less risky means. "I have decided to set a plan into motion that requires that these humans remain alive and loyal just long enough to serve us one last time."

"I see," Jinora breathed. "I knew there had to be an excellent explanation."

"Of course there was," Agrigore glowered, allowing himself to look as insulted as possible. "You see, the humans will be helping us to bring about the Intergalactic Council's total annihilation."

The Special Unit

Mr. Salcedo's farm had become somewhat of a safe house for the Resistance. Its members were able to convene there, under the protection of several barriers – all constructed by Mr. Salcedo, himself. And because of this, the house had become probably the busiest place in the Underground. Teams were constantly arriving under the pretense of collecting food for transport to their local market or to fulfill food rations. Then, once inside, they would make their reports or receive new missions. Some of them stayed for days at a time, building strategies or taking part in what they called 'think tanks.'

This was all quite exhilarating to Hanu, seeing the harried faces of the soldiers as they brought news to the Hierarchy. Sometimes there'd be hushed meetings in the hallways between small clusters of people, and occasionally someone would run out of a spare room with a loud, "I figured it out!" It was like being in the City of Fire again, except the distinct lack of privilege.

Since their arrival in Underground City, Hanu had become less of an informant, having no more information than they did on the settlement in the Uninhabitable Zone, and more of a liability. Which is why he wasn't allowed in any of the meetings, and was promptly shooed away when he was caught trying to eavesdrop. The last time, when he was discovered pressing his ear up against a door, he was asked to leave the house by a stern looking captain he'd never met before. Which is why he made sure to not even look like he was eavesdropping this time, or doing anything that might cause him to be removed again. Two days had passed since he saw the mysterious woman, and he preferred to not be alone in case she was interested in following him.

And, with very little else to do, Hanu found himself on a couch in the conservatory on this particular afternoon. The sun peeked through grey clouds occasionally, warming his face through the windows and lulling him into a deep slumber. He rarely slept well enough to dream lately, but today was an exception.

He found himself drawn sharply into a large room. A wide window in front of him revealed some sort of stellar phenomena. Three ghostly pillars illuminated the inky cosmos with a greenish glow, and distant stars winked whimsically at him. Though the nebula was quite large, Hanu got the feeling it was actually very far away.

He ran a hand across the window pane, allowing an expecting smile to stretch across his face. Then he turned and was shocked to find that it wasn't Yaar behind him. His stomach fluttered, then swelled with nervous intrigue as his brain was able to process what his eyes were seeing. There was a great variety of different beings standing around a long and narrow table. It was dizzying to take in the sight of them.

"You are Hanu Manel," said a peculiar individual.

Hanu thought it could have been a woman, by the look of its beautifully large eyes and strikingly silver hair that flowed from a ponytail. But it wore no shirt, baring blue-silver skin, and Hanu could clearly see that there was no further evidence of femininity.

He took an unsure step toward the table. This wasn't the first time he'd accidentally happened upon a conference. Only this time, it seemed like they expected him to be there.

"I am," he said faintly.

He was too distracted by his own fascination to give proper effort in the conversation. His eyes fell on a rather large being that towered over the rest. His prominent brow bone and brawny physique were the first things Hanu noticed. The being smiled delightfully and gave him a small nod.

"I am Thalor," said the first one. He took a step forward and offered a small bow. "And the Intergalactic Council wishes you well." He extended a sweeping hand, indicating his counterparts.

"Thanks," Hanu said.

His eyes swept the table and fell on a very slender woman who appeared to be mostly made of smoke; her edges seemed to taper into nothingness. He'd seen this being before, in the Tome of the Earth.

Thalor's face firmed with an air of urgency. "We must deliver news with expedience," he said. "We've been summoning as many humans as possible to inform you of our new developments."

"I see," said Hanu. He raised his brows expectantly. "Thank you. And, uh... what are the developments?"

Thalor took an even breath. Then he dipped his chin to get a better look at Hanu. "We've been informed that it is now time to withdraw our members who have been volunteering on Earth. Your Faedon will no longer be allowed to assist in this conflict."

A streak of nausea ripped violently through Hanu's stomach. He sputtered. "Wh... why not?"

"Not because we want to," Thalor clarified. "And this is in no way a reflection of our faith in you. But our destiny has shifted, and we have fulfilled the amount of assistance we can offer your people as you journey toward sovereignty. Further action on our part will result in both our detriment."

Gravity shifted, but not because of anything the ship had done. Shock had caused Hanu's knees to buckle, his head to swim. He stumbled back, finding the ledge of the window to steady himself. Then he struggled to suppress a sudden flash of heat that coiled in his stomach. The alien studied him closely through unblinking eyes.

"You're afraid," he said.

"And angry," said a very old and brown little creature.

Hanu searched the room, but the small consolation was lost as he realized the Nergal wasn't Yaar. It was somebody he had seen before, though. She limped around the table, which had been far too tall to suit her. Old and beardless, she wore a tight lipped expression. It was the oldest of the Nergal.

"I know you," Hanu said. He steadied his legs under him. It was difficult to do, as this was the least helpful Nergal that could have shown up for him at the moment. She never possessed the warmth of Yaar or the quirky candor of some of the others. He racked his brain to retrieve her name. "You're... Meni, right?"

She gave a slight nod. Her eyes were dull, drooped under several sets of wrinkles. "You have felt nothing but frustration with us as of late. That we have allowed you to remain one step behind."

"Those are his *personal* feelings," said the smoky woman. She tilted her head at the Nergal, making the edges of her essence wave and flicker like a flame. "They're not for you to share."

Thalor leaned in just a little so as to make proper eye contact with Hanu. "And that proves we have exhausted our ability to help here," he said.

Meni pursed her lips together.

Hanu shook his head. He furrowed his brow, silently agreeing with the smoky woman. But defending the privacy of his feelings would have to wait. That wasn't the most pressing concern at the moment.

Thalor continued, gesturing toward the ship as a whole with a broad motion from his arm. "Understand, Hanu, that the Provenience is not your savior," he said. His face bunched up in an unflattering scowl. "We are not your gods, or keepers. And it is entirely our fault that we've allowed you to fancy us as such."

"I never thought you were gods or anything like that," Hanu protested. Then he scoffed. "But you're obviously more advanced than us, so what's the harm in helping us end the war?"

"The Faedon were created to help you see your own potential – not favor ours," said Thalor. Then he smiled in a fiercely apologetic way, nodding toward his counterparts. "We're merely a federation of scientists and environmentalists. We never intended to be known by your world in the first place. But our destinies became intertwined when we meddled with Earth's affairs long ago, and now our duty to one another is over."

Hanu sputtered, trying to understand. "But you're here now. And you could still –"

"We could do no more," said the old Nergal. Her face twisted with a shadow of contempt. She spit her words out with deadly precision. "*Yaar* has done quite enough for you already, and his actions have affected us all. If nothing else, Hanu, find satisfaction in knowing he went as far as committing such a cruel act against you in the name of doing more."

An explosion of anger and indignation and steep confusion muddled Hanu's words. "That doesn't make any... What does that even... Yaar's the only one who's even bothered to –" He threw his hands up stubbornly, but was interrupted before he could formulate a proper response.

Thalor raised his voice. "Our infractions are not to be blamed on any human," he said, hushing the two. He paused for quite a bit of time, blinking leisurely at Hanu, until the boy crossed his arms in silent resignation and pinched his lips together. "Our only task on the Provenience had been to maintain the dimensional stability across the sector of galaxies that lie within our jurisdiction – to ensure that no civilization threatens the natural order of the cosmos. We will resume that task now."

Hanu shook his head, allowing his shoulders to drop pitifully. "But the Ancient Ones *are* threatening the natural order," he said, almost in a whisper. "They're killing off a whole civilization down there. You're not gonna stop that?"

Thalor shook his head. "It is deeply unfortunate, but overall inconsequential to the integrity of the fabric of this reality," he said. Hanu sucked in a sharp breath, ready to argue, but Thalor's sympathetic eyes silenced him. Then his face was suddenly serious. "Your species is a precious one," he said. "Earth's timelines have converged, and now there are no more options. Year One is going to happen, and there is absolutely nothing you can do to stop it. You must only think about the manner in which you wish to experience it."

The air was knocked from Hanu's lungs. He gasped a shallow breath, shaking his head fervently now. "You're lying."

Thalor spoke more urgently. "You are a species worth saving, Hanu. But you have to *be* worth saving. You can save yourselves."

Hanu massaged his forehead irritably. "Hold on," he said. "So we're worth saving, but you're not gonna save us? Why did you even bother bringing me here?" He paced the room, trying to suppress the insults that were forcing their way to the forefront of his mind. "Where's Yaar?" he blurted, searching the room.

Meni shook her head sharply. "He can no longer visit you. He will not be coming back to Earth."

"Why?" Hanu desperately searched the length of the table, but only saw apologetic faces – none of which would be any help. He scanned the walls, but found that there were no doors. It didn't come as a surprise. If they wanted him to have access to the rest of the ship, one of them would create a door.

Then, for just a moment, he and the Nergal locked eyes. She had been holding out a clenched fist. Hanu watched it expectantly, thinking she would reveal something, but then he realized what she was trying to say. She slowly opened it. "Do not underestimate your own power," she said. She straightened herself to her full height. Her eyes softened ever so slightly. "Yaar must carry out his new destiny now." She drew in a deep breath and gave Hanu a little nod. "He behaved as a fool. But his lessons were sound, and you must never forget them. Be open to new perspectives. Be willing to trust your choices."

Thalor placed his hands on Hanu's shoulders. He squeezed them, turning Hanu on the spot until he could see his own reflection in the window. His face was drawn and pale; gaunt.

Thalor offered a small smile. He leaned in. "Yaar told you how to fight," he said. "Nothing has changed. Humanity will use its new dimensional energy. It is humanity's choice."

Chapter Six

〴〵 〴〵 〴〵

Hanu woke with a start, and realized that someone had fallen through the front door in a puddle of blood. It was a young woman, maybe in her late twenties, wearing large, panic-stricken eyes and a gushing hole in the shoulder of her EAG. He jumped from the couch in a flash, dizzy and disconcerted, but quickly made himself useful. First he tried to lift her, wrapping her good arm around his shoulders, but she only winced and groaned, and fell back to the floor. The smell of her blood pushed the memory of the dream to the back of his mind.

"Help!" Hanu cried as he adjusted her. He tried to untangle the mesh from around her ankles. It looked as though she may have leaned against the screen door while trying to open it and toppled straight through.

"Candace!" she called feebly. She wrapped a bloodied hand around Hanu's wrist. "The medic. Go get her."

Hanu could hear footsteps coming down the stairs. It was a rather burly man. "She's not here," he said. "Help me move her." And before Hanu realized that the man was talking to him, he was already picking up the woman's upper part.

Hanu grabbed her legs and apologized as she screamed in pain. Then they steered her to one of the spare rooms where they were met by several other soldiers. Someone swiped the contents of a large table onto the floor and they laid her across it.

"What happened?" asked the burly man.

"It was the biggest... Ancient One I've ever .. see.. seen."

A man with a ponytail on the very top of his head unzipped her suit and calmly peeled it off. "Brandy, did you finish the job?" he asked coolly while inspecting the wound.

"I d... did," she said. Her face had gone pale and her teeth were chattering. "They didn't know what I was... th... there for."

Then the man turned to Hanu. "Find a vein," he said. Then he stuck a gloved finger into the wound. Hanu grimaced as she screamed again. The man didn't slow, though. Next he ordered another soldier to go and find *O negative.*

Hanu looked around, bewildered. Then he realized that they were going to inject her with something, because the burly man pulled out a needle and began filling it with medicine from a vial. Hanu extended the woman's arm and began pressing on the soft part of her wrist. He had no idea what he was doing, but he didn't have to say so because the man was already pushing him out of the way. "Take off her shoes," he barked. "Elevate the feet."

Hanu walked around the table and yanked off her boots, one at a time. They hit the floor with loud thuds. Then he peeled off her sweaty socks. But there was nothing he could immediately see that would effectively prop them up. Hanu scanned the room for a moment and saw a bookshelf lined with encyclopedias. Perfect. He grabbed the thickest volumes he could, and dropped them onto the table. Then he hoisted her legs on top of them; her flesh was stone cold, and surprisingly heavy.

"I c... copied everything using th... encryption co...," Brandy slurred. Hanu adjusted the books so that they were in a neat stack, but mainly he wanted to hear what she had to report. He moved as slowly as time would allow. The burly man injected her with a familiar yellow liquid, then inserted a catheter into the spot where he poked. "A.I. sub... subroutines... and overwrite protocols – all in the sh... ship."

And with that, two people darted from the room.

"And did you use the alternating encryption sequence?" the ponytailed man asked. Brandy nodded. Then she grimaced and looked as though she would be sick – a symptom of the lemon that Hanu recognized all too well.

"Good, honey," he said. And he closed his eyes for a moment, breathing a sigh of relief. Just then, the soldier came back with five bags of blood. "Listen, Brandy, you need a blood transfusion," the man explained. "Don't you worry about anything else, okay?"

Brandy allowed her head to relax into the table as the burly man attached the first bag to her IV. The ponytailed man stroked her forehead, sweeping her bangs out of her eyes. "You did it, girl."

Hanu stopped pretending to secure Brandy's feet somewhere around the third bag of blood. She had warmed considerably by then and her wound was already salved and bandaged. She was now ordered to rest, which meant that she wouldn't be divulging any more secrets. So, he slunk away quietly after being thanked, grateful that he wasn't spotted by any of the higher-ups.

Moments later, he slipped into a washroom to clean the dried blood from his arms and neck, then he changed into one of his cleaner shirts. And when he was sufficiently freshened up, he allowed himself to collapse onto the toilet, exhausted and afraid. For a while, he only held his face in his palms. He would have to sort out his dream and what happened with Brandy separately, and he didn't know where to begin.

He rolled the information around in his mind, then decided the most pressing thing would probably be that Year One was, indeed, coming. Hanu's stomach grew uncomfortably tight, and it was suddenly hard to breathe in the tiny bathroom. On top of that, the Intergalactic Council was no longer going to be helping Earth. It wasn't as though they offered any real help, in Hanu's opinion, but he was smart enough to know that their withdrawing from the planet would change the dynamic of things for the worse. Whatever they've seen coming must be pretty bad in order to leave after all of this time, regardless of if they were just a cosmic maintenance crew. And whatever kept them here before was no longer worth the trouble.

Hanu pounded his knees with his fists. If he could manage to get hold of Yaar one last time, he might squeeze some last bits of help from him. Yaar had always been a rule breaker; he always gave Hanu more than he should have. But that had apparently gotten everyone in some sort of trouble. Hanu suddenly stood, his face twisting into an uncomfortable scowl. He remembered something else. The old Nergal said that Yaar had committed a cruel act against him. He folded his arms indignantly. What could she possibly mean by that? He racked his brain, recounting every single encounter he could remember with the creature. It was rather difficult, but he pinched his eyes and thought hard. They had talked. And laughed. Schemed against the Ancient Ones. They eavesdropped on conferences. And when Hanu was a child, they played games – all sorts. He couldn't recall a single harmful action Yaar could've taken against him.

He decided to disregard the old Nergal's accusation. He would only focus on proving Thalor's prediction wrong. After all, they'd been wrong before, which meant that they weren't infallible. They admitted that they made a mistake by interfering on Earth in the first place, so as far as he was concerned, it was possible that humanity would still be able to help stop Year One.

As for what he overheard with Brandy, he would take the information to a trusted source. He stood up and gave himself a firm shake, then slunk upstairs to the last room on the second landing and knocked three times.

After a few moments of hushed voices and a dull thud, the door creaked open and a freckled face appeared. It belonged to Sarah Salcedo.

"What's your clearance code?" she whispered.

"Chief Executive Alpha One," Hanu said very seriously. The door swung open to reveal a very dim room with a table fixed right in the middle. On it, a lamp shone over a large map, and several kids were placed around the table.

Hanu recognized most of them. There was Maximus and Jerry, who were brothers, a girl named Cecily, another girl that called herself Foxtrot Lovehound, and Sarah's younger brother, Daniel. Then there were two new children that introduced themselves as Kavel and Kezra.

These were all children of the soldiers who came here to work. And they were lucky to have such imaginative hosts. Sarah's room had become the headquarters of the *Special Unit*, who were assigned to only the most impossible information gathering missions. They were essentially the backbone of the entire Resistance, according to Sarah.

Hanu sometimes joined in as the guest of honor, having nothing better to be involved with. This proved to be quite informative at times, so much so that he stopped being angry that he'd resorted to playing pretend with a bunch of eight-year-olds.

"We were just talking about the quiet lightning," Sarah said. "Nobody knows if it's a natural phenomenon or not."

But Hanu interrupted. "I actually have a special report," he announced. His eyes flashed mischievously. Sarah produced a fold out chair from under her bed for Hanu, and Max pointed the lamp toward his face for dramatic effect.

"You're on surveillance duty, Shanks," Cecily said to the teddy bear that was sitting in a chair next to the door. "We're all ears, soldier."

Hanu proceeded to tell them about what had just happened downstairs, minus the bloody parts. The children oohed and aahed occasionally, but were otherwise silent. Then, when his story was over, there were questions.

"So what do you think they retrieved?" asked Sarah.

"Data of some sort, obviously," said Kavel.

"Obviously, it was data," Hanu agreed quickly. "But do any of you know what kind? Has there been any talks about this mission Brandy went on?"

"Well... there is one thing," Sarah said reluctantly. "But I don't know if this has anything to do with it."

"Okay, shoot," said Hanu.

"So, I heard something about a huge attack on Underground City," Sarah said. Then she quickly added, "We're not in trouble, though."

"What do you mean, not in trouble?" asked Kezra. "We're *in* Underground City!"

"What exactly did you hear?" Hanu asked.

"Okay," Sarah said, squeezing her eyes tight as if trying to relive the memory. "When I was looking for my doll's shoe the other day, some people were in the hall and one of them said that they were going to be able to control the attack on Underground City, and that they were taking extra precautions to keep everyone safe."

"Alright..." Hanu said, thinking very hard. "Maybe they were stealing the information on how we would be getting attacked. That way they could stop it?" Or at the very least, that's what he'd hoped.

"That's possible," said Jerry.

"That's what I would do," Foxtrot Lovehound agreed.

"I don't know," said Kavel. "The barriers are getting attacked every week, and they've managed to hold... there's really no reason to risk it when we can just keep adapting our defenses."

The group grew thoughtfully quiet for a moment, and you could hear the rustle of movement in the neighboring room or an occasional cough from somewhere in the hall.

"So, wait," said Sarah, backtracking the conversation. "She got stabbed by a super big Ancient One?"

"In the shoulder," Hanu confirmed. "And come to think of it... so did I."

"It's a flaw in the suit's design," Daniel piped up. "The EAG allows for a free-flowing motion around the trapezius, but as a result, the fibers become less porous there. The polymer particles can't properly soak into it in that area, causing an ineffective response to force."

"Yeah, yeah," Sarah waved a dismissive hand. "He's been telling my dad that for months, but there's not much they can do about it, really. I'm worried about the big alien, though. Do you think they're getting healthy again?"

"Maybe something to do with Year One?" suggested Max.

"Speaking of," Hanu said darkly. He leaned into the table, allowing the light to cast a long shadow into the room. "The Intergalactic Council won't be giving us any more help."

Sarah wrinkled her nose. "Well, it's not like they were doing much, anyway," she said.

Daniel snorted. "They've literally done nothing."

"Agreed," said Kavel.

"Here, here," said Cecily.

Hanu shrugged, nodding agreeably. "I guess you're right," he said. But it didn't stop his stomach from twisting with unease. He began to tell them what Thalor said about Year One, but then he hesitated, remembering the look of terror on Camille's face that day in the field when she learned about the war. He couldn't bring himself to disillusion these children, especially not with a future in which he was determined to change the outcome.

Just then, there was a loud knock at the door, which made everybody jump. Cecily mumbled something about firing Shanks, and Sarah snuck over to the door.

"Clearance code?" she demanded.

"Secretary of Steak."

It was Akesh. Sarah opened the door wide enough to let him slide in, but he didn't take a seat around the briefing table. Instead, he gave everyone a high five, kicked off his shoes and jumped into Daniel's bunk.

"*Pillows*," he groaned, squirming on the soft sheets. Then he folded one of the pillows in half, punched it a few times and pinned it to the bed with his head. "Do carry on," he said, now fully prepared to watch the meeting.

"You do realize that *Secretary of Steak* isn't a real position, right?" said Kezra. "It's Secretary of State."

Akesh gasped. "Secretary of Steak is a *very* real position," he said, thoroughly offended. "Do you realize how delicious steak is? Have you ever eaten it before?"

"I don't know, actually," Kezra laughed heartily. "I guess it's no worse than Chief Executive Alpha One."

Then Akesh sat straight up, suddenly remembering why he came in the first place. "So what have you learned about the weird lady?"

The children shrugged.

"Nobody's heard of her," Hanu sighed. "Salcedo's looking into it, though."

"We were thinking maybe a spy," said Sarah. "But daddy said they'd know if there was an intruder here."

"Or maybe she has something to do with the lightning," Hanu said thoughtfully. "I saw lightning in the sky that day, right before I spotted her."

"Oooh," said Cecily. "That could be possible!"

"I think it's a hostile alien," said Akesh. Then he fell back into a laying position. "Yep. I'm calling it – she's gonna make trouble for us."

Foxtrot Lovehound scribbled in very small letters on a piece of paper: *follow-up assignments*. Then she cleared her throat officially. "Now it's time to assign new missions," she said, pulling out a pair of glasses and placing them on her nose.

"I second that motion," said Akesh.

"And I third," said Daniel, giggling.

"And I fourth," Kavel added.

"Stop that!" Foxtrot yelled. Her eyes darted threateningly from Daniel to Kavel. Max and Jerry giggled silently into their hands and Kezra's nose flared as he lost the struggle to hold in a laugh. Foxtrot pursed her lips together, trying to suppress a laugh, herself. "I hate it when you do that!" she squealed.

Then she smoothed out her paper and took a deep breath. "Mission 359," she said, having regained her composure. "The job will be to gather intel on Project Living Library."

Several hands shot up at once.

"What's that?" asked Akesh.

Foxtrot pulled her glasses halfway off her face. "From what we've been able to gather, it's a data collection project that Arrangement started," she reported. "But now the Hierarchy seems interested in some of the information it contains, especially concerning their quantum teleportation technology. We want to know what they plan on doing with it."

"Our dad is personally on that project," said Kezra. "So I think me and Kavel should take it."

"Agreed," said Foxtrot. And the rest of the children groaned collectively. Then she scribbled their names into her notebook. "Next is mission 360," she continued. "Liaison between the Special Unit and the higher-ups regarding the Mystery Lady."

Again, everyone's hands shot straight into the air. Kezra bounced up and down, flapping his hand around. "We just got the last mission, dude," said his brother. "Put your hand down." But Kezra ignored him.

"I'll do it," said Sarah. "I have twenty-four hour access to my parents. Plus, I know how to talk to them."

"Oh, they'll talk alright," said Daniel, pounding a fist into his palm.

"Then it's agreed," said Foxtrot, all business as she wrote in their names next to the assignment. "Those are all the new missions we have for today. The meeting is adjourned."

For a while everyone cautiously looked at everyone else.

"I second that motion," Hanu said reluctantly.

Market Daze

Weeks went by and Hanu hadn't seen or heard anything about the mysterious woman. He all but gave up on it, convincing himself that she very well could've been a figment of his own imagination. And he didn't find any other clues as to what type of data Brandy had stolen from the Ancient Ones, either. Unless you counted that Salcedo farm had become even more busy since, and they almost immediately set a team to manufacture borosilicate glass – whatever that was.

The lack of information on Hanu's end left him with an anxious feeling. He could tell something big was brewing in the Resistance, and it put a terrible strain on him to know that he wouldn't be allowed to do anything to help. At best, he relied on gathering whatever information he could from Sadie and hoping he could deliver some useful bit of insight to the Hierarchy, but so far that wasn't the case. Still, it was nice spending time with her, being as she had chosen to isolate herself for so long after the funeral. She had allowed Hanu to pick her brain freely as of late, and it seemed to ease both their apprehensions a bit. But on this particular day, he would have to pick it at the market, because Ester and Vanessa wanted new gloves.

"Keep up, guys," Sadie yelled over the crowd. She had been pulling Hanu along by the elbow in order to keep from getting separated, but he broke away to grab Akesh, who stopped to admire a box of fancy rings.

"Catch up," he told Akesh, tugging at his arm. He tried to help him weave through the walkway, but Akesh didn't seem to need it. He barreled through the crowd in a straight line, nudging people one way or the other to clear them from his path. Hanu followed closely in his wake, apologizing to people as needed.

They caught up to the girls just in time to see a merchant pull out about thirty pairs of gardening gloves, all with different patterns. "We could've met you here *after* all this," Akesh groaned.

"Yeah, but then you'd miss the debate about stripes versus polka dots," Vanessa teased, holding up two pairs, side by side.

"Personally, I'd do a simple black," said Sadie, who was admiring a tight leather pair that she'd tried on.

"What happened to your old gloves," Hanu asked. Then he quickly wished he didn't. Until recently, Sadie had been wearing fingerless gloves, just like Andy used to.

"It's just time for a change," she said simply. And with an uncharacteristically cheerful smile she removed the gloves from her hands and tried on the next pair.

Hanu and Akesh waited patiently as the girls made their trades – each, a pair for a bag of carrots that they'd harvested from the wildlife preserve. Then they made their way toward the courtyard, which was a great deal less busy than the strip. Akesh unfolded his newspaper as they walked, which he traded for a bag of cherry flavored gum – a total loss, in Hanu's opinion. "Look at this," he said excitedly. "There's a music festival going on in a couple weeks – it's called Riverfest."

"Cool!" Vanessa shrieked, grabbing the paper for a better look. "Moira's band played this festival before, remember Ester?"

Sadie snatched the paper from him. "I can't believe they're still gonna do Riverfest," she said, reading the announcement herself.

"Why wouldn't we?" Hanu asked, looking around at the cramped market. Just beyond the Gazebo that marked the end of the courtyard were a half a dozen rows of tiny houses with thatched roofs. "The City of Fire could use some cheer."

Sadie smacked her lips. "The City of Fire could use –" She pinched her lips and forced her eyes closed as though the words would spill out of them if she kept them open. She took a deep breath. Then she smiled before opening her eyes again. "You know what, it won't even matter," she said. Then she glanced over the newspaper again before handing it back to Akesh.

"What do you mean, it won't matter?" Hanu eyed Sadie cautiously, hoping the question wouldn't reignite her temper. But the grimace she was wearing told Hanu he shouldn't press it.

Ester was looking at the newspaper now, walking sideways in order to see it from Akesh's hands. "I noticed they're not announcing anything about any of the recent attacks on the barrier," she said matter-of-factly.

"They don't want to scare everybody, do they?" said Akesh.

It was a good point, Hanu noted.

"Yeah, but you can't keep a whole city oblivious to reality," argued Ester, who'd stopped reading by now and was dusting off a wooden table in the courtyard.

Then Akesh mumbled something about liking oblivion before emptying out the contents of his pockets onto the table and digging in. Of all the things he could have traded his hygiene products for, he came up with a handful of bouncy balls, half a bar of chocolate that wasn't even sweetened and a large bag of peas.

Hanu, who came with three pairs of socks, a used set of snorkel gear and a pineapple, managed to bag a bottle of shampoo, a new backpack and three blueberry granola bars for his next visit with Garion. He was proud of himself for not having traded any of his food rations this time.

Ester grabbed the shampoo and inspected the bottle. Then she opened the lid and sniffed. "I love lavender," she said. Then she held the bottle to Vanessa's face and gave it a little squeeze.

"That's awesome," Vanessa said. Then she leaned across the table to where Hanu was sitting, her face an inch away from his as she held a yellow lock to his nose. "I have the same kind, see?"

Hanu jerked back suddenly, almost falling out of his seat, but the smell of her sunbaked hair lingered in his nostrils. Vanessa sat back down slowly, her face wearing a mixture of confusion and embarrassment. Hanu looked at the table, his face burning.

"Let me smell," said Ester, sniffing the side of Vanessa's head. She knew full well what happened and, thankfully, she wasn't going to tease him about it. "Oh, it does smell good!"

Vanessa quickly recovered, smiling at Ester, but Hanu was beginning to panic. He tried to think of a way to redeem himself. He picked up her gloves, hoping to say something nice about them, but Sadie plopped down next to him.

"So what's new at the wildlife preserve," she asked Vanessa. "I hear you guys are more farmers than vets nowadays."

"Tell me about it," said Ester. She shuffled a deck of cards she hadn't managed to trade off. Ester never wanted to do physical work, whether it was with plants *or* animals, but was kicked out of Intelligence for having betrayed Underground City. She was lucky enough to be pardoned for her crime, but unlucky enough to be stuck working with Vanessa, having no other prospects for employment. "If *some* people got jobs," she looked meaningfully at Hanu and Akesh. "We wouldn't have to slave away so hard."

It was true, Hanu had no job, nor did he have any intentions of settling into one, being as he still had plans to join the Resistance as soon as they would have him. He had submitted his official application, along with the proper waiver, since he was underaged and didn't have a parental endorsement, and he eagerly awaited their response. Akesh, on the other hand, just flatly refused to acknowledge the prudence in having a job at all.

"I like it, actually," Vanesa said, flipping through a book

she'd just traded for a jar of peanut butter. "It gives us a little variety in our work. Plus we have so many visitors coming in to collect data on the animals, it – Holy crackers!"

Vanessa jumped sharply as a man dumped a wooden box onto the pavement right behind her with a sharp *clack*. He straightened up his vest – his bare chest underneath riddled with curly hairs – and stepped on top of it.

"Ladies and Gentleman," he announced to the courtyard. "I present to you a humble message today."

A couple of people paused long enough to figure out where the commotion was coming from, but mostly people just went along with their business. Hanu squinted to get a good look at the man. He wasn't quite old, but he had a very tired face. Nonetheless, he continued to bellow into the crowd.

"We are at a moment in history where we must make a stand," he said. A man and a woman stopped to listen. "Our values, our beliefs... our strength of will are called into question by time itself, and therefore we must arm ourselves with knowledge and truth. I will reveal to you today a few truths."

The man went on about the meaning of destiny and other such things, making elaborate hand gestures and pausing dramatically occasionally, until he'd gathered a decent audience. By this time Hanu and the others had gotten up as well and were exchanging dubious looks.

"And therefore, I must divulge to you that nobody, and I mean *nobody*, in Underground City is safe," he said. "At this very moment there's a war being waged right... there." The man pointed at an arbitrary place in the sky with an overdramatized look of fear on his face.

Someone who was standing towards the very front threw his hands up and stalked away. Several people laughed and a woman standing just behind Hanu whispered, *I bet he's City of Fire*, to a friend.

"Oh yes, I'm talking about the Ancient Ones," the man said. "They've brought the fight to our front door and now we need to end it, once and for all."

"This is a joke," Sadie said, embarrassed for the man.

"Well, he's not lying," said Hanu.

"I think he's actually talking about the barriers," Ester said. "They've been blasting at them for weeks now."

The man continued. "I tell you that we must say goodbye to our beloved city and return to the surface," he said. "The end is near and we will all perish, or we will all rise!"

A very small number of people clapped, cheering the man on, but the majority scowled disapprovingly at him. A few more people started walking away.

"What's the point in returning?" shouted a man in a straw hat. "They'll eventually leave... an' besides, they ain't no threat to none of us here."

"They *are* a threat to us," the man assured him. "They're going to kill us all before Year One."

Then there was a fresh outburst of sighs and moans from the crowd. Several people interjected at once and someone yelled that the man had gone crazy.

"Oh yeah, so then what's Year One?" a woman goaded.

"It's the beginning of oblivion," the man said very seriously. "And it's the end of humanity."

The four of them eyed one another, nodding agreeably at his words. The man was telling the truth alright, except he had an awfully weird way of delivering it. For a while, Hanu thought about pitching in to help him explain, but a quick count of angry faces in the crowd discouraged him from doing so.

The man wasn't deterred at all, though. "They need to kill everyone, now that they can sustain themselves," he explained. "And they're closer to achieving that goal than you think!"

"You shouldn't speak about things you know nothing of," yelled a man over the bunch. "Are you Arrangement?"

"Well no, but –"

"Are you a journalist?"

"Not exactl –"

"Well then shut your mouth!"

At this, several other onlookers yelled angrily at the man, but he didn't back down until he'd finished having his say. More people crowded into the courtyard to witness the commotion, shoving Hanu and his companions further in. Some of them had begun chanting, *"Thrive, don't survive!"*

"Mark my words," he yelled. "The Ancient Ones will set foot in Underground City very soon. Just like they did in the City of Fire! What will you do then?"

A minute later, when the whole thing had become one large shouting match, they decided that they would leave. Hanu ducked his head, following Akesh, who expertly created a path through the throng. Then, when they were just clear of the crowd Hanu heard a familiar voice.

"Hunny!"

He searched the market, wide eyed, hoping to find the little girl before she yelled again. But he was too late.

"Hunny, over here!"

Sadie slapped Hanu on the back, amused. "Over there, *Hunny*." She pointed at a little girl in a purple romper. Sunglasses were propped on top of two pigtails and she clutched a silver purse in one hand while she waved with the other.

Rachael parted the crowd, with two girls following. "Hey, Hunny," she smiled bashfully.

"Rachael," said Hanu. He smiled awkwardly. "What are you up to?" He tried not to make eye contact with any of his friends. His only concern was getting the conversation over as quickly as possible.

"Me and the girls were looking for new purses," she said, holding up her sequined bag so he could see it. "Do you like it?"

"It looks great," he said. The girls squealed and giggled, which made Hanu's neck grow warm. Then he couldn't figure out what else to say for a moment, until he realized the appropriate thing to do would be to introduce everyone. "Uh, listen Rachael... these are my friends," he said. "This is Sadie, Vanessa, Ester and Akesh."

Each of them greeted Rachael, then she introduced her friends, whose names Hanu didn't catch because he was busy thinking about how to end the encounter. Then one of the girls squealed again. "I can't believe we met your boyfriend!"

Hanu stammered. "Wait, that's not –"

"Rachael!" A woman in a green jumper was making her way toward them, balancing an oddly shaped bag on top of a stack of boxes. "I need some help over here, girls."

"Okay," Rachael called over her shoulder. Then she said a quick goodbye. "It was nice meeting you all. I'll see you soon, Hunny!"

Then the girls skipped off and disappeared into the square, leaving Hanu to interpret what had just happened. Sadie burst into laughter and Akesh simply said, "*Wow*."

"That was not what it looked like," Hanu finally said. "That girl... that's not even..."

"She's like *ten*," Vanessa scowled, making the bottom of Hanu's stomach fall out. She started up the hill that led out of the market and onto the main road, looking thoroughly scandalized.

"But she's not my girlfriend," he yelled, marching right behind her. Akesh followed suit and Ester had to grab Sadie, who was doubled over with laughter by now.

"Weird how she thinks she is," Vanessa said rather coolly. "That's your business, I guess."

Hanu stopped at the top of the hill. "But I don't even... That's not who I like."

But Vanessa was already stalking away, leaving Hanu in a puddle of misery and helpless confusion. Ester appeared behind him, straightening out her tee-shirt and breathless from having to drag Sadie halfway up the hill.

She patted him sympathetically on the shoulder. "I think it's cute you have a not-so-secret admirer," she breathed. Then she barked an ironic laugh. "Of course, that doesn't help you one bit, now does it?"

Reggie's University Woes

The clandestine class ship, Mako, was rendered helplessly idle somewhere between Underground City and University. "Override that safety protocol and get this ship moving," Reggie yelled into the bustling and noisy cockpit. "And somebody, turn off that damned alarm!"

He grabbed the panel, bracing himself as the shuttle rocked violently. Several crewmembers slid across the floor, grabbing for nearby furniture legs.

"We'll be crushed if we engage thrusters without the tunneling sensors," said Pants from behind a console. His thick locks danced wildly around his face as he leaned in closer. Reggie squinted to read his lips through the dark glow of the emergency lights. "We need to reinitiate the cloak. Then we can maybe move ourselves another mile or two and hide out."

Reggie hobbled to the holoscreen that flickered along the adjacent wall. He jammed a finger at a button, but his hand went straight through. Then, cursing, he banged the emitter several times. The holoscreen flickered a bit more before smoothing out, and he tried for the button again. The secondary light systems came on and Reggie was able to read the output on his diagnostic tool. "Try remodulating the cloaking frequency, and get ready to send as much power as you can to those thrusters," he yelled. He rubbed his chin hairs, thinking hard about what he should do next.

Another crewmember rammed into him from behind as the ship lurched again. "Sir, we'll need to reinforce our shielding soon. At this rate, we'll be completely exposed in about four minutes."

"I'm working on it," Reggie barked, thoroughly irritated for having been asked to lead the mission in the first place. Andy was always better at making split second decisions than he was, and on top of that, Reggie barely knew how this vessel worked. He was used to piloting the smaller, sleeker stealth flyers. "Somebody cut the noise – "

Just then the alarm was silenced. The cabin had gone relatively quiet, allowing everyone to bustle to and from their stations with a more manageable amount of stress.

"The cloak's back online," reported Pants. "But we're still in trouble if we run into something down here."

Reggie jumped over a railing that separated the main floor from the surrounding stations to reach the console where Motley was. He winced, clutching his leg.

"Any luck on the pulse bypass?" he asked the man.

Motley crouched under the console, letting a light that was attached to his forehead illuminate the circuitry. He prodded at a clumsy looking device in the grid. "It burned out after the first EMP," he reported. "It's a dud."

"Well, we better get outta here before they decide to hit us with any more," said Reggie. "Pull it out and reroute power into the shields."

"Aye, sir."

Reggie scrambled to get to the holographic map at the captain's station. He searched for a place more north, just behind a large mineral deposit. "Take us to these coordinates," he ordered the crew at navigation, punching in the location. "Engage thrusters at half speed, and let's hope our shield will take care of the rest."

The crew jerked slightly as the ship moved toward its new destination. They each held their breath as the hull groaned, anticipating another onslaught of weapons fire, but the seconds turned to placid minutes. Reggie rubbed his bleary eyes, finally breathing a sigh of relief.

"I need three people keeping a visual on that map," he said, crossing the room. "Report on EMP activity and navigate around anything in our flight path with a density greater than seven point eight five grams per cubic centimeter."

Several crew members rushed to his station as Reggie shuffled through the debris that now littered the floor. Scanners, notepads and random papers were scattered about as if a tornado whipped through the cabin, and a liquid had leaked from somewhere up high, creating a dark puddle in the carpeted floor. He found what he was looking for several feet away from where he'd left it, buried under the contents of a spilled emergency medical kit – a thin box, no bigger than a briefcase. He pulled the thing up onto the nearest console and opened it, checking to make sure the contents hadn't been scrambled too much.

The first device was the most delicate. He inspected the glass housing on the fist-sized canister, which was, thankfully, perfectly intact. This was the transmitter for the other six devices in the box. He inspected each of the other units, in turn, and then placed them back into the box. Then he latched it back up and carried it to his station.

"Report," he said, sliding the box under the console.

"We have four more miles to navigate," said Motley. "So far we've had to maneuver around one large object – inanimate, non-technological."

"Good," said Reggie as he dropped himself into his seat. He closed his eyes tight, hoping to get some inspiration on how he would complete his mission.

His goal was supposed to be a simple one – re-establish the abandoned Deprogramming station that was hidden under the university. But when they arrived to replace the emitters for the deflection field, they were ambushed. Maybe their presence somehow tripped an alarm, or perhaps a trap that the Ancient Ones set, he thought. And if that were the case, then maybe the Deprogramming station had already been infiltrated. Maybe it wasn't safe.

"We've arrived at our destination," said Pants. He crossed the room back to his own station and slowly pulled back a lever. With an almost inaudible whir, the vessel slowed to a halt.

"We'll regroup here," said Reggie from his seat. "Put Adam Lilley through, will you?"

"On it," said one of the more eager crewmembers, punching

the dial at her station. "The monitor's blown. We'll have an audio connection only, I'm afraid."

Moments later Mr. Lilley's voice crackled inside the ship. "Adam here. Go ahead, Mako."

"This is the vessel, Mako," Reggie reported – his voice thick with apprehension. "We were ambushed after crossing under the city."

"Have you found cover?"

"Affirmative. Only after we were pushed eighty-two miles from our target. How should we proceed?"

The crew anxiously awaited their orders, but none came. For a while there was only silence, and they weren't sure if Mr. Lilley was thinking of a plan or if the signal had dropped. Then they were certain that the communication had failed, because they could now hear a faint fizzling sound coming in fast from a distance.

"Everyone, to your stations!" Reggie jumped to his feet and braced himself for impact.

Fwoom!

An explosion just outside the craft rocked it horribly, and Reggie was certain the hull had buckled. But when he opened his eyes, everything was still intact. He scanned his console, flabbergasted by whatever it was that happened. Pants frantically adjusted his equipment, and the other crew members scrambled to assess the damage.

"What *was* that?" somebody asked.

"It wasn't an EMP or a dampener missile," Reggie reported,

reading the feedback from his computer. "Damage?"

"Shields at twenty-three percent and failing, and we have hull fissures," said Motley. "Not big enough to compromise structural integrity, but it might be problematic above ground."

"I don't think they know we're here," said Pants. "It looks like they're taking blind sweeps."

"Let's not stick around to find out," said Reggie. "Pants, I need you to alternate our cloaking frequency, and Motley will work on getting that shield back up. Somebody, take over navigation. We're retreating."

The crew scrambled to ready their stations. They, too, had very little experience working on such a specialized ship, and were happy to return, able to say that they'd done all they could.

"But, sir," Pants interjected. "This might be our only chance to secure the station."

"We can't secure the station if we're dead, Pants." Reggie rubbed a temple with shaking hands. "We have no idea what just hit us, and we're already crippled as it is."

"But, think, what if we tried approaching with the alternating frequency and – "

"I respect your persistence, Pants, but this command is mine." He looked the man reassuringly in the eye. "We can discuss our next approach once we're back in Underground City, but right now we can't waste another – Oh, my god!"

A large, scaly woman suddenly appeared out of thin air, and was watching the interchange from the captain's seat with relative interest. It was the Nagi.

The crew drew their weapons.

"Who are you," Reggie demanded. He moved himself slowly around the railing.

Her large, yellow eyes followed him lazily. "I think you'll find it's not all that important who I am," she said, adjusting a thick cloak around her legs. The dim cabin lighting danced lazily on her iridescent skin.

"Okay, what do you want?" asked Reggie. He trained his gaze on her, ready to give the order to shoot, if he needed to.

The Nagi rose from the seat and strode over to Motley's station, not at all phased by the fact that their weapons were all trained on her. She picked up the pulse bypass, which was strewn haphazardly onto his console, and inspected it. "This is a nice piece of technology," she said. "Shame it didn't work for you."

"You've been spying on us?" Reggie's eyes darted between the woman and the nearest crewmember. It was Kayrin, a younger and much less experienced soldier. Did she have the gall to tackle the woman, to retrieve the pulse bypass before she disappeared?

"Not spying, exactly," the woman said. "Your ship triggered the sensor network and almost ruined my plans. I peeked in to see who you were."

Reggie thought about shooting the woman, but something told him she might disappear – and maybe reappear with a vengeance. He decided he would buy himself some time to think. "You know who we are, but we don't know who you are," he said. "Doesn't quite seem fair, now does it?"

She ignored him, though, turning the equipment in her hand to inspect it. "This... this piece of technology you've developed really piqued my interest. What do you call it again?"

The crew shifted nervously, eyeing Reggie for orders. "It's a pulse bypass," he obliged.

"Ah, a pulse bypass..." she smiled. "Next time, consider using a viscous coupling unit inside the main reinitializer. It's losing far too much momentum when it transfers the electrical power back into the ship."

Reggie narrowed his eyes at her. "Are you an engineer?" he said. Then his face contorted with a mixture of impatient frustration and confusion. "As a matter of fact, *what* are you – and better yet, how did you get onto my ship?"

"I am a Nagi," she said airily, dropping the piece back onto the console with a thud. She took a cautious step over to one of the consoles and surveyed the various buttons and levers on it. "And I only boarded your ship because I require refuge."

There was confused silence for a moment. "Well you can't take refuge here," said Reggie. "We're under attack, in case you didn't know."

"Not anymore." She typed a series of commands into a nearby console, and Reggie made a mental note to create some sort of password requirement. "There are detection networks around the cities now. You triggered an automatic targeting sequence, but they believe they've destroyed you. They will take no further action." Then she double checked her work. "With the proper shield frequency, you will be able to avoid detection."

Reggie motioned for the crew to lower their weapons. Then he and Motley moved to the console in unison in order to study her alterations.

"So why do you need refuge?" Reggie asked.

"My ship was just destroyed, and therefore, I will be needing passage back to the surface."

"Then that was you just now?" Reggie gestured toward where the explosion came from. "You sacrificed your ship to save ours?"

"Well it was more like a lucky accident," she said, looking at the structural reports.

"Yeah, lucky," he laughed. "So are you part of the Intergalactic Council, then? I've never seen anyone like you in the Tome – "

The Nagi rounded on him, making him jerk back. Her eyes narrowed with fury. "I would have destroyed the Intergalactic Council by now if I wasn't preoccupied with the Ancient Ones."

"Woah, okay." Reggie raised both hands. Then he squinted at her. "So what were you doing down here, anyway?"

The Nagi rolled her eyes. "Proving that curiosity *does* kill the cat." But the crew continued to stare expectantly at her. "Some of the students at University have been attempting to construct a device that would open a portal. I've been observing." Then she sighed and dropped herself back into the captain's seat.

"Your vessel is ready to be moved back toward University. I will leave once we get close enough."

Reggie hesitated. He knew they wouldn't be able to survive another attack. He eyed Pants meaningfully, hoping for a vote. But Pants shrugged, wild-eyed, leaving him to make the call. "And you're sure they won't detect us now?"

"I assure you," she said, staring confidently into his eyes. He allowed himself to be mesmerized for a moment.

"Okay," he said. Then he moved briskly back to his station, doling out new orders. "Pants, we'll need those thrusters at half speed, and Meyer – you'll monitor navigation. I want eyes on that map the entire way there."

The crew rushed to make the necessary changes, preparing both the ship and themselves. Then they moved back toward the Deprogramming station.

Agrigore's Plan

Agrigore wasn't surprised at all when an invitation to the fortress arrived. Three very young and very serious looking couriers stood dutifully at attention as he fumbled with the front gate, which he only opened wide enough to stick his arm through. He snatched the small scroll from the foremost messenger's hand and slammed the gate closed again before they could bow or say who it was from.

Then, without even a word he rushed back up the path that led to his temple. He read and re-read the invitation several times before tossing it onto what was left of the desk in his study. He hastily pulled up a chair, but then thought better of sitting in the rickety thing. He chose to stand instead, pacing the room while eyeing the piece of paper.

Saleel had asked Agrigore to join him for dinner. *A gesture I've learned from your pets*, he taunted in the note. It was terribly disturbing to him. This gesture wouldn't be the same as when the humans did it; it was no activity of fellowship. For the Ancient Ones, to be in close proximity with others during feeding aggravated their most violent qualities – greed, aggression, and mistrust. The Luminous Great had invited him to dinner most likely to kill him, and then justify his own actions.

Agrigore was almost impressed by Saleel's cunning, but he knew this was not an original idea. He, too, had studied the private writings of the ancient rebellion leader, Safthon. He killed his Deh counterpart in this manner, and was exonerated in the affair. He claimed that his partner had surprised him during a meal and that he'd acted instinctively, pleading that the court grant him reprieve. He was allowed to continue his work on the governing body. Then, unrestrained, he was able to manipulate enough of the government officials to stage a larger coup against the Deh.

Agrigore made a resolution to not be tricked by any of Saleel's manipulations. He immediately set to cleaning the temple – leaving no trace of discord, just in case the Luminous Great decided to have his guard look for evidence that could sully his reputation while he was away at dinner.

It took quite some time to collect the bloodied gauze and poorly made tinctures from the debris. He was careful to burn those things in the furnace. Then he collected the splintered bits of wood and organized them into a neat pile at the rear of his temple home. He could justify getting rid of his furniture as a matter of preference. And he would use the wood on cold nights to warm himself. Then, when he was satisfied, he turned his attention toward himself.

He preened what was left of his chest feathers, wondering what kind of weapon could create such a change in his anatomy. He could see that the membrane was now protecting greenish, fleshy looking scales. These scales seemed to be spreading from the wound, covering nearly half of his breast plate. It was curious, because he'd never seen anyone develop scales. You were either born with them or you weren't.

Thankfully, the worst of the pain had subsided in the last couple of days, so he wouldn't have to worry about suddenly collapsing in public. Agrigore chewed a sprig of oregano and spit it into a cloth. Then he applied the poultice to his wound, wincing as he squeezed it tighter into his chest.

After he was satisfied with this, he put on his best tunic and walked down the path toward the front gate, making a silent pact with himself that he would return home that night after dinner, whatever it took.

ᚻ·ᚲ ᚻ·ᚲ ᚻ·ᚲ

Lost in thought, his feet moved him through the city faster than he would've liked. He arrived at the fortress seemingly in no time. But at least he was prepared – or at least, he was as prepared as he could have been.

After the standard entry ritual, he was guided to a great hall. It was a rather large and junky place, with obtrusive stone and wooden structures scattered about, creating several labyrinthine paths through the room. Agrigore's eyes followed the wall, which was made with a sturdy stone and contained a couple of markings in the old language – decorations, as the humans would call it. But Agrigore knew that these markings weren't merely part of the decor – they meant that somebody had already claimed this space as their hunting ground. And by the sound of it, something was in there that needed hunting. It was crashing violently through the maze, grunting its displeasure all the while.

Toward the center of the room, the ceiling domed, allowing for a row of seats to be placed just behind a railing on the second floor. Agrigore could see that several people had taken seats in this part of the room. He felt strangely as though he were in an arena.

One of the spectators shifted nervously in her seat and Agrigore recognized that it was Jinora. She smiled a guilty grin, flashing a glance between the other spectators – members of Saleel's guard – then back to Agrigore.

"Have you spoken against me?" Agrigore whispered under his breath. He tilted his head, getting a better look at her face through his left eye. Was she changing allegiances and offering him up as a sacrifice? He didn't have long to interpret the look on her face, though, because just then, he detected that someone had entered the room and was standing right behind him.

"You are a very prompt guest," Saleel beamed. He was dressed minimally, sporting a thin loincloth and three shiny metal bands around his neck. He approached Agrigore with outstretched arms, motioning into the room. "How do you like it?"

"It's elaborate," Agrigore said, allowing his eyes to sweep the room one more time. "Your private hunting grounds?"

"Not nearly as elaborate as the ones back home," Saleel said.

"I use it for training, too, from time to time."

Agrigore wanted to make a point that there wasn't really much to train for on this planet, being as its inhabitants were practically defenseless, but he was certain that Saleel would find a way to use that statement to somehow prove that Agrigore's thinking was, once again, inferior to his own. He allowed his face to relax into a cunning grin instead. "I may have to have one installed, myself."

"Well, today you get to give it a test run," said Saleel, walking toward the entrance of one of the paths. He listened for a brief moment and then pounded abruptly on the metallic wall. Agrigore could hear the hefty animal scurrying somewhere inside of the maze. He smiled wickedly.

"Do you remember the zecrone?"

Agrigore tried to hide his sudden apprehension. The zecrone was a violent abomination; one which should have never been created. Bred for its girth and hardiness in the harsh environment of one of their previous planets, it was a reliable food source, until it had become too aggressive to control. It was not wise to pursue the creature for sport.

"So, is this how you unwind after a long day?" Agrigore teased. He moved toward another entrance, hoping to hear which way the beast was headed.

"I was hoping it would be a nice bonding experience," Saleel said. "After all, you're my second-in-command. We should be spending more time together."

Agrigore eyed the spectators, wondering if any of them were

tracking the beast as it crashed around in the maze, but none of their faces revealed a hint of where it could be.

"Oh, them?" Saleel barked a laugh, slapping Agrigore's back cheerfully. "I invited the guard, of course – and your apprentice as well – so that we may all hear of your new plan to destroy the Intergalactic Council."

Saleel opened a large wooden trunk that Agrigore hadn't noticed before. Inside was a number of different types of weapons – staffs, hooks, spears and shields. He beckoned for Agrigore to choose one, grabbing a smaller hand knife for himself. He held the blade up to the fluorescent lighting, casually inspecting it. "I have to say your apprentice was eager to brag about it when I summoned her a couple days ago. She wasn't quite clear on all of the details, though... I know you'll enlighten us."

Agrigore chose a double bladed spear and hastily took his position just inside one of the maze entrances. Saleel took the entrance opposite of him, stepping into the shadows. The pale yellow light that emanated from his chest reflected off of the metal rings around his neck, making him light up like a target. Then, with a maniacal grin, he turned on his heels and ran into the maze.

Agrigore followed suit, positioning himself just inside the first corner of his path. For a few moments it was dead quiet; he couldn't hear the zecrone or Saleel. He took this opportunity to get himself oriented. Jinora hadn't betrayed him, but he knew that if he didn't produce an acceptable plan, they may both be annihilated. The guard would simply have to agree that it was a hunting accident.

"Don't lose your position," he whispered to himself. Then he pushed past some debris, further into the darkness of the maze.

"So what's the big plan?" came Saleel's voice from above.

Agrigore grappled his way up a thick tree trunk, balancing the spear in his beak as he went. Then he toppled onto a lower branch and positioned his spear to ambush the beast. "I have to admit, I was cautious of your approach," he said. He glanced over the maze, to the wall where Saleel was perched. "Killing members of the Intergalactic Council is undoubtedly a risky move, and I do not wish to entice them to interfere with our plans here."

Some of the members of the guard had begun to lean in, and Agrigore could tell they were trying to lock in on his position. He braced himself as Saleel jumped into the tree, then he scaled the trunk, moving strategically away from him. He listened for the zecrone, making sure it hadn't made its way into the tunnel he was approaching. He knew he wouldn't be able to contend with the creature head on, especially not within the confines of the maze.

"You have made those concerns known," said Saleel lazily from somewhere behind him.

Agrigore cleared the tunnel in large strides, but found himself caught in a series of nets as he tried to climb the next wall. His spear slid just out of reach. "I was thinking," he said, untangling himself as quickly as he could. "Instead of killing off its members one by one, why don't we destroy the entire ship at once." He freed himself from the netting and tried to put as much distance as he could between himself and Saleel.

"How do we do that with our current resources?" Saleel said.

Agrigore rounded two more corners before – thwack! A yellow flash barreled past him, barely missing his face and crumbling the wall behind him. "You should be a little more vocal," Saleel warned, shaking the dust from his fist. "I thought you were the zecrone."

"You should probably cover up," said Agrigore, careful not to look too directly into his superior's eyes. "That thing will see you coming."

"I want it to see me," Saleel pulled his knife from the wall, sending small bits of stone crumbling over their feet. "That makes it more thrilling, wouldn't you agree?"

The creature roared angrily from behind Saleel. He rolled out of the way just in time for Agrigore to see two sets of horns charging down the path.

"Absolutely," he said. Then he jumped high into the air in order to grasp onto a slanted stone structure. He used an uneven rock jutting out from it as a foothold, and climbed above the path, closer toward where the spectators were seated.

Then it was quiet again, which let Agrigore know that the hunt was still on. He slid underneath a canopy to hide himself from the guard, but stayed safely above ground in order to avoid the beast. He had no interest in hunting; he only wanted to survive. And he had to have an incredible plan in order to do that.

Minutes later, Saleel peeked around a corner, sneering at Agrigore. "Well... how do we do it?"

Agrigore slid as stealthily as he could onto a beam that ran almost the whole length of the hall. "Do you remember the electrodynamic conversion chamber we've been using to trap them?"

"Oh yes, that's one of my favorite toys," Saleel's voice traveled closer to his position.

Agrigore could hear a commotion right underneath him. Did Saleel find the zecrone, or did the zecrone find the two of them? He lowered his head to have a peak, only to be grabbed by the neck and thrown to the floor. Agrigore crashed through several layers of wooden planks and caught himself on what could have been a marble tabletop.

"In the very first conflict," he groaned, clutching his side. Saleel was already jumping down to meet him, though. Agrigore held out a hand to halt him. "When they came before, Safthon wanted to pull their vessel in – he knew it would collapse under the physics of this dimensional space. That's how we will do it."

Saleel paused his onslaught. It took a moment, but his gratified smirk turned into sober comprehension. "We will be prepared this time," he whispered. Saleel jumped down from the table. "How do we kill them?"

Agrigore slid off the table, careful not to allow his torn tunic to reveal his injury. "We will create an electrodynamic field large enough to draw their vessel here," he said, dusting himself off. "We will pull them in right before opening the portal for Command. The nuclear blast will herald in our new age and eradicate all opposition at the same time."

"Yes." Saleel began mumbling excitedly to himself about drawing up a preliminary design, but Agrigore realized he still hadn't completely justified his actions thus far.

"I've been trying to assess if I could trust the Council to install the modified technology in one of the cities," he lied. "Our most skilled personnel are restoring the nuclear silos. It would be difficult to spare even one or two of them for the task."

Saleel reluctantly agreed. "We're in danger of falling behind as it is."

"For this reason, I believe we need to use the humans – keep them complacent and faithful – so that they can help us to carry out this perfect plan."

"Your simple-minded dependence on humanity baffles me," Saleel spat. "You will set them to do your work, all the while some of them continue to try and infiltrate our facilities."

Agrigore tried to maintain a certain level of resolve as he eyed his superior. "We are stretched thin, are we not? We must continue our pursuit of Underground City as well."

Saleel conceded. "We will construct the technology," he said. "Then we will see if we can trust the Council to install it."

Agrigore stood to his full height, then nodded firmly. "Let us continue the hunt."

"No." Saleel's eyes darted the room. "We shall get started on this new plan right away."

A satisfied grin danced on the corners of Agrigore's beak. He looked to the spectators and saw that Jinora had relaxed into her seat. The guards were leaning further into the ring, though, rather interested in the new plan. Then Saleel turned and quickly made his way toward the entryway. Agrigore was right on his tail.

"You will submit your formal proposal tomorrow," said Saleel. Then he turned and extended a hand.

Agrigore grasped his forearm, a sign of mutual respect. But as Saleel squeezed back, a shock ran up his arm, making the wound in his chest throb uncomfortably. He yanked his arm back, realizing too late that what he'd done was a great insult. Saleel looked at him through narrowed eyes.

"I wish to begin the task right away," said Agrigore, hoping to explain away his strange behavior as eagerness.

But Saleel wasn't fooled. He glared at him suspiciously. "See to it that you do."

What was in the Basement

Sadie managed to round up the gang for dinner at Salcedo Farm. And since it had been a few days since his last appearance there, Hanu decided it would be safe to return – especially since he'd be coming with his own food rations this time. He threw on his best tee and a clean pair of jeans, and headed toward the market where the gang agreed to meet.

They hadn't really had a chance to interpret what they'd seen at the market the last time they were together, but as they set out toward the farm, the silence of the empty streets allowed them to share their observations privately.

"He wasn't wrong at all," said Sadie. "The Ancient Ones aren't gonna waste their time on ineffective tactics. They're adapting; they're gonna find a way in soon."

"Yeah but we should go up there and do what?" Akesh asked for the third time.

"Go up there and stop them from dropping the bomb," Hanu answered. "But the real question is why did he have to act like a total weirdo? Nobody's gonna take anything he said seriously."

Akesh laughed madly. "I don't know, I was diggin' that vest."

Vanessa strained under the weight of a watermelon, shooting

a dirty look at Akesh before adjusting the thing in her sweaty palms. It was he who insisted that they choose the watermelon at the market, despite the group's protests that it would be too heavy to carry to their destination. Then, after about a half a mile, they'd given in to his complaining and decided to take turns carrying it.

"Seriously though," she said, pulling down the skirt of her sundress. "Who was that guy? He seemed too intense to be a local, but too... *loopy* to be City of Fire."

"He didn't do us any favors," said Ester thoughtfully. "I would've tried presenting evidence first – data, footage... it's more real if you see it for yourself."

"I think he's City of Fire," said Akesh. "That's all you guys ever talk about is the Ancient Ones." Sadie stuck her tongue out at him playfully.

"I wonder if he was talking about the attack that's coming," said Hanu. His stomach was uncomfortably tight. "The one Sarah was talking about – the one they're gonna try to control." He suddenly turned to Sadie, who had gone rather rigid. "Hey, by the way, do you know anything about that?"

"I'm not sure about any attack." She scoffed. "I think you need to check your sources."

"Or maybe they're already here," Akesh said in a spooky voice.

"We'd *know* if they were here," said Vanessa. But she looked over her shoulder anyway, as if the Ancient Ones would be strolling up the street behind them.

"Think about it!" said Akesh excitedly. "The Mystery Lady, Hanu. What if she's really here to bring Underground City down from the inside out? What if she's a hybrid?"

"I don't know," said Ester. "She *has* been freaking everyone out."

Sadie gasped. "I forgot to tell you guys! Reggie ran into her on his last mission." She held out both hands to halt the gang. Vanessa took this opportunity to pass the watermelon on, and dropped it into her arms. "She *is* an alien," Sadie said. Then she scowled at the watermelon.

"Ha!" yelled Akesh, pointing at Hanu. "I called it alright. She's hostile, too, isn't she?"

"Well, not really. But sort of," said Sadie. She hiked up the watermelon and continued walking. "She's out for revenge on the Ancient Ones, too, but she also hates the Intergalactic Council for some reason. Sounded like she was plannin' an attack on 'em, from what I heard."

"They're definitely becoming less popular with me," Hanu said darkly. He picked up a dried up stick from the grass and threw it toward the ziggurat as hard as he could. Then, after it hit the side of the building with a satisfying smack, he continued. "She'll have to make her move fast, 'cause the Intergalactic Council's moving as far away from Earth as they can."

Ester sighed. "Just in time for Year One."

"Wait, how'd you know about that?" Hanu asked.

Ester hiked up her backpack, then wiggled a bug away from

her nose. "Intelligence is one-third intuition, remember."

Then it dawned on him. "Hey, you *are* an intuit," he said to Ester. It had been so long since she was in her white coverings, that he almost forgot she could practically read the future. "They said Year One was gonna happen no matter what – "

" – and that we had to decide how we would experience it." Ester frowned. "That's about all I know, too, Hanu."

Hanu tugged at the hem of his shirt nervously. "But what about Year One, though," he said. "I mean, do you see how it happens? Do we survive it?"

Ester's feet slowed. "I don't see how it happens," she said.

Akesh wrapped an arm around her neck, pulling her along in order to keep up with Sadie, who was marching briskly through a stretch of tall grass now. "Mainly, I think he wants to know if we're alive by the end of it," he said. "You know, do we die?"

"I just don't know," Ester said firmly. She eased herself from his grasp. Her face was suddenly somber. Then she shrugged. "I don't see anything. I don't see people dying, or explosions, or fighting." Sadie stopped walking and Vanessa ran into the back of her. Then they backtracked to where Ester was standing. She stared at them, stone-faced. She took a deep breath and bit her lip. "I don't see anything at all beyond the next couple of weeks. It's just blank."

Vanessa was the first to speak. She wrapped her arms around Ester in a hug. Then she smiled. "We're supposed to decide how to experience it, right?" she said. "Maybe we just haven't made that decision yet."

Ester smiled in an unsure way.

"Well, I know one thing," said Sadie. "We're not goin' out like cowards." Then she continued marching toward the farm, hiking up the watermelon against her hip.

Hanu followed suit, making his way toward the main road that would lead to the farm, but nobody felt like talking anymore. For a while, he watched his sneakers as they kicked through the grass. Then he saw a flower. Then another, and another – deep pink bunches among the green. He picked a stalk and held it up to the last of the sunlight, admiring the cluster of blooms.

"Those are Hollyhocks," said Vanessa, trailing behind the others. She stopped to smell one, tucking her hair behind an ear. Then she scowled. "They don't smell very good, I guess. They're beautiful though."

Hanu put the flower to his nose, determined not to do or say anything that would make him look like a lunatic. Its scent was rather flat. "You're right," he said.

"They smell like dirt." She chuckled. She continued walking. Hanu followed, rolling the flower between his fingers, unsure of what he could say next. A great deal of anxiety started to well up inside of him, starting as a squeezing sensation at the pit of his stomach and rising up into his throat. He could tell he would be saying something stupid at any moment, so he started to walk a little faster to catch up with the others. But she wasn't finished talking. "I used to put them in my hair, you know, before all of this." She gestured over the city behind them. Hanu glanced at the sea of buildings and homes, all dotted with grounded flyers and escape pods. The two giant pyramids loomed in the distance, overlooking it all. "I just don't have the time anymore," she said. "They never made me smell any better, but they have amazing medicinal properties. That's why I like 'em."

"Well," Hanu said. His feet stopped as he looked at her. His throat was dry by now and his tongue was numb. He snapped the stalk down to a more manageable length and held out the cluster of flowers. "There's no reason you can't put this one in your hair now."

Vanessa smiled at him. It made Hanu's stomach lurch in the most pleasant way. She inched closer, until she was right on him. Then she leaned in, tucking a lock of hair behind an ear. She gestured for him to tuck the flower in next, which he did with incredibly shaky hands. Then he smiled, daring himself to look into her eyes. She didn't look away, and he was able to admire the deep amber of them in the dusky evening sun. She leaned in closer, making his heart beat at double pace. Then Akesh yelled from further down the path.

"Hurry up, guys!" he said. Then he cried out a protest as Ester poked him in the arm.

Vanessa bit her lip. "Thanks," she said.

Hanu regained control of his tongue just enough to say. "It matches you." He glanced at the maroon paisley on her sundress. "You know, cause it's pretty. It goes with your outfit."

Vanessa blushed, then turned sharply up the path. And Hanu, satisfied with his relative control over the word salad, followed.

Ten minutes later, they were kicking up dust on the narrow, gravelly road that led to the farm. Sadie shoved the watermelon into Akesh's arms, then she punched him in the shoulder, making him wince. Ester breathed a sigh of relief, wiping the sweat from the back of her neck with a towel from her pocket, and Hanu gave his legs a good shaking. Vanessa, who was used to walking miles at a time on the preserve, strode contentedly up the path with her flower bobbing happily on the side of her head.

The Salcedos were already in the kitchen when they arrived, along with about a dozen soldiers. Mrs. Salcedo greeted them warmly before taking their bags of rations and setting them to their tasks.

Hanu was to help Rambo and Deeds peel potatoes, and the girls were split into the other groups, who were either chopping vegetables, harvesting herbs from the field or supervising the chickens as they roasted on the open fire in the yard. Akesh followed Mrs. Salcedo around, claiming to be her personal assistant, but managed to only help by tasting everything she touched – to make sure nobody had attempted to poison it, of course.

This gave Hanu the perfect opportunity to listen in on the going-ons of the City of Fire. Rambo was what Sadie liked to call a *social butterfly*. He'd never heard of the term, but pretty much what it meant was that she liked to talk a lot. Hanu didn't know much about Deeds, being as he usually reported straight to Adam before vanishing into thin air, but he was always cordial with Hanu.

The two sat at the kitchen table now, barely visible behind about a hundred potatoes. Hanu grabbed an apron from a hook along the wall and immediately got to work.

"All I'm saying is Underground City has become just as useless as Capital City," said Rambo, stabbing a potato with her knife and pulling it from the pile. "The majority of them don't even realize what's going on."

"Well, you can't blame 'em," said Deeds. He dropped his potato into the peeled pile and grabbed another one as well. "Arrangement's been keeping it on the hush. Notice how they didn't make any kind of statement or announcement about what happened to the City of Fire."

Rambo gave a small nod, considering his argument. "True, but what about that lady down at the distillery today," she retorted. "I gave her facts and she flatly refused to see the –"

"Cause you can't just drop all of that on somebody!" Deeds interjected.

Hanu sank down in his seat, thinking he may have been assigned to the wrong group. Then Deeds suddenly turned to him. "Help me out, Hanu," he said. "Do you think it's possible that Underground City is brainwashed?"

Hanu laughed nervously. "Well... it depends on what you mean, I guess..."

"Okay," Rambo said, putting down her knife. "I asked a lady, hypothetically, if she thought she would be able to live on the surface if she had to migrate up there and she flipped! It was like she malfunctioned at the very *idea*."

Deeds held up a finger to interject. "First of all Hanu," – and he rolled his eyes dramatically at Rambo –"she gave this lady the most morbid doomsday scenario before asking that. You didn't even know the lady, Rambo!"

"It was *hypothetical*," Rambo said, slamming a hand on the table at every syllable. Several of the soldiers stopped what they were doing and looked at the three of them. Hanu shrunk down further behind the pile of potatoes.

Then Deeds threw his head back and laughed. "Oh, you should have seen it, Hanu," he wheezed. "This lady flipped."

Rambo was laughing now, too. A tear escaped from the corner of her eye as she slapped the table some more. Hanu peeled his potato a little faster, hoping to be finished before things got any more confusing.

After a ridiculous amount of time, their laughter died down, and they were looking at him again.

"Well," said Hanu. He didn't think he'd really have to answer the question. "I actually kind of agree with Rambo."

"What – *how?*" Deeds demanded. Rambo smiled mockingly at him.

"I was at the market the other day," said Hanu. "And this guy was telling people about the Ancient Ones and Year One and all of that, but they just got angry with him. It's like they don't even wanna know."

"Total denial," agreed Rambo. "It's mind control."

"It's normal," argued Deeds. He picked up another potato. "It's a lot to take in for people who've been living in peace for so long."

"Come on," said Rambo. "This is not a normal response, though. And check out how Arrangement's been acting, Deeds."

"Okay, total denial there."

"It's like they want them to be unaware... *unprepared*," said Rambo darkly.

"So Arrangement has been overtaken," Deeds joked. "It's official. They've been infiltrated and we have to –"

"You shouldn't go yelling things like that," said Adam Lilley, who had just come in through the kitchen door and was handing Mr. Salcedo a large black box. Then he grabbed a knife and pulled up a chair.

He smiled at Hanu and gave him a little wink before grabbing a potato from the pile. Hanu nodded in return, fighting down a small panic. The last time he spoke with Mr. Lilley face to face, he was being told that he was too young to go on the mission to the District of Operations. Hanu, of course, completely disrespected him by going anyway. And since things ended up the way they did, Hanu never really had a chance to fully clear the air with him about it.

"Sorry, sir," said Deeds. He sat straight up in his seat and cleared his throat. Rambo grabbed another potato and peeled it as quickly as she could.

The two of them remained very silent for a while, seemingly

nervous. It never dawned on Hanu before, but Mr. Lilley *was* an important man in the Hierarchy. Naturally, he would solicit this kind of respect from the people in his command. He kicked himself just a little more, having realized the severity of his offense.

Hanu peeled his potato carefully, considering what he might say to Mr. Lilley. He would, of course, have to say *something*. It would be rude not to, especially since they still had quite a large pile of potatoes to get through; they would be there for a while.

He wasn't sure if he should mention anything about the District of Operations, though, being as Adam's demeanor had considerably relaxed since the last time Hanu saw him. He wouldn't want to re-stress the man. And he didn't want to pester him about his recent request to join the Resistance, either. He didn't want to be seen as impatient – that wouldn't help his case at all. So he decided on small talk instead.

"So, um…" Hanu cleared his throat. "Mr. Lilley, how are things going with you?" Then he held his breath, wondering if it was proper protocol to ask a person of his rank how things were going.

"Oh, you know," Mr. Lilley sighed. He continued to peel his potato, and a smile danced on the corners of his mouth. "We've been busier than ever. How about you – settled in okay?"

"Yes, sir," said Hanu. He feigned a confident smile. "There's lots to do around Underground City. We've all gotta play our part." Hanu had no idea what he was saying, but he definitely wasn't going to choke up and let his chance to impress Mr. Lilley pass him by.

"You got it," smiled Mr. Lilley. "It takes every last one of us."

ᚻᛁᚳ ᚻᛁᚳ ᚻᛁᚳ

Dinner went by smoothly enough. They managed to get through all of the potatoes without so much as a hiccup from Hanu. He said all the right things and even made a few jokes – juvenile though they were, he got one or two belly laughs from Mr. Lilley. Then after the food was prepared, all of the staff in the house circulated through the kitchen, creating a cacophony of silverware scraping against plates and light-hearted chatter.

The Special Unit came down just long enough to collect a whole chicken and a large bowl of soup, then disappeared back through the living room doors, soup sloshing onto the stairs as they went. Then, when everyone was mostly finished and people were unbuckling their utility belts or leaning back in their seats, a soldier stood up and tapped the side of his glass delicately with a spoon.

"With the Coordinator's permission," he started. "I'd like to propose a toast."

With a gentle smile, Mr. Lilley raised his glass. "Here, here!"

Then everyone grabbed their glass or rushed to get one, hastily pouring a splash of water or tea inside, until the whole room had a drink raised. Mr. Salcedo, who dashed to the basement for a couple bottles of wine, returned breathlessly and, realizing he was too late, uncorked a bottle and raised it for himself.

"I propose a toast to the family we've created here," he said, extending his glass out to the room. "And to the bonds that make us strong. We've endured many challenges, especially recently, but here we are on the verge of making real change in the tides of history."

The room erupted into cheers and murmurs and applause. Hanu looked meaningfully at Sadie, who was clapping one hand against her glass. "What are they talking about?" he mouthed.

Sadie shrugged her shoulders and continued clapping, but the gratified grin that stretched across her face said otherwise. Ester looked just as confused, but Vanessa and Akesh – who were sitting in the living room – didn't seem to care.

"May we always recall our own strength," he continued. "And may we always have family to fight for, to rely on, and to protect."

"To family," they all said. Then everyone clinked their glasses together or raised them high in the air before drinking.

Hanu raised his own glass, then took a sip of his cherry juice. Then he returned to his seat next to Akesh, content with knowing that this wasn't just a regular dinner – it was a celebration of some sort; the Hierarchy had accomplished something big. And he didn't have to know what it was in order to be happy, too.

The other guests continued with their various conversations as well. Then, as people started clearing out for bed or getting back to work, Hanu decided he would slip out as well. He had made a good impression all around – he even helped Mrs.

Salcedo with the dishes – so he would leave it at that, and hope the Hierarchy admitted him soon.

He gathered his belongings and prepared himself to make the walk to the recreation annex, hoping nobody else claimed his sleeping spot. Then he took a turn through the first floor of the house. He would have to say goodbye to at least one of the girls or Akesh before heading out.

But the first person he ran into, just inside the hallway, was Sarah. He literally ran into her, sending a tray full of metal couplings across the hallway floor. And thankfully it was carpeted, or else the whole house would've been put on alert.

"Sorry," he said, quickly picking up the pieces and putting them back on her tray.

"It's okay," said Sarah. She clanked two of them together, making a deep ringing sound. "It's not like they can break."

"I guess not," laughed Hanu, struggling to reach one that fell under the storage cabinet. "What are these, anyway, and why do you have... so... *many?*"

Sarah didn't answer Hanu immediately. Instead she looked up and down the hallway then, when she was certain they were alone, she leaned in close. "If I show you something, would you keep it a secret?"

Hanu was just about to brush it off as child's play, but something in her wide mahogany eyes told him that this was more than a *Special Unit* kind of secret.

"Sure, I can," he said, thoroughly curious.

Sarah led him further into the hallway and opened a small

and rather old-looking door just behind a short flight of stairs. It wasn't a very tall door – Hanu had to duck to get inside – but it was very heavy. Then they were in the basement, which was equally unappealing. Cobwebs blanketed stacks of old, rusty parts and the wooden furniture looked like it should've been recycled decades ago. Hanu was ready to be disappointed by whatever Sarah would produce from this room, but then she lifted up a dusty carpet and revealed a trap door.

"I'm not sure if we should be here." Hanu had suddenly become nervous. There was no way he could afford to be busted snooping around here.

"Oh, lighten up," said Sarah. "And don't forget my couplings."

She pulled the handle on the trapdoor and opened it, revealing a brightly lit staircase. These stairs led to a large, sterile looking laboratory.

Hanu felt as though he had entered a different building altogether – perhaps they snuck into Intelligence through a back door or something. He stepped off the last stair and held his breath, thinking an alarm would sound at his intrusion.

"Come this way," Sarah giggled excitedly, beckoning him to a smaller room to the left.

"What *is* this place?"

"It's Daddy's lab," she said, tapping a button on the wall. The door silently slid open. It was a storage room. "He's been teaching me and Daniel down here for years, and now I get to do jobs alone, like deliver equipment and keep track of inventory."

"I don't think you should've brought me here," said Hanu. His eyes drank in the grandeur of place, but he dared not touch anything.

"I think it'll be okay," she said, dropping the couplings into a large bin full of identical parts. There could've easily been hundreds of them. "We won't be here for long. I just had to deliver these and – Oh, I never told you what they were!"

Sarah tucked the bin back under a cabinet and pulled Hanu just outside the storage room. She pressed her face against a long panel of glass, looking into a sealed off room. "They're gonna attach these things to some of their ships soon," she said.

Hanu squinted through the glass. There were rows and rows of canisters, each containing a fist-sized device made of thick wires, two flat discs and a bulbous protrusion at the bottom.

"Daniel actually did some of the research that helped to create them," she said proudly. "He's such a prodigy."

"But what *are* they?"

"Oh," said Sarah. "Let me see..." She concentrated very hard on remembering; her lips pursed and her eyes squinted. "They absorb the energy from an EMP... and use it to restart the systems in the ship."

"That's helpful," said Hanu. "So when the EMP shuts down the systems, they'll come back on right away?"

"Exactly," said Sarah. "It was Daniel's idea to experiment with magnetic hematite." Hanu ducked his head closer, inspecting the wires. They were bulky looking, and very shiny.

Then, in the reflection on the glass, he saw something moving. "What's that?" He turned around to see that just inside the opposite room, a single machine was working on something. Its mechanical arm glided back and forth over a round, flat disc.

"Oh, that," Sarah whispered, sneaking over to the room. She peeked into the window as if she were afraid of it. "That's the Living Library – well, the disc is, anyway. The machine is just encoding the information into it."

Hanu gasped. He hadn't realized the Hierarchy was already in possession of the Living library. But it would make sense, since Kavel and Kezra's father was on the project. He took another look at the disc. It was no bigger than a fist, and only an inch thick. "It's so small... What does it do?"

Sarah sighed. "Well, from what Kezra reported two days ago, Arrangement had been cataloging as much information as they could for after Year One – that way, no matter what happened, the story of humanity would be remembered." She crossed her arms. "Daddy says it represents their lack of faith in humanity, but for some reason, he still offered to encode it for them."

He squinted at the machine, remembering what Mr. Abbott had said to River. "Arrangement said we'd been using too much of the power supply," said Hanu. "They were gonna have to put the project on hold. Maybe he offered to do it as a compromise."

"Well I guess it worked out for everyone," she said. "It *does* seem to require a lot of energy, though. The machine's been doing that for four days straight now." She pointed at the disc. "The crystal holds forty-two thousand terabytes of data. It's an actual *library* of everything."

Hanu looked dubious. "Everything?"

"Well, all the pertinent information – genetic records of plants and animals, teachings of all of the greatest philosophers, historical data, scientific knowledge and the arts – stuff like that. It doesn't contain a record of what toast tastes like."

Hanu scoffed. "Or a record of the Last Stand of the City of Fire, apparently."

"But it had loads of information on quantum teleportation." She peeked back through the window, grinning widely.

Hanu inched closer to the glass, studying the small disc. "Were Kezra and Kavel ever able to figure out what they're gonna do with that info?"

Sarah frowned. "No, not yet." Then she strode back to the staircase. "We better get out of here," she said. But somebody was walking down the staircase when they got there – a very *unhappy* somebody.

"Okay, let's hear it," said a very tight-lipped Mrs. Salcedo. She put her hands on her hips and tapped a sneakered foot impatiently.

"Mom!" whined Sarah. She stomped her foot as if her mother had been the one caught wrong-doing. Hanu closed his eyes tight and said a silent goodbye to his days of scavenging for action at Salcedo Farm.

"Well?" sighed Mrs. Salcedo. She tucked a curtain of chocolate brown hair behind one ear. "Let's hear why you brought a guest to your super-*secret* job."

Sarah grabbed her mother's hand and took a deep breath. "It's only Hanu, though, mom," she began sweetly. "And you've always said how much you like Hanu, so I didn't think you'd mind.... Please don't tell dad."

But Mrs. Salcedo wasn't buying it. She turned her nose up, refusing to look into Sarah's wide, begging eyes. "Oh no, Little Miss," she smirked. "You said you'd be *responsible*."

"But I *am*," squealed Sarah. This, of course, did nothing to help her claim, though. "Hanu helped me to bring those couplings down, didn't you, Hanu?"

Hanu, who was thoroughly desperate to not be kicked out, nodded fervently. "Yes, ma'am," he agreed. "She needed help, that's all. We delivered the couplings and were heading right back up."

Mrs. Salcedo walked around the lab, silently inspecting the place. Hanu wasn't sure what she thought she might find – perhaps that they'd used up all the plastic gloves or played with some of the delicate instruments that hung in the cabinets along the countertops. This gave Hanu a chance to give a very stern look to Sarah, who silently apologized with her eyes in return.

But, thankfully, Mrs. Salcedo found that everything was in order. She rounded back on the two of them. "Alright," she said, looking back and forth from Sarah to Hanu with intense eyes. "No more visitors down here, you understand? This is not a playground."

"I promise," said Sarah. Then she quickly added, "and you're not telling dad, right?"

Mrs. Salcedo crossed her arms again. "If I didn't tell your father, then how would you learn your lesson?"

Sarah opened her mouth to argue, but thought better of it. "Oh you're right, as usual," she conceded with a frown.

Hanu was alarmed all over again. He shook his head dumbly at Mrs. Salcedo, who was too busy grinning amusedly at her daughter to notice. Then, after a few moments of this, she must've caught sight of his pitiful face, because she changed her mind. "Alright you, two," she said, giving Hanu's shoulder a little squeeze. "I won't tell if Hanu doesn't. Not very many people know about this place, and we like it that way."

"Not a word, I promise," Hanu agreed.

"Good," said Mrs. Salcedo firmly. "Now off to bed, both of you."

Hanu started up the stairs. "But I wasn't going to be sleeping here tonight –"

"Oh, you'll sleep here tonight, if you know what's good for you," Mrs. Salcedo said kindly. "Besides, it's far too late to be roaming around on the streets. *Curfew.*"

Adam Lilley's Plan

Twenty minutes later, Hanu was slinking through the door to Daniel's room. A pale streak of moonlight seeped in through the open window, allowing him to navigate to the bunk bed with relative ease. He tiptoed past Akesh, who was asleep, hanging halfway off the daybed under the window, and set his bag down in an empty spot on the floor. Luckily, Daniel slept on the top bunk tonight, because Hanu was able to slip into the bottom one without disturbing anyone. But just as he settled into the mattress, Akesh rolled right off the daybed and onto the floor with a thud.

"What... Whodat?" he blurted.

Daniel moaned slightly and pulled his blankets tighter around his head.

"Shhhh..."

"Oh, Hanu," Akesh said groggily. "I thought you left."

"Stop talking so loud," Hanu whispered. He crept closer to where Akesh was, easing onto the foot of his bed. "I was trying to leave, but I got hung up."

Akesh had a nice view of the Salcedos' yard from the window. Hanu could see over the orchard and well into the city. Lights twinkled innocently from many of the buildings, but the night was otherwise quite still. He watched in silence for a while, wide awake from the night's events.

"Hey, do you think Underground City'll be attacked?"

"Oh, I doubt it," Akesh yawned. "They haven't gotten in yet."

It wasn't enough to convince Hanu, though. He pulled a thin sheet around his shoulders, resting his chin on the window pane. He thought about telling Akesh about what he'd just seen in the basement, but thought better of it. Akesh never knew how to keep a secret. "Things are happening," he said. "I wanna be able to fight when it's time to fight."

"Mmmhmm."

Hanu squinted into the yard. Several large, black containers were stacked there. They were barely visible in the shadow of the trees – dozens of them. They certainly hadn't been there earlier. "Would you ever join the Resistance?" he asked.

"Nah," said Akesh. He punched his pillow. "I don't really have anything to fight for."

Hanu thought about his mother and sister. His stomach churned; it felt queasy and hollow. He hoped they were happy, but he also hoped that they felt some bit of despair that he was gone. He knew that the mother he saw in the District of Operations was just an illusion, but he feared that what she said was true. Hanu couldn't just be normal, and it had cost her a great deal of sorrow.

"But what about your family," he asked Akesh. "They couldn't have been that bad."

"Pu-lease..." Akesh rolled his eyes. "They're idiots... all six of them."

"I'm sure they did the best they could," said Hanu. "They just didn't know any better."

"They *should've* known better," Akesh said, sitting up now. He glared out the window, too, saying nothing for quite a while. Then he sighed grumpily. "My dad deserves everything he's gonna get when Year One comes. Jarret, Comey, Lance... all of them. They never let up on me. They made fun of me every chance they got; made me feel like a moron for not thinking like they do."

Hanu wasn't sure what to say to this. Akesh had never spoken about his family before in all the years he'd known him. He'd never been so angry, either. Hanu patted his best friend's shoulder sympathetically. "I'm sorry," he said. "My mom's the worst kind of idiot. She actually works for the Council."

Akesh gave his blanket a little shake and was about to lay back down when something caught his eye. "Hey, look at that," he said. Soldiers were starting to file out of the house – all wearing EAGs. Then several vessels materialized on the lawn in a shimmer. They quickly loaded the black containers into the ships, one by one. "Where do you think they're going?"

"I don't know. Maybe to the surface." Hanu said. The stacks of containers disappeared into the ships within a matter of minutes, then the soldiers began to board.

"Oh look, there's Sadie." Akesh perked, grinning as he pointed at the porch.

Sure enough, Hanu saw her red ponytail whipping behind her as she descended the porch steps. She said something to Mrs. Salcedo before trotting to the ship that was just below the tree line. Hanu watched enviously as the ships prepared to leave. Then his stomach suddenly knotted up. "Do you think they're heading into a fight?"

But Akesh didn't answer. He was preoccupied with the orange and blue lights that danced just inside the ship's afterburners. The two of them watched in awe as the ships simultaneously rose into the air, sending a flurry of birds retreating from the trees. Then, in an eerie silence, they disappeared into different directions of the night. A crackle of lightning slithered across the sky in the east.

"Something's definitely happening," said Hanu. "And I want in."

Then he slunk into his own bed, allowing Akesh to yawn and punch his pillow. Then, sooner than he expected, the boy was snoring again.

Hanu smoothed a woven blanket over himself, then rolled to face the wall. But he wasn't nearly ready to fall asleep yet. He was thinking about the war. And how he might contribute. Then, with a pang of unease, he thought about what Thalor said – that nothing's changed. Humanity would use its new dimensional energy to continue the fight. He grumbled a frustrated growl. Yaar wouldn't be coming to Earth anymore. Couldn't offer any further help. He wondered if he could speak with him telepathically. After all, the Nergal said that they had made a game of it. It was one he'd never mastered, but maybe now that he was desperate enough, he would make more progress.

He took a deep, even breath, then furrowed his brows in steep concentration. He felt rather stupid, doing this, but it was the best approach he could come up with. He thought about the Nergal, and about the tall desk, and about the brown, spongy inside of his ship – willing the Nergal to send him a message. But after several fruitless minutes of hard thinking, he relaxed his muscles.

Nothing was going to happen.

He sighed, then rolled onto his back, allowing his heavy heart to pin him down. His lip suddenly quivered. He pushed out a sorrowful whisper. "I'll never forget you, Yaar."

Then his eyebrows furrowed again. He found that he was a bit dizzy. The words felt strangely familiar, like deja vu. It made him feel vulnerable. Desperate for his mother, for some reason.

Without warning, a prickly dread struck the pit of his stomach. Then he was violently nauseous as icy, cutting pain arrested him again. He clenched his jaw to suppress a scream that burned his throat. Then he tried squeezing his eyes, pushing the vision away, but he failed. The smell of musky, sharp sweat that comes from terror filled his nose. It mixed with a copper that he could taste. His eyes darted, but he couldn't see the darkness of Daniel's room. There were eggshell colored walls, blurry as he squinted in pain. He rocked. He needed his mother. His eyes darted, then he saw someone familiar. It was

Yaar. Hanu's heart throbbed. It raced even harder. He reached out to him, but the creature didn't take his hand. He only watched, wearing a sad, sorrowful expression.

Hanu yanked himself upright, hitting his head on the wooden bars on the underside of the top bunk. He grabbed his face with both hands, allowing a sharp groan to escape him. His lungs were tender as he gulped in sharp breaths. His heart raced, barraging against his chest, making him feel faint. Daniel stirred in the top bunk, rolling and grumbling. It made Hanu squint into the room. It was dark. And quiet. Akesh snored loudly under the window. Daniel settled, then his breathing was slow and even again.

Hanu laid tenderly over his pillow, allowing it to cool his face. But it helped very little. His eyes darted as he puzzled through what just occurred. Was it possible Yaar actually did do something cruel to him? Hanu was reaching out to him. Why didn't he take his hand? And if this was a memory, why didn't he remember more? Why didn't he remember sooner? It seemed to be pretty dramatic. And those types of things aren't easily forgotten.

Then a faint suspicion crept into his mind. Could it be possible that the Intergalactic Council implanted the vision in order to make it easier for Hanu to let go of the Nergal? Or, maybe, it was as simple as his memories being all mixed up. After all, he'd endured so much torture while being held prisoner in the District, he wouldn't be surprised if his brain was even a little scrambled.

He puzzled over the experience for what seemed like hours, but he found that he couldn't come up with a reasonable conclusion yet. He needed clarity. And he would have to find it on his own. The fifth dimensional sphere was quite far enough already, and Hanu had a sneaking suspicion that Yaar was a great deal even further away now.

With shaking hands, he smoothed the blanket back over himself. Then he squeezed his eyes shut, knowing he wouldn't be getting any sleep. He was more lost than ever. Something terrible may have happened. And Hanu hadn't a clue what or when. And most pressing, Year One was on the horizon and he was armed with nothing more than a whispered reminder that humanity would use its new dimensional energy to solve its problems.

Whatever that meant nowadays.

⸕·≺ ⸕·≺ ⸕·≺

The next week and a half was painfully uneventful. The farm was no longer abuzz with soldiers coming in to receive their orders or members of the think tanks shuffling up and down the stairs on their breaks. And without a steady source of Hierarchy gossip, Hanu had become quite bored. So much so that he allowed Akesh to recruit him for a little construction project just beyond the fence to the south of the property.

"I say we should give 'em another day," said Akesh, inspecting a long row of clay bricks on the ground. He pressed a thick twig into one of them. "They'll be dry enough to stack tomorrow."

Hanu poured a bucket of water on the makeshift oven that they'd built, making it hiss and crackle angrily. "If you ask me, we should've made a lot more." He eyed the clearing on the edge of the forest that they'd designated for their hut, then counted the bricks again.

Akesh tried to brush his bangs from his eyes but only managed to wipe dirt on the side of his face. "Nah, there's plenty," he said confidently. He held his hands up to scale the imaginary house. "Especially if we make the roof from sticks. The ones I saw up the road didn't have all that many."

"Okay," said Hanu. "So what did they use for the doors?"

Akesh paused hard, holding his chin in his hand. "That's actually a good question. I don't remember."

"Well, we'd better start hiking," sighed Hanu.

They didn't get a chance to go anywhere, though. Along the narrow path that ran along the property fence, they could see that Sadie was approaching. "Hey," she yelled. "Is this where you're building the mansion? I heard there would be a mansion."

"It's actually just me and Hanu's new hangout," laughed Akesh. "We definitely don't have enough bricks for a mansion."

"How did you know we were out here?" Hanu asked, walking through the grass to meet her.

Sadie cut through the tall grass as well, hiking up her backpack. "Well you know," she said, pointing to the fire. "I think all that smoke mighta gave you away."

Akesh grimaced. "So everyone knows we're – ?"

"Nobody really cares," Sadie waved him away. "We thought you were just setting stuff on fire, but I saw the bricks."

It wasn't unheard of for anyone to build their own home, especially among the refugees. But the boys preferred to keep their project a secret so the younger children didn't get in the way trying to *help*.

"We're actually making a lot of progress," Akesh said proudly. "There'll be a kitchen, game room and two bedrooms – one for each of us. We haven't really worked out the bathroom, though."

"Oh yeah?" said Sadie, studying the construction site. She tapped one of the bricks with a sandaled foot.

"No combat boots today?" asked Hanu. Then he noticed she actually wasn't wearing *any* of her uniform, which was rather unlike her. Instead, she wore loose fitting pants and a tee-shirt.

"We were ordered to take it easy before tonight's mission," she said. "I'm probably gonna head to Moira's house. Wanna come?"

"Not today," Akesh said, dragging a wooden bench to the center of the clearing. "We've built a lot, but we need a few more things, and now we gotta figure out what our doors are gonna be made from."

"Just make them from wood, like that bench," she said simply. "That's what those people back there did."

"Oh," said Hanu. Then he sat on the bench before Akesh got a chance to position it properly. Akesh didn't mind, though. He just moved on to setting up the rest of the furniture. Hanu patted the seat next to him. "Come and rest your feet," he said. "You're our first house guest."

"Ah, I should've brought the champagne," Sadie joked. She dropped herself onto the bench, which was actually sturdier than it looked. She stretched her legs out in front of her.

Hanu drummed his fingers on his knees. "So, does that mean they'll be processing those applications?" he said. "You know, with everyone being on break, I guess they have plenty of time to sort through those, huh?"

Sadie melted further into her seat, allowing her head to rest on the back of the bench. She took in a deep breath, then squeezed her lips together. "Why do you want to join so bad?"

Hanu was taken aback. "I... I want to help," he started. Then he cleared his throat, realizing he didn't sound too convincing. He'd been focusing for so long on becoming a member of the Resistance, that he almost forgot why he was even trying to do it in the first place. "I want to know what's going on, you know... so I can help stop Year One. I want to be able to jump in and make a difference."

"You do that anyway," Sadie said. She laughed mirthlessly. "Hanu, you jump in anyway – even when the Hierarchy tells you not to."

"Well, I wouldn't have to if they'd just let me join," Hanu defended. "See how they can avoid all the confusion if they just give me an assignment?"

"That's the problem," Sadie said. She scoffed, wearing a look of reluctant admiration of his stubbornness. "You don't follow the orders they give you as it is."

"I would if I knew all of the *information*," Hanu said. He scoffed, folding his arms. "If I knew what was going on, I wouldn't be in half the situations I end up in!"

Sadie sighed, then rested an elbow on the back of the bench. "So you're saying if you knew what the Hierarchy was doing you would go along with it?"

"As long as what they're doing is getting rid of the Ancient Ones, yes," Hanu agreed.

Sadie watched Hanu with scrutinizing eyes, then she looked over her shoulders. "They don't need any more recruits," she said quietly. Hanu leaned in closer. "Everything we needed to do is already set in place. You just have to keep a clear head when it happens, and follow the instructions."

"What instructions?" Hanu said, glancing over the tree line. "What's happening?"

Akesh stopped adjusting a wooden statue and began arranging some flowers in a tin can vase, shifting nervously from one foot to the other.

"Don't freak," she warned, looking Hanu straight in the eyes. She paused for quite a bit, allowing him to lean in further before she told him. "We're lowering the barriers."

"What do you mean – like, the ones around the farm?" Hanu was confused as to how surrendering to Arrangement would help stop Year One.

But Sadie shook her head, eyeing him meaningfully. "No,

not those."

Then Hanu realized what she was talking about. He jumped out of his seat. "That would leave us wide open to attack, wouldn't it?"

"Shhh... I'm not even supposed to be telling you this, you idiot!" Sadie forced Hanu back into his seat. "Yes, but we've been preparing for that."

"So you're going to force Underground City to fight?"

"No, not at all. The citizens will be taken care of, we just need to destroy Underground City to force everyone above ground. That's the only way – "

"Seriously?" Hanu looked expectantly at Akesh, who simply dropped the rest of his flowers haphazardly into the vase and shrugged. "We're literally going to destroy the city?"

"Shut up," Sadie said, glancing over her shoulders again. But Hanu had already begun marching toward the farm.

She threw her arms up. "You see this," she yelled, following him down the path. "You're doing it again... you're acting without knowing all the details." But Hanu didn't stop. He didn't even look back over his shoulder. Sadie gave up on her half-hearted chase. "Don't tell them it was me that told you!" she yelled after him.

Minutes later, Hanu threw open the backdoor of Salcedo farm. He found Mrs. Salcedo at the kitchen table, having her afternoon cup of tea. Mr. Salcedo was busy at the spice rack, collecting the largest of his bay leaves.

"Come in, Hanu," said Mrs. Salcedo pleasantly. "We're

getting started on lunch. Do you want us to deliver yours to the new hangout?"

"No, thank you," he wheezed, crossing the room to confront Mr. Salcedo. "You can't lower those barriers."

The Salcedos looked at Hanu with inscrutable expressions. "You're not supposed to know about that," Mr. Salcedo said matter-of-factly. Then he continued to measure out his spices.

"But the fact of the matter is, I do," Hanu hissed. "Year One is less than a month away, and you're about to send everyone to the surface? I think you've all gone insane!"

"It doesn't really matter what you think about it, Hanu," said Mr. Salcedo. He pinched a bit of salt into a pot of boiling water and sprinkled a few bay leaves into a soup. "It's what's going to happen, and when it does, it'll be for everyone's benefit."

"You can't speak for everyone," Hanu began to argue, but then a stern voice came from the living room.

"And neither can you."

Hanu turned on his heel to find Adam Lilley and three soldiers blocking the doorway to the kitchen. Though nobody was in uniform, they still had a very formal demeanor about them. "You do not understand the amount of consideration that went into making such a decision," he said. "And you have no idea of the level of care we're prepared to give to these civilians during this transition."

"But what about the people who don't *want* to go back to the surface," Hanu argued. "And the people who were born down here – it's not fair to just force them to uproot their whole lives just for us. That should be *their* decision."

One of the soldiers made a move toward Hanu, but Mr. Lilley stopped him. He leaned against the doorframe. "I understand what you're saying, Hanu, but you're young. You don't get the big picture," he explained. "We weren't meant to stay down here forever, hiding from the Ancient Ones – "

"Yeah, but we also weren't meant to ambush anyone, either!"

"There's no other way," Mr. Lilley said simply.

"Can't you find another way, though?" Hanu pleaded. "Isn't destroying the city taking it too far?"

Mr. Lilley beckoned to one of the soldiers, who secured Hanu by the wrist. "Everything is in place, Hanu. You'll be staying upstairs until it starts, just as a safety measure."

Hanu allowed the men to escort him to one of the rooms on the top floor. He didn't struggle or attempt to argue Mr. Lilley down. He almost instantly regretted reacting the way he did, actually, realizing too late that if there was ever an interview in the recruitment process, he just blew it. He stepped into the room and turned on the light. There was a small cot, a wooden stool, and a rectangular window on the back wall.

Mr. Lilley offered him a sympathetic smile, then closed and locked the door with a series of clicks. Hanu already planned to wait until everything died down again, then quietly sneak out of the house. The only problem was, an hour later when he opened the window and tried to climb onto the tree outside, he found that he couldn't leave.

He could feel the cool breeze that rushed through the leaves as it entered the window, but no matter how hard he tried to stick his arm out, he just couldn't. Time and time again, he slammed his limbs into an invisible wall before he realized that there was a barrier surrounding the room, making it impossible for him to leave.

"Of course," he groaned, throwing himself down on the cot. Then he noticed something strange going on. He could see light shining into the room from the hallway through the crack at the bottom of the door. And there was a shadow. Someone was in the hall, spying on him.

Hanu tiptoed over and put the side of his head onto the cold floor, hoping to get a look at who it was. To his surprise, he saw two pairs of shoes – both small and familiar. "What are you two doing here?" he asked.

Sarah and Daniel jumped in unison. "Oh, it's really you," Daniel said excitedly.

"We didn't think they would ever have to use this room," said Sarah, kneeling down to try and look under the door. "Especially not for someone like you."

"What kind of room is this," Hanu asked Sarah's eyeball. "Is this the prison room or something? There's a barrier that won't let me out."

"Basically," said Sarah. If Hanu could see her whole face, he would be able to see that she was blushing apologetically.

"It's actually a pretty simple design," said Daniel. Some of his red curls slid under the door as his eye appeared. "But I think it's genius. The atmosphere on the property is shifted slightly out of phase with the rest of Underground City, right? That's why Arrangement can't enter without a special modulating frequency. They've only adjusted the atmosphere in the room to sync with the rest of Underground City, which means you can't *leave* without the modulating frequency."

"Yeah... *impressive*," Hanu said sarcastically.

"But it's meant for legitimately dangerous people," scoffed Daniel. "Not emotional teenagers."

"Well at least *you* know I'm not dangerous," Hanu chuckled. "So, uh, can you let me out?"

"Oooh..." Sarah bit her lip. "We're definitely not allowed to let you out, I'm sorry."

Hanu frowned. "Well, it didn't hurt to ask. "

"We're actually not even supposed to be up here," said Daniel. "We're not allowed to talk to prisoners."

"But since it's you," said Sarah, squinting her eye. "We figured it's only right that we pay you a visit."

"And ask you what happened," added Daniel.

"I protested." Hanu cringed, thinking about how furious Sadie must be with him right now. A small part of him was relieved that a locked door and barrier were in between him and everybody else at the moment. At least this way, Sadie couldn't beat him to a pulp.

"Is that all?" asked Sarah.

"Well, I yelled at your dad, too."

"Don't we all from time to time," Daniel laughed.

"I also yelled at Mr. Lilley," Hanu admitted. "But that's kind of it."

"Well, that's not really a reason to imprison somebody," said Daniel. "But more importantly, what were you protesting?"

"That's the thing," said Hanu. "The Hierarchy is about to do something crazy, but I can't tell you what it is. They're keeping me here so I don't tell anyone else."

"Oh, please tell," said Daniel, shivering with excitement.

"No!" yelled Sarah. "That's why he's in prison now. If he tells us, then everyone will get mad at him."

"Not if *we* don't tell anyone," Daniel reasoned.

"No, Sarah's right," said Hanu. "Besides, you two are just going to freak out – just like I did."

Then Hanu could hear footsteps climbing up the staircase. Sarah and Daniel scrambled to their feet and slunk down the hall before he could say another word.

※·※ ※·※ ※·※

Hanu spent the next eight hours either pacing the room or staring at the ceiling from his rickety cot. For the most part, he appreciated the peace and quiet that imprisonment naturally provided. It gave him time to mull over what he'd just learned, and gave him an opportunity to try and fit all the pieces of his reality together. He came to the conclusion that as much as he hated the way Arrangement was ignoring the problem, he didn't have to agree with what the Hierarchy was doing.

What if something went terribly wrong and the citizens of

Underground City ended up being killed because of it? How could they guarantee the safety of each and every one of their lives? Nothing was black and white anymore, and he hadn't yet learned to navigate the shades of gray.

"Psst."

Someone was at the door, and Hanu was certain it wasn't the man who came every three hours with rations. He crept toward the door, laying his head against the cold floor once again. It was Akesh.

"Hey, down here," said Hanu.

After a moment of fumbling, Akesh's eye appeared in the crack under the door. "Are you okay in there?"

"I think so." Hanu licked his lips. "I'm not really sure, actually..."

"Yeah," Akesh laughed nervously. "Everyone out here's on edge now."

For a while there was silence, and Hanu had a difficult time staring into Akesh's eye, so he opted on playing with a piece of lint that blew under the door from the hallway. He flicked the ball of fuzz a few times and then a thought struck him.

"Wait a minute," he said indignantly. "Why didn't they put *you* in here? You know about the plan, too."

"Yeah, but I didn't go yelling about it." Akesh scoffed. "You pretty much did this to yourself." Hanu squinted his eye as angrily as he could, and Akesh must've gotten the message because he quickly added, " Sadie's words, not mine."

Hanu closed his eyes and took a breath, accepting the fact

that Akesh was right. When he opened them again, he was much more pleasant. "So what should we do now, then?" he said productively.

"What do you mean," said Akesh. "There's nothing we can do except wait – "

"And let them wreak havoc on the city?"

Akesh's eye focused on the ball of lint. "Yeah, I mean their plans are pretty much set in stone."

"You don't think what they're doing is wrong, then?"

"I don't know," said Akesh, agitated. "They said everyone would be safe. They said there was a plan for everyone to be taken care of – even you."

"Does everybody agree with it, then?" asked Hanu. "Do you agree with it?"

Akesh was silent for quite some time, and Hanu knew he was probably regretting having come to visit him. Akesh had never been one for arguments, or having very strong opinions about anything.

"I hate everything about the surface," Akesh whispered. "I think they're all stupid... but I'm not gonna fight the Hierarchy, Hanu. If they think they can get rid of the Ancient Ones, then we should be helping them."

Hanu rolled onto the floor, spreadeagle. He looked up into the ceiling, but his mind's eye was recounting his last memories of the City Of Fire – when it was being burned to the ground by the Ancient Ones. His stomach writhed as he thought about all of those citizens scrambling, trying to find safety, as enormous blimps scorched everything from overhead. He would have never imagined that the Hierarchy would purposely allow this to happen again. The whole idea was absurd. Yet that was, in fact, exactly what would be happening.

"I don't know if I can let them do that, Akesh." Hanu said quietly. "The whole thing sounds crazy."

Hanu could hear shuffling on the other side of the door, then the sounds of Akesh's footsteps grew fainter up the hall. But he only continued staring at the ceiling, hoping to come to a different understanding of Adam Lilley's plan.

He wondered if Ester knew about it, being an intuit and all, or if her ability to see the future had run out at this point. If she did know, though, wouldn't the intuits in the Intelligence department know as well? Arrangement might have already developed their own countermeasures.

The light outside had begun to fizzle and fade, casting long shadows into the room. Hanu remained on the floor for a very long time. He actually considered falling asleep exactly where he was, but he started to notice how uncomfortable he had grown. There was a faint buzzing in his ears. It wasn't the most awful sound, but it was very annoying. Had it not been so quiet, he might not have noticed it at all. He sat up and shook his head grumpily, but it didn't help.

Then, with a loud moan, Hanu pulled himself off of the floor and shuffled toward the window. He hoped to get some fresh air, but when he arrived, he saw something very strange. Half a dozen craft were silently hovering over the woods to the east, between the farm and the mountainside. Some of them were large, bulky machines that Hanu had never seen before and others were sleek and angular, like the City of Fire's stealth class flyers.

It was odd to see the craft just hanging in the air. As a rule, when the Hierarchy needed to come or go from the city, they did so as secretly as possible. They quickly loaded their vehicles under the cover of the Salcedos' barrier, and they always engaged their cloak before taking off.

He watched these strange vessels, trying to interpret what they might be doing in Underground City, until the buzzing in his ears made it too hard to think. He crossed the room.

"Hey, anybody out there," he yelled, pounding on the door. "Something's going on. I – I think something's happening outside." Hanu was afraid nobody would hear him. He rushed back to the window, double checking that the craft were still there. They twinkled menacingly in the sky as the last of the daylight crept from the city.

To Hanu's surprise, the door was suddenly clicking and, in a flash, it swung open. It was Adam Lilley, dressed in full uniform. He studied Hanu for a brief moment. "You applied to join the force," he said.

"Yeah, but that's not important right now," Hanu urged, digging his fingers into his ears. He shook his head. "Don't you hear that? And look –"

He crossed the room again, beckoning Mr. Lilley toward the window. Mr. Lilley ran a hand against the barrier. "Interesting," he said more to himself than to Hanu. "The room is picking up on the frequency."

"What..." Hanu stammered. "What frequency – ?"

"You always seem to find things out," Mr. Lilley laughed. "Find some loophole, or stray bit of intel that turns the tides in some unpredictable way." Hanu shook his head, ready to deny that he was doing any of it intentionally, but Mr. Lilley continued. "I guess it helps that you're persistent... But you throw yourself in danger's way time and time again, despite my attempts to keep you safe."

"But, Sir –"

"Why did you apply to join the Resistance?" he demanded, looking Hanu square in the eyes. "What was the reason?"

Hanu was prepared for the question now, having a whole day to replay his conversation with Sadie in his head. "I want to help stop Year One," he said decisively. "I want to help get rid of the Ancient Ones."

"And how do you propose we do that?" Mr. Lilley asked, brushing the hairs on his own chin with a gloved hand.

"I, uh... I don't really know," Hanu said.

Mr. Lilley pulled Hanu closer to the window, pointing into the sky. "You see that lightning?" Hanu nodded, watching the sky light up in a flash. "You notice it's been going on for months now, right?"

"Yeah, I noticed."

"That's what it looks like before a barrier fails," said Mr. Lilley. "We can't defend these people for the rest of their lives and stop Year One at the same time. Not unless we're willing to go to extremes." He took a deep breath and looked at Hanu. "We only get one chance to pull it off and you have to play your part, because any half-witted attempt to stop this plan could result in the death of hundreds of thousands of people."

A certain type of thickness suddenly came into the room. Hanu could feel the weight of it pressing on his chest as he looked into Mr. Lilley's eyes. He plopped down on his cot and ran a hand through his mop of hair. Mr. Lilley watched him rather patiently, but Hanu knew he wouldn't be able to wait much longer. "What do I need to do?" he sighed.

Mr. Lilley extended a hand. "Things have already begun," he said, hoisting Hanu from his cot. He beckoned him through the door which, thankfully, allowed him out into the hall. "I've made arrangements for you to ride with the little ones."

Mr. Lilley led Hanu down the hall and down the staircase, which was rather busy for it to be so late at night. Rambo and Deeds rushed past them, carrying a very large metal chest. Deeds offered a quick, "Pardon," before grunting the rest of the way down. Another soldier Hanu had never seen before squeezed by.

"There's a cargo vessel in the yard," said Mr. Lilley, walking briskly through the kitchen. "Once aboard, you'll get the rest of your instructions."

Hanu trotted to keep up with Mr. Lilley's purposeful strides. He shuffled down the stairs on the back porch and straight toward the trees that lined the yard, but his knees buckled halfway though. Thirty more ships rested in the sky just off to the south, just as ominous and silent as the others. "What is this?" Hanu whispered in horror.

"They're the evacuation fleet," Mr. Lilley said, doubling back. He grabbed Hanu by the arm and pulled him quickly through the trees. A giant craft was waiting in the clearing on the other side.

Mr. Lilley walked straight up to it and pounded three times. Then a small hatch opened, revealing a dimly lit corridor. "This is where we part ways," he said, giving Hanu's shoulders a squeeze. His eyes glinted in the moonlight, but the darkness hadn't erased the trepidation from his face. "You're a Dissenter at heart, and I respect that. Now is the time to lay low, though. You've done more than enough."

Hanu gave Mr. Lilley his best smile, despite the fact that he suddenly couldn't feel his legs. Things had moved along so quickly that he didn't have time to think about how nervous he was until just now. After all, he hadn't entirely committed to the plan. He only made an agreement that he wouldn't do anything stupid.

But since Mr. Lilley was now watching him expectantly, he turned and started up the ramp and into the ship, dragging his heavy feet along the thinly carpeted floor. Then he offered a final wave goodbye as the hatch swung closed and sealed with a hiss.

Exodus

"Hello?"

Hanu shuffled nervously into the hallway. Bluish lights lined the floor, illuminating his path into the larger part of the ship. A rather childlike voice called from further inside the cabin.

"Keep walking, I'm in here!"

Though the lighting didn't improve much once he was in the cabin, he could make out most of the room. There were the typical control panels and stations, equipped with cushy seats. He could also make out several tubelike compartments lined in neat rows on the far end of the room. Someone was typing something into one of the computer screens.

"I'm ready for you over here," she said loudly, motioning for him to come in further. A dull glow from one of the consoles revealed a soft face with premature worry lines. It was someone Hanu recognized, though he couldn't quite remember why.

"Hey... I know you," he said, walking a little more quickly now. "I've seen you before – "

"Yes," the woman said. She double checked her work against the glowing screen on a notepad. Then, when she was satisfied, she crossed the room to meet him. "I'm Cameron, remember? We rode together from the District of Operations a few months ago."

"Oh yeah, you're Pants' partner right?" Hanu said.

He attempted to smile, but he knew his face was most likely wearing a painful grimace. Memories of their encounter with the Ancient Ones in the Uninhabitable Zone had suddenly flooded his mind.

"I *was*," she said, scrunching up her face. "But for the last three months I've been overseeing production at one of the metallurgy outposts. He got reassigned to someone else."

"I see," said Hanu. He ran his hand along the rail that separated the platform he was on and the recessed floor at the forward end of the room. He was happy to be back on a craft, though this one didn't look like it was equipped for much action. "So, Mr. Lilley said I would get my instructions here," he said. "What am I supposed to do?"

"Oh," said Cameron. She threw her notepad on the nearest console and motioned for Hanu to follow. "Come on, you'll be back here with these guys." Hanu followed Cameron toward the wall of tubes. "All the necessary systems for this transport are fully automated, so there won't be a crew," she explained casually. "Your job is to get prepared for life on the surface."

As they approached the compartments, Hanu noticed that some of them were occupied. He pressed his face against the glass siding on the first one on the row. It was Daniel. The boy's round face was illuminated by a carousel of colors as he stared, slack-jawed, into the abyss. "What's wrong with him?" he asked, waving a hand back and forth, but Daniel didn't notice.

Hanu slid his face along the side of the glass to find the source of the light. A screen was fixed at the front of the compartment, exactly at eye level. It was projecting two-dimensional images of people – a man was walking through what could have been a general store, then there was a diagram of a trade interface.

"It's what we call learning on the fly," Cameron interrupted. She pressed her face against the window for a quick look. "Don't worry, he's okay. There's just a lot of information to take in before getting to the surface. We had to prepare them somehow."

Daniel's eyes darted back and forth rapidly, as though he were tracking something very fast across the screen. He blinked tiredly. "So where exactly is everyone going to evacuate to?" said Hanu. He bit his lip. "I think the Council would notice if hundreds of thousands of people showed up out of nowhere all of a sudden."

"Don't you worry about the Council," said Cameron. "They're practically useless now that the Ancient Ones have fled to the Uninhabitable Zone."

There was a scout on the screen now, with portions of his anatomy being highlighted. Its arm blinked several times, then an infographic appeared on the screen. "Just steer clear of 'em and you won't have to worry about the arm," Hanu snorted.

"You practically lived on the surface your whole life, huh?" said Cameron.

"Yeah, I guess so," said Hanu, allowing himself to be transfixed by an aerial view of Capital City.

"I guess you don't need this part of the directions, then," said Cameron, fidgeting with one of the clasps on her utility belt. She glanced at her wristwatch. "I have to pick up a whole bunch of passengers. What do you say about helping me out instead?"

Hanu pulled his eyes away from the screen. "Help you? Yeah, I'd like that."

"Alright," Cameron chuckled. "I guess I won't really need help, but I'll be a lot less nervous if I had some company."

She strode through the dim cabin and pulled up an extra chair at navigation. "I'm locking you in here, right next to me," she said, magnetizing the seats to the floor with the flick of a switch. "Strap in."

Hanu joined her at the console. He sat quickly, pulling his safety strap over his shoulder with shaking hands and scanning the blinking console with wary eyes. Cameron began the launch sequence, double checking the flight path and adjusting the atmospheric settings. Then she picked up the radio. "Songbird ready for takeoff," she said.

Someone on the other end immediately responded. "Clear for takeoff, Songbird."

Cameron engaged the thrusters, monitoring several points on the console and turning delicate knobs. "Look, Hanu," she said seriously. "I heard you weren't too happy about the plan when you heard what we were going to do. I didn't like the idea either, but the bottom line is, we were only going to waste our time and resources trying to protect Underground City while the Ancient Ones carried out Year One. After that, they'd have nothing left to do except come after us with their full force."

Hanu nodded, watching the ground get smaller through the viewscreen as they cleared the property line of the farm. They headed toward the city. And though he didn't agree with what they were doing, he felt a small sense of ease, knowing that nobody really wanted to carry out this plan, but they agreed that it was necessary.

The feeling was short-lived, though.

Moments later Cameron stopped the thrusters and they were hovering over a very neat looking neighborhood. Its wide, cobbled road was lined with dozens of tidy homes – each a perfect square with a single spruce tree in the backyard.

"I trained hard over the last three weeks for this part, and I'm still not ready," she admitted, avoiding looking Hanu in the eye. Then she sighed. "To be honest, I should've secured you in one of those information chambers because you won't be ready either."

"Ready for what?" asked Hanu. His mouth had suddenly gone dry.

Cameron unfastened her safety belt and motioned for Hanu to do the same. He followed her to the recessed platform. It was circular in shape, and couldn't have been more than twenty feet in diameter. The surrounding machinery offered very little light, but it was enough for Hanu to have a decent look. The floor contained a series of vents and the ceiling above it was lined with thickly coiled wires. "This is a transport pad," she explained, stepping down onto the platform. "Our passengers will be arriving through here. Our job is to keep them safe and guide them into the information chambers."

"Okay," said Hanu, inspecting the contraption. "That sounds easy enough."

Cameron checked her watch again. "We're about two minutes ahead of schedule," she said nervously. "When it's time, I'll activate the transport and then you're going to have to help me, Hanu. They'll be a little tired and... *confused*."

Hanu suddenly understood what had been making Cameron so nervous. He shifted from one leg to the other as a spot deep within his gut writhed with guilt. "We're kidnapping them out of their beds," he whispered. "They don't know we're coming for them."

"They don't," said Cameron. Her voice was determined now. "And there's no easier way to do this Hanu, so we just have to get through it." She quickly stepped off the platform and rounded on a small console that was perched at the far end. Hanu watched in horror as she pulled up a map of the area below them and drew a perimeter around the neighborhood with her finger. The system isolated all of the life signs in the area, which she assigned for transport.

Hanu fought down an impulse to march over to her console and cancel the command on the holoscreen. It would've been easy. There were two options at the bottom of the display – one that said 'activate' and another that said 'cancel.' It would've taken no time at all to sabotage her. But then what? He knew it would do no good and, besides, Mr. Lilley had already warned him of the consequences. He swallowed down the afternoon's rations, which were bubbling in his throat, and prepared himself for what was to come.

Cameron leaned on the console with both hands and closed her eyes, steeling herself. Then she looked at her wristwatch again, counting down the seconds until it was time to begin. "Their safety is our priority, Hanu," she said firmly, then she activated the command.

A second later, fifty people appeared on the pad, engulfed in an electric blue sphere. Hanu jumped at their sudden appearance. He expected a flurry of discordant scrambling or at the very least an onslaught of indignant cries, but neither of those things happened. For a while, Hanu stared disbelievingly at the silent wall of humans looming on the dark platform.

Cameron withdrew the map from the holoscreen and activated an audio file labeled, 'Introduction.' Soft music began to play, then a woman's crisp voice spoke. "You have just experienced a transport," she said. "Right now you are safe, and with your loved ones on the Cargo Class vessel, Songbird. Because it is becoming unsafe to remain in Underground City, the City of Fire's Hierarchy is transporting you to a place where you have the greatest statistical chance to survive and thrive."

The hairs on Hanu's neck began to prickle as a growing sense of unease replaced his guilt. The passengers, who were mostly middle-aged and elderly, all wore identical flat expressions as they slumped in their huddle. Some of them were dangerously close to falling to the floor. He circled the platform toward

Cameron. "Something's wrong with them," he said, but the recording drowned out his panicked warning. "Right now you are safe," the voice repeated. "You will now be guided to an information chamber for more details about your new home, and how to best adapt. Please direct any questions to your attendant, who is here to guide you and keep you safe."

Then the woman's voice was quiet, leaving only the soft music until the entire recording was finished. "Stay calm," Cameron said, and Hanu knew it was equally a reminder to herself.

Hanu stifled his jitters with a deep breath and gave a reluctant nod. "I can do this," he told himself quietly. "There's no other choice."

Cameron stepped down onto the platform and placed a gentle hand on the nearest body. It was an elderly woman wearing a robe and thick, fuzzy socks. "Mrs. Canlas," she said, double checking the woman's identity against a roster she pulled up on her notepad. "You have a husband, right?" The woman's sagging eyes made no attempt to focus on Cameron as she grunted a mild confirmation. "Yes, I see you do," said Cameron, searching the surrounding bodies. "Here you are, Mr. Canlas."

Cameron quickly locked the couples hands together and guided them up the small step and toward the chambers. Hanu quietly followed. He wasn't quite sure how he could help, so he dawdled behind, watching the elderly couple shuffle toward their destination. Cameron hurried them along, circling them anxiously like an excited sheep dog retrieving lost members of its flock.

"Wha... what's this now?" said the old man. He stopped to stare at a flashing button on one of the consoles, brushing it gently with a wrinkled finger.

"That's what regulates the distribution of power in the room," said Cameron. She motioned for Hanu to open the door to the nearest chamber, sweeping him away from the console. The man obliged, following his wife toward the row.

Hanu pulled the latch on the chamber door and was surprised to find that it was a rather cozy space. The inside was noticeably cool and the floor was covered in a thick mat. Hanu offered the woman a dull smile as she obediently took her spot in the chamber, consoling himself with the fact that they would at least be comfortable. Mr. Canlas followed, nestling himself in the chamber with his wife. Then Cameron locked their hands together again and adjusted the screen to meet them at eye level. Then, finally, she secured the door.

She glanced at her watch. "We have about forty-three minutes to secure everyone."

Hanu knew what he had to do, but was reluctant to agree. A shiver crept down his spine as he looked at the huddle of zombies across the room. "I got it," he sighed.

Cameron moved swiftly toward the platform, checking her roster. Hanu followed, focusing on putting one foot in front of the other. "You'll take Ms. Middleton," she said, pulling a young woman from the crowd. "I'll take the Offermans."

Hanu placed a clammy palm on Ms. Middleton's shoulder

and guided her toward the chambers. Her cooperative feet staggered up the step as she stared blankly ahead. His eyes darted around the room, trying to focus on anything besides the heinous crime he was helping to commit. They passed the Canlas', whose faces were now glowing with the light from their screen. "You'll be nice and comfortable in here," Hanu said as he placed Ms. Middleton in an unoccupied chamber. Then he nauseously ran to meet Cameron back at the huddle.

The two of them worked silently, taking the passengers one, two and sometimes three at a time to their places with very little trouble. One man complained about having to use the bathroom, but agreed to wait until morning, and a very old lady wouldn't be settled in her chamber unless she had Charlie, her Great Dane, accompany her. Thankfully Hanu was able to find Charlie among the remaining passengers on the transport pad, and he didn't seem to mind twisting his body around to lay at his owner's feet.

Cameron secured the last passenger with fourteen minutes to spare. They walked up the row, inspecting their work, then quickly returned to their station at navigation. For a while Cameron stared at the console, saying nothing. Hanu took this time to collect himself as well, clasping a hand to his mouth in disbelief and watching the eerie sight across the room.

"What's wrong with them," he finally asked. "They weren't this confused all on their own. They didn't even look confused, really. Something was done to them."

Cameron took a deep breath and leaned back in her seat. She

seemed to be thinking hard about how she might answer. Then she swallowed hard. "Our ships are emitting a frequency that isolates parts of their brains and makes them fall asleep." She avoided looking at Hanu, who was wearing an expression of sheer terror. "I guess confused isn't the word," she added thoughtfully. "I felt a little confused when they tried it on me, though."

"You mean they did this to you, too?"

"Of course," said Cameron. "I wouldn't do this to someone else without knowing what I was putting them through."

Hanu continued to watch the blank faces flashing in the screen light. "Will it hurt them to be like this for so long – you know, with some parts of their brain asleep?"

"Nah. Not for the amount of time they'll be in there. We would've put them all the way to sleep, but this way seemed to be more efficient," she said, nodding at the chambers.

Hanu thought about how the passengers might react once they were fully awake. By that time they will have lost their homes, belongings, and entire way of life. They would have nothing more than the memories of a world that no longer existed. He wrestled with the Hierarchy in his mind.

"You know," Cameron said. "We actually got the idea from your friend's ship."

"Wha – ?"

"Your friend," she repeated. "The guy with the super advanced ship. He would talk to her. What was her name?" She tapped her chin. "Oh yeah... *Donna*."

"Oh yeah," said Hanu. Then a thought suddenly came to him. He shot straight up in his seat. "Where's Garion?"

"Relax. He's being transported, too." Cameron searched her database. "He should be aboard the Mako in about ten minutes."

"Wait, but what about Donna?"

"Who?"

"The SHIP!"

"Oh, right," Cameron laughed. "I think it's still in storage at the farm, actually."

"And nobody thought to rescue Donna, too? The Hierarchy didn't plan on giving it back?"

"This has been the most complex mission we've ever carried out," she defended. "Hopefully that's the only oversight we'll encounter. We're rescuing *him*, at least."

"But you might as well not even rescue him if you leave *her* behind!" Hanu jumped out of his seat, pacing the length of the navigation console. "Can't you call somebody?"

"For a ship?" Cameron scoffed. "*Please...* We couldn't possibly spare personnel for that. We didn't even have enough people to collect the wildlife – they're working double time!"

"No, you've got to spare somebody for this," Hanu said. "Or at least have this... *Mako* drop him off. He can pilot Donna out of here and it'll be done."

Cameron reluctantly grabbed her radio. "Songbird to Mako."

Silence.

"Mako, come in."

Cameron looked at Hanu apologetically. "They might not be able to hear us. There's like a hundred fifty other passengers aboard that ship."

Hanu continued pacing the room, baffled. He could feel that he was working himself into a frenzy, which is exactly what he always did, so he took a deep breath and reminded himself of what Mr. Lilley said – hundreds of thousands of lives were at stake. Then he stopped short. A hint of a plan edged its way into his mind.

He wouldn't have to risk any of *their* lives, he reasoned. He would only have to risk his own. Hanu slunk back into his chair in thoughtful silence. "We finished early," he said slowly. "And technically, you don't need me."

"Yeah."

"And I've watched Garion pilot Donna a million times…"

"Hanu, I'm not going to let you out of my sight – "

"But I helped *you*," Hanu complained. "Now you have to help me!"

"I'm helping you," Cameron said coolly. "I'm helping you to not get blown up when they lower those barriers."

Hanu threw his hands up, incredulous. "You know, even if I got blown up, nobody would notice. What are you really risking?"

Cameron crossed her arms stubbornly. "I'm being held accountable for your safety, and *I* would notice."

"Look, everyone always treats me like a child, and I know I

act like one sometimes, but right now I'm really trying not to." Hanu forced himself to stare into Cameron's determined eyes. "You know as well as I do there's no way Garion will fit in up there. His ship *is* his home. And we both owe him one for getting us out of the Uninhabitable Zone alive."

With a defeated sigh, Cameron reached into her pocket and pulled out her notepad. She pressed it against a port on the console, downloading information from the database. Then she offered it to Hanu. "These are the coordinates where the Mako will be. Don't dawdle. More than likely he'll already be on the ship by the time you get there."

The notepad was in Hanu's pocket in a flash and Cameron was changing the flight path. She moved the ship back toward the farm, leaving Hanu to go over his plan in his mind. He would program the coordinates into the navigational system and Donna would be able to do the rest. Then, whoever was piloting the Mako would more than likely hail him, and he would be able to explain that he was returning the ship to Garion.

"I'm transporting you down from the pad," said Cameron, bringing the ship to a halt. Hanu checked the viewscreen. They were now nestled in the shadow of the farm.

"Wait, you can't just let me out through the door?" Hanu said, eyeing the platform.

"Oh no, I'm not landing this thing until we're safe on the surface. Which reminds me – " Cameron checked her watch again. "You have to be clear of the city by eleven o'clock. That gives you a little under forty minutes, understand?"

"Right."

"Okay, just stand right here," Cameron said, pushing him toward the center of the pad. Then she rounded on the console. "Whatever you do, make sure you're *completely* out of the city by eleven." Hanu nodded assuredly. Then, without another word, she activated the transport.

Hanu collapsed to the ground right outside the Salcedos' shed in an electric blue sphere. He shot to his feet, coughing and dusting off his jumper. A quick glance around told him that nobody saw him arrive, so he pressed himself against the side of the shed to stay hidden.

The Songbird silently retreated into the night, moving swiftly for such a large craft, leaving Hanu alone. He crept over to the double doors but found that they were locked. It was only a mild deterrent, though, because a vent that was protruding from the side of the building was just large enough for him to crawl through.

Once inside, Hanu fumbled through the darkness, following the faint glow that was emanating from under the doors. The rich smell of damp cedar and hay filled his nose as he navigated several bulky obstacles, knocking down a couple of heavy sounding pieces of metal along the way. The fact that he had not bumped into anything that could be considered a ship added to his anxiety, as he realized that Donna could have very well been moved to a different location long ago.

His efforts were rewarded, though, as he swiped blindly

along the wall. A large switch activated a number of lights within the shed, revealing a collection of oddly shaped machines, including a weary looking Donna.

Hanu wasted no time jumping in through the hole where the door used to be. Tool boxes and broken parts lined the floor, but for the most part, the cabin was considerably cleaner than it was the last time he was there. He picked up a bulky potentiometer. The inside of it had been fried, leaving a black scorch mark running along the outside of its casing. There was an identical one in the console, shining and new; someone had been making repairs.

"Let's hope you're fixed enough to fly," Hanu said, eyeing the empty door frame. Unfortunately they hadn't gotten around to repairing that. But she'd flown without it before. Hanu knew it was possible to do so again. He cleared stray instruments from the main console, hoping to find the navigation panel.

Two minutes later he found the projector that should've been displaying a map. He wiped the sweat from his brow, double checking the time on his notepad: thirty-one minutes before eleven o'clock. He ran a hand across the dead panel. He would have to start the machine, but realized he had no idea how to do that. He pressed a few buttons, hoping one of them might bring her to life, but then remembered that she responded to voice commands, too.

"Uh... power on," he said.

Nothing.

Hanu licked his lips and tried again. "Donna, power on."

With an abrupt hum, Donna buzzed to life, flooding the room with soft light and a much needed supply of fresh air. Hanu recognized the navigation panel now, which was displaying a topographic map of the farm and surrounding mountains. He hastily typed in the coordinates from the notepad and Donna charted a course.

"Donna, take me to these coordinates," he commanded.

The machine emitted a single flat tone.

"Wha – ?"

Hanu checked the map again. The destination was clear; Donna knew exactly where to take him. He scanned the room, hoping to find the source of the delay. Maybe a blinking light, warning him of a system malfunction. Or maybe there was a specific launch sequence – just like Cameron had done aboard the Songbird when he arrived. He racked his brain, trying to remember how Garion commanded the ship. He sat in one of the thick chairs at the console, sending a thin layer of dust flying into the air.

"Uh, Donna – full speed toward these coordinates," he said. "Propulsion at twenty-six hundred hertz – no, twenty six *thousand* hertz, and a variance of one thousand hertz."

Another flat tone.

Hanu checked the time again: twenty-eight minutes. He continued scanning the room, looking for ideas. His eyes fell on the door frame, and with uneasiness mounting in his gut, he thought maybe she wouldn't move – even for a short flight –

without it being secured somehow. He tried to remember what Garion had done when they were out in the Uninhabitable Zone. They were being surrounded by the hybrids when Garion rushed through the door. Then he engaged some sort of force field, but what did he call it?

"Donna, engage a force field around the door," he tried. But nothing seemed to happen. He walked over to the door and stuck his hand straight through. He squeezed his face in his hands. "Um, activate the... Briggs... Brigance..."

Donna emitted her flat tone.

"Higgs field!" Hanu crossed the room. "Donna, activate the Higgs field on all sides." And with a reassuring hum, the machine emitted two cool tones.

"Okay," said Hanu, putting the whole sequence together again in his head. "Donna, take me to these coordinates at twenty six thousand hertz, with a variance of one thousand hertz – full speed."

Hanu sighed in relief as Donna floated effortlessly through the side of the shed, leaving no trace of her stay behind. He returned to his seat, checking the time again. He only lost three minutes in the ordeal. "Donna, windows on all sides, please."

The machine obediently made the walls dissolve, showing scores of ships hovering balefully throughout the city. They navigated through these like a ghostly minefield, and were soon right on top of a large, sleek looking vessel – the Mako.

Hanu crossed the room to get a better look at it. There were no lights on, or movements in the windows, or anything else that could've indicated that anyone was aboard.

"Donna, radio the Mako."

Static fizzled over the communication system as Donna attempted to connect to the right frequency. Then a flat tone. He tapped the notepad with his finger, thinking about how he might contact the Mako. One option would be to park Donna directly under the ship, in case they were still scanning for life signs. In that case, he would be detected. But he thought better of it, opting to avoid being blasted with that frequency and being zombified for the remainder of the operation.

The minutes slipped away and Hanu resigned to hoping Garion would put up enough of a fuss about Donna that the pilot would come looking for her. If the old lady on the Songbird had the wits to put up a fight for her dog, then Garion would certainly do the same for Donna. But would he be able to pilot her in such a state?

"Donna, are you capable of following other vessels?"

Two dulcet tones confirmed.

"Follow the Mako when it moves."

Two more tones indicated that Donna had received the instructions. Hanu fidgeted with the notepad, pacing the wall. Though he felt accomplished for getting along so well with the ship, he started to feel as though something might be wrong. The Mako remained silent, unmoving, and a flash of lightning crawled through the sky above. He checked the time. They had fourteen minutes to clear the city.

"Wait a minute..." Hanu crossed the room and studied the

map. He zoomed in on the building below and isolated the fifth floor, searching the layout. "Donna, belay that last order," he said, highlighting the coordinates of Garion's prison room. "Take us here instead."

Three seconds later, he was smack dab in the middle of what appeared to be a battle ground. An explosion sent bits of burning furniture and charred clothing against Donna's windows. For a split second he considered pulling Donna back out, but he caught a glimpse of someone he recognized crouching behind a desk at the far side of the room. The man shielded his neck and face from the brunt of the explosion, but there was no mistaking him by his fluff of hair.

"*Reggie?*" Hanu disengaged the Higgs field and climbed out of the ship.

"Donna!" came an elated cry. Garion, who was crouched in a golden bubble, gestured excitedly at Hanu. His hair fell wildly around his head and most of his chin was smeared with ash.

"Pick up the emitter," coughed Reggie, extinguishing a small flame that singed through a tuft of his hair.

Garion did so, which caused the golden barrier to disappear. He grabbed the blackened bars of his cell, smiling fondly at his ship.

"What are you doing here," Reggie asked, moving quickly toward Hanu.

"I could ask you the same thing." Hanu shuffled through the debris to meet him. Smoldering bits of wood, power tools and fragmented lengths of rope littered the ground, all covered in a thick layer of ash.

"I'm fighting the clock here." Reggie glanced at his watch with a look of consternation.

Hanu understood now; this had become a rescue mission. And one that wasn't going so well, at that. "Eleven minutes," Hanu said, checking the time on his notepad. "So you couldn't transport him out of the cell from the ship?"

"There's a barrier around the room that's stopping me," Reggie explained. "These bars are no joke, either. I've tried just about everything I can think of."

For a minute, nobody spoke. Garion hummed quietly in his cell, thinking. Then all of a sudden he laughed. "Donna!"

The two stared expectantly at the craft as it emitted its usual cooperative tones. Garion paced the room. "Donna, can you measure the vibrational frequency of the alloy in these bars?"

Two cool tones.

"Now," Garion stopped pacing. "Identify the frequency that would destabilize the molecular bond of this metal."

Hanu and Reggie held their breaths, waiting for the confirmation. It came in two more tones.

"Okay, good," said Garion. "Now Donna, is it possible to produce a beam of radioactive particles that deliver short bursts of that destabilizing frequency?"

The three of them waited while Donna calculated. Then there were two more tones.

"You might want to stand back," warned Garion. Reggie pushed Hanu into the ship and jumped in behind him. "Donna, target the metal bars and deliver the beam now."

All at once, the entire cell fell to the floor in a pile of fine, gray sand. Then, in two enormous strides Garion was aboard the ship. "It feels good to be back," he beamed, running a hand across the transparent wall.

"It'll be a short reunion if we don't get out of here," said Reggie, checking his watch again. "Six minutes 'til go time."

Seconds later, Donna was parked awkwardly inside the Mako. She phased through its hull, giving them access to the large, flat platform that recessed below the navigational console. The lights were dim on this ship, just as they were on the Songbird.

"Thanks for the lift," Reggie said. He jumped down from the door hole. His boots hit the ground with a loud thud, which reverberated off the walls, but the rows and rows of complacent passengers didn't seem to notice.

"I was hoping I could come with you," Hanu said to Garion. "I can help you with repairs, you know."

Garion stretched back in his seat with a sigh. He pinched his lips together, thinking. Then he sat up, and his face was serious. "Things are accelerating," he said, watching Reggie make haste of his launch sequence. "I've lost a lot of time. There are a few things I still need to do."

"I see," said Hanu flatly. He made for the door, not entirely surprised.

"Wait."

Garion fumbled through the rubble, brushing small parts

and bits of paper aside until he found what he was looking for. He smiled sheepishly. "Thank you for saving Donna… I owe you my life." Then he pressed a shiny, round button into his hand. "Keep that on you… I'll come find you when I'm finished."

Hanu turned the shiny thing in his hand. It was smooth and hard, and fit perfectly in his palm. He placed it in his front pocket. "What are you going to do?" he asked.

Garion chuckled, brushing a ringlet of curls from his face. "First, I'm grabbing my door from the Uninhabitable Zone."

Hanu jumped onto the steel floor of the Mako, looking back just in time to see Donna disappear through the wall.

Reggie followed suit, moving the Mako swiftly toward the border of the city.

"What are we doing now?" Hanu asked.

Reggie activated the cloak and adjusted the frequency of a series of shields. They watched the map as their position moved closer to hundreds of blinking dots on the horizon. Hanu activated the viewscreen on the panel. "Next, we let the Ancient Ones in for a surprise," Reggie said, pulling the ship straight through a ribbon of crackling lightning.

Hanu checked the time on his notepad. It was eleven o'clock. The radio crackled in, *Detonation sequence has begun.*

Just then, Reggie was forced to maneuver through a drove of blimps, surrounded by smaller ships, as they burst into the city. They raced inward at full speed, whirring and humming as they readied their weapons.

Hanu braced himself against the console, holding his breath for fear that they might be detected. The sky fizzled; it glowed with an illuminating light. He adjusted the viewscreen. It was emanating from somewhere down below. He squinted to find the source. It was coming from one of the pyramids, growing more intense by the second as a roar grumbled through the city. A wave of nausea crept up into his stomach, though he wasn't sure why. Then he was forced to look away just as they crossed the border into the ground. Blinded, he forced his eyes to focus on the map. When his vision returned, he could see that the blinking dots had started to disappear from it, one by one, in rapid succession.

Reggie sank into his seat, smearing sweat from his face with a sleeve. Then he wheezed a cackling laugh. "I think we did it!"

Hanu stared at the map a while longer, wondering what Mavis would say about her precious city, destroyed in the blink of an eye. He pulled up a seat, regretful and angry and just a little numb. He allowed himself to feel the shock of it for a while longer. But he knew he wouldn't be able to completely mourn the loss just yet. There was somewhere they needed to get the passengers to. And hopefully, it was somewhere safe. Hopefully, the Hierarchy would be able to make good on its word.

₭·⟨ ₭·⟨ ₭·⟨

Reggie docked the Mako just under the surface of University City at what used to be a Deprogramming station.

"We were beginning to worry," said a young woman as they

opened the hatch. She walked briskly onto the ship to inspect the passengers, beckoning for her soldiers to follow. "You're the last group. If all goes well, we can call this a successful mission."

Her team of soldiers boarded the ship dutifully and began removing the passengers from their chambers. They gathered them in the cavern, which was a great deal larger than Paula's Deprogramming station, and a great deal more inviting, too. Elaborate carpeting covered most of the tiled floor and colorful paintings lined the walls tastefully.

When everyone was unloaded, another recording was played for them. This one informed them that they would now be implanted with their own trade interfaces, and reminded them of the technology's specifications.

Hanu, who had been trying to make himself as quiet and helpful as possible, worked hard to restrain himself as the soldiers began implanting the things in the obliging citizens' arms. One of the passengers passively grumbled something about hating needles as he held his right hand out, allowing the soldier to place a black pincer on his forearm. The passenger flinched slightly as it punched the interface under his skin, then withdrew his hand without complaint.

Reggie, who couldn't ignore Hanu's look of bewilderment any longer, leaned in and whispered to him. "If you had watched the video you'd understand why we had to do it."

Hanu nodded numbly, relying on the fact that the Hierarchy's choices had been somewhat understandable up until this point, even though Hanu didn't always agree with them.

"These people are going to need access to food, water and their basic necessities," he explained. "Most importantly, though, they'll need to be able to fool a scout if something goes wrong with the plan. Name, address, occupation – they'll need an identity."

The soldiers quickly finished the implanting process and were now guiding them toward a vehicle on the other side of the station.

"Are they gonna remember anything?" asked Hanu.

"You mean all of this?"

"No... well, yeah," said Hanu. "But what about their lives in Underground City? Are they brainwashed?"

A man in white coverings began scanning the passengers with a medical tool, reading their life signs on a holographic display. Reggie crossed his arms, watching the silent boarding. "They'll remember it all," he said simply. "It'll feel like a dream for a day or two, but they'll have their full memories. They'll have a lot of other knowledge as well – how to blend in up here and a full history of the planet. It's up to them to decide what to do with it, though."

With a quick goodbye, the woman in charge closed the hatch on her vessel and they disappeared, leaving Hanu and Reggie alone in the Deprogramming station.

"You think they want us to turn off the light on the way out?" Reggie smirked, climbing the ramp back into the Mako. Hanu followed, still mildly shocked from the night's events. "So where do I drop you off?"

Hanu stopped abruptly on the ramp. He glanced at the place where the ship had disappeared. "I think I'm actually supposed to be with them," he admitted, grimacing. "I was on the Songbird with Cameron when I remembered Donna and – "

A hearty laugh popped out of Reggie's mouth. "You mean to tell me they were just gonna put you on the surface?"

"Well, yeah."

"That wouldn't have worked." Reggie laughed again, shaking his head this time. "Why aren't you in the Resistance yet?"

"They don't need me," Hanu said. His voice had gone hollow. He gestured toward the Deprogramming station. "Clearly, the Hierarchy already has everything worked out."

Reggie walked back down the ramp, grabbing Hanu by the shoulders. His face was tired, but his eyes were as intense as they'd always been. "Clearly, you saved Garion's life today," he said. "And probably mine and all of those passengers. Seriously. I don't know if I would've been able to leave him there when time ran out."

Hanu allowed a smile to creep across his own face. "I guess I *was* pretty helpful."

Reggie stood up straight, wearing an amused grin. He snapped his hand to his forehead in a salute. Hanu watched in puzzlement, unsure if he was supposed to return the gesture.

"I, Reginald Stubblefield, Lieutenant of the 117th Recovery Division, hereby instate you, Hanu Manel, as a Cadet in the

Resistance of the City of Fire."

Hanu laughed sheepishly. "Uh... thanks."

Then Reggie slapped Hanu on the back and started up the ramp again. "Now," he said, glancing at his watch. "I'm due at the District of Ops. What do you say you come help the 117th?"

"Of course." Hanu puffed out his chest, strutting quickly up the ramp.

The Recovery Division

The Mako crossed silently over the city. This one's streets were organized into neat rings around a conglomerate of old-looking buildings – the university. Reggie set himself to finding a proper uniform for Hanu, tearing through several storage compartments as the boy tested all of the tools on a spare utility belt.

"If all went well," Reggie grunted as he replaced the panel on a locker. He tossed a pair of boots at Hanu's feet. "They should've arrested the Council, and are evacuating the other employees and their families from the District of Operations by now."

Hanu dressed hastily, pushing his legs through the armored suit. "What are we supposed to do?"

"Our assignment won't start 'til tomorrow. They might need help with evacuations, though."

"Okay. That'll be easy enough." Hanu tried to hide the apprehension in his voice. He clipped on the utility belt and adjusted his collar.

The viewscreen showed that the Mako was moving over barren wasteland now. They were crossing the Uninhabitable Zone. And when civilization appeared again, it was Capital

City. The outer rungs were dark and quiet as its inhabitants slept peacefully in their beds. The closer they got to the center of the city, though, the busier it became. The Entertainment District twinkled with flashing marquees and neon signs. People roamed the streets in droves as festivities carried on, despite the time of night. Further into the city – in the Business District – searchlights and smoking flares illuminated the streets to reveal a different scene. Droves of countless citizens were spilling around the buildings and into the parks as they were pushed further away from the District of Operations. They clamored in a mass of confusion as weapons fire crashed against the wall.

Reggie parked the Mako along the flattest strip of land he could find near the District palace, then they trotted toward the building, ducking behind parts of the building to avoid being seen. Hanu tried to ignore the screams erupting in the distance as explosions echoed in the night sky. A strong smell of sulfurous gun powder and stale sweat hung in the air. They dashed into the main hall, which had been transformed into a well-established headquarters.

Heavy looking consoles, weapons lockers and shield emitters had been transported in, and turrets were mounted at every window. The whole room was abuzz with officers scrambling to deliver and receive information. Hanu tried to make his face only as visible as necessary, afraid Adam or one of the Salcedos' would discover him. Reggie made a beeline toward the tactical station. It was attended by a man with a dark mark on one side of his face. *Motley.*

"Status?"

"Two Council members have escaped, but that's not our most immediate problem," Motley reported, reading the map on his console as he uploaded an update to the database. "The perimeter is just about secured – they're evacuating the last of the citizens now – but it seems like the scouts have reverted back to their original programming. They've started attacking the wall." He paused to upload a set of instructions to one of the teams. Then he pulled up a map of the grounds and pointed to a large square building. "We set up camp at the theatre," he said. Then he pointed to a spot along the District wall. "Relieve two members from the 733rd here, so they can help overwrite those subroutines again over at Communications. Then report back to the theatre and try to get some rest."

Without another word, they turned on their heels and started toward the tunnel. They cleared the palace stairs and jogged across a lush lawn. Hanu followed closely behind Reggie, squinting to focus only on their destination. He prepared to be as helpful as he could.

"So what are subroutines?" Hanu asked thoughtfully. "I've heard that word before."

Reggie didn't break his stride as he stole a glance at Hanu. "A subroutine is a set of programmed instructions," he said. "For a computer or a machine."

"Or an artificial intelligence; a scout," he said. Then his eyes widened as a flash of understanding came over him. He laughed. "*That's* what Brandy stole – the overwrite protocols for the scouts!"

"There's no way we would've been able to take the District with the scouts protecting it," Reggie said. "We reprogrammed them to help us instead." Then he suddenly broke his stride. "You have got to be the nosiest kid I've ever seen," he laughed. "How did you even know about that?"

"That one wasn't my fault," Hanu said. "I just happened to be there when she returned from that mission... she was pretty beat up, too."

But Reggie was barely listening now as he tracked a fizzling projectile above the District wall. It floated lazily toward them, then crashed with a muted thud against an invisible barrier. Another came, then another, forcing them to jog a little faster. As they approached their destination, they realized it was nothing more than a hole that someone blasted through the wall. It was converted into a checkpoint, with soldiers scrambling in and out, ducking to avoid swipes from angry protesters. Dozens of civilians were pressed against a barricade, threatening to spill into the clearing as they cried in protest.

Soldiers lined the barricade, attempting to quell the uproar with very little success until a small ship appeared overhead. The protesters watched in quiet curiosity as it landed in the street behind them. Then a door promptly opened and allowed a very angry Mavis to climb out. She pushed her way through the bewildered protesters.

Reggie halted one of the Captains who happened to be rushing by and told him to send two of his best men to

Communications. Then he rushed out to meet Mavis, with Hanu on his heels.

"You *cannot* be serious," Mavis hissed. Her face was contorted with anger. She tried to lift the metal bars of the barricade, but they proved too heavy for her.

"We had to do what was necessary," Reggie said. He reached out a sympathetic hand, but she swatted it away. He wasn't offended, though. "You can still help," he said. "You can help Capital City to see the truth."

This made Mavis even more furious. "You've killed us all!" She rattled the bars, causing another uproar among the protesters.

Then they could see that someone else was making their way through the crowd. "Hey!" They yelled from a distance. "Over here!" Hanu squinted to see who it was. An explosion further down the wall lit up the sky, causing a fresh wave of screams as everyone ducked. Then he could see that it was River. She waded through the crowd, followed closely by two intuits. "Wait for us," she yelled.

Mavis didn't wait, though. She continued yelling at Reggie, who couldn't do much more than nod sympathetically. "First you turn our city into your own personal war ground, then you steal our technology!" she said. "Wasn't that enough?"

River finally reached the barricade, short of breath and sweaty. "We want in," she breathed, gesturing toward the stern-faced intuits. Mavis continued yelling, swiping at Reggie with a balled up fist.

"So does everyone else," Reggie said distractedly as he avoided the blow.

River shook her head. "You don't get it," she said. Then her face lit up as she recognized Hanu. "Oh look, you made it to the Resistance after all!" She beamed fondly at him before rounding back on Reggie with a serious face. "I want to help," she said. "I know we've been fighting, but Project Living Library might be of more use to the Hierarchy now that we're on the surface."

This made Mavis even angrier than before. She yelled rudely at River as she attempted to shuffle sideways to where she was standing. River did her best to ignore some of the more inappropriate words Mavis used to describe her during all of this. She avoided eye contact with the old lady while Reggie considered her offer, and chose to smile awkwardly at Hanu instead. Her intuit counterparts stood by patiently, unfazed by the old woman's tantrum.

Reggie scoffed.

"Everything about Project Living Library is opposite of what we're trying to do!"

"It was," she admitted. Then she gestured toward the horde of angry protesters. "That was when we thought they'd be dead. But you all are bent on saving them, so we might as well help."

After careful consideration, Reggie conceded. He pulled back the barricade and squeezed River and her companions through. Then he beckoned for one of the soldiers. "These three go straight to headquarters." Then Mavis was storming back through the crowd, toward her ship. "Hey, Mavis," he yelled behind her. "Remember, your apartment is in the Business District. Your cat's already there. He'll be hungry!"

Hanu eyed Reggie. "Do you think she'll make trouble?" he asked.

Reggie laughed heartily. "Oh, yeah. She'll be back."

The rest of the protesters were subdued easily enough after that, especially after the scouts stopped attacking the wall and started helping to escort the citizens into their homes. Then, when peace was restored at the checkpoint, they trudged warily toward the theatre.

Dozens of other soldiers converged on the building as well. Their tired and, sometimes, bloody faces moved quickly through the night, ready to take whatever rest they could.

The seats in the theatre were replaced by rows and rows of flimsy looking cots – just like the one in Hanu's prison room on the farm. Dim lights were fixed along the walls, offering only the necessary amount of illumination. As they navigated toward a cozy spot in the room, Hanu searched for familiar faces. Then, with a sudden drop in his stomach, he realized he had no idea where Vanessa and Ester ended up. He knew vaguely where Akesh was, but that brought very little relief as he realized none of his friends would be with him in the District of Operations. They had been smuggled and scattered throughout the continent, and he would no longer be able to directly protect them. Hanu nursed an incredibly heavy hole that suddenly bored its way into his gut as his thoughts fell back on Vanessa. He had finally gained control of the connection between his brain and mouth in her presence, yet there was so much he hadn't been able to tell her yet. Like how he admired how hard she worked, and how she possessed a special type of courage, working with animals as she did, that he could never have. And how the softness of her cheeks made him feel. He clenched his fists, fighting against the hard emptiness of his loss.

Reggie found an acceptable area and threw Hanu a blanket, which was nothing more than a thin square of fabric, then he dropped himself into a cot. "Good work out there today," he said. "Rest up."

Hanu chose a cot and stuffed the blanket under his head. It was absurd to think that he would be able to sleep, though, after the day's events. Instead, he lay in his cot, watching the other soldiers triage their wounds, or pace the aisle, or excitedly recount the details of their missions with friends. In the distance, explosions boomed like firecrackers. Hanu listened to the sounds of the Resistance with an equal amount of heartache and excitement and angst.

"So what's next for us?" he asked Reggie quietly. "What's the Hierarchy going to do now that we have the District?"

Reggie rubbed his chin. "Next, we have to convince the people on the other side of that wall to not fight us."

〟·〉 〟·〉 〟·〉

Despite Hanu's expectations, the Hierarchy didn't bother to celebrate their victory. In fact, for the next several days, they worked even harder than before. And not in a way that Hanu was prepared for. The 117th Division was assigned to recycling duty, and their assignment was to dismantle a small fleet of ships, part by part, and deliver them to the engineers.

Sure, manual labor required very few technical skills – which worked out, because Hanu had exactly none – but the task was nearly impossible without the necessary tools and equipment to transport the parts. By the second day, all of the lighter pieces – the doors, bulkheads and most of the consoles – had been cleared out. They dragged everything they could onto the transport pads, and delivered them that way, but now they were stuck having to move the bigger objects by less convenient means.

It was advantageous to be a manual laborer, though. Hanu had plenty of time to acclimate to life as a soldier, and there were plenty of opportunities to hear all of the latest rumors.

According to one of the incoming pilots, the two council members that escaped had resurfaced, and were organizing an army. A woman at the munitions lab heard that the Ancient Ones hadn't once emerged from the Uninhabitable Zone to help the Council, and that the citizens had been in an uproar about it. And another soldier briefly recounted a rescue mission underneath the Business District that had failed. But the real news came on the fourth day when Reggie was summoned for a staffing.

They were scaling the hull of one of the smaller craft when the call came over the radio for the team leads to assemble at the palace. Reggie pulled the strap on his harness, doling orders as he slid to the ground.

"Feelix, you'll be lead for now – make sure everyone's out of here by nineteen hundred hours," he said. He gestured at Hanu. "You're coming with me."

"But I'm not a team lead," Hanu said, catching up to him in the yard.

"Yeah, but you'll need to be assigned to a squadron." Reggie squeezed out of his harness. "I'm sure we can fit that into the meeting."

Hundreds of people were gathered at the palace when they arrived minutes later – some wearing EAGs and others wearing civilian clothing. The Hierarchy had turned the back end of the main hall into a briefing room, fitting several rows of benches along the length of the room, and a pulpit was fixed on a raised dais. They joined Cameron, Pants and Motley, who were already seated near the front.

"Why are you here?" Cameron hissed. Her eyebrows furrowed steeply with alarm.

"Relax," said Reggie, leaning back in his seat. "He's in training. This is just a little field trip."

Cameron looked like she would explode. "But he's not even a soldier!"

"Of course he is," Reggie said. "He was enlisted almost a week ago."

"By *who*? All of the recruiters have been reassigned."

"By me." Reggie smiled at Motley, who looked away quickly, determined not to be involved.

"You're a Lieutenant." She crossed her arms. "You can't recruit people."

Reggie waved her concerns away. Then he pat her reassuringly on the shoulder, which made her even more angry. "I've never steered the Hierarchy wrong before."

The matter would have to be settled for the time, though, because Pants shushed them both as people began settling into their seats. Six officers were now sitting on one side of the dais and nine intuits in white coverings sat on the other, waiting patiently for the meeting to come to order. Hanu remembered several of these intuits from the time he visited Intelligence with Garion. One of them was Deanna, and there were a few whose faces were familiar, but he couldn't recall their names. Hanu wondered how they came about joining the Resistance. Maybe they switched allegiances when they realized what the Hierarchy had planned.

His wonderings were cut short, though, because he spotted someone else he knew. He almost didn't recognize her with her bangs pulled into her ponytail, but it was definitely Ester sitting in the second row. Hanu stood and was about to flag her down but at that moment, Adam Lilley's voice came over the speaker system, forcing him to crouch down in his seat.

"Year One is twenty-six days away and we're coming up on a few deadlines," he said. "There are also some new developments that will be shifting our priorities." Mr. Lilley took a deep breath and straightened himself up as best he could. "We've still been unsuccessful in our attempts to evacuate the citizens from the twelve establishments in the Business District. The sonic tractor that was holding the generator steady just under the surface has started to malfunction."

"The generator?" Hanu wondered out loud. Then he rounded on Reggie, wide-eyed. "The *pyramid* generator? The one from Underground City?"

Reggie nodded. "We sent them a courtesy warning before we surfaced it, but it backfired on us," he whispered. "Some of the citizens refused to leave when they realized their businesses would be crushed."

The officer who was working the display screen changed the view to a schematic of a machine. Then Mr. Lilley continued. "It would be unwise to try and take the tractor offline for repairs, as the ground may shift in ways we can't anticipate, so we'll be constructing a brand new sonic tractor to take over once the civilians are cleared out. I've assigned the 33rd Research and Development Division to begin construction on the project." At this, one of the scientists that was sitting behind Mr. Lilley stood dutifully, then sat back down. He must've been the one heading off the mission.

Then one of the officers pulled up a holographic map, which identified a city to the north. Hanu perked up quite a bit at this, being as this was the city that housed the Flush. "We haven't been able to establish contact with Medical City for two days now, which means we'll have to send a modified reconnaissance team." Mr. Lilley looked at his notepad. "I'll need the 51st and the 117th Recovery Divisions."

Reggie shot out of his seat and was standing at attention. Hanu crouched down even further as Mr. Lilley searched the crowd for the team leaders. But it was no good. When Hanu looked up, he found the man glaring at him. Hanu met his gaze, trying to look as apologetic as possible. Mr. Lilley's face went from puzzlement to anger to a very reluctant surrender. Cameron shot Reggie a dirty look. "You'll be searching for the assimilation team there," Mr. Lilley continued. "Be prepared to assist and, if necessary, evacuate them from the city."

The rest of the meeting went smoothly enough. Or at least, Adam didn't shoot any more disappointed looks in their direction. There was an update on the status of the scouts, whose systems had to be decompiled since they were being remotely sabotaged, and a pair of engineers were assigned to try and write a program from scratch.

Then there was the matter of the civilians. The seizure of the District of Operations left hundreds of families homeless and jobless, which put all but a halt on many businesses. The system began to crumble sooner than they anticipated, and they didn't take into account that the population would reject their attempts to restructure the economy.

Mr. Lilley's most pressing concern was regarding the citizens' willingness to take cover under the District's protective barrier once the time came, and was concerned the Hierarchy wouldn't be able to convince them it was for their own good. He reported that all of his efforts at addressing the public directly resulted in physical aggression, and informed them that a media team would be formed to compile a number of transmissions that could be broadcasted through the civilian channels. Ester and one of the intuits that came with River was assigned to lead this project.

Finally, Mr. Lilley reported on Year One. As far as things stood, the Ancient Ones were in control of a nuclear silo, and there was very little they could do to stop their launching it on schedule; therefore, a preemptive attack on the Uninhabitable Zone would take place in twelve days. At this, there was a bit of applause, but it was short-lived as someone shouted a question from the back of the room. Hanu recognized the voice immediately.

"Mr. Lilley, have you had a chance to read my report?" asked River. "Have you considered augmenting your plan to include using the Living Library?"

Mr. Lilley squinted to find where her voice was coming from. Then he spotted her. "No, I haven't had a chance to read the report," he said. "I'll assign someone to get right on it."

Then he was about to conclude the meeting when River interrupted again. "Who, Mr. Lilley?"

He hesitated.

"Who are you going to assign to read the report?" she clarified. Then she took a step closer. "You're about to send a biomolecular cascade into the Uninhabitable Zone, which will ensure that the environment never supports life again. With all due respect, Sir, I think you should be looking into alternatives that both benefits the environment out there as well as offers a less destructive means of getting rid of the Ancient Ones."

Mr. Lilley blinked several times. His eyes, tired and heavy, searched the woman's face. "While I'm thoroughly curious about what your proposal could be, please understand we've carefully constructed every step of our plan. We may not be able to make a change, but we'll consider."

River didn't seem to be satisfied, though. She glared at Mr. Lilley with pursed lips. Then someone in the front row stood up grumpily.

"I'll have a look at the report," said Paula. She gave River a quick nod, then glowered at the others in the back as if warning them to not interrupt any further. "Now can we get out of here? These benches are doing nothing for my back."

Hanu tried to get Paula's attention with a quick wave, but she had already grabbed her bag and was shuffling out of the row. Then the meeting ended just as abruptly as it began. Mr. Lilley thanked everyone for their service, and was gone from the pulpit.

Hanu slipped through the aisle to try and catch Ester while avoiding Mr. Lilley at the same time. Reggie jumped over a bench to catch up to him. "Hey, you can't just go running off," he said. "We need to sneak you onto someone's roster."

"But I need to find Ester," Hanu said, craning his neck to look over the crowd. She was already walking off the dais. Hanu darted through a space between two people, nearly knocking them down, and ran straight into Mr. Lilley.

Reggie squeezed through the crowd and nearly ran into the

back of Hanu. "Mr. Lilley, we were just looking for you," he lied. "Hanu here was – "

Mr. Lilley raised a hand to shush him. He massaged his temples with the tips of his index fingers. "I could build another brig and put you in it until this is all over... I can drop you off in the Residential District with a host family."

Hanu shook his head, grasping for words.

Mr. Lilley ignored him. "Or," he said. "I could ship you off to a metallurgy station underground. But if I did either of these things, I know for a fact that you would find your way back into a uniform." He closed his eyes and took a deep breath. "And since you're so willing to risk your life, there's no point in me trying to stop you anymore."

Reggie clapped his hands. "Alright, so he's – "

"You're training him," Mr. Lilley snapped. "And he's taking all of your commission."

Then he stalked off.

Reggie raised a brow at Hanu. A grin crept across his face. "I only get paid if we get through Year One, so I guess we should just focus on that for now."

But Hanu wasn't listening. He had gone back to searching the crowd for Ester, who was nowhere to be found.

ᚻ·ᚲ ᚻ·ᚲ ᚻ·ᚲ

The next morning, the 117th and 51st Divisions reported to the shipyard in full uniform. Hanu buzzed as they stood at attention to receive the details of their assignment. It would be his first mission as an official soldier in the Resistance.

They were soon separated into four vessels, with Hanu stationed with Reggie, of course. Their plans were simple – the Mako and another craft, Bertha, would approach the city from below to conduct initial scans while the other two, Big Mack and the Honey Badger, waited at a safe distance above ground. Hanu had a simple job; he was to scan for anomalous readings in the atmosphere. So he placed himself dutifully at the appropriate console aboard the Mako, which had been converted from its previous state to accommodate their mission.

They wasted no time once aboard. The launch sequence took no more than a minute and they were underground. Hanu anxiously scanned his panel, ready to identify any fluctuations on the many charts or gauges that he was in charge of.

A few minute's study of the panel revealed that the information was organized well enough even for a novice like himself to understand. The devices measured the atmospheric pressure, soil and air composition, radiation levels and all sorts of other breakdown of any given area within a certain distance around the ship.

A soldier at the helm, whose name was Delores, reported the distance from their target every few minutes. They were a hundred fifty miles from the city. Then eight-five miles. Then sixty. Then, at forty miles, Reggie ordered a slow ascent toward a position just a quarter mile under the surface.

Gilbert, at tactical, chimed in every once in a while with, "No other vessels detected." Or if they scraped against a dense pack of minerals or underground structure, he'd say, "Shields are holding steady,"

Hanu wasn't sure at what intervals he was supposed to report, so every once in a while he firmly announced, "No environmental anomalies." Everyone seemed to go with it.

When they got closer, though, something strange happened. The power in the cabin flickered for only a second, but when it came back on, all of the alerts on Hanu's console were triggered. The temperature gauged at minus two-hundred degrees and the radiation detector was reading deadly amounts of beta, gamma and several other types of radiated particles.

Hanu's eyes frantically scanned the console. "The environment is – " But the lights flicked again and the readings returned to normal. He hesitated, looking at his crew's expectant faces. The place between his eyes folded with confusion. "There was a spike in... *everything*," he said. "But it's normal now."

"What do you mean by everything?" Reggie crossed the room to read his data. He studied the console for a moment, then reported. "Temperature dropped, massive amounts of radiation and – what's this?" The computer was unable to identify a mass of unknown particles, so it created a series of complex equations and in an attempt to make sense of them.

An engineer named Basse looked over Reggie's shoulder. "I've never seen anything like this," she said. "What about life signs in the area?"

Hanu widened the search parameters on his map to scan the

city. "This can't be right," he said, double checking the data. "It says there are only fifty-two people on the surface."

Reggie ordered a full stop and picked up the radio. "Mako to Bertha, what's your position?'

A voice crackled a response. "We're stopped about sixteen miles from your port quarter."

Hanu checked the map but, strangely, there was no indication of the other ship's position.

"Did you guys just get some abnormal atmospheric readings?"

"Negative."

Reggie scratched his beard. His face bunched up as he re-read the data. Then he slowly raised the radio back to his lips. "Bertha what's your life sign count for Medical City?"

After a period of silence, the voice crackled back in. "We actually can't get a reading."

Everyone double checked the data from their stations, looking for any slight deviation or malfunction that could've affected their systems. Reggie changed the frequency on his radio. "Big Mack, come in."

Nothing.

The Honey Badger had gone silent as well. Reggie changed the frequency again. "Bertha, standby at your position," he ordered. "I'm sending a team to the surface from here. We'll report back at 0700 hours."

"Copy that."

Reggie studied his crew. "Basse, Jaeger, Hanu – you're with

me." He double checked the tools on his utility belt and beckoned them to the transport pad. "Gilbert is in charge while I'm gone. I'll be sending updates every ten minutes."

Hanu double checked his own utility belt, making sure each tool was accounted for. He unlatched his spare pocket and took out the round, black button Garion gave him. He rolled it in his hand, then put it back and secured the latch again. Reggie found an isolated part of the city and programmed its coordinates into the transport pad. Then, with a final systems check, an engineer named Ebner activated their transport.

The team landed outside of an abandoned diner in a dry ghost town. The sun hadn't risen yet, being as it was so early, and a slight fog laid over Medical City like a blanket. Hanu squinted into the haze to get a better look at the dozens of crumbling buildings and weed-eaten lots that lined the street, but the streetlamps offered very little help.

"What the... " Reggie opened his notepad and searched for life signs. The team followed close behind, inspecting the surrounding area. "There's an active rescue buoy in the area."

Reggie reported the circumstances of their arrival to the Mako, and quickly charted a path toward the buoy. Then the team cut through an alleyway to get to a large neighborhood, surveying the city in disbelief as they went.

There appeared to be a mountain in the distance, which Hanu never noticed in all of his years living at The Flush, and in all directions, a dark fog marked the outskirts of the city. A cold prickle crawled up his spine. This wasn't the city he once knew at all. They cut through a row of backyards, easily bypassing their wooden fences, which had rotted and fallen to the ground. The backdoors to these homes were either left wide open or broken, with shards of glass littering their porches. They cleared the neighborhood easily enough and approached a run-down plaza. The signal from the buoy was coming from an entertainment outlet.

"What happened here?" Basse whispered.

Reggie peeked around a corner of the building. "I don't know, but I bet whoever's in that store can tell us."

They followed Reggie's lead through the alley. The front entrance of the place was just as ugly as the rest of the town. Glass was shattered at the door and the advertisements in the window were too faded to read. They crept into the lobby.

A man was shouting angrily in one of the back rooms of the building. Reggie silently signaled for them to follow as he secured the back hallway. It was lined with several different types of rooms – a bowling alley, a roller rink, a theatre. There was a crash and then more swearing. They were getting closer.

They followed the angry voice to a large open room. They hid just around a bend in the hall, waiting for an opportunity to creep in. The man continued to shriek. "You insulate little man, why can't you follow a simple order? I'm telling you to jump. We'll die if we stay here!"

The four of them peeked into the room and saw that the man was standing on some sort of screen. He was wearing a tattered shirt and EAG pants, and his hair and beard were wildly overgrown. He was punching the air in frustration. A few feet away, a small holographic version of himself stood on an animated platform, punching the air as well. He jumped up and down, and then cursed again as the holographic character failed to jump to the next platform.

He roared angrily. "If you want to stay here, then that's on you!" Then he peeled a stringy attachment from his arms and legs and ripped it from the screen just before his character was crushed by a boulder. He kicked the projector, making the arena flicker. Then, without warning, he pulled a knife from his utility belt and threw it into the hall. It landed in the wall three inches away from Basse's face. "Don't think I didn't hear you," the man yelled wildly as he charged the hall.

Jaeger screamed, then tucked himself and rolled into the hall. Reggie froze, allowing the man to choke him around the neck with partially gloved hands. He sputtered, choking on his own spit. Then he said thickly. "*Andy?*"

Andy's eyebrows shot straight into the air. He cursed, then stumbled backward, releasing his hold on Reggie's neck.

"No way..." he breathed.

Andy shook his head, wincing as though he were hurt. His lip quivered as he allowed Reggie to pull him into a tight hug. Hanu watched on, frozen to the spot by disbelief. His lip quivered as a growing sense of relief washed over him.

After a minute of confused sputtering all around, Andy slapped Reggie on the back. "You look good, man!" He scanned the room, nodding at the others. Then he found Hanu and clasped him on the shoulders with a beaming smile. "And you haven't aged a bit, Hanu. How did you guys find me?"

"We tracked your rescue buoy," said Basse, reluctantly shaking his hand. "It led us right to you."

"Oh yeah," said Andy, rubbing his face thoughtfully. "I haven't thought about that thing in at least three years…"

"Wait, that's impossible," Hanu said, scoffing. "You were only missing for four or five months. We thought you were killed when the City of Fire was destroyed."

"*What*?" Andy's mouth hung wide open. His eyes darted from Hanu to Jaeger to Basse, and finally fell on Reggie. He put his hands on his hips. "City of Fire destroyed… no."

Andy shook his head, pacing toward the window and back. He swiped a pile of stuffed animals from a nearby bench and lowered himself down gingerly.

"What's the last thing you remember?" Reggie asked. He took a cautious step forward.

Andy squeezed his eyes shut. "There was a call over the radio – Hanu had closed the portal. Then we were leaving the District of Ops – had to scramble to avoid the scouts. I ended up with Wiggins, Shaw and Frazier. We were hit." He jumped up from the table. "Yeah, we were hit, but flew as far as we could before we crashed in the Uninhabitable Zone… And we were able to hike it here. We blended in well enough for a few months, actually." Andy gasped, then he clapped a hand to his mouth to steady his quivering lips. He let out a dreadful laugh. "It was gone in a flash," he whispered, snapping his fingers. "Just like that!" He leaned against the table to steady himself. "It was Year One... Year One happened."

Basse shook her head. "Year One hasn't happened yet," she said. "It's still twenty-five days from now."

"No." Andy shook his hairy head. He fought back a sniffle. "Year One happened seven years ago. I've been waiting for you to come rescue me ever since." Then, to everyone's alarm, he began bawling into his gloves.

Hanu broke from the collective stupor first. He leaned against the bench and gently patted Andy along the shoulders. As he did this, he studied the man, allowing himself to be relieved by the fact that, no matter what had occurred in this dilapidated city, Andy was alive and they were all together again.

Reggie put the radio to his lips. "Ground Team to Mako."

"Go ahead, Ground Team."

"We just found Anderson Nanton," he reported. "The whole city is stuck in some sort of alternate reality or something."

Back Again

The ground team set off toward their transport coordinates, but not before helping Andy collect some of his most cherished possessions – including a very heavy rectangular briefcase, which he insisted he couldn't leave. By the time they left, Jaeger and Basse were each carrying a mesh drawstring tote while Reggie was in charge of a large duffel bag. Hanu was fortunate enough to only have to carry a couple of rolled up maps.

The sun had risen considerably by this time, which allowed for better visibility. It was hardly an improvement, though; they could now see just how dreary and decrepit the city really was. Graffiti had been painted on many of the buildings and bits of trash were either lodged in fences or collecting in the gutters and the grassy, overgrown fields. The fog had lifted in the immediate area, but seemed to create a wall around the city in all directions. And what had earlier appeared to be a mountain turned out to be a huge mound of uprooted buildings.

Jaeger gasped. "What *did* that?" he asked.

"Shockwave," said Andy. He limped awkwardly across a street, pulling the briefcase behind him. "It swept everything west of the Flush that way." He drew a line through the city with a finger, showing the path of the blast.

Hanu tried to recognize the exterior of the Flush in the mound, but its plain white bricks weren't particularly remarkable against any of the rest of the city's architecture. Nevertheless, he took a moment to mourn the devastation of his long-time home, then followed the ground team across the street. The sidewalk on this side was wider, and lined with various marquees, statues and signs. He squinted into what could've been a general store. The aisles had all been toppled, and boxes were stacked unceremoniously throughout the storefront. "Where did everyone go?" he asked.

"Dead," Andy said simply. Then he gazed over a row of houses toward the hazy horizon.

Reggie signaled for them to follow him into an alley, wasting no time in his effort to get them back to the transport location. He double checked the navigation on his notepad. "Exactly how did they die?" he asked.

Andy shook his head. "About four or five days after the shockwave, when they started to realize nobody would be coming to save us, people started leaving in droves. They packed up and followed the path along the Maglev strip. I didn't like that idea, though – something seemed off." Andy looked darkly at the others. "Once they walked into that fog, nobody ever heard from them again."

A chill ran up Hanu's back. He glanced warily over a shoulder, hoping the feeling of being watched was just his imagination. He squinted, trying to make sense of it all. "Maybe communications stopped working after the shockwave hit," he suggested.

"No, they're dead, alright." Andy spit on the ground. Then his eyes darted instinctively up and down the street. "Frazier and Shaw convinced Wiggins to give it a shot after about a month of being stranded. I refused, but right after they left, I changed my mind and tried to follow. They were already gone, though." Hanu moved closer. Andy shook his head again. "Once you get so far into that fog, you start to see trees, grass – some of the thickest anyone's ever seen... Some kind of creatures live out there. Massive creatures with sharp claws and scales... fifty times bigger than any of the Ancient Ones... and they were *hungry*."

"So you're saying there are monsters out there?" Basse said in a panicked whisper.

Andy shot her a grim look. "We're safe as long as we don't try to go into the fog," he said. "Speaking of – how *are* we leaving?"

"We've got a ship waiting for us," said Reggie, beckoning them into the alley. He rubbed his chin hair nervously. "I'm hoping since we were able to transport in, we'll be able to transport back out."

The team was nearing their destination. They were two streets from the coordinates when someone in a tattered, brown overcoat came crashing out of one of the houses with a large hunting bow. Everyone stumbled to a halt as he screamed.

"You stay right there or I'll shoot!"

He trained an arrow right at Basse, who had made the mistake of lagging behind. She raised her hands slowly.

"Back off, Chinatown." Andy took a cautious step forward. Basse cringed as the man adjusted the grip on his arrow.

"Stay back, I'm warning you!"

Andy stopped, narrowing his eyes at him. "Look, man, it's bad enough you're in my territory, so how about this – I'll forgive you for trespassing if you just walk away now and go back to where you belong."

The man's eyes darted wildly between Basse and Andy. Then he glimpsed Andy's briefcase. "How about *this*," he said, nodding at the box. "I won't kill your friend, if you drop what you're carrying and back away slowly."

"It's not food." Andy scowled. "It's nothing of value to you."

The man sneered. "I'm not an idiot," he said indignantly. "There's nothing else worth lugging around this dump. It's food and it's mine, or she dies."

Basse whimpered.

"Wait," Hanu said. His tongue moved without his permission. But everyone was looking at him. He took a small step forward. "You don't have to kill anybody. We're heading back to our ship. Come with us. We have plenty of food."

The man let out a hearty cackle. "*You can join us on our ship*," he mocked. "Only the Ancient Ones ride around in ships... You're just as crazy as your friend here."

"But it's true – " Hanu started, but Andy raised a silencing hand.

The man continued jeering at him. "What else? You and your friends off to find a way to the Underground? You gonna fight those big ol' mean Ancient Ones?"

They allowed the man to continue his onslaught, raising their eyebrows at Andy all the while.

"Don't bother arguing," Andy whispered.

The man finally fell silent, and his amused grin was replaced by a cold grimace, reminding them that he meant business.

With a sigh, Andy lowered the briefcase to the ground and backed away. The rest of the ground team followed suit. Then, when they were at a safe distance, the man walked toward the briefcase.

"Are you sure you wanna let him have it?" Reggie asked quietly.

Andy was moving his legs backwards so slowly at this point, he might as well had been standing still. "Not a chance," he said under his breath.

The man crouched near the briefcase, then realized he would have to use at least one hand to hoist it. He almost reached for the heavy box, but hesitated, realizing that it would leave him open to attack. But that was all Andy needed. At that moment, the man's arrow slipped and Andy reached for his throwing knives. He threw one right at the man, narrowly missing his hand. The knife landed in the box with a quiver. He threw the second knife, which ricocheted into the street as the man darted. Then, realizing he'd lost his upper hand, he skirted off between two houses.

"I'm gonna have to remember to punish him," Andy said grumpily as he picked up the briefcase.

Basse erupted into shaky laughter. Then she craned her neck to double check that he was, in fact, gone. "What was that about?"

Andy stuffed his knives back into his utility belt. "This is how we've been surviving," he said. "After all these years, food's runnin' out... everyone's gettin' desperate."

Reggie nodded them along, taking his place back at the front of the formation. He checked his navigation. Hanu was reluctant to move, though. He stared at the spot between the houses where the man disappeared.

"Hey, come on," Jaeger called over his shoulder.

But Hanu didn't move. He looked from Andy to Reggie, knowing what they would say, yet still unable to stop himself from asking. "How are we going to save these people?"

"We don't have time for that," Basse huffed.

Reggie paused long enough to sigh and drop his shoulders, but Jaeger looked mildly interested. Andy continued hobbling along with his briefcase as if he didn't hear the question at all.

"We'll put in a request for a full evacuation once we get back," said Reggie. His eyes warned Hanu not to argue. "We're already five minutes late for our rendezvous with Bertha."

Hanu reluctantly complied. He caught up with the group, making a silent resolution that he would follow up on the evacuation, himself, if he had to.

They arrived at their coordinates a minute later, rounding from the alley behind a row of houses and onto the street where the abandoned diner was.

"Where's the flyer?" Andy asked, sweeping a hand awkwardly in front of himself as he stepped into the street. "Is it cloaked?"

"It's about four miles beneath the surface," said Reggie. He dropped the duffel bag and pulled out his radio. "Ground Team to Mako, we're ready. Activate the transport."

The team realized too late that nobody had warned Andy about how the transport actually worked. Moments later, he was yelling inaudibly and clutching himself on the transport pad in the Mako. It took two whole minutes before he was fully able to calm down.

When he settled, he took a turn around the transport pad, then inspected the panel on the console. "I was gone," he whispered. His face hung with a mixture of amazement and grief. "*Quantum teleportation...* You guys mastered teleportation?" The entire crew watched cautiously as Andy took a turn about the ship. He slid his hands fondly over the various knobs and controls. "How come you didn't come for me sooner?"

Reggie played with the sensors at Hanu's station, trying to understand the strange readings they had gotten. "It's actually only been four days since we lost contact with the assimilation team here," he said. "Maybe time started moving faster inside the city because of whatever it was that caused that shockwave..."

"We would've come sooner if we had any idea you were there," said Hanu. He grabbed Andy's shoulder reassuringly and smiled. "Everyone's gonna be so happy to see you."

Andy's face melted into a mischievous grin. "And it'll be good to get back into action. Twenty-five days until Year One, you say?"

There wasn't enough time on the way back to headquarters to explain everything that had happened in the Underground since the night they closed the portal. They arrived in the District of Operations, and an astonished Andy was struck with a fresh wave of questions.

"So, if Year One is still gonna happen, why are we on the surface?" His eyes had grown alarmingly wide by this time, demanding a reasonable answer. He hiked up his briefcase.

"It was a strategic move," Reggie reassured him as they strode up the granite steps toward the main lobby.

"I didn't like the idea, either," said Hanu. He made it a point to stay silent about the Intergalactic Council's warnings. He skipped a step to keep up with them. "We're here now, though, and things have been working out so far."

"So what's in the briefcase?" Reggie asked, watching Andy struggle with the thing.

"I think it has something to do with the shockwave, actually," he said. "I found it at the courthouse in Medical City, along with two dead council members."

Adam Lilley was waiting for them just inside the doors. He beamed, greeting Andy with a strong handshake and pulling him into a warm embrace. "I heard about your misadventure," he said. He held Andy at arm's length, inspecting him. His tired eyes sparkled affectionately. "Are you in any condition to debrief with us before getting some rest?"

Andy nodded agreeably, allowing Adam to guide him toward a makeshift cubicle toward the end of the hall. As they crossed the room Hanu heard several gasps and squeals. Andy nodded a greeting at several of the awestruck comrades, and a few people clapped and cheered. When they arrived at the cubicle, though, Mr. Lilley invited Reggie and Andy in, but halted Hanu at the door. "You've done a great job on this mission," he said. "And I know you three have a special relationship, but I'm going to ask you to leave this one alone."

Hanu looked Mr. Lilley in the eye, ready to prove himself a disciplined member of the Resistance. He wanted to mention the others in Medical City that were still trapped, but figured he would have to wait. He nodded firmly. Mr. Lilley smiled and closed the cubicle door, which was nothing more than a recycled curtain from one of the crafts they had dismantled.

Hanu turned around. Everyone in headquarters had gotten back to work, making calls or searching data files. He shuffled back toward the door, prepared to leave, but then something strange caught his eye – someone was watching TV.

Two separate stations were broadcasting muted reports. One of them was projecting a miniature holographic display of a news anchor delivering the mid-morning news. The woman mouthed words silently, but Hanu had a good idea of what she was saying. The headline that flashed along the bottom of the screen read: *Dissenters Tighten Grip on District as Freedom Forces Target the Wall.* The second projection showed footage of masses of people flooding the streets in the Entertainment District. They wore colorful clothes and held up glittery signs that read things like, "*Make Peace, Not War,*" and "*The Ancient Ones Will Forgive You.*" They were protesting.

Hanu walked over to the console to get a better look at the spectacle, and as he approached, he saw a familiar face poking out from behind the screen. It belonged to someone he forgot he was looking for.

"Ester!"

She jumped. "Oh, I thought you would end up finding me," she said. She rounded her desk in order to pull Hanu into a hug.

"How did you get here," he asked excitedly. "Where's everyone else?"

"Um, let me see..." Ester cupped her forehead with both hands. "Sadie's been on a mission to the City of Water Sourcing, but she's due back tomorrow, and Akesh and Vanessa are here in Capital City with a host family – it's actually the Salcedos; they're taking care of a lot of the soldiers' kids at a remote location."

Hanu sighed with relief. Then his stomach fluttered and he had to hide a grin from Ester. Vanessa was safe. And so was his best friend. Hanu couldn't ask for anything more than that. Then he had a thought. He scrunched up his face. "Vanessa and Akesh aren't children of any soldiers, though."

"Well," Ester said. "They asked if I thought they'd want to return to their own homes, and I didn't think they would. The Hierarchy really thought about *everything*."

"Wait." Hanu shook his head. "They asked *you*? How long have you known about this?"

"Just since that night at the farm, when they had their celebration," Ester said. "Mr. Lilley pulled me aside and asked if I could help recruit some of the intuits from Intelligence. Hold on – " She pulled up a third screen. This one showed a woman in white coverings giving a speech. She had a simple face, wearing no make-up or exuberant jewelry, and her hair was pulled back into a ponytail. Her eyes were sincere and somber as she spoke, but Hanu couldn't hear what she was saying, either. Ester pressed into the hologram of the woman with her index finger and dragged her over to the projection of the protesters. The protesters fizzled and dissolved as the woman was superimposed over the feed. Then Ester did it again, dragging a new image of the woman over the news anchor's feed.

Hanu waited patiently as she examined some numbers on one of the gauges in her console. It started at over forty-thousand, but quickly began to drop. Then it slowed and eventually stabilized at somewhere around eighteen-thousand.

"Sorry," she said as she logged the numbers in her notepad. "Today's our first day hijacking the airwaves, and we have to record all sorts of data in order to interpret how the citizens are responding."

Hanu nodded at the screens, all three of which were now

projecting the woman. "So what is she saying?"

Ester played with a knob, allowing Hanu to hear a few seconds of the broadcast. "She's giving basic reassurances for now," she said matter-of-factly. Then she turned the volume back down. "We're starting by letting the public know that we're here for the interest of the people. As the days move on, though, we'll slowly start disclosing some of the more... *uncomfortable* truths about the Ancient Ones."

They watched the woman mouth her message, and every once in a while Ester entered a timestamp into her notes when the numbers dropped. "Right now we're just seeing how long they watch before they change the channel."

"This was *your* idea, wasn't it?" Hanu watched in amazement as she logged her data. He studied her console, which looked vastly different from anything he'd seen thus far – a huge circuit board with hundreds of channels covered the majority of her desk, and dozens of wires zig-zagged across the thing in a rather confusing way. "That guy at the market... You said you would've given the people proof, and that's exactly what you're doing, isn't it?"

Ester giggled nervously. "When I said it back then, I didn't realize I would have to actually put the plan into action." She put her hands on her hips, glancing around her work station. "I'm really nervous it won't be enough to change people's minds."

Hanu grinned at Ester, his chest swelling with indomitable pride for the girl. "You're doing something really important," he said. "It's gonna work."

Ester grinned, too. Then she suddenly punched Hanu on the shoulder. "Hey, you're doing something important, too, soldier."

"I guess I am," Hanu said.

Ester gestured at Hanu's EAG with a nod. "So have you been out on a mission, then?"

Hanu jumped with a start. "I have – and there's so much to tell you," he said, tousling his hair with both hands. Then he spewed out his entire morning in one breath. "We found Andy... He was alive this whole time, except time didn't move the same for him, somehow, and everyone was trapped... Year One had already happened and we got attacked by one of the fifty-two people left that survived out of the whole city – and guess what – "

Ester grabbed Hanu by the shoulders. "Wait," she laughed. "You mean to tell me that Andy *survived* ?"

"Yeah... He's talking to Adam now." Hanu pointed over his shoulder toward the cubicle.

"Oh that's fantastic!" Ester yelled, making some of the nearby workers look up from their desks. She pulled Hanu into a hug. "I know it's been really hard for Reggie, too, you know. I'll make sure to catch him and say hi." She quickly closed down her projectors, which had finished broadcasting their messages by now and had begun playing the regularly scheduled programs again. "And you say time moved differently for him?" She bit her lip. "How is that possible?"

"Nobody has a clue," said Hanu. "I guess that's what they're figuring out now."

Ester had an uneasy look on her face. "So, these survivors," she said. "They're trapped in Medical City somehow?"

"It's the strangest thing I've ever seen," Hanu admitted. "Andy said there was some kind of shockwave that warped the city. For him, seven years have already passed since the day we closed the portal."

"I doubt they'd have any answers in this morning's briefing," she said, checking her watch. "We're supposed to be meeting in about ten minutes." Ester logged the last of her data and closed her notepad. Then she shut down the rest of her station and started for the briefing room.

"Wait," Hanu said, stopping her. "Those survivors will starve to death unless we rescue them."

Ester nodded her understanding. "I'll make sure we have a plan for them."

Hanu watched her leave, confident that Ester would do exactly what she said she would. Then he gave himself a firm nod, fighting against a quiet unease that crept up slowly on him. The world was unraveling, and he knew that despite their relative successes so far, the hardest part of the fight would soon be upon them.

The Nagi's Gift

The following week and a half passed quickly, bringing the Resistance several more victories. The 51st Division was able to recover the remaining survivors from Medical City, and a group of scientists – led by Mr. Choyce's apprentice – had already begun to collect data on the anomalous atmosphere surrounding the city, which they called the "buffer zone." On top of that, Andy was recovering nicely. He was given leave of duty for a couple of weeks in order to acclimate to the current timeline, but chose to come back early to help the Hierarchy with their plans to stop Year One.

The scouts hadn't stopped their barrage on the wall, but the number of citizens who supported them had begun to dwindle. The volunteer forces slowly went home, leaving fewer and fewer troops camping at the perimeter of the District of Operations. Unfortunately, though, that didn't stop them. They merely changed their tactics from launching explosives at the barrier to tunneling from underneath, to trying to sneak imposters through the gates. All the while, everyone's level of stress had reached an all-time high as the clock ticked closer to Year One.

Reggie, who'd spent most of his time in briefings nowadays, ordered Hanu to take this particular day off. But he knew he wouldn't be able to sit around idly, so he volunteered to help the 36th Division supervise a group of civilians who were visiting the holding facility. According to the Intelligence Division, a good enough portion of the population was ready to be shown *hard evidence* of the Ancient Ones' and the Council's wrong-doings, so the Hierarchy set up a schedule of tours for key parts of the District. The holding facility and its built-in research lab was the most attended attraction. It wouldn't start for another couple hours, though, so he rested in his rickety cot, staring at the vaulted ceiling of the theatre.

The other soldiers fumbled through the dim lighting to dress, or they sometimes coughed or blew their noses, but the theatre remained otherwise very quiet. He rolled over, grabbing the round button from the pocket on his utility belt. It was just as shiny as ever, and just as quiet, too. It hadn't beeped or buzzed, or produced a holographic screen, or done anything else that Hanu expected it to do. He rolled it between his fingers. Then he squeezed it as hard as he could with both hands. There was a small click, and then it vibrated.

Hanu jumped up in his bed, holding the button at eye level. He tapped on it, then he shook it, waiting to see if it did anything more. But the seconds ticked by and the button remained shiny and quiet. He shoved it back into his pocket and secured the latch.

An hour later, Hanu prepared for his role in the holding facility as best he could. He practiced his personal testimony as he dressed. "I personally spent a few weeks here as a prisoner," he mumbled, zipping himself into his uniform. "I had to endure all sorts of torture at the hands of the Council."

He kicked his bag of accumulated items further under his cot and headed for the doors, ready to meet the other cadets at the courtyard in front of the holding facility. Then he stepped into the thick air. A damp breeze smelled of rich soil, and clouds were rolling in from the south. He strode across the theatre's neat lawn toward the sidewalk.

And someone was waiting for him.

"I see you're fitting right in," said Garion.

Hanu whipped around to see the boy leaning smugly against Donna. The silvery orb was massive, yet seemed to blend in on the busy sidewalk. Hanu would've walked by them without ever noticing.

"You're back!"

"Well, just for a little while," said Garion. "I'm not finished with my work, yet, but I got your call, and figured I can at least drop in."

"My call?"

"Yeah, through your tracer."

Hanu pulled the button from his utility belt.

"It helped me find you," said Garion. He took the button from Hanu's hand and held it up to the sunlight that peeked through the clouds. "I designed it with a crude communications interface, but never bothered to make any use of it." He squeezed the button. It clicked, then vibrated, and Donna made a buzzing sound. Garion put the button close to his mouth. "Hello?" he said. Then his voice echoed inside of Donna. *Hello?* Garion smiled, then he put the button back to his lips. "Do you like ice cream?" he asked. His voice echoed again inside the craft.

"*Hey!*" Hanu grabbed the button from Garion's hand. He held it to his own lips. "I could've been having a private conversation, you know!" And his voice echoed indignantly from inside of Donna.

Garion laughed. "I didn't think you'd *press* it," he said. He took the button back from Hanu and placed it in the front pocket of his jumper. "I never told you to press it. I told you to keep it on you."

"Well, I did, so... there you go," Hanu tried to scowl. He glanced over Garion's shoulder, noticing that there was now a door where the hole used to be. "So she's back to normal now, huh?"

Garion slapped the side of the ship proudly. "Took a few days to find it, but I did."

Hanu watched in quiet allowance as Garion admired Donna, just as he often had. It had always been bizarre to Hanu that someone would be so emotionally attached to a machine, but it was only just now that he thought about how long the two might've been together. Being gifted a long lifespan, but cursed to be the last of his kind, how long did Garion spend alone with his ship? But he would have to wait to figure that out, because he had a more pressing question at the moment. "So what kind of work are you up to, anyway?"

Garion bunched up his face. "Well, after you closed that portal, I thought it would be all over," he said, kicking a tuft of grass with a thick boot. "But when it wasn't, I realized I was going about it all wrong... After all, there's a reason people like me were left here."

"Oh yeah?" Hanu shifted uncomfortably on the spot. He was rather afraid Garion might leave if he said the wrong thing.

"Yeah, but I can't seem to find the exact information I need," said Garion. "I suspect it's in the original Tome of the Earth, but I have no clue who's keeping it nowadays."

Hanu nodded toward the palace. "The Hierarchy can probably help with that, you know."

No, they couldn't," Garion scoffed. "I've asked just about every official on the planet I could think of – even *Mavis*."

Hanu laughed. "Even if Mavis knew, she probably wouldn't tell you."

Garion chuckled. "I guess you're right about that."

A gust of wind danced through the street, sending Garion's curls in all directions and blowing past Donna's hull with an eerie whistle. "What kind of information is it?" asked Hanu. "Maybe I can help."

Garion frowned. "Trust me, you wouldn't be able to help. This is more of a... *biological* matter."

For a while, Hanu didn't know what to say. He and Garion looked at each other in uncomfortable silence while the breeze carried on, whipping their hair into their faces. Hanu made a mental note to get a haircut soon. He gestured toward the street. "I was headed over to the holding facility to volunteer," he said. "You wanna come with me?"

Garion pulled the collar of his jumper tighter around his

neck. "I think I've had my fair share of prison," he laughed. "But I guess it beats standing out here."

When they arrived at the courtyard they found that the 36th Division was already gathering into a crowd on the tiny lawn. Garion slouched as they made their way through the mass, hoping that nobody would notice his giant form. It wasn't working, though, because Donna – who had been bobbing along dreamily behind them – was now scraping so close to the ground that people had begun to duck in order to avoid being hit.

Then, when they got to a favorable clearing at the far end of the lawn, Garion plopped down into the grass, and so did Donna. Hanu chose to stand, though, having grown restless from laying in his cot all morning.

In a matter of minutes, the Captain of the 36th Division came to address the volunteers. He looked very young to be a captain, with a tall and thin build and a no-nonsense expression on his baby-smooth face. He introduced himself simply as Tim.

He doled out the instructions quickly and efficiently. It was a pretty straightforward job – they would supervise the tourists, making sure they stayed with their respective groups. They were to be friendly to the guests, and – as Hanu hoped – they were encouraged to share their own personal stories, if asked. Then the captain called them one at a time to come to the front and receive their patrol assignments.

When he was called, Hanu strode quickly toward where Tim was standing. "Can I supervise on the second floor?" he asked, looking over the man's shoulder to better see his roster. The map indicated that Hanu would've been assigned to the grounds. "I was once held prisoner there for a few weeks."

Tim blinked at Hanu. "And who's your friend?"

Garion waved casually from behind him. "I'm sort of helping out today, too," he said. Then he quickly added. "I'm here in more of an emotional support capacity, if you know what I mean." Garion glanced meaningfully at Hanu.

Tim looked at Hanu, then Garion, then he leaned over and looked at Donna, who was still perched on the lawn. His eyes jolted with a hint of recognition. Then he rolled them in resignation. "Please, just don't make any trouble," he said, crossing Hanu's name from the grounds. He penciled them into the lobby on the second floor.

⧙·⧘ ⧙·⧘ ⧙·⧘

They arrived at their patrol station before anyone else had. Hanu's chest was suddenly very tight as he took a turn around the room, reminiscing on a time that seemed so long ago. It felt as though nothing had changed – from the chairs lining the walls to the delicate instruments and knobs on the desk – everything was how he remembered it, right down to the last stapler. "I was pretty crazy, breaking into this place," he said. "Just plain reckless."

"I think it was brave of you, actually," said Garion, who had been rifling through one of the drawers behind the desk. "You see someone that needs help, and you help them."

"Yeah." Hanu smoothed his hand across the double door at the back end of the room. "Even if it means sacrificing myself."

Garion dropped a heavy instrument back into a drawer. "I'm starting to think that's the only way we're gonna stop Year One. We've all gotta sacrifice something."

"I'm starting to think I'm just being stupid." said Hanu. He leaned against the doors, unable to bring himself to open them. "What if something goes wrong and we don't stop Year One?"

"You can't think like that – "

Hanu scrunched up his face. He fought against the suffocating feeling in his chest, but it was starting to overwhelm him. He sighed a heavy, miserable sigh. "The Intergalactic Council thinks it's inevitable."

Garion stood straight up. "When did they say that?"

"Probably a few months ago, by now," said Hanu, trying not to look him in the eye. "They seemed pretty sure."

Garion closed the drawer and rounded the desk. His eyebrows bunched up as he scowled, thinking, then his face melted into a stubborn grin. He grabbed Hanu by both shoulders. "The only destiny we have is the one we're willing to accept," he said. Then he straightened himself up. "They told you that, and you joined the Resistance anyway, right?"

"That's right," said Hanu.

"Well, it seems to me that you still haven't really accepted it then, huh?"

Hanu was quiet for a moment, struggling with his own doubts. "Year One happened for Andy somehow," he whispered. "Maybe that's what they were talking about when they said it was meant to happen. Maybe it's our job to stop it from happening to the rest of the world."

Garion nodded agreeably. "You think we can do it?"

Hanu laughed. "I guess we have no choice," he said. Then he pushed through the double doors and stepped into the hallway. Garion followed. Then they both regretted having done so immediately after walking in.

His stomach churned, his senses arrested by the faint smell of urine and industrial grade cleaner. He clenched his fists, forcing himself further into the hall. As he shuffled along, he searched for the speaker that was perched along the ceiling in the hall. He could almost hear the pledge of allegiance being played.

His feet suddenly slowed. He found himself wanting to recall if he'd experienced anything here that would cause the icy, stabbing sensation that had been resurfacing in his memories as of late. Anything that would offer a better explanation than the ones Hanu had been generating as of late. So far, his mind had gone to such morbid thoughts as Yaar actually being evil, performing some sort of mind control on him. But he recoiled from the thought of the memory altogether. It made his whole body clench up, like when you're peeling a bandage off, but are too scared to look at the wound. He shook his head, unwilling to chase the curiosity.

"At least you had neighbors," Garion mumbled darkly as he peeked through the mesh of one of the cells.

Suddenly, a woman's voice came from near the end of the

hall. "Trust me, having neighbors didn't make it any easier," she said.

Hanu stopped short. "Who's there?"

There was a rustling sound coming from one of the cells, then grunting. Hanu rushed down the hall, thinking they may have forgotten a prisoner when they took the District.

He stopped short at the second to the last cell, nearly causing Garion to run into the back of him. There was a cloaked woman, teetering on a slender stool in the middle of the room. She had removed the tiles in the ceiling, and was unscrewing one of several small canisters that were housed just behind them. She didn't stop, or even try to hide what she was doing. She wrenched the canister free and stored it in one of her cloak's inner pockets, then began unscrewing the next one.

"Hey, I know you," said Hanu.

Garion was in awe. "How do *you* know a Nagi?"

"A what?"

"Snake beings," said Garion, eyeing the woman. "Keepers of knowledge... I thought they went extinct."

"Well, we haven't," she snapped. "And you would do well to worry about your own existence instead of speculating on mine."

"What are you doing here?" Garion asked.

The Nagi freed the next canister, but hesitated before putting it in her cloak. "You know, the young one is right about one thing," she said, gesturing toward Hanu with the nod of her head. "The Intergalactic Council knows Year One's going to happen. Such a tragedy, isn't it, that they'll do nothing to help you?"

"How did you hear that from way over here?" asked Hanu.

The Nagi knocked on the wall of her cell. "Voices carry a long way when they vibrate through the walls." She tucked the canister carefully into her pocket. "And it would be naive of you to think that what happened in Medical City was Year One."

Hanu leaned into the mesh. "What do you mean?"

"The city was destroyed by the Council." She adjusted her stool and began unscrewing the next canister. Then she paused thoughtfully. "Well, mostly. I may have had something to do with it, too, actually."

"You were there when it happened?" asked Garion.

"I was trying to figure out what those council members were building there. And I found out." She shook her head, then began unscrewing the canister again. But Hanu and Garion continued watching her, their eyebrows raised expectantly, so she stopped. A dark purple tongue pressed her lip up as she thought, perhaps deciding how much she cared to divulge. She watched them for a moment, unblinking. Then she took in a swift, conceding breath. "Turns out the Ancient Ones ordered the Council to summon the Intergalactic Council's vessel and trap it within the city."

Garion sputtered. "Why would they want to do that?" he said. "That would start a war between them?"

"Not a war," said the Nagi. She glared at Garion with cold eyes. "It would've been a mass execution." She continued working on the canister, leaving the two to grimace at one another in desperate disbelief. She continued, unconcerned with their feelings. "It was a desperate move," she said. "They weren't supposed to do that until Year One actually started, but you scared them well enough when you took over the District of Operations. They thought the Intergalactics had begun to help you."

"Clearly it didn't work," Hanu said. A cold dread had begun to edge its way into his gut. "So what happened to make time end up moving faster?"

The woman grunted as she pulled out a particularly stubborn piece. "It was more like a time *jump*," she said. "And that was probably my fault."

Garion scowled. "What did you do?"

The Nagi sighed. "It took two days for the Council's little army to place the emitters around the city," she explained. "By the time they initialized them, I realized what they were doing. I destroyed about a dozen of them, which helped – the vessel only flashed into the atmosphere for a fraction of a second before it escaped. But by stopping those emitters, I disrupted the dispersion of free-floating tachyons into the ionosphere. I'm thinking that's what caused the space on either side of the emitters to fracture into two different time periods."

A chill crawled down Hanu's spine, making the hairs on his neck prickle. He raised a shaking hand to his mouth. "One seven years in the future," he whispered.

The Nagi confirmed it with a firm nod. "And one millions

of years in the past," she said.

"What kind of emitters were they?" asked Garion. "We should probably go and collect them before – "

"They were all destroyed in the blast," she said, raising a halting hand at him. "The only part of the system that survived was the initializer, which is already safe, here in the District."

"Wait," Hanu said. He tittered nervously. "How is it that they almost trapped that *whole* ship? I'm sure they didn't just send out a friendly invitation and the Intergalactic Council just came skipping along."

She held up a canister. "Simple electrodynamic field emitters are designed to inhibit particle conversion," she explained. "But with the right modifications, you can take it a step further and stimulate targeted mass materialization *into* the containment field."

Garion's voice had gone hollow. "You can pull anything or anyone into this dimension."

"And what exactly do you plan on doing with those?" Hanu asked, eyeing the canister suspiciously.

"Oh, don't worry," said the Nagi. A satisfied smirk edged at her lips. "I wasn't going to use these for myself. I've been modifying them for *you*." She stepped down from her stool, tucking the thing into her cloak. "Whether they like it or not, the Intergalactic Council will help you fight the Ancient Ones. Or they'll die with you."

Hanu's neck was no longer prickling. His ears and scalp were now alarmingly hot. "We can't *force* them to help!"

"Besides, we already have a few plans of our own," said Garion.

"Oh, right." She scoffed. "I know all about your plans, Garion, and we might as well count you out."

"What does she mean?" asked Hanu.

"Nothing," Garion said sharply.

"That's why you won't say it out loud," the Nagi teased. "It doesn't even *sound* like a good plan. You're going to merge with Saleel, but you can't learn how to win a fight against wills from a book, now can you? You either have the resolve or you don't. There *is* no intellectual or technological solution for that."

"Hey, you're pretty rude," Garion said, his face etched with a deep scowl.

Hanu narrowed his eyes at Garion, barely understanding what was going on. "Are you really going to... do...?" Hanu asked, but Garion stalked off.

Then there was clamoring and shuffling at the doors to the lobby just outside the hall. The Nagi pressed her face to the wall. "Time is running out," she said, raising both her eyebrows. She leaned in. "You'll have to summon them – it's your only chance at survival and you know it." Then she hesitated, studying Hanu with quiet, unblinking eyes. She reached into her cloak and pulled out a small vial, then squeezed it through the bars of her cell. "I guess I am pretty rude," she said. "You can have this as a peace offering. It's antivenom. You'll know if you ever need to use it."

Hanu picked up the vial. It held a clear liquid and a thick

needle was capped at one end of it. He secured it in his pocket.

Then, a moment later, a group of eccentrically dressed civilians burst through the double doors, escorted by several soldiers. The one who was leading the tour scanned the hall nervously as the group filed in. "This is where they kept many of the test subjects," she said.

The civilians groaned their disapproval, poking disconcerted faces into the cells and frowning at one another.

Panicked, Hanu glanced back into the Nagi's cell, but she had already gone.

#·⟨ #·⟨ #·⟨

Hours later, Hanu grumpily descended the puddle-soaked stairs outside of the holding facility. The tours were a huge success, with many of the citizens vowing to write letters to the media or organize canvassing parties. But Hanu was forced to expend a lot of energy pretending to care when they ogled him sympathetically or tearfully interviewed him. He was mostly preoccupied with silently cursing the Nagi for chasing Garion off. He also wondered how he might stop him from merging with Saleel because, if he remembered correctly, the loser of that merger would have to basically be the other one's slave.

Hanu squeezed his temples between his fingers as he searched the courtyard for signs of Donna. Then, when he couldn't find a trace of either of them, he stomped his way through the wet grass, determined to go straight back to sleep once he got back to the theatre. He was so determined, that he walked right past Donna for a second time.

"I thought you would never leave," Garion said.

Hanu jumped. "Stop *doing* that!" He backtracked toward the sidewalk.

"I went to the Hierarchy to report our run in with the Nagi," said Garion. "A lot of what she said checks out against all the data they collected at Medical City."

Hanu nodded, sliding his hands into his pockets. "And what she said about you?"

"Well, let's just say she wasn't lying about any of it."

"So you'll really merge with Saleel?"

Garion sighed. "If the opportunity comes along, yes. If there's a small chance I can disrupt their plans, then I'm gonna try."

Hanu opened his mouth, prepared to argue. But he thought better of it. He settled on giving Garion a rueful smile, hoping the gesture conveyed some measure of encouragement, but he silently plotted to keep Garion as far away from the Ancient Ones as possible. "Let's go," he said, glancing at his watch. "Reggie and Andy should be off duty by now. They'll be happy to see you."

Don't Start Now

The next morning was a lazy one for the majority of the residents in the theatre. A handful of the higher ranking officers dressed and slipped quietly through the doors, leaving everyone else to sleep in or otherwise recover from the night's events.

It all began with an announcement. Somewhere toward the late evening, Mr. Choyce, accompanied by Mr. Lilley and a very sour-faced Paula, paid a special visit to the theatre to notify the soldiers of a timely breakthrough. The scientists had successfully completed their third field test of the new sonic tractor, and would proceed with moving the generator to the surface within the week.

This prompted Deeds to make a follow-up announcement that he and Rambo had coincidentally discovered several kegs of the District's finest lager at a brewery only three days earlier. Then he offered to show anyone who knew how to operate a Nomad where to pick them up.

The relocation of the pyramid naturally garnered a mixed reaction, but the news of the lager was overwhelmingly well-received. In less than an hour, the entire camp was making their toasts – to teamwork, to luck, and to stopping Year One.

One of the intuits fashioned up a radio, and someone had

produced a sack full of tiny explosives that fizzled and danced when you threw them onto a flat surface. Soon enough, Reggie was stumbling around with Andy tucked firmly under one arm, introducing him to anyone who would listen as the '*First Time Traveler in History*'. This was typically followed by another toast, or at the very least, an explosion of raucous laughter and high fives. By the early hours of the morning, several people were passed out on the outskirts of a makeshift dance floor, and the ones still dancing had sloshed a good amount of liquid into the carpet.

Garion, who had allowed Ester to, literally, gamble him out of his boots, now stretched across three cots. He shared one of these with Hanu, who had the misfortune of falling asleep near his feet. Hanu didn't know it, but there were several times in the night when he was in real danger of having a toe lodged in his mouth. Sadie was one of the last to fall asleep, having defended her title as arm wrestling champion nine times in a row.

It was no later than nine o'clock in the morning when the cacophony of snoring was broken by a high pitched whistle. It wasn't enough to wake anyone until moments later, when an ear-shattering crash rocked the theatre, knocking glass fixtures from the walls.

"Who said that?" Hanu yelled, pushing Garion's feet away from his face. A siren started up in the distance.

Dozens of now alert soldiers scrambled from the theatre, hopping over cots and zipping up EAGs along the way. Garion scrambled for his boots as another explosion erupted nearby.

Hanu pulled Ester by the leg. She fell from her cot onto the floor, still clutching her blanket. "No," she groaned. "Year One isn't for another two weeks." She pulled the blanket over her face and tried to roll over again.

"They might've moved the date up," Hanu said with a shaky voice. He crouched over her, hoping his uniform would protect the both of them if the ceiling decided to come crashing down. "We have to get somewhere safe."

Andy crouched behind Hanu, pulling a radio from his belt. "Nowhere is safe from a nuke," he said. "Let's hope this is just their warning shot." He turned the volume up and pressed the radio to his ear. "They need security personnel to Salcedo's place," he said, motioning to Sadie. She gave a quick nod before sprinting off toward the other end of the theatre. Then Reggie signaled for the rest of them to follow.

"This way!" Hanu yelled. He grabbed for Garion's arm to pull him along, but he was already sprinting in the other direction. Hanu cursed, then pulled Ester toward the rear exit, following closely in Andy's wake.

"We've got one ship in the air," Andy yelled over the siren. "Intelligence is about to broadcast the footage."

On the count of three, Andy kicked open the door, and a flood of sunlight blinded them momentarily. Hanu could see that a greenhouse had been blown to bits, leaving huge chunks of fiberglass sprawled up and down the street. They sprinted toward the palace. Overhead, a handful of stealth flyers gave chase to the massive orb. For such a large vessel, it maneuvered around the advancing forces with relative ease. Though it probably could've disabled the flyers easily, it didn't seem interested in defending against them. It merely rolled and zipped, blasting randomly into the District of Operations. Some of its projectiles failed to detonate. A long, cylindrical shell pierced the ground near the tunnel, shining ominously in the morning sun.

"What's going on?" Hanu yelled loudly. He only just realized that the siren stopped. Weapon's fire from the turrets chased the orb, exploding overhead.

"Not sure," Andy said. He pushed Ester along with one hand and blocked the sun with the other as he studied the craft's movements.

They rounded the corner to get to the palace, and found that a large chunk of the main hall had been blown away. Debris littered what was left of headquarters – tools, bricks and oddly shaped splinters of wood were scattered in equal parts. Several different teams navigated through this, either trying to secure or make use of what was left of the building.

Ester swiped a heavy bar and some plaster from her circuit board, then grabbed her headpiece. "Deanna, are you there?" She opened ten channels. Hanu peered nervously through the hole in the wall, flinching whenever the craft zipped overhead. Another crash in the distance told them they were still in danger.

Where's the feed?" Ester asked into the headpiece. She moaned impatiently.

Pants and Motley jumped through the hole in the main hall,

and Andy helped them to mount heavy looking ammunition into the turrets. A group of intuits rushed by, nearly knocking Hanu down as they passed. He recovered, then searched the area, hoping to make use of himself. A stray wire from Ester's console splayed among the rubble. He picked it up and threw it at her.

Ester gasped, then shoved the thing into the console with a shaking hand. "Got it," she yelled triumphantly, pulling up a broadcast of a familiar reporter. From her vantage, the silvery orb looked much larger as it zoomed in and out of the distance. She may have been standing on top of a building.

Ester pressed an image into the hologram and dragged it into each channel, one at a time, until they were all broadcasting the report. Ester checked the gauges. One hundred forty thousand viewers were now watching the Ancient Ones attack the District.

Hanu was about to suggest they take cover when a second, smaller orb zoomed into the feed, joining the chase. His ears grew suddenly hot. It was Garion.

Donna rolled in the air, matching the speed and agility of the larger orb. She bounced around the Ancient One's vessel, forcing it lower into the atmosphere.

"What does he think he's doing?" Ester cried.

Hanu was transfixed; unable to pull his eyes from the terrible scene. He held his breath as the larger orb hobbled toward the ground. Whoever was filming adjusted the camera, then zoomed in. Hanu could see that there was some sort of distortion between the two ships.

"I'm not sure," Hanu said hesitantly. "But he just might be winning."

The larger ship plummeted to the ground now, skidding to a halt into one of the fields behind the residential area. The woman continued her report, speculating on the events as they happened. "It looks like there might be some possible negotiations," she said hopefully as Garion climbed from his ship.

But Hanu knew better than that. He slammed a fist down on the console, making all ten of the channels flicker. Ester squealed irritably.

Then there was a commotion at the doors. Three soldiers had their weapons drawn, and were shouting at an intruder on the stairs. Hanu's hand moved reluctantly toward the gun on his utility belt. A moment later, he recognized who it was. Pants ordered them to hold their fire as the Nagi marched straight up to one of the intuits – an older man named James.

"That wasn't an attack, it was a distraction," she said. Her eyes were strikingly baleful. "The Ancient Ones have just implanted their emitters around your perimeter and they'll be summoning the Intergalactic Council soon." A cold dread froze Hanu to the spot. His eyes moved from her to the shiny metal tube that was sticking out of the ground just outside the palace. She was telling the truth. "You must summon them first; leverage the enemy's strategy for your own advantage," she said. "There's no more time to sit on the fence about it."

The man's scruffy eyebrows joined together as he frowned. "None of us here are authorized to make that kind of decision," he said simply.

The Nagi picked up a radio from a nearby console and offered it to him. "Then contact Adam Lilley."

"This isn't the time," James urged.

Hanu tore away from the raucous and focused on the screen. He could see that about twenty of the Ancient Ones had already spilled onto the field. They clicked their beaks irritably, posturing and snapping at one another in a confused frenzy. They did this until everyone had scattered into a perfect circle around Garion. Saleel, who was markedly larger than the others, remained in the middle with him. He stalked pompously toward Garion, who was puffing his chest out just about as far as it would go. He was still nowhere as large as the bird-giant, though.

Hanu's stomach twisted with a sick and heavy nausea. "We have to do something *fast*," he breathed.

"We do," said the Nagi. She strode quickly toward Ester's desk to get a better look at her screen. After a moment's glance, she turned back to James. "I'll tell you what," she said. "Since they've landed in such a providential spot, I'll summon the Intergalactic Council for you, and their ship'll crush half the Ancient Ones' line of command. The emitters I modified for you are in place just off the field there. Just tell me where the initializer is."

Hanu didn't mean for his eyes to dart toward the makeshift

cubicle, or what was left of it anyway. But at that moment, he realized that the initializer was safe in the District because Andy brought it here in his briefcase.

But the one look was all the Nagi needed. She dashed toward the cubicle, dodging many of the soldiers along the way. They grabbed, kicked and dove at her, but she maneuvered around them with relative ease.

Andy reached the cubicle first. He pulled the briefcase from under a broken chair, but couldn't do much else before the Nagi was right on top of him. She grabbed the box, yanking him right along with it. But he didn't let go. She exposed two large fangs, lunging right at his face, but he blocked the bite with his forearm. She struck again, but he wasn't fast enough to block it. He fell backward, narrowly avoiding her fangs. Then, before his knives could reach her, the Nagi disappeared.

Andy cursed loudly. Pants, who had been attempting to radio Adam, kicked the ruins of a desk so hard he hurt his foot. He changed the channel and sent an alert to all units.

Ester suddenly let out a terrified gasp. "Garion's down there, too," she whispered.

Hanu crossed back over to her desk, afraid to see what was transpiring on the field. He forced himself to look at the broadcast. He could tell that Garion had been fighting Saleel, and that he was losing badly. His clothes were torn and blood was oozing from several gashes in his face and neck.

"We have to get him out of there," Hanu said through gritted teeth, but the soldiers had all become preoccupied with locating the Nagi. He swallowed down a hopeless desperation that was welling up from the pit of his stomach. Garion wouldn't be getting any help.

Ester cupped her forehead in both hands as she paced the length of her desk. "Think..." she mumbled to herself.

Hanu resolved to race toward the residential area and hope Garion would survive that long. He grabbed a spare gun from the rubble and started toward the hole in the wall, but before he could get a good stride, he tripped and fell on top of a smooth platform.

"Ow," he groaned, grabbing the side of his face. Then he jumped up quickly, realizing what he'd uncovered. He cleared as much clutter as he could from the transport pad. "Hey, somebody help me!"

Ester sifted through the debris, searching for the targeting console. "I don't know if this is going to work." Her voice was shaking.

"You have to keep the sensor steady," James said. He propped up a bulky looking tripod. "This'll help."

Ester practically threw the targeting console at James, who mounted it with a click. Then he swiveled it into the general direction of the residential area.

Ester raced back to her station. "Make it quick," she said.

"I think these are life signs," James said uncertainly.

Hanu looked over the man's shoulder at the complicated readings. The system seemed unable to classify the Ancient One's signatures, but one was markedly different from the others. He pointed to it. "That's gotta be him," he said.

Ester suddenly wailed. "Get him! Get him right now," she cried, stomping her feet like a tantruming toddler. *"Hurry!"*

Hanu isolated the signature and activated the transport. A moment later, Garion was writhing on the pad. His screams grew muffled as his face swelled, and he was clutching his side with a bloody hand.

"What's happening," Hanu yelled wildly. He dropped himself onto the pad by Garion's side.

Ester was sobbing uncontrollably, trying to lift Garion up by the shoulders. But that didn't stop him from flopping around pitifully on the pad, staining it with blood. "He stabbed him," she screamed. James peeled her hands from Garion's jumper. "He stabbed him with something."

The intuit pulled Garion's chin up, studying his face. More than half of it was purple with bruises and his tongue was so swollen it started to ooze out of his mouth. Hanu's stomach dropped.

"Whatever he stabbed him with was dipped in poison," James said definitively.

Thick tears welled in Hanu's eyes. He tried to blink them away, but they spilled out – onto his hands, the floor, and along Garion's bruised and bulging face. He rasped and choked, grasping at the boy's jumper. He squeezed his eyes tight, shutting out a sudden and unexpected memory of fire and overwhelming heat. And the determined look on a dead man's face. Hanu wailed. He'd already lost Harris, and now he would lose Garion.

Ester was yelling something to James, but Hanu could hardly bring himself to understand. It was something about a medic. Or anyone who could provide an antidote.

Then Hanu gasped. He wiped the tears from his face with clumsy hands, then took another look at Garion. Vomit trickled from his mouth as he sputtered for air.

"It wasn't poison," Hanu said, fumbling with his utility belt. "It was venom."

He found the vial in his spare pocket and jammed the needle into the thick part of Garion's thigh. Garion jerked at the impact, then he wretched, spilling more vomit onto the pad. James rolled him onto his side, where he labored to suck in air. Then he coughed and went still. Hanu put his head to the boy's chest. He could hear his heart beating, faintly. He was breathing. The antivenom was working.

But they wouldn't be able to rest. The air was suddenly thick with a deceivingly sweet, earthy smell. Hanu searched the hall in an attempt to identify what it could be. It almost smelled like rain. It would be soothing if it weren't so thick. Hanu found that it was suddenly difficult to breathe. Everyone else felt it, too. James stood up slowly. Ester's tear-soaked face was painted with bewilderment.

"No," Andy shrieked. "Not now. Don't start now!"

Everyone looked to the sky. Storm clouds were gathering at an alarming rate. They billowed and pulsed, rippling toward a singular point in the sky right above the residential area. A strong wind followed, whipping everyone's hair into a frenzy as it sucked papers, books and broken bits of furniture from the building.

"Get down," Andy yelled. He forced Motley to the ground.

Hanu threw himself onto the pad, pulling Ester along with him. Garion coughed and groaned. "What's going on," he asked. Ester opened her mouth, but no words came out.

James took cover under a nearby desk and Hanu attempted to pull a metal sheet over the three of them. Garion's feet hung out from the bottom, but it was the best he could do. "I don't know for sure," he said. "But I know it's not good."

A brilliant light flashed in the sky. Hanu squeezed his eyes shut, but the light had already gone. He blinked several times, and was surprised to find that his eyes didn't hurt at all.

Ester snapped out of her stupor. She rubbed her eyes, then grabbed Garion, trying to pull him further under the sheet. The wind whistled, then roared as heavier objects were pulled into the air. Then there was a deafening crack, and the rubble suddenly fell to the ground around them.

Hanu coughed violently as a cloud of dust invaded his lungs. Blood was spilling down his chin; his nose was bleeding. He squinted at Ester. She was coughing, too, splattering blood onto the transport pad. She cupped her forehead with both hands, then said something to him, but Hanu could only hear ringing in his ears.

Andy stumbled toward the hole in the building. He faltered. Then he fell to his knees. At first glance, the sky seemed to have returned to normal. The crisp morning sun had reappeared and was shining benevolently over the District of Operations. But in the distance, hundreds of gnarled, ghostly towers peeked over the District wall through a thicket of sour looking fog.

The Intergalactic Council

A stabbing pain seized Hanu's side, threatening to cripple him, but he forced his legs to keep moving toward the residential area. Nomads and Convoys began to zoom by, stopping occasionally to pick up a few lucky passengers, but Hanu wasn't one of them. Then there was screaming and confusion in the distance as the checkpoints were opened and civilians poured in from the Business District. He maneuvered through these terrified citizens, determined to get to the massive spaceship that had flattened the entire east side of the District. It was the Provenience.

The ship itself had to have been a mile long, and was made of the starkest black material Hanu had ever seen. It was strikingly out of place against the trees and District wall behind it. Several rows of windows told him that it was comprised of at least a dozen decks. He sprinted toward the thing, fueled by nothing more than a sliver of hope that the ones who were inside felt like helping to put their city right again.

As the soldiers neared the crash site, their path became more difficult to navigate. The ground was broken and uneven as sidewalks were shifted, sending large slabs of concrete jutting out at random angles. The road had become an obstacle course.

Chapter Seventeen

The vehicles, which were now useless, were abandoned at the perimeter of all of this, and the soldiers now scaled the wreckage to get to the ship. Hanu jumped from a particularly tall mound of what used to be part of a gym, and into a clearing.

He tried to keep his body moving, but it seemed like the more he tried, the heavier he felt. And finally, he allowed his body to slump into the grass as he gasped for air.

For a while, he thought he would pass out. Little flashes of light were flickering in and out of his field of vision. He wiped his face with an armored sleeve, leaving a mixture of blood and sweat on it. Then he forced himself to breathe slower and more evenly. A minute later, though, he realized that something curious was happening. The flashes of light were still there, crawling around in the grass and in the air in ribbons. They were traveling toward the ship in fractalizing patterns.

Six flyers suddenly materialized overhead, bringing Hanu's attention back to the Intergalactic Council's ship. It was less than a quarter mile away now; he could see the disheveled troops gathering around one end of it. He pulled himself up and hobbled through the field after them.

By the time he got there, Adam Lilley was ushering the mob away from the ship. Hanu ignored him, pushing through the crowd to get a better look. He could see Paula was standing in front of what might have been the ship's door. It was a rather ordinary looking hatch, actually. She studied it curiously, hands folded casually behind her back, as she waited for something to happen.

Adam, on the other hand, paced the length of the crowd irritably. There was a vein bulging in his neck that Hanu had never seen before, and the red rings around his eyes had returned. "Did anyone check for anomalies?" he said. He shook each of his legs awkwardly, as if they had fallen asleep and he was trying to get the blood flowing back through them properly.

One of the soldiers stepped forward. "All of our sensors were de-calibrated during the event, Sir." He coughed into his sleeve, and dried blood peeled from under his nose as he wiped his face. "Analog sensors gave basic readings, none of which were anomalous, but we've manually detected gravitational eddies throughout the District of Ops."

"They're concentrated here," said a woman. She adjusted her broken glasses. "There's a nine mile radius around this ship, beyond which is a temporal buffer zone. Beyond that – "

"Oh, I know what's beyond that," said Adam. He took a deep, steady breath. "But I'm talking about *here*. Did anyone check for radiation? Temporal fluctuations?" The soldiers shrugged uncertainly. This made Adam angrier than ever. "Then why are you all standing here?" he yelled. "Why would you come racing here without knowing –"

He cut himself off, choosing to walk away instead. He rubbed his temples while eyeing the soldiers.

Hanu fought back the urge to ask him why he had come if *he* didn't know about those things, either.

Paula sighed. Well, we're all here now," she said testily. Let's try and show the Intergalactic Council humanity's best."

Adam nodded agreeably, trying his best to regain what little composure he had before it all. He clapped a nearby soldier on the back and smiled apologetically. "Okay," he said calmly. "Does anyone know if this is being broadcast…?" He looked over the District wall, allowing his voice to trail off.

Hanu stepped forward. "There were plenty of survivors on the other side of the District wall," he said encouragingly. "Ester's broadcasting everything, including the details we know and an invitation into the District for refuge."

Mr. Lilley offered a hollow smile. "I guess they don't really need convincing anymore," he said, more to himself than the others. He glared over the District wall.

Hanu looked, too, forcing himself to squint into the fog. There was an entirely new, and thriving, civilization out there. Twisted spires reached into the thick sky – massive, unearthly buildings that dotted the landscape in a sinister way. Shiny, silver vehicles zoomed through it all. It was an advanced city, but it wasn't built by humans.

He fought down a bout of queasiness, clutching his gut as he admitted to himself that the Nagi had killed most of Capital City. There was a sucking sensation where his heart was, but he tried not to think about it. He had to hold himself together. It was the only way he would be any help. And they needed all the help they could get if they were going to bring them back.

Paula suddenly moved toward the door, knocking three times on the ship's hull. Her knuckles clanked hard against the metal, but it was doubtful the ship's inhabitants heard it. The soldiers began shifting nervously. Some of them tended to their wounds and others gave in to the gravitational pull, sitting down in the rubble. Other than that, though, there was silence.

Half an hour later, one of the intuits raced across the clearing. It was Deanna. She stopped just short of the ship, panting and coughing to clear her throat. "There's a message," she breathed. She rested her hands on her knees. "Sir, there's a message coming from the ship."

"What does it say?" Adam crossed the field.

"It's telling me... telling *us* that they aren't supposed to be here." Her face twisted as though she were trying to remember something very difficult. "They won't be able to help us fight the Ancient Ones." Adam began to jog toward one of the flyers, but she stopped him. "I don't know if you can talk to 'em through the comm system," she said.

"Deanna, if they've opened a channel, they'll be able to receive audio from our end."

"They didn't open a channel, though."

Adam snapped. "Well, how did they communicate with us?"

Deanna eyed the soldiers warily. She took a step toward Mr. Lilley. She hesitated. Then she squeezed her eyes shut. "They're talking directly to me," she said. "In my head."

Adam threw his hands up. "Of course," he said, scoffing. Then he stalked off angrily, but thought better of it. He turned back around. "You tell them that their ship ruined our city. They can at least come down here and help us fix it."

"They're saying they can't fix what they haven't done," said

Deanna. She squinted again. "It'll further pollute our timeline."

"Pollute our timeline?" Adam gestured in outrage toward the District wall. "There's no more timeline left!"

Deanna shrugged wildly. "That's what they said!"

"That'll be all," said Paula, hushing Mr. Lilley. Then she reached up and squeezed Deanna's shoulders gingerly. "What exactly did they say?"

Deanna squeezed her eyes shut again as she drew in a rattling breath. "They said... they said that consequences are about to unfold as a result of their being here."

Paula gave her a reassuring nod. "Alright," she said. "What kind of consequences are we talking about, exactly?"

Deanna continued, staring uncertainly into Paula's steady eyes. "They're saying their arrival here has... *irrevocably* changed our time-space constitution," she said. "And it – "

Paula's face fell. "Irrevocably?"

"Yes," Deanna's eyes furrowed. "They're saying we shouldn't have pulled them here."

Adam exploded. "But we didn't – "

Paula silenced him with a firm look. Then she pointed at the District wall. "What's going on out there?" she asked Deanna.

Deanna peered over the wall, saying nothing for a while. She took a slow and thoughtful breath. "The matrix that contains their reality is coded differently than ours," she said, gesturing toward the ship. "The Provenience entered our dimensional space so suddenly they couldn't activate the necessary phase shielding, so their ship... it created fissures in the fabric of space-time."

The soldiers murmured amongst themselves, but Paula silenced them, allowing her to continue. "The planetary matrix attempted to repair itself, using the coding from the ship's energetic output," she said. "But their jump triggered a tachyon condensation, which resulted in a temporal displacement." Then she turned to Paula with a stern look. "Just beyond the temporal fissure, the planet has aged forty-two years."

Hanu finally surrendered to the weight of the unusual gravity. He dropped to his knees, his eyes wide in disbelief as he searched his comrades' distraught faces. He struggled to catch his breath as he realized the Intergalactic Council had been right all along; Year One was going to happen, and they were all staring straight into the evidence of its occurrence.

"There's got to be a way to fix this," said Paula coolly. "If we have a scientific understanding of the process then we can reverse what was done."

Deanna shook her head at Paula. Then she blinked several times. "They're gone," she said. "The voices are gone."

Adam fought very hard to control himself, taking several deep breaths before speaking again. He brushed a tear from a rose-red cheek. "We're not done here," he said to Deanna. He took a step back and looked up at the ship. "None of those people out there asked for this, and we didn't, either. We aren't the ones who pulled you down. You can at least come out here and talk to us face to face!"

For a while nobody spoke. They only looked up, watching

the silent ship. Paula studied Deanna warily, but no more messages seemed to be coming through. The soldiers eventually began to file away, shuffling haggardly back toward camp in small droves. But the ones who stayed behind were rewarded when a lone alien appeared. For a moment or two, nobody seemed to notice her there, but soon there were gasps as her thin, smoke-like form strode toward where Deanna was standing.

A hint of recognition gave Hanu a jolt. He'd seen this alien before. He stood, tugging at his neighbor's elbow to pull him to his feet.

The alien smiled reassuringly at Deanna, giving her a small bow. Then she smiled at Paula before rounding on Mr. Lilley. "The only assistance we can provide you is to leave here as soon as possible," she said. Her wispy face was gentle and regretful.

Mr. Lilley hesitated, alarmed by her appearance. "You're clearly far more advanced than we are," he said, swallowing hard. "At the very least, help us to understand more about this temporal fissure. That'll help us to determine what actions we should take next."

"You are the authorities of what's left of humanity," she said. Then she glanced over at the soldiers, allowing her eyes to fall on each of their faces. As her gaze met Hanu's, she smiled a wry smile. "You will have to determine for yourselves what actions you should take next," she said. "It's as simple as making one choice."

Hanu's eyes had gone red. He sniffled, losing the fight against fresh tears that were now spilling down his cheeks. He looked away from the alien, but he still felt her eyes on him.

Adam shook his head stiffly. "We've already sacrificed too much," he whispered. Then he glared over the wall, squeezing his fists so tight his gloves groaned under the strain. "How can you say it's up to us?"

Paula stepped forward. "The most pressing thing we might need to know is the nature of the consequences that will be unfolding from all of this. What's going to happen now?"

The alien wiggled her nose irritably. "It seems the matrix contained here within the temporal fissure will suffer the same displacement if we do not leave here quickly enough," she said, glancing at the massive ship. "However, our technology is not built to interact with the physics of your dimensional space, so we must modify our systems and chart a course toward your nearest stargate."

"Wh – wait," Adam stammered. "You can't help us, *and* you can't leave.

"We have already begun to modify – "

"Join us at our headquarters," interrupted Paula. "We'll do what we can to help get you out of here... and you'll have a chance to stretch your legs, so to speak."

The alien hesitated. "But we will not be able to offer you any help."

Paula raised a silencing hand, allowing her face to melt into a reassuring smile. "You've been known to inspire us from time to time," she said. "I'm afraid your absence could send the wrong message to the masses. Does your Universal Injunction stop you from helping to keep our hope alive?"

ᐂ·ᐟ ᐂ·ᐟ ᐂ·ᐟ

In a few short hours, the briefing area at headquarters was restored to a functional space again. The floor was cleared of most of the debris, and the benches were back in their neat rows. The podium was, unfortunately, blown to bits, but it allowed the soldiers to place a rectangular table at the edge of the dais to accommodate their guests of honor.

Hanu arrived as early as possible in order to help with this transformation, but not necessarily because he cared about how the place looked. In reality, he wanted to sneak into the meeting, and he knew that helping to clean up would provide a perfect opportunity for this.

His efforts paid off when the commanding officers started to arrive. At first, only a handful of them straggled in. Some of them huddled together, speaking in hushed tones, and others sat alone, staring numbly into space. Then, dozens more arrived, quickly filing into the first rows. And finally, Hanu spotted Reggie's fluff of hair bobbing in the throng. He moved through the crowd and squeezed into the seat next to him.

"Mighty bold move, sitting front and center," he said casually. He studied the intuits as they took their places on the dais.

"I'm still in training, aren't I?" whispered Hanu.

Suddenly, there was a confused clamoring at the back of the room that signaled the arrival of the Intergalactic Council.

Citizens and soldiers, alike, crowded the entryway to get a good look, and several photographers sprang from the crowd and began taking pictures. Adam gave up on trying to keep them out of the briefing room, and focused on guiding the visitors toward the dais instead.

Reggie sighed. "I guess he has bigger problems to deal with at the moment."

Six aliens marched in a procession toward the front of the room. The smoky woman, who introduced herself as Fiara, took the lead, and Hanu recognized Thalor and the Nergal from the Tome of the Earth – Galedeus. There was a woman with three horns on her chin and a couple more individuals that Hanu had never seen before.

The fact that they hadn't bothered using a uniform, just like Arrangement, baffled him. He shook his head disapprovingly. One of them wasn't even wearing actual clothing – a skirt of wet-looking foliage covered his private areas, but the rest of his blue-green skin was otherwise exposed. They looked more like a collection of hitchhikers than space travelers, in his opinion.

Adam seemed to have gotten himself together considerably since the last time Hanu saw him. His face was clean and he smiled bravely in an attempt to hide the sorrow in his eyes. He pulled out a stack of speech cards. "I'd like to start by saying that today we witnessed and survived one of the most devastating turns in human history." The civilians erupted into terrified murmuring, but Adam raised a hand to silence them. "We *survived*," he repeated. "Which means we still have the ability to act, and to turn the tides of this moment in our favor. This morning, our barriers were infiltrated by a single ship, which was manned by some of the highest ranking members of the Ancient Ones' military." The citizens in the back grumbled, and one person yelled about needing proof of said military.

Clearly, Ester hadn't gotten around to broadcasting that information to the public yet. "The Ancient Ones had been planning all along to colonize this planet, and Year One is nothing more than the date and celebration for the arrival of their militant mothership. You can see the proof out there." He pointed through the hole in the palace wall, speaking directly to the citizens in the back who still had doubts.

A cameraman, who was recording the meeting, zoomed in on the foggy distance. Ester, of course, would be broadcasting this through the usual channels, but it was doubtful that anyone was still out there to watch it. By the size of the crowd spilling into headquarters, it didn't look like anyone had declined the Hierarchy's invitation when they opened the District gates to survivors.

Adam Lilley went on, recounting the day's events, including relevant background information regarding the Ancient Ones' agenda, as well as a brief introduction to the Nagi and her possible motives. The soldiers waited patiently through this part, then perked up considerably when Fiara stood up to address the room. There was immediate silence.

"The Ancient Ones have, indeed, been untruthful in their dealings with you," she said, confirming Adam's claims, in case any of the citizens were still doubtful. "But you are no longer swept up in their illusions, which means you have much work to do."

The soldiers erupted into applause, and Fiara paused for a moment, allowing them to do so freely. "There will be a time on Earth when your descendants recount the events that are occurring right now," she said. "Let them remember that it was by human determination, strength, and the righteous use of your own free will, that you survived these dark times." The soldiers cheered again, but Hanu rolled his eyes grumpily. He knew that this was nothing more than a nice way of saying that they wouldn't be helping at all. She continued. "The Ancient Ones have threatened your way of life, and the Nagi has done a great disservice to you," she said. "But it will be you, as a species, that takes the necessary steps in order to transmute the condition of this planet."

Dozens of hands shot into the air. "What kinds of steps?" "How can we fight the Ancient Ones now?" Someone up front stood up. "What if we use our free will and choose to let you help?"

She smiled gently at the man. "Dear friends, you must understand that free will is much more than being able to make a choice. With free will comes the great privilege – and great responsibility – of becoming self-aware; it is about forging your own destiny, without interference from an outside source." She scanned the quiet room. "What is the reason you seek help outside of yourselves? Who are you? You don't look so helpless to me."

A few people in the back of the room clapped uncertainly, but the rest of them remained quiet. Hanu looked away from her, feeling exposed, even a little ashamed. He certainly *felt* helpless. He didn't know how not to feel that way.

Then there was a sudden hum in the room. It sounded like one of the fans in the ceiling vents was malfunctioning. Several people ducked.

Hanu realized the sound was, in fact, coming from the alien with the leafy skirt, who slowly rose to his feet. For a full thirty seconds, he did this, smiling candidly at the onlookers. Then he finally spoke. "Rejoice, even in the dark," he said. "For that is where your roots grow strong." Then he sat back down.

Fiara smiled gently at him, allowing the room to process this. Then she continued. "We leave you with those words of wisdom," she said. Then she sat back down, leaving the soldiers feeling rather flat. Hanu eyed Paula, who wore an inscrutable expression.

Adam thanked Fiara with a small nod, then looked over the briefing room. Though he was smiling, his face had gone slightly green, and it looked as though he'd be sick. "The Intergalactic Council will be mining for a few raw materials in order to make modifications to their vessel," he said. "They'll be leaving as soon as possible, due to the effect their ship is having on our atmosphere." Then he rubbed his hands together rather nervously. "In today's attack, we took advantage of Garion's distraction," he said. "Right before the Nagi pulled the

Provenience into the District, we were able to tractor the generator to the surface in the Business District." At this news, the soldiers perked up once again, buzzing amongst themselves. "One advantage is that it's still intact out there, and another is that the Ancient Ones either don't know we're here, or don't view us as a threat."

One of the scientists in the front row stood up. "We're still running a few tests," he announced. "But it looks like we may need to augment the generator in order to produce a large enough cascade to affect the entire planet. We'll be tunneling under the structure later today to see if we can incorporate photovoltaics – "

River interrupted.

"Why don't we incorporate a photovoltaic system into the Living Library's mainframe?" she yelled. Hanu's eyes darted around the room and found her just left of where he was sitting.

The leafy alien stood up once more, humming loudly. The soldiers mumbled curiously among themselves, but nobody else spoke up, in anticipation of what the alien would have to say. Some of them tittered nervously. Hanu glanced over his shoulder, scanning the room. His eyes found Andy, who was sitting three rows back. The man stared dumbfoundedly at the alien, his eyes furrowed intensely as he silently mouthed, "What's going on?"

Then the alien finally spoke again. "Please, tell us more about this Living Library."

River stood nervously. "It's a catalog," she said. "A record of

Earth's history, arts and sciences, as well as a bank of its genetics. Some of us believe we could trigger an overwrite mechanism in the quantum field by –"

"It's a beautiful project," said Adam. "It really is, but frankly, we can't waste our time on theories – not to mention it requires a phenomenal amount of energy to catalyze the reaction, and we have a finite amount. It'll take more than what we can spare to experiment with this kind of technology."

The aliens looked at one another curiously. Then the one with three horns on her chin took a turn speaking. Her voice was gruff, though inquisitive. "What intention did you have for such an experiment?"

At this, one of the intuits on the dais spoke. "If we could encode an ultra-fast laser with the information gathered in the Living Library, and deliver a series of blasts into the atmosphere, we believe it would trigger a charge density wave that alters the nature of our matrix. The information contained therein would act as a tuning fork, guiding this change and favorably altering the value of particle interaction within the Higgs field."

"Essentially, we were going to try and revert the planet back to its original state," River said. Then her face was more serious. "Bloody wars are what got us into this mess – we can't solve our problems with the very same thinking that created them." She scanned the quiet room, taking a rattling breath. "We don't need to commit genocide. If the environment is no longer fitting for them, the Ancient Ones will be forced to leave."

The civilians in the back clamored loudly, shouting

questions. Then nobody could hear anybody anymore. Hanu shrunk into his seat, feeling rather embarrassed at their behavior as the members of the Intergalactic Council watched all of it transpire. His gut was writhing terribly all of a sudden and the sucking sensation was sneaking back into the hollow part of his chest. Adam raised his hands, but it still took a full minute and a half before he could speak. "In theory, this would be the most favorable option," he yelled. "But right now we need to focus on getting rid of them directly, and a biomolecular cascade has proven effective on several occasions." His voice contended with the chatter. "As soon as the generators are modified, we'll move ahead with our original plan."

Hanu's stomach suddenly squirmed. It wriggled with an uncomfortable nagging that told him something important was happening. Before he could stop himself, he shot straight out of his seat. "Maybe that's why Year One happens," he blurted. He squeezed his eyes shut. Reggie slapped his hands to his face, and there was another uproar. "Think about it," he shouted. "If out there is forty-two years from now, then whatever we're about to do doesn't work."

Pandemonium broke loose at this point. The civilians were shouting for answers and the soldiers were bickering amongst themselves. One woman in a sundress ran from the room, crying.

Adam scowled at Hanu. "We don't have time to debate this," he said.

"But that's just the problem," Hanu said. He felt terribly

guilty for giving Mr. Lilley a hard time, but he couldn't back down now. "Fiara just told us that it's about transmuting the conditions of the planet and all of that – well that's exactly what River's plan would do! If it's going to – "

"But we can't defend ourselves with ideals alone!"

"Or maybe we can," Hanu said. Then the room grew quieter. "What if we can, Mr. Lilley?"

"Or," yelled a balding man from the dais. He stood up. "Or, maybe we decide to activate this library and – surprise, it doesn't help in any way – we all die because the Ancient Ones are still running loose out there."

Hanu rolled his eyes. "The Intergalactic Council said it themselves; their ship ripped the fabric of our reality and it repaired itself – "

River interjected. "The mainframe is built. We just need time to see if our calculations are correct."

"How much time do you think you have to figure that out?" The man was puffed up like an angry bird.

"Gee, I don't know," Hanu said coldly. "Probably the same amount of time it'll take to modify that generator." Then he squeezed his lips shut. The words had come out of his mouth before he could stop them.

Reggie slumped in his seat. His shoulders jiggled up and down as he suppressed a laugh.

The man walked to the edge of the dais. "You mark my words," he said slowly. His voice was rising, along with his temper. "The surest way to get this planet back is to obliterate the ones who took it, and sitting on morals and ethics isn't going to get you around the fact that you're going to have to fight them at some point."

"It might be the surest way, but it's not the only way."

"The chance is too great!" The man stomped his foot angrily; his face blooming a deep crimson. "You clearly don't understand the responsibility of protecting the lives of others!"

Hanu's ears started to burn. He stood up, grasping for words to spit back out at him. "And clearly, you don't understand how to do anything besides turn red when you're angry!"

Then he shuffled out of the row and stomped away from the briefing area.

Revolution Day

Hanu worked hard to be as invisible as possible over the next four days. But not just because he was hiding from the bald man. That was actually easy – hiding among the crowd of civilians who had taken over the theatre and surrounding buildings. The main reason he wanted to be invisible, though, was that there was just nothing to do while the scientists were busy modifying the generator, and that left everyone available to be as miserable as possible, with nothing to distract them.

Hanu was able to visit Garion in the new medical tent, which was erected about a quarter mile west of the palace, but when he wasn't there, he was utterly annoyed. First of all, nobody was able to sleep, so they had no choice but to sit around, sad and cranky, at all hours of the day. Second, he often found himself in charge of comforting a nearby stranger who had burst into tears, or listening to a roommate at the theatre go on and on, teary-eyed, about the friends and family they'd lost. It forced him to think about the people *he'd* lost, like Vanessa, Akesh, Sadie and the Salcedos, as well as his own family – and he was trying really hard not to do that. At least for the time being. That's why he spent most of his time at the buffer zone. He sometimes found one or two other souls wandering around down there, but they mostly stuck to an unspoken code of silence.

He snuck over to the buffer zone as often as he could, to stare off into space, unhindered, or to punch something without feeling guilty for causing a scene. Or sometimes he would study the wall in hopes to find some sort of inspiration for reversing the anomaly. It was intriguing that the border between the two worlds was surprisingly distinct. The soupy atmosphere was contained to one side by an invisible wall, while the ruins of the Business District remained relatively undisturbed on the other.

On this particular day, he sat grumpily on the ground, just a few yards away from the wall of thick fog. He was both disgusted and fascinated by the ghostly shadows in that other world. He stared at it, noticing that the air on his side was slowly starting to match its color and consistency. Each day the Intergalactic Council stayed on the planet, the District looked more and more like it.

Lost in his own thoughts, and didn't realize that someone was approaching. It was the leafy alien. He was moving so slowly that nobody would have noticed him, really. He ambled toward Hanu, smiling pleasantly.

Hanu thought about casually getting up and walking away as if he didn't see him. There was plenty of time to do so, but the alien started making that humming noise again, and Hanu accidentally looked him in the eye. It was too late to walk away now.

He smiled awkwardly. "Hello."

The alien continued to hum, crossing what was left of the street. When he got to where Hanu was, he lowered himself into the grass. "Good day to you," he said.

"I'm not sure if you can call it that," Hanu said gloomily.

"Nonsense," said the alien. His eyes were very small, but they twinkled warmly. "I heard today is your revolution day."

"My what?"

The alien took a deep breath, and Hanu could feel the ground vibrating slightly. "Hmmmm..." It would've actually been quite soothing if he hadn't been annoyed to begin with. "You've made one full revolution around your star," he said. "I heard that is something to celebrate on your planet."

"There's nothing here to really celebrate," said Hanu. But the alien continued smiling, so he quickly added. "Next year, I'll have a huge celebration... if I survive that long."

"I heard that it is an Earth ritual to make a goal for the upcoming year," he said. "A large celebration next year sounds like a worthwhile objective. I also heard that everyone is to give treats to the person who is celebrating their annual revolution." The alien shoved his hand into his leafy skirt.

"No!" Hanu yelled, alarmed. "I'm, um... too old for treats now."

"Oh." He withdrew his hand.

Hanu smiled at the alien, hoping he hadn't heard of any more rituals. "Thank you," he said. "This is more excitement than I can handle right now, though."

"Okay."

The two of them sat in silence for a while. Hanu scooped up a handful of pebbles and rolled them around in his hand. "So why do you do that anyway?"

"Hmmm...."

"Yeah, that."

"Mmmm..."

Hanu waited awkwardly while the alien finished.

The alien smiled, then he continued. "My species is almost strictly telepathic," he said. "It takes a great deal of energy to speak, so I must pull energy from the atmosphere when I am required to communicate in this way."

"Oh."

"Your planet is particularly dense, I must say." He chuckled. "It's a great deal more difficult to adjust than I anticipated."

"Trust me, I know what you mean," said Hanu. "I'm having a hard time adjusting, and I was born here."

The two continued staring into the fog, content with saying nothing for a while.

"So, uh... I'm Hanu. Do you have a name?"

"Hmmmm...."

Hanu flicked a couple of sharp rocks across the ground. They tumbled toward the wall of fog.

"I don't have a name, but I can be distinguished from others by a certain *feeling*," he said.

"Well, what do non-telepathic people call you?"

"You may call me what you feel is appropriate," said the alien.

Hanu laughed. "You probably shouldn't say that to too many Earth people," he said. "Some of us are known to make up some really rude names."

Then something happened at the buffer zone that caught Hanu's attention. There was a fizzling sound, then someone fell out of the soupy fog and onto the ground in a puddle of a cloak.

For a few searching moments, Hanu tried to distinguish what had happened. Then, enraged, he shot straight up and stomped toward the disturbance. "I can't believe you would show your face around here!" he growled at the Nagi.

She dusted off her robes, coughing. "You'll want to be careful where you step," she said. Her eyes darted through the rubble.

"The only thing I want is to rip your arms and legs off," he yelled. "You killed my friends!"

The alien followed Hanu, humming with a sense of urgency. Hanu got there first.

"I found a way to fix everything," she said warily. She held a hand up, stopping Hanu. He clenched his fists, deciding which way he might lunge in order to get hold of her. "It was never the dispersion of tachyons that was the problem. But I've figured out how to move through time. I can even go backward."

Hanu went stone still. "Don't lie."

She lifted an oddly shaped box from the debris and waved it in Hanu's face. "Tachyon field drive."

"The last thing you used on us ended up killing everyone!"

He lunged at the case.

The alien appeared right behind Hanu at that moment and grabbed him with surprising strength. Hanu flailed his arms and legs, clawing at the air.

"Let's talk about these feelings," said the alien. "Surely there's a peaceful way to resolve whatever – "

"No, he's rightfully angry with me," the Nagi admitted. "But he's right, Hanu. There's a way to solve our problems."

She placed the box on a nearby slab of cement. "I've been collecting tachyon particles here," she said, pulling out an awkward looking piece of equipment. "The field drive takes them, and creates something like an inverse polaron dispersion that allows me to literally travel to any point in time between now and forty-two years in the future."

Hanu stopped struggling. "How does that help you to go back in time?" he demanded.

"Well, I realized if I could deliver a steady pulse of tachyons to the conversion chamber, I would be able to travel further forward – or even *backward* if I wanted – but I would need to stabilize the particles between a set of magnetized coils in order to store enough of them to do that. So basically, I just need a vessel – "

"And you think we're just gonna give you a ship and trust that you'll go back in time to fix all of this?" Hanu scoffed. "You're *not* on our side."

"I'm not," said the Nagi in a dignified way. She put the piece back into its case. "I couldn't care less about humanity. I think you're a bunch of weak, ignorant brutes. But I'm willing to correct the mistake I've made."

Hanu hung limply from the alien's arms, scowling at the Nagi. She dusted off the rest of her robes unapologetically. "How do you know that thing works?" he asked.

"I've had forty-two years to develop and test it," she said. "It works." Then she started off toward headquarters.

There was a flutter in his stomach.

"Wait, where are you going?"

"To Adam Lilley."

Hanu struggled to free himself from the alien's grip, assuring him he wouldn't be violent. "I'm coming, too," he said.

The Nagi paused, throwing her hands on her hips. "Of course you are."

The alien smiled wider than ever. "Excellent!" he said, striding until he was right on her. He extended a moist hand. "Bob."

She scrunched her face. "What?"

"You may call me Bob," he said. Then he started humming again. This made the Nagi even more confused.

"We were coming up with a name for him," Hanu explained. He smiled awkwardly. "I guess he chose Bob."

"But he's humming." The Nagi said, eying Bob.

"Yeah, well that's... that's how he gets his energy to talk."

The Nagi stared at Bob with mild interest. "Well, Bob, it's nice to meet you," she said, shaking his hand. "I don't have a name, and I certainly don't want one.

ⵘ·ⵉ ⵘ·ⵉ ⵘ·ⵉ

The small flicker of hope that had ignited in Hanu's chest was quickly extinguished. Not only did the Hierarchy deny giving the Nagi access to a ship, but they tried to confiscate the tachyon field drive. This ended badly for the soldiers, of course. Two of them suffered broken noses and another three were left in a heap. The Nagi escaped in a flash, unharmed, taking the technology with her. Hanu slipped out of headquarters before anyone could ask him any questions, or further aggravate him in any way.

Determined to avoid Bob, he weaved through the new shanty town that had formed on the palace lawn. As he cleared the last row of tents, he kicked a pile of heavy rocks. They scattered across the grass and ricocheted off the tunnel wall in a satisfying way. He was angry with the Hierarchy for being so bone-headed about the Living Library, and he was angry with the Nagi for killing his friends. But he was mostly angry at himself, for getting his hopes up about getting them back. He continued toward the gate, hoping she would just steal one of the ships that were lined along the northern wall of the palace.

Further along the path, a voice echoed in the distance.

"Hey, Hanu... wait!" Garion was shuffling between a row of tents.

"You're up," Hanu said, his chest bubbling with a muted delight. It was easy to forget that not all of his friends were gone.

"Ester said you've been hanging out over there," said Garion, gesturing over the wall. "I wanted to come visit *you* for once."

The two crossed the expanse toward the outer wall, dodging debris and an ominous looking emitter along the way. "It's pretty depressing over here," said Hanu. "But at least it's not crowded."

"I guess only the brave come here," said Garion, staring down the wall of soupy fog. He shuddered. Then he sighed. "I wasn't much help, huh?"

"Well, according to Adam, you distracted the Ancient Ones long enough for them to get the generator moved to the surface. That counts for something, right?"

Garion made a noise that said he didn't agree, but wouldn't argue. They walked in silence for a while. "I heard they were going ahead with the same plan as before," he said.

Hanu rolled his eyes. "It's the safest bet," he said flatly.

"Doesn't really feel right, does it?"

Hanu looked at the wreckage at the buffer zone. "I guess we can still go ahead with the Living Library after all the Ancient Ones are gone," he said. "I just get a nagging feeling the Intergalactic Council is trying to tell us something." He screwed his face up. "It only takes one choice," he said in a mocking voice. "They keep saying that, like we haven't already been making choices."

"They're doing their best, I guess." Garion scowled. Then he sighed. "I wonder if we'll even be able to create a blast that big."

"I wonder if they've lost their minds," said Hanu.

"Do you think we should start a protest?"

"Sure, why not." Hanu chuckled. Then he stopped in his

tracks. Just ahead, the Nagi was slinking along the wall of fog. "It is my revolution day, after all..." He watched her for a while, allowing a radical idea to unfold in his head. "Hey Garion," he said slowly. "Where's Donna?"

"She's docked with the other ships," he said. "Why?"

Hanu raised a mischievous brow. "Would you happen to know where to find a set of magnetized coils?"

The Visitors

Garion grunted from underneath the console of his systems regulator manifold. Then he poked his head out. "Grab that soldering pen, will ya?"

Hanu scooped up a handful of tools from the floor and sorted through them. He didn't know what a soldering pen was, but assumed it had to be long and thin. He was wrong.

"It's the bulky one," said the Nagi.

"Oh, right." Hanu dumped the tools back onto the floor. Then he wheezed, coughing into his sleeve, as he offered Garion the instrument.

Garion cursed loudly as two pipes fell from underneath the console and hit him in the face. Then he grabbed a cloth from his front pocket and wiped away the sweat that was pooling in his eyes.

The Nagi sighed. "You'll *have* to take a break."

"I've almost got it," said Garion. He groaned as he squeezed the two pipes back into place. "Besides, it looks like we're not gonna make it much longer."

Hanu felt the Nagi's eyes on him as he coughed into his shirt. He gasped for air.

"I think you're right," she said.

Hanu mustered a faint smile, though everyone knew that he wasn't faring well at all. The environment in the District of Operations was collapsing at an alarming rate, and neither they, nor the Hierarchy had made as much progress as they should have in their separate endeavors. The Intergalactic Council was nearly able to lift off, but after a week and a half on Earth, the radiation levels started to spike and the air was so dense that breathing was now a full time struggle.

There was a knock at the door, making everyone freeze. Garion eased himself from under the console. "Donna," he whispered. "Windows, please."

Hanu ducked, alarmed, even though he knew the transparency of the walls only worked one way. Garion ducked too, for some reason, knocking the panel covering down with a loud clatter.

Hanu's eyes grew threateningly wide. "They'll hear us!"

"Shhh..." hissed Garion.

An alien held her face to the door, nearly scraping it with the three horns on her chin. She sniffed curiously. Fiara, Thalor and Bob stared contentedly at Donna's hull.

The Nagi glared at the door, her jaw set firmly. "It doesn't matter," she said. "They already know we're here."

"How do you know?" Hanu whispered.

"We don't have to see you to know you're there," Thalor called.

Hanu's eyes darted wildly from Garion to the Nagi. The slits in her eyes narrowed as she continued to glare. "Don't open it," she said.

Garion beckoned for the soldering pen, and began to ease himself back under the systems regulator.

Thalor folded his arms. "We could enter this vessel with ease, if we wanted to thwart your plans," he said.

Garion huffed, then unfolded himself from underneath the console. "Donna, doors, please."

The four of them entered, letting in a puff of thick, hot air that irritated Hanu's throat further.

Fiara beamed, fondly inspecting the cabin. "This ship is a relic. You've kept it well, Garion."

"Thanks," he said. "But... how do you know about my ship?"

"I was there when it was forged," she said.

Thalor inspected a bulkhead that he'd just hit his head on. "It was your grandmother's," he said. "On your father's side."

Garion grew quiet as his eyes darted the bunch. Then a small dimple appeared at his cheek. "You knew my family?"

"They were part of our crew on the Provenience for a while," said Thalor. He crouched onto a nearby stool, letting his silvery ponytail graze the floor. Then he stretched his legs in front of him. "Your grandmother was our primary cartographer on our very first mission to this system, and your grandfather was a very skilled linguist." He smiled affectionately at the memory. "When they applied to the mission, we had no clue they had ulterior motives."

Garion's grin quickly faded. "What do you mean, *ulterior*?"

Thalor waved him off. "They were noble, of course. But ulterior, nonetheless." He raised both eyebrows at Garion, who hadn't decided yet if he would remain offended. "During a time when the Deh were forbidden from pursuing the Anuh, your parents found the means to track them down and confront them. They applied to join our investigation of a quasiparticle leak that to your planet."

"They knew the Anuh were here," Hanu guessed.

Thalor gave a small, amused nod. "Indeed. When we arrived, we discovered the Anuh here. They had been experimenting with awfully dangerous portal technologies that would've destroyed this whole sector of the galaxy, and our job was to put a stop to it."

Bob sighed somberly. "Your grandparents cared a great deal about what happened to this planet, though for different reasons," he said. "They sacrificed much."

"Including your crew," Garion said. His face was bent with a guilty grimace. "They tricked you into fighting their battle."

"Oh, yes," said Thalor. He folded his arms gently across his chest, wearing a grin that reeked of scandal. "We were unwittingly thrown into the midst of it. The Dehan crew members launched an assault on an Anuh shrine as soon as we arrived. And they were quick to retaliate."

Hanu's eyes darted between Garion, who slumped against the navigation panel, and Thalor. He leaned in closer.

"At first, we only wished to retreat," said Thalor. "But we'd sustained such heavy damage – and with the Universal

Injunction already violated – we decided to end the conflict swiftly."

"So, did you win?" Hanu urged.

The three-horned alien barked a laugh, making everyone jump. "Of course we did," she said. "Now, understand – most of the battle took place out of phase of the planet's harmonic sphere, but Safthon – their leader at the time – knew that our systems would decompile if he knocked us into alignment with it." She raised an eyebrow and paused dramatically, allowing Hanu to lean in further. Garion's eyebrows furrowed expectantly and the Nagi watched her through intensely focused eyes. "He opened a triaxial singularity, hoping to force us into this atmosphere, but we countered it, pulling everyone into our dimensional sphere instead."

Bob shook his head disappointedly. "It was a tragedy."

Thalor sighed. "We did the best we could to save their physical forms," he said, shaking his head along with Bob. "We escorted what was left of Safthon and his crew back through the singularity in a small fleet of our shuttles. The Anuh didn't put up much of a fight after that, though. When the rest of his command saw the condition Safthon was in, they evacuated, thinking we would damage *them* as well."

Garion nodded. "So, they broke off the fight when you injured their leader?"

Thalor leaned back in his chair, tilting his head thoughtfully. "I guess you can say they lost their conviction, yes. They fled through their artificial portals, which we sealed."

"Then you left," said Hanu. Then he quickly smiled, trying to hide his accusing tone.

"Not exactly," said Fiara. "We were stranded, ourselves, for a time. The singularity closed much faster than we accounted for."

Bob began to hum, but nobody paid attention.

"We spent a great deal of that time getting to know the humans that lived on the planet back then," said Thalor. "One hundred forty-seven of us – including your grandparents, Garion – remained on Earth for three centuries. The humans often came to our mountain, where we camped, asking for solutions to their problems."

Fiara scowled, making the smoky edges of her face pull in close. "They relied far too much on our solutions," she said to Hanu. "We were your gods once, you know. As much as we tried not to be, they couldn't help making us their deities."

"I've heard that before," Hanu said through a scratchy throat. He tried not to cough.

"We realized, too late, that we had crippled you," said the three-horned alien. "It's truly our greatest regret."

Bob stopped humming and opened his mouth to speak, but Hanu interrupted. "And that's why you won't help us now."

Fiara nodded softly. "We learned firsthand why the Universal Injunction was set in place. All we could do was to hole ourselves up on our mountain top until we could leave." She squeezed the soft material of one of the spare chairs and smiled into one of Donna's consoles. "We experienced our own challenges during that time, of course. Manufacturing neural-ships for our Dehan crew was most difficult."

"*Neural*-ships?" Garion said, raising his brows for clarification.

"On your home world, your species had evolved an instinct to merge with their technology in place of their Anuh counterparts," she explained. "If the biological process of merging began, and there was no neural-ship available, the individual experienced incredible psychological damage. Many of the Deh in our crew hadn't undergone their merging yet, and when they started, there weren't nearly as many of your ships as there should've been. So we ended up creating them with some of the resources from our ship, and materials found here on the planet."

Hanu was thoroughly confused. "How could they merge with a ship?"

Bob jumped excitedly. "The neural-linking circuitry is able to interface with the consciousness of its pilot," he said. "It's as close to a bio-ship as you can get in this dimension." Then he smiled an accomplished smile, seating himself in a spare chair.

Garion rested elbow on a nearby console, grinning in childish awe. "So, is Donna linked to me, then?"

"No," said Bob. But then he started humming again.

"It's actually still merged with your grandmother," said Fiara.

Garion shook his head. "But my grandmother's long gone."

"Loved ones are never really gone," she said, patting the side of a bulkhead. "Especially yours." Then her face melted into a sharp scowl. "The hybrid children were a separate challenge altogether. We underestimated the foresight of our Dehan crew, and the lengths to which they would go to protect Earth. But thankfully, you children never required a merging process."

Bob interjected, raising a finger. "You were quite sickly as a child," he said to Garion. "Your grandmother tasked Donna with watching over you."

"By the looks of it," said the three-horned alien. "She's done a good job." She stooped to get a better look at the underside of the console Garion had been working on. Then she looked at him seriously. "And speaking of a good job... I trust you know what you're doing with that tachyon field drive."

Garion broke from his reverie. "We do," he said cautiously.

The Nagi, who had been rather rigid during all of this, glared at the alien. "You are quick to interfere with others' plans, though you break your own laws to interfere when it suits you," she spat. "You will not disable our attempt to save ourselves."

Hanu held his breath, anticipating the Nagi's attack. But she only glared expectantly at the alien.

"Be easy," said the three-horned alien. She picked up one of Garion's tools and rolled it in her hands. "We technically wouldn't even be here if we hadn't noticed a fluctuation in the particle field," she said. "We followed it here to the buffer zone – and then we found you."

The Nagi didn't relax, though. She set her jaw. "Do you plan on stopping us?"

Thalor's lips curled into a wry smile. "Now that would be a direct violation of the Universal Injunction, wouldn't it?" The Nagi cocked her head curiously at him. He clarified. "You've come up with this plan all on your own," he said. "Therefore, we cannot deny you the experience."

She wasn't convinced, though. "The Intergalactic Council has regulated the pursuit of time travel."

"We must prevent anyone from destroying the fabric of the cosmos," said Thalor. "Your species, unfortunately, championed an unstable method of time travel, so we were forced to intervene. But your new field drive is more than promising, and the benefit of using it far outweighs the risk."

"What do you mean?" asked Hanu. He blew his nose with the spare handkerchief from his back pocket.

Thalor shook his head sternly. "Your planet is dying," he said. "Our ship is ready to leave, but the atmospheric shift here is destabilizing the planetary grid. It's going to collapse in on itself." He stole a glance at the Nagi. "The destruction of the planet in this way would restructure the entire galaxy, and we just can't allow that."

Hanu stopped, the handkerchief still raised to his face. All of the air was sucked from his lungs. It was as if the room itself was holding its breath. "Oh," he said. He cleared his throat and placed the cloth back into his pocket. "I see." Then, he was suddenly aware of everyone's eyes on him. Everyone, except the Nagi, who lowered her gaze in disgrace. Hanu found only the slightest satisfaction in this; knowing she had the decency to at least be ashamed of herself for what she'd done. "So we're like the last hope, then."

Garion forced a hollow chuckle. "Well, it's a good thing we're prepared."

"That remains to be seen," said Thalor. He ducked under the console. Garion followed, watching him closely. "You won't be able to counter the isolytic reaction when the tachyons are filtered through the coiling system," he said. "The drive is gonna blow the moment you try to activate it."

The Nagi looked thoroughly scandalized. "How would you even know that?" she asked. "You barely even looked at it."

Thalor poked his head out from under the console. "I scanned you before we knocked." He smiled, flashing a small diagnostic rod.

"Your ship requires a quantum funneling chamber," Fiara said. "It'll collect the excess energy generated by the coils and use it to stabilize the structural integrity of the drive itself."

"But we don't have one of those," Garion said. "I wouldn't even know how to begin building something like –"

"It would need to be done properly," Fiara said seriously. "We will do it."

The Secret Mission

The visitors worked diligently for several hours. Fiara and the three-horned alien took turns constructing the device, while Bob and Thalor scanned the buffer zone for potential threats to their plans. Hanu sat idly by, blowing his nose or forcing small talk with the others or resting, when appropriate.

Then, after the sun disappeared over the eerie towers in the distance, Fiara popped the front panel back over the systems regulator. "It's ready," she said with a sure smile.

Garion nudged Hanu, who had found a comfortable spot on the floor in the corner. "Hey, wake up."

"I never went to sleep," Hanu said grumpily. He rubbed his eyes, irritating the red rings that had formed there.

Bob rose sleepily from one of the chairs and stretched his legs, giving his leafy skirt a good shake. Thalor, who had been deep in thought for the last half-hour, continued to stare down the soupy wall of the buffer zone. "You mustn't forget what I said, Hanu." He turned to the boy. "The only way you will prevail is by following your innermost voice. Your choices can be powerful."

Hanu met his intense gaze. Then he gave a feeble nod.

"We can't waste a minute more," said the three-horned alien. She extended a hand to Hanu and pulled him to his feet. Then she beckoned for the Nagi and Garion to follow. "You'll have to generate three short neutrino bursts before you initialize the tachyon field drive," she said, typing a complicated algorithm into a newly installed console. "They're modified to open a singularity, but you'll need to activate the drive as soon as the mouth becomes visible. You'll have two seconds at most, you got it?"

Hanu gave a shallow nod, running a hand over the lever that would activate the drive. He glanced at Garion, who looked just as nervous as he felt. The Nagi watched placidly as the alien doled out her final instructions.

"The algorithm I've programmed will take you to the morning you summoned the Provenience," she said. "Your ship is small, so you might not get a second chance. Don't alter the algorithm, and don't put unnecessary stress on the neutrino emitters."

"Right, short bursts." Garion smiled, nodding just a little more confidently now.

Bob, who had just finished humming, gave his final words. "Don't go interfering with things you don't have to," he said. "It can change the future in ways that you can't predict."

Then the members of the Intergalactic Council gathered at the door. "Oh," said Thalor. "This is probably most important. When you enter the time-space at your destination, your consciousness will try and revert to a single point. You must act quickly and decisively, as the process becomes exponentially more intense the longer you're there."

Then the Intergalactic Council said their goodbyes, and the three of them were left standing alone inside the ship.

"Okay," Hanu said wheezily. "Let's get to it."

The Nagi gave a determined nod, taking her place behind the upgraded console. "Take us into the stratosphere, Garion."

Garion quietly obliged, programming the coordinates into the navigational panel. Then, on his command, they were airborne.

They quickly reached their destination, hovering quietly above the brown, unearthly city before anyone spoke. Hanu licked his lips, tasting the blood that leaked through the dried cracks. "Three neutrino bursts," he said to the Nagi. She pressed the button, but nothing happened. She pressed it again, harder this time, and a dull beam shot from the underside of the ship toward a focused point just in front of them.

"Not so hard," Garion hissed.

"Three of them," said Hanu.

The Nagi pushed the button two more times, sending smaller zaps into the same focal point. Then, after an incredibly long moment, the space just ahead of them contorted. The air twisted and crumpled, pulsing rapidly.

"Is that the mouth?" asked Hanu.

"I'm not certain," said the Nagi." Her hand hovered over the lever.

"Wait," said Garion. "Not yet."

A second later, a rift appeared. A small tunnel, filled with an electric blue gas.

"Go!"

The Nagi flipped the lever with a lightning-fast hand. Then, a blinding white current emerged from inside the singularity and pulled Donna in.

Hanu couldn't do much more than clench his jaw and close his eyes. The ship rocked violently as it traveled through the tunnel, making it hard to hold down the bile that was churning in his gut. Twenty-two seconds later, though, he was rewarded for his efforts. Donna was suddenly free-falling toward a shining palace over the District of Operations.

The Nagi climbed to the nearest console. "The navigational array is down," she reported.

Garion crawled toward the systems regulator and pulled the panel off. He checked the readings. "Donna, reroute auxiliary power to the navigational relays." And with a compliant tone, they slowed to a halt.

Hanu took this opportunity to catch his breath. He threw himself into one of the seats. The Nagi followed suit, breathing in a deep sigh of relief.

Garion let out a feeble laugh. "We made it," he said. "Donna... windows, please."

The ship became transparent, and Hanu jumped from his seat. "No." He crossed the room to get a better look through the window. "No, no, no, no, no..."

Garion rushed to the window, too. Capital City was there – whole and bright and bustling. But something wasn't right. Yellow and Red banners littered the Entertainment District, and a ferris wheel towered in the distance.

"This can't be right," Hanu said. "This can't be the right time."

Garion checked the console. "The readings are exactly where they should be," he said. "And none of us touched the algorithm.

"It had to be the neutrinos," said the Nagi, looking at her own console. "The button was stuck. The excessive neutrinos probably compromised the tachyon acceleration."

Garion crossed over to the Nagi's console. "The emitters are nearly blown," he said, looking over her shoulder. He typed into the keyboard. "The quantum funneling system was knocked out of alignment, too. I'll initiate a system overhaul before we try again."

Hanu suddenly jumped. "I know when this is," he said, pointing excitedly out the window. He squinted into the distance, reading a countdown banner on a rooftop patio. "This is almost three years ago... three days until the Bowl party."

The Nagi slipped from behind her console. "Three years?"

Garion chuckled. "Well, at least things are back to normal," he said. The Nagi scowled.

Hanu studied the bustling city in silence.

"What are you looking for?" Garion asked.

"I don't know," said Hanu. "Anyone that I know, I guess. My mom..." And with a sudden flutter in his chest, he squeezed his face against the window. His eyes darted the Business District, longing for a glimpse of a man who was long gone. His face twisted with grief. "Harris is down there somewhere."

"I doubt you'll find them among all these people," he said, squinting into a throng of campers. Then he went back to analyzing the field drive. "Where are *you*, anyway?"

"I don't know," Hanu said quietly. Then he noticed Garion's eyes on him. He gave it some thought. "I guess I'm still at the Flush," he said. " Can we go there?"

The Nagi screwed her face up. "You want to go to the Flush?"

"Why not?' Garion said. He reached over to the navigation panel. "We've got time to waste, apparently." He programmed the coordinates, sending Donna floating lazily toward the north.

"We busted my friends out of that holding facility, you know," he told the Nagi as they left the District of Operations. She wasn't very interested, but nodded politely, at least. They passed over the Business District. "Just up there, under the ferris wheel, there was a secret path to Deprogramming, and over here's where I hid in a pile of garbage when we first escaped." He stopped short, then he fell quiet. He suddenly didn't feel like talking anymore.

He watched quietly as they passed over the Residential District. A single black Convoy caused his heart to skip a beat. He jumped. "That must be us!" he said. "They're taking us into the District for override."

The Nagi perked up considerably, watching the vehicle wind its way down the maze-like streets back toward the city. Donna followed the vehicle back through the Entertainment District and past the Fountain of Hope. "Hey, this is when we escape," he said, grinning. "This is when the Convoy flips."

The vehicle travelled further into the Business District, but nothing out of the ordinary seemed to be happening. The Nagi raised her brows in anticipation. Hanu squeezed his face into the window. The surveillance tower was just ahead, but no sign of turbulence. He groaned impatiently. "Why isn't it flipping?"

Garion sighed. "Donna, target the left side of the vehicle at these coordinates," he said, typing into the console. "Fire a de-polarization beam now."

The convoy flipped violently all of a sudden. It rolled several times before grinding along the sidewalk and straight into the surveillance tower. The tower groaned on the way down, crashing into a department store.

"I can't believe you shot us!" Hanu yelled, glaring wildly at Garion.

"But it wasn't flipping," said Garion. "It didn't look like you were gonna make it."

"But you *know* I was gonna make it," he said. "I'm standing right *here*, aren't I? That means I made it!"

"Come on, you were getting nervous about it, too," Garion laughed. "There's no way you were gonna escape."

Hanu scowled indignantly at Garion. Then his face furrowed. "So... was it you all along then?"

Garion shrugged. "I don't know, actually."

They both looked at the Nagi, who had crossed her arms and

was leaning against a wall. "Seems like some version of a causal loop to me," she said. Then she gestured toward the field drive console. "Try not to shoot anybody else, though."

Garion returned to his work at the console, ejecting the drive from a cylindrical compartment. Then he began his overwrite protocols.

Hanu went back to looking out of the window, though he was still quite disheveled. "I can't believe you shot us," he repeated grumpily. Then he narrowed his eyes to watch the scene unfold below. Tui and La were scrambling up one of the main streets. The scout must've already sent the alert, because a man at a sidewalk cafe made the mistake of grabbing one of them. The other twin grabbed the chair he was just sitting in and broke it against his back as the first one punched him. Hanu winced, watching them cross the street toward a department store. Then a fleeting thought crossed his mind. "They don't know what's coming next, but it's pretty bad." He turned to Garion, who had finished programming the overwrite and was watching Vanessa and Ester slink through an alley and toward the Entertainment District.

"We can't interfere," he said. "That'll risk changing the future in ways you can't predict, remember?"

"Yeah, I guess shooting people is the exception," Hanu said. He raised his brow at Garion.

"Well, you'd already escaped once, so I didn't really change anything, did I?" Garion said.

The Nagi rounded on her console. "Besides," she said. "We

don't have time for that anyway. The overhaul is complete, and we need to jump again while the tachyons we have left are still stable."

Garion pulled Hanu from the window. "We can't forget what we came here to do," he said. "Let's finish the mission."

Donna was back in position over the District of Operations within seconds. Hanu checked his readings, then gave the Nagi a swift nod. "Three small bursts," he reminded her.

The Nagi placed her hand on the button, then hesitated.

"It shouldn't stick this time," Garion assured her. But still, she didn't move.

"It's not that," she said quietly. She took a rattling breath. A shadow crossed her face. "We're going into a future where my people don't exist," she said. "But they exist right now... The Ancient Ones haven't invaded my home world yet. I haven't been captured."

Garion shook his head. "There's no way we can stop something like that," he said, wide-eyed.

"I'm not asking you to." She removed her hand from the button. "I don't mind making my own sacrifices."

"But we can't just *leave* you in the past." Garion scoffed, rounding from behind his own console. But the Nagi already disappeared into thin air.

Garion stopped in his tracks.

Hanu threw his hands in the air. "Okay, that's the last thing we need."

"What do we do?" asked Garion, crossing to the window as

if he might catch a glimpse of her.

Hanu shrugged incredulously. Then he rubbed his temples, squeezing his eyes shut. But a sudden jolt in his stomach paused him. He wiggled his fingers. They were suddenly numb.

"What's going on?" Garion said.

"I don't know." Hanu gave his arms a shake and found that the feeling had returned quickly. He rubbed his stomach. It had returned to the usual amount of queasy. "We have to act quickly and decisively, right?" He placed a hand over the button. "Three blasts?"

Garion swallowed hard. "Right. Three blasts."

Hanu pressed the button three times and waited for the anomaly to appear. Then Garion flipped the switch, and they were tumbling through the tunnel once more.

Donna shot out of the singularity with a jolt, and Garion – who was prepared this time – rerouted auxiliary power to the navigational array.

"I don't know how many more times I can do this," Hanu groaned, clutching his stomach. He pulled himself from the floor and leaned over his console.

Garion was typing fervently into his keypad. "I don't think we'll have to worry about that," he said.

Just then, a fleet of stealth flyers zoomed straight toward Donna, and Garion was able to engage the phase variance just in time for two of them to pass straight through without harming them. Hanu whipped around to see a giant orb maneuvering around the flyers' onslaught. It shot long, narrow missiles into the District of Operations with explosive force.

"Great," said Hanu in a harried voice. He popped up, running a hand through his hair. "Let's find the Nagi."

Garion scanned the city below. "That might be kind of hard, being as she's no longer here to tell us exactly what her plans were." He steered Dona toward the palace. "Let's just destroy the initializer."

Below, several soldiers were loading newly positioned turrets, and personnel scrambled in and out of the building, but the palace remained, otherwise, untouched. "We're just in time," said Hanu. "They haven't bombed headquarters yet."

Just then, Garion doubled over, grasping his stomach with both hands.

"Are you okay?" Hanu rushed over to help, but Garion was already beckoning him toward the door. Donna had already landed in the lobby of Headquarters.

"Let's go," he said. "I'll be fine."

Hanu helped him to his feet and was heading toward the door, but then he felt it, too. In a heartbeat, his body was suddenly numb, then the feeling came back with an intense prickling sensation all over. His stomach dropped, and he thought he'd be sick for sure this time. Then, moments later, it was gone. He looked at Garion. "What was that?"

"I don't know," Garion slurred. "I feel a little out of it."

Then a sudden explosion sent debris against the side of Donna's hull, making the two of them jump. Dozens of people fled from the newly-formed hole in the main hall, pulling comrades along as they went.

"Alright," said Hanu, grabbing the bridge of his nose as he squinted through the settling dust just outside of the ship. His body was getting numb again. "Let's just destroy it from here," he said thickly as he spotted the case among the rubble of the toppled briefing room. "Pulverize it, Garion... like you did with those bars in the prison cell, remember?"

Garion straightened himself up as best he could, but Hanu knew he wasn't okay. The color had completely left his face. "Donna," he said. "Identify the vibratory frequency of the contents of this briefcase," he said, manipulating the targeting scanner from his console. Two compliant tones. "Destabilize the molecular bonds of the contraption," he said.

But whether the plans were carried out or not, there was no way to be sure. The briefcase remained seemingly undisturbed in the rubble. Hanu could only stare at it through his tired eyes. Then he collapsed to the ground next to Garion's limp body.

⧼·≺ ⧼·≺ ⧼·≺

Hanu came to, only moments later, to find that he was running up the stairs toward the palace. He faltered, missing a step, and scraped his shin along three steps. Thankfully his EAG bore the brunt of the impact and he was unharmed by it.

Andy pulled him to his feet. "Look sharp," he said, stealing a glance at the orb in the sky. It was barrel rolling out of the way of several blasts from the turrets. Hanu studied Andy with deep confusion, but allowed himself to be pulled up the stairs, nonetheless.

He tried to keep up as they navigated through the debris at the entryway. He followed Ester toward her circuit board. She cleared the debris from her desk top, then opened ten channels.

"Wait a minute," he whispered, realizing he'd already done this before. Hanu rubbed a hand over his chest, trying to quell a fresh wave of nausea. His eyes darted from Ester to the place where he and Garion had just been. Then he ducked behind an uprooted satellite dish, dry heaving. Fortunately, though, nobody witnessed it, because Andy had already run off to help Pants and Motley, and Ester was searching for the footage Deanna was streaming. He found the stray cable and tossed it at her.

Then he remembered the briefcase. He started toward the upturned briefing room, stumbling over himself as he went. He reached the briefcase and fumbled with its heavy locks. Then he dumped its contents onto the floor. Sand. He sighed a breath of relief, dropping to his knees. "We did it," he whispered through dry, cracked lips.

But more blasts from the turrets reminded him that the battle wasn't over. The orb was heading toward the residential area now. He could see it through the hole in the wall, descending awkwardly to the ground.

"Garion," he breathed. Hanu sprinted toward where the transport pad should've been and began to dig through the rubble. But finding it wasn't as easy as it was the first time.

"What are you doing?" Ester hissed from behind her console.

Her face was twisted with angst.

"We need to transport Garion out of there," he panted.

"The transport pad!" She popped up. "Hanu you're a genius!" She scanned the floor and spotted the thing just behind where Hanu was. They were swiping the rubble from its smooth surface when Ester hesitated. "How did you know Garion was down there?" she asked.

"A hunch," said Hanu, not caring to go into the details. He searched for the targeting scanner now. "Look, he's gonna get stabbed with the Nagi's venom, so we're gonna have to be ready, got it?"

Ester screwed her face up. "The Nagi?"

But Hanu was already beckoning toward James, who was huddled with several other intuits behind a communications console. James trotted toward them.

"Do me a favor," said Hanu, shoving the scanner into his hands. "Target the life signs on the far side of that field in the residential area. Transport the one that doesn't match the rest."

"What's a Nagi?" Ester asked, following him to the console.

"The alien, remember?" He was moving so fast, he didn't notice the confusion written on her face. "The lady with the yellow eyes."

The broadcast showed that Garion had already taken a few blows from Saleel. Twenty aliens surrounded the pair, watching Garion attempt to tackle the Luminous Great. Hanu called over his shoulder. "Now would be a good time to grab him, James!"

"Almost there," he said, pulling the tripod from the rubble.

Hanu watched fervently as one of the Ancient Ones stepped from the circle and grabbed Garion by the hair, snatching him away from Saleel. It was Agrigore. Several of the others attempted to stop this, but he pecked and slashed them away. For a brief standoff, he stood there with Garion in one hand, like a rag doll, posturing at the others.

"They're gonna stab him now," Hanu said. He shoved a jittery hand into the spare pocket of his utility belt. "I was hoping we wouldn't have to use the antivenom – " But it wasn't there. He searched his leg pocket. Nothing. "Oh, *no*."

Hanu searched the ground around the console, looking for the narrow vial. It was nowhere to be found. Ester searched, too, whipping her hair from her face as she scanned the ground. "What does it look like?" she asked.

Hanu groaned. "Just get him out of there, James." He turned back to the broadcast. Several soldiers were slinking onto the field. The Ancient Ones filed onto their ship with the alien that was holding Garion bringing up the rear. He tapped the console anxiously. "Hey, you need to get a lock on now, James."

But it was too late. The orb shot straight into the air and over the District wall.

Hanu watched the orb shrinking over the city and toward the Uninhabitable Zone, dumbfounded. "They were supposed to stab him," he said. He turned to Ester, who had been watching him with great confusion. "They weren't supposed to take him. They were supposed to stab him."

Agrigore's Resolve

Agrigore was becoming increasingly aggravated as the human ships continued their assault. He paced the length of the dim control room, barking orders at his subordinates. "Rotate the shield harmonics on the projectile and release it into the drum," he said. "And prepare to mount the next one once it's deployed." He returned to the weapons array, but not before shooting a cold look at the helm, where Saleel was sitting.

Agrigore had spent a great deal of energy preparing to lead this morning's ambush in the District of Operations, and he knew that in return, he would receive high honors from Command when they arrived. But Saleel was adamant about accompanying him, and he couldn't figure out if it was due to Saleel's lack of trust in him, or if he wanted to claim all of the glory for himself. Either way, Agrigore was terribly annoyed.

Once they were in range of the palace, with the surrounding grounds quiet and calm, he slammed the deploy trigger – probably harder than he should have. The first of the projectiles was a small bomb. The second would be an emitter.

The human ships maneuvered out of the projectile's way, some attempting to blast it off its course, but its shielding held. They continued with their plan, carrying it out with precision, rolling and ducking as necessary. They placed all of the necessary emitters with relative ease. Then, right as the Ancient Ones were about to retreat into the Uninhabitable Zone, a smaller orb appeared. They avoided a collision with it, but it gave chase. Agrigore clicked his beak irritably. He knew he'd have to put forth a little more effort to avoid damage from this ship. The smaller orb buzzed around their hull, like a bug, somehow forcing it downward.

"Report," he demanded. Several crew members scrambled to understand the malfunction. Then somebody was able to identify the problem.

"He's emitting a scalar pulse, Lord," said Xananda. The screen at her station was showing a partial diagram of the wave format. "It's degrading all of our primary systems."

Agrigore crossed the room grumpily. "Our shields are in place, are they not?" He stole another glance at Saleel, who had been calmly observing all of this.

"They've been completely disabled," Xananda reported. "And there's something else you should look at."

Agrigore made his way toward Xananda's station, bracing himself against her console as the ship was shaken by another blow. He examined the readings that were now populating on the screen, jerking his neck testily.

"There's an embedded carrier wave," he said. Suddenly he paused, clenching his fists. Then he gave himself a quick shake. "It's carrying a frequency, but I am unsure of what it means."

Tameus, who had been struggling at navigation, managed to

set the ship down without further damage. Saleel was the first to speak.

"It is a call," he said. He stood up and took a deep breath, looking rather feverish now. He rattled his feathers. "It seems the hybrid wishes to weigh himself against me."

Agrigore labored to suppress a hot wave of rage that rolled through his gut. He steadied his hands by holding them firmly behind his back. Then he cleared his throat and followed the Luminous Great down the main ramp.

By the time they spilled onto the field in the Residential Area, the entire crew was worked into a frenzy. Garion walked straight up to Saleel without wasting any time. "No interference from your crew," he said, eyeing them suspiciously.

"No interference," Saleel agreed. Then, without another word, he puffed himself up and lunged straight for the boy.

Garion narrowly dodged the swipe, bringing his elbow into the side of Saleel's face two times before the bird-giant slammed him to the ground. He moved with surprising speed, and was on top of him, bringing his fists down into Garion's face. Garion grabbed one of his arms, then wrapped his free hand around Saleel's neck, but he was in no condition to properly defend himself. He was still rather exhausted from his previous mission, and was quickly overpowered. The barrage continued.

Agrigore was careful not to let his primal instincts overcome him. He didn't care to join in on the frenzied jeering, hissing or rattling. He watched intently as Garion continued his weak attempt at merging, knowing that once the two had exhausted their physical strength, they would still have to face one another in a battle of wills. Every once in a while, the hybrid would land a decent blow, sending feathers into the air, but the fight was mostly one-sided.

Garion's energy was all but spent, and Saleel would merely have to take command of his will. But a strange feeling was coming over Agrigore. Something was twisting in the pit of his stomach; the flash of anger had returned, but there was also a terrible desire. He acted without thinking, grabbing the hybrid by the hair and clutching him closely.

The crew shouted their disapproval – screeching, clicking and tearing at his tunic – attempting to pull Garion from his grasp. He fought them off, hiding his own sense of guilt and confusion.

"I trust you'll have a most valuable explanation for your actions," Saleel breathed.

Agrigore's eyes darted through the grounds as he searched for an acceptable reason and, thankfully, he easily found it. A handful of soldiers were sneaking across the field, weapons raised. "My Lord, if we would have continued this, we would have been ambushed," he said, gesturing toward the humans. "Let's not forget that I command this mission. I will not compromise Year One for this."

The crew filed agreeably back onto the ship, regaining their composure as they went, and Agrigore immediately set them to work. "Engage thrusters at full-speed," he barked, dropping Garion's barely conscious body into a small cargo hold along the helm. "Do what you can to restore the shields."

Saleel returned to his seat and quietly nursed a swelling eye. They reached the Uninhabitable Zone within minutes and docked at the east end of the main palace. Then, on Saleel's command, they filed off the ship toward his private briefing room. Agrigore hung back, hoping to steel himself against any more public mishaps.

He busied himself, shutting down the orbs' systems, one by one, and applying the locking protocols. He was careful not to make eye contact with Saleel as he did this, and was forced to stop himself from interfering as the Luminous Great grabbed up Garion and forced him through the ship's door.

Once alone, he dropped himself into the central chair, analyzing his own mental state. What was driving this strange behavior? He was afraid of the answer, but with Year One so close at hand, he couldn't afford any more of these inexplicable impulses.

⪦·⪥ ⪦·⪥ ⪦·⪥

Garion fought against Saleel's grip, but to no avail. The Ancient One steered him with relative ease though the main hall and into a maze of passages. They descended a short flight of stairs and entered the first room on the right, where several others were already gathered.

The air was rife with a controlled excitement as the aliens busied themselves among the awkward machinery. Large tables, equipped with satellite dishes and portable consoles made up stations around an open floor, and three large cells lined one of the far walls. Saleel dropped Garion into one of them.

"Wait here," he said, barely hiding a triumphant smile.

Garion gripped the bars with both fists and glared at his captor, determined to stare him down. "I'm not finished with you," he said. But Saleel had already moved on to collecting reports.

"The relay network is functioning at ninety-four percent," said Jinora from behind a console.

"Ninety-four will do," he said. "And what of the secondary containment field? Can we achieve full integrity?"

Jinora bowed slightly. "Luminous Great, it's taking longer than we anticipated, but –"

"How much longer?"

Tameus, who had been programming a sequence of codes into a handheld device, interrupted. "It seems as though they've erected a structure in the Business District. It's blocking our signal from reaching the emitters in the District of Operations."

Agrigore studied the image on Tameus' holographic map. It was a pyramid. "Do what you can to bypass the interference," he said. "Once the emitters are online, launch the missile – for Capital City first. But remember, double containment will not be activated until the projectile is within a quarter mile of the City. You cannot pull the Intergalactic Council into the District until then."

Garion doubled over, suddenly winded. He'd done nothing to interrupt their plans. They were going to destroy the

Intergalactic Council along with everyone in Capital City, just as the Nagi said they would. "They're not gonna fall for the same trick twice!" He shook the bars, hoping to make enough of a distraction to hinder their activities. "They're not stupid, you know!"

But nobody bothered to pay him any attention. The crew continued doling out their reports.

"We now have access," said Jinora. "I have rerouted the signal through the surveillance towers; they will transmit the signal to the emitters."

Saleel nodded his approval. "Then let us proceed," he said. "Initiate the sequence."

Without hesitation, Jinora crossed the room and typed a passcode into the keypad of a computer along the wall. Then she turned on her heels. "The missile is now being launched toward the upper atmosphere. In thirty-six minutes, it will reach the District of Operations."

Garion squeezed his eyes shut, hoping it would delay the inevitable. He was watching Year One unravel right in front of him, and he couldn't do anything to stop it. But a distant roar told him that now wasn't the time to wallow in self-pity. He searched the room, hoping to find a way to sabotage their plan. He tugged at the bars, and was relieved to find how malleable they were – these cages were meant for much weaker beings. But he knew he couldn't just rip through them without a plan.

Thankfully, everyone was too busy at their stations to notice the slight blend in the bars as he thought up his next move. They were so busy, in fact, that they didn't notice that Agrigore had entered the room.

Garion was the only one who saw as the disgruntled alien shuffled toward Saleel, who was monitoring the bomb's trajectory on one of the holoscreens. His face was gaunt and a dull, green glow throbbed from his chest as he moved in closer. He clicked his beak warily.

Garion watched curiously, then the others began to notice, too. The room went rather quiet, and the air was suddenly thick with angst. But Saleel remained aloof, watching the screen as Agrigore stared down the back of him.

"Two challenges in one day," he said, slowly turning to face Agrigore. "But you know well by now that you cannot take my title by force."

"I don't care for your title," Agrigore snapped. "I want you to neutralize the missile."

Agrigore sneered. "Neutralize it? Have a change of heart about your beloved pets?"

Garion was watching intently, but it was growing harder to concentrate as a rush of elation swept through his chest. Beads of sweat welled up on his face, and a low hum was fogging up his brain. The others were feeling it, too. They paused their tasks to close in on the two of them.

It was harder to see now, but he could hear Agrigore's voice. "We've done enough to ourselves," he said angrily. "And we've done enough to them. It ends now."

Then without the slightest warning, Agrigore's body crashed

through the wall of onlookers and through the bars of one of the unoccupied cells. He quickly recovered, and was on top of Saleel in a flash.

Garion decided to forgo making a plan, and took this opportunity to bend the bars of his cell and slip through. He slunk behind a row of consoles, careful to be seen as little as possible by the jeering bystanders.

He peeked over one of the desks, uncertain of what he was looking for. It displayed a schematic of a large ship, twenty-three decks tall and almost six miles long; it was Command.

Suddenly, a foot crunched down into the console, right next to his face. He was frozen to the spot, afraid he'd be noticed, but all eyes were on Saleel and Agrigore, who were now pecking the feathers from each other's necks. Garion fought down an urge to watch the battle, reminding himself of what was at stake.

Agrigore was overpowering Saleel, making him dig his foot deeper into the console. He left a long, peeling gash in the paneling as he launched himself at Agrigore. This gave Garion an idea.

He crawled toward Jinora's station and removed the front panel, exposing the circuitry. Then, in one swipe, he snatched the wires out, causing the thing to spark and smoke.

He rose cautiously from underneath the console, nursing his singed fingers. The lights in the display had gone out, and the meters and gauges were no longer measuring anything. He sighed a breath of relief, knowing that at the very least, they wouldn't be able to pull the Intergalactic Council down.

Then he realized the room had gone quiet. He braced himself for an onslaught, but quickly realized that nobody would be pursuing him. The Ancient Ones were incapacitated. Their eyes had all gone white as their pupils rolled to the back of their heads, and their bodies were as still as statues as they huddled in on a single spot in the room.

Garion crept from around the console to see that at the center of it all, Agrigore was crouched on top of Saleel's chest, pinning his head down with two taloned claws. Their faces were mere inches apart, and they would have been staring into each other's eyes if their pupils hadn't also relocated to the back of their heads.

Garion watched, dumbfounded, but only for a moment. He took advantage of the opportunity this presented, and slunk over to the computer from which Jinora launched the missile. He studied the keypad, trying his best to translate, as everything was in the old language. "Come on," he groaned, attempting to override the launch sequence. He was able to pull up the command on the holoscreen, but an authorization code was needed to do anything further. He glanced over his shoulder at the petrified giants, certain that none of them were in a sharing mood.

Then, for a few scrambled moments, he racked his brain for another plan. But he knew he couldn't allow too much time to slip away. A clock on the console counted twenty-seven minutes until detonation.

Garion gripped the handle on the maintenance panel below

the computer and pulled hard, revealing a large circuit board and various wires and tubes. He kicked the circuit board as hard as he could, hoping that his boot would protect him from another shock, and with a violent spark, the lights on the control panel flickered and faded. He took a step back, wanting to be satisfied with his handiwork, but the distant roaring continued to grow. He hadn't stopped the missile from launching, and he knew it.

As quick as a flash, Garion ran into the hall and back through the maze. He skipped up the flight of stairs and burst through the double doors at the end of the main hall.

"Donna!" His eyes swept the skies, looking for the orb. She was nowhere to be found, though. He climbed the ramp to Agrigore's ship, but when he tried to cross the threshold, he was thrown to the ground by an invisible force field.

Garion pulled himself to his feet, dusting off his clothes with his singed hands and coughing through tender lungs. He fixed his gaze over the dry desert. The Ancient Ones would be busy for a little while, but Command was right on their doorstep. With a resigned sigh, he sprinted toward Capital City.

Year One

Donna was floating lazily toward the theatre, and Hanu was right behind her. He sprinted up a crumpled, uneven walkway toward the machine, but it was becoming more difficult to navigate around the people who had begun pouring through the gates and were now being ushered toward Headquarters.

He slipped past a group of elderly women, and was suddenly whipped around as someone grabbed him by the arm. It was Sadie. Before he could stop himself, he scooped her into a hug. "You're *alive*," he breathed, fighting back a tremble in his lip.

Sadie huffed impatiently. "We need to report to the rec center," she said. All of the mischievous playfulness had left her eyes and was replaced by rigid consternation. "That attack wasn't the worst of it. We're getting our orders now."

Hanu straightened himself up, giving her a serious nod. Then he glanced over his shoulder at Donna, who was now settling onto the theatre lawn. The ship was unable to find her pilot, and Hanu knew Garion would be in trouble without her. But there was no way he'd be able to deliver the ship to him and he knew it. Not at a time like this. He fought down the tugging sensation in the pit of his stomach and followed Sadie back through the crowd.

They jogged across a clearing toward the recreation center in silence, and Hanu was able to see the clear, blue sky beyond the District wall. His chest swelled as he was able to fully appreciate that he and Garion had accomplished their mission. He allowed himself a small grin, realizing that all of Capital City was alive. And now their only task would be to keep it that way.

Hanu followed Sadie to the recreation center, where a throng of civilians were crowding the front entrance. Sadie pushed her way through, making a path for Hanu and several other soldiers. Then raced past an indoor court toward the gymnasium, where hundreds of others had already gathered to replenish their ammunition and receive their orders. Dozens of team leaders bustled through the gym, accounting for their soldiers.

A stage had been fashioned up from the bleachers, but it wasn't Adam who was delivering the briefing. Instead, Paula was addressing the soldiers.

"It's going to take nine minutes to re-establish the barriers," she said. Her face was placid as she delivered the news, and her voice was just as matter-of-fact. "We'll be vulnerable until then. As for the technology that the Ancient Ones have driven into the ground, preliminary analysis reveals that they are field generators. We are unable to dismantle them at this time." She paused, allowing her eyes to sweep over the crowd. Her lips quivered as she faltered for the slightest moment. Then she steeled herself before speaking again. "Year One has come two weeks ahead of schedule, therefore we will be moving forward with Scenario Omega." She glanced at her wristwatch. "You have twenty-six minutes to complete your duties and return to the base. That is all." And with a swift nod, the soldiers were dismissed.

Everyone suddenly buzzed to life, moving swiftly and precisely. The soldiers filed through the doors in orderly lines and the team leaders radioed for their missing soldiers. Several of the intuits gathered at the front of the gym, putting their heads together as they whispered among themselves.

Hanu whipped around to Sadie, wide-eyed. "She means this is it?" he asked. "They're dropping the bomb, like, now?"

Sadie swallowed hard. "This is the real deal, Hanu." Though her voice was shaking, her grip was firm as she squeezed the back of his neck. Her lips curled into a nervous smile. "Let's give 'em hell."

Sadie grabbed a couple of guns from a nearby locker and secured one to her belt. Then she tossed the other to Hanu. And without another word, they filed toward the exit. Hanu squeezed his eyes closed, trying to remember where he was supposed to report in scenario Omega. His stomach had grown quite tight and it was making his brain go fuzzy.

They followed the flow of the foot-traffic until they were out on the open lawn. Everyone was clearing out quickly, jogging systematically toward their duty stations. Then, before he could say a proper goodbye, Sadie gave him a hearty slap on the back and disappeared into a large Convoy with several other soldiers.

"Twenty-six minutes," Hanu told himself. Then he gave himself a little shake, determined not to waste the time. He scanned the vehicles that were now rolling out of the parking lot from behind the building and saw a familiar face. Andy was flagging down a Nomad.

"Hey, over here!" Hanu yelled, sprinting toward the vehicle. "Room for one more?"

Andy clapped Hanu on the back as he approached. We were looking for you," he said.

Reggie, who was driving the Nomad, skidded to a halt a little harder than necessary and threw the passenger door open. Ester was already in the backseat, looking dangerously unprepared for the occasion in their white coverings. "Get in," said Reggie, "We're gonna have to book it."

Andy scrambled into the vehicle, leaving Hanu in the street. He stared uncertainly at Reggie, feeling rather faint. Then he glanced over the wall. "This isn't right," he whispered.

Reggie glanced impatiently at his watch. "Hey, this isn't the time to back out."

Hanu shook his head. His mouth had gone incredibly dry. "This is where we choose how we want to experience Year One," he said. He couldn't help but face the uncomfortable wriggling, squirming sensation that had been haunting at the pit of his stomach. The Intergalactic Council had lectured them over and over about their choices. Thalor told him that nothing had changed. Humanity would use its new dimensionality and make a choice. He was able to close a portal, cut the Ancient Ones' access to them off by choosing to forgive them. It was the path of least resistance. "I think I'm gonna try and activate the Living

Library," he said. "And that means I'll need your help."

Andy exploded into a fit of anger. "Are you crazy?" he said. "We've got twenty-five minutes until a nuke falls out of the sky. We need to evacuate those civilians out there!"

But Hanu was already waving down River, who looked like she was having a hard time finding a ride herself. "Hey!" he yelled. "Over here!"

"Get in," Reggie hissed.

"What do we have to lose?" Hanu said, ducking his head into the vehicle to get a better look at Reggie.

"Well, your life, for one!"

"We're gonna have to leave you now," said Andy. He moved to close the door, but Hanu grabbed his hand, stopping him.

"I've seen what happens if we lose this fight," he said. "And I think I'm willing to make that sacrifice, if it means we don't have to give our planet up to Command."

Just then, River appeared right behind Hanu, panting. "Are you guys headed to one of the evacuation sites? I need a lift."

"No, we're not," said Hanu. "We need to get to the Living Library.

"Wrong," said Andy. "We need to get to the Entertainment District and help with transports." And he made another attempt to shut the door.

Hanu was too quick, though. He stuck his foot in the Nomad this time, stopping the door. "Look, whatever the Hierarchy is going to try won't work," he said. Then he hesitated, looking at their harried faces. "In forty-two years from now, there *is* no more humanity."

"How would you know that?" Ester asked, her face screwed up dubiously.

"You don't see anything past today because there's nothing *left* for us after today," he said. "I've seen it."
She shook her head. "But – "

"Wait," River scoffed. "You're trying to activate the Living Library right now?"

"Don't you see?" said Hanu. "This is what the Intergalactic Council's been trying to tell us all along – it'll be us that transmutes the conditions of the planet. It's so obvious now!"

But River was shaking her head. "Hanu, if we tap into that generator and our plan doesn't work, we'll have wasted that energy. It's already depleting faster than it can be produced. It's powering both the barriers *and* the cascade. We will have left the Hierarchy with nothing to stand on."

Reggie drummed on the dashboard impatiently while Andy squirmed in the passenger seat. Ester leaned in on Hanu with an apologetic face. "She's right, Hanu. If this is a mistake, we'll have blown our last chance at survival."

Hanu wrestled down a writhing in his gut. He tousled his hair in frustration, gazing over the horizon. Then he realized the sky had begun to bulge. An unnatural fold was forming in the atmosphere as a very large something stretched into it, forcing its way through. The four of them watched in terror. Then, there was a twinkle in the distance as something caught the sun's reflection; it appeared silently, glowing faintly on the horizon.

It was the nuclear missile, moving toward the groaning distortion, ready to open the sky and let Command through.

Then Hanu had an idea. "Not if we use a different power source, altogether," he said. He jumped into the backseat of the Nomad, gesturing for River to follow. "We'll use the bomb."

Reggie whipped around in his seat. "What?"

"The bomb," said Hanu. "It's gonna release a ton of energy – enough to rip the sky. What if we used that energy to deliver the encoded laser blast? Then it can do that thing you were talking about – rewrite the atmosphere – as the matrix tries to repair itself. That's exactly what happened when the Provenience landed."

River scoffed. "This is crazy," she said, climbing into the Nomad. She checked her watch. "Hanu, we have a little over twenty minutes. We can use this time more wisely if we – "

"Look, we can use Garion's ship to house the mainframe. We'll take it up into the atmosphere and harness the energy from there."

"That won't work," said River. "That ship won't be able to house that kind of energy without being destroyed. It'll fall apart!"

Hanu racked his tired brain. He looked into the sky through the Nomad's window. "Reggie, take us to Donna," he said. "I think I have a plan."

Reggie looked at Andy, awaiting his silent vote, but Andy shrugged his shoulders in bewilderment. Then he looked to Ester, who shrugged a little more agreeably. A moment later, they were speeding toward the theatre.

It didn't take long to get to Donna, and Hanu jumped out of the Nomad before Reggie could properly park it.

"We only have nineteen minutes left," Ester warned as she caught up with him at the ship's door. She eyed the shimmering missile warily. "Whatever you're gonna do, it has to be quick."

But Hanu had already run into his first problem – he didn't know how to get into Donna, now that she had her door. He rubbed a hand across the ship's smooth exterior, unsure of where it was even located. He took an angst-filled breath. "Donna, doors please."

And thankfully, a ramp rolled from the ship with a cool hiss. The four of them entered the cabin, and Hanu immediately scanned the consoles. He didn't find what he was looking for. It didn't deter him, though. "Donna," he said, glancing over the white walls of the interior. "Since I can remember the Intergalactic Council landing on Earth, and the last mission we went on, then that means you can, too, right?"

Reggie and Andy exchanged confused looks with Ester. River furrowed her brows. Then she shook her head. "This is a ship," she said. "It doesn't have a memory."

Hanu ignored her, though.

Two affirmative tones.

"Okay, would you happen to remember the blueprint for the quantum funnel?" He drummed a console impatiently with his fingers.

River watched incredulously, her eyes wide and curious.

Reggie crossed the room, monitoring the sky through the door.

Two more tones.

"Good. Now, can you alter the matrix in the room to create the quantum funneling chamber and control panel?"

Then, after a few uncertain moments, the room transformed to reveal a newly installed console.

Hanu ran a shaking hand across the thing. "The funnel should keep the mainframe from collapsing. Now we just have to find it, right?"

"I don't think there's enough time," said Ester. She was at the door now, too. "That bomb is getting really close."

Hanu squeezed past Andy to get a look through the door. The missile was shining even more brightly now, gleaming ominously in the sky. Hundreds of soldiers scrambled in the distance, working to evacuate Capital City's citizens into the District's protective barrier.

River shook her head. She uncuffed a key from the inside of her jacket. "We haven't run out of time until it's detonated," she said. "Hanu, take this thing to headquarters. That's where we've kept the mainframe."

Moments later, they were in one of the lower floors of the palace tower. "I'm not sure if we'll be able to lift it," said River. She jumped from the ramp and placed the key inside of a heavy looking door. "It's pretty big."

Hanu sighed when he looked into the room. The mainframe was so large, he wasn't sure that it would fit into the ship even if they *could* lift it.

"This won't work," said Reggie, shaking his head pitifully. "How are we gonna…"

"We're in this too far," said Ester. She walked briskly around the machine, studying its design. She poked and prodded at the thing, then tried unsuccessfully to lift it from the floor.

Andy checked his watch. "Fourteen minutes," he warned.

"We need to teleport it," said River. "Does that ship have a teleportation pad?"

There was a jolt in Hanu's stomach as he realized the task would prove to be impossible. "No," he said numbly.

"We haven't run out of tricks yet," said Ester. "What if we activated the phase variance and moved the ship over the mainframe so that it's inside the cabin? Then, maybe, we can bring the ship back into phase and the mainframe will be materialized into the cabin."

Reggie scoffed. "Yeah, except we don't know how the bottom of the ship is gonna interact with the floor when the two come into phase. What if we damage the mainframe?"

Just then, Andy jumped. "Of course," he said. "We've already done it before. What if Donna scans the mainframe, and then duplicates the blueprint, Hanu?"

River gasped. "Like she did with the funnel!"

"Of course!" Hanu sprinted back to the ship. "Donna," he called from the ramp. "Can you scan the mainframe and use the blueprint to create a duplicate inside of the ship?"

Two cool tones.

"Okay," said Hanu. He climbed aboard and targeted the

mainframe with the scanner. "Scan it now, and replicate it inside the ship."

The four of them waited in silence. A low hum told Hanu that Donna was in the process of scanning, and though he was certain she would be successful, he couldn't help but hold his breath.

"We may not make it in time," said River, checking her watch.

But suddenly the floor shifted, making Hanu jump aside. He pressed his body up against the wall of consoles as the room shifted to accommodate the duplicate of the mainframe.

"I'm gonna have to borrow this ship when this is all over," said Andy. He folded his arms. "Garion really hasn't been using it to its full potential."

"Well, let's just hope we make it that far," said River. She scrambled to unlock the hatch to a small compartment on the very top of the original mainframe then pulled out a crystalline disc. "Don't forget the actual library," she said, balancing on the tips of her toes to hand it off to Hanu. Then she shut the hatch and secured the machine before climbing the ramp. "The mainframe will embed the information into the laser as it's produced. But we still need to find a way to deliver the pulse."

"Got it," said Hanu. But when she reached the door, he didn't step aside. "I think I'm gonna go alone," he said.

"That's ridiculous," said Ester as she moved to push past him.

Hanu kicked his leg out, halting her. "I needed your help,

and you helped," he said. "I'm not selfish enough to risk your lives."

Reggie raised a brow. "But Hanu, you – "

"It only takes one person to press the button," said Hanu. "You guys stay. I might not make it back, and if I don't, tell Garion I'm sorry about his ship."

River checked her watch irritably. "I guess we can't waste our time arguing you down," she snapped. "Are you sure this is what you wanna do?"

Hanu drew in a steadying breath, then gave her a nervous grin. "This is how I choose to experience Year One," he said with a definitive nod. "It'll be Year One for us, not them."

Ester squeezed Hanu into a tight hug. "Make it back," she said.

Hanu nodded. "Right."

Andy extended a hand, giving Hanu a firm handshake. Reggie clapped him on the back, a mischievous smile creeping across his face. "I always knew you were City of Fire," he said.

River sighed, folding her arms. "You're stubborn, you know that?"

Hanu gave a feeble laugh. Then he squeezed into the ship and retracted the ramp as soon as they stepped off. Then the door closed with a hiss, leaving him in the quiet.

"Donna," he said. "Take us into the stratosphere at twenty six thousand hertz, with a variance of one thousand hertz – full speed. There were the usual compliant tones, but he couldn't tell if they were moving or not. "Donna, windows on all sides, please."

It had never made Hanu sick before, but as the windows turned transparent, his stomach lurched terribly at the sight of the palace growing smaller. He was floating above the city in no time, staring down a grossly distorted sky. The missile was much larger from this vantage point, barreling menacingly through the atmosphere.

Hanu tore his eyes away from the sight. He moved to the mainframe, placing the disc into the small port along the top of it. It clicked into place. "Donna." He licked his lips. His throat was incredibly dry. "I need you to route power through the mainframe to produce an ultra-fast beam. Can you do that?"

Two affirmative tones.

"Is there a way you can deliver a series of pulses from the mainframe into the atmosphere?"

Two more tones.

"Okay," he said. "Before we can do that, though, we need power. "Donna, can you collect the power from that nuclear missile into the quantum funnel, and feed it to the mainframe?"

Several seconds passed, and Hanu thought he would have to ask in a different way, but Donna finally answered with two cool tones.

"Okay." He took a deep, rattling breath. Beads of sweat had begun to pool along his brow, despite the coolness of the ship. He glanced at the timestamp at the navigation console. Seven minutes remained. But he would have to act even faster than that, because the Ancient Ones were going to pull the

Intergalactic Council down at any moment.

He squeezed his eyes shut. "Donna, harness the energy from that nuclear bomb into the quantum funnel and route it into the mainframe. Then, use the mainframe to produce an encoded, ultra-fast pulse and deliver a series of these pulses into the atmosphere."

Then Donna was incredibly silent for a few moments. Hanu squinted as the light reflected off of the missile and shined on Donna's hull, then there was a crackling. He scanned the console, confused, then suddenly there was a terrible roar. A deeply orange light ripped from somewhere on Donna's hull and headed straight for the bomb. It blasted right through the thing, cracking it open and spilling radiated heat into the atmosphere.

"No," he cried. His heart raced, beating hard against his chest. He braced himself as the ship was wrenched backward. "I didn't say to detonate it." But Donna didn't seem to be listening. He groaned, struggling to pull himself upright again.

Then he was whipped forward as Donna shook and steadied, and Hanu realized she was pulling the explosion into her. Several alarms began to blare, but were immediately stifled as the ship's insides were warped. Dry, toxic heat leaked in. A violent jolt threw him against the far wall as Donna's hull buckled. He squeezed his eyes tightly as he slammed against it.

Then there was silence.

He had been pulled from the ship. Taken to another place altogether. He was too afraid to open his eyes to see it, though.

But it felt cool against his scalded face. And it was quiet. Serene. He was lying on his back. He groped at the ground and found he was in an incredibly squishy field of grass. The smell of salt air found his nose, beckoning him upward. He rose slowly, then squinted into the haze that permeated the atmosphere, trying to recognize where he could be. It was an unfamiliar place.

In the distance, there were tall, pointed mountains overlooking a sparkling ocean. The water lapped up against them playfully, spraying them with white, bubbling foam. The sight would've been overwhelming had he not been so tired.

Hanu ran a hand through his scorched hair. He couldn't bring himself to understand what had happened to him. Nonetheless, he took advantage of the calm, drawing in an exhausted breath.

"It takes all of the fun out when you don't act surprised," said a familiar voice.

Hanu whipped around. He grinned. Further along the field, there was a brown creature, with a wrinkled little face and wispy whiskers protruding from underneath a long beard.

The Living Library

"You."

The Nergal wore a deeply contented smile. "Me."

"Wha – *how*?" Hanu was incredulous. He dragged himself up from the ground and trudged toward where Yaar stood. "They said you wouldn't be allowed to come to Earth anymore."

Yaar gave Hanu a wry smirk. "Well, this isn't exactly Earth, now is it?"

Hanu took another look around. "No, I guess it's not," he said, noticing the wall of haze that surrounded the beach. It was both familiar and ominous. "What's in the fog?" he asked warily.

"Nothing at all," said Yaar. He gazed into the distance beyond the field. "But it could be something one day. Anything, really."

Hanu shook his head, confused. "So it's just blank?"

Yaar nodded. "Quite so."

It still didn't make much sense, but he decided not to pursue it. Instead, Hanu sighed deeply, incredibly relieved by the softness of the fresh air. His stomach no longer ached. "What is this place?" he said, bouncing on the balls of his feet. He looked down and realized he'd lost his boots. The velvety foliage squished between his toes.

Yaar watched the waves in the distance lap up against the shore. "I guess you can say it's a place in between worlds."

"How did I get here?" Hanu asked.

"You made a choice."

Hanu nodded rather seriously. "I chose to activate the Living Library."

Yaar squatted along the foliage, then beckoned for Hanu to do the same. "Our absence served its purpose then," he said, smiling warmly.

"But we haven't accomplished anything," said Hanu. A hint of apprehension tugged at his chest. He dropped down beside the Nergal. "We're actually right in the middle of Year One right now. At least, I think we are."

"The consequences of your collective efforts will now become quite real," said Yaar. He sighed, content to continue watching the waves wash along the shore.

Hanu followed suit, allowing the rhythmic sound of their crashing to lull him into a quiet thoughtfulness. He sat in the grass with Yaar, saying nothing for quite a while. Until he remembered there was something he'd been meaning to ask the Nergal. He didn't quite know how he would say it, though.

"You're breaking the rules by meeting with me, aren't you?"

A coy grin drew up Yaar's eyes. "There's something to be said about a healthy opposition to certain rules."

"It's not the first time," said Hanu. A jitter started up in his stomach, working its way to his hands and making them shake. The memory of icy knives tearing through flesh edged at the forefront of his mind. A stony fist squeezed his lungs. He needed Yaar to tell him it wasn't really his memory. That it was someone else's. He pushed the words out. "You did something to me, didn't you? Something you weren't supposed to do."

Yaar met Hanu's eyes with a steady gaze. "I did."

Hanu looked away, his mouth hanging open as if he were trying hard not to taste something very bitter. He didn't expect the Nergal to be so forthcoming. "Oh," he said. He cleared his throat, adjusting the collar of his EAG. He ran a hand numbly along the length of his arm. His suit was broken, gnarled in some places and torn in others, leaving parts of his flesh exposed to the elements.

Yaar watched the boy, a gentle smile reaching his eyes. "If you would like to have the memory back, I will give it to you."

Hanu stammered. Then he drew in a breath. "I don't know if now's the time," he said.

"Now may be the only time," said Yaar. He raised his eyebrows.

Hanu nodded. "Okay, then."

Then, without any warning, a familiar dizziness struck the boy. The edges of his consciousness were drawing in, pulling him into a black nothingness. And though he knew he was being swept into a memory, he fought it, because he knew it wouldn't be a pleasant one. But when he finally came to, he found that he was wrong.

He was wearing blue and yellow pajamas – his favorite – and sitting across from Yaar at a small but elaborate table. Rings of various sizes were drawn along its surface, inside of which were colorful marbles. His eyes swept the plain room. There were no doors or windows, but it didn't cause him any alarm. This was the room Yaar had always constructed for them to come and play.

Hanu cradled a nearby marble in the crook of his index finger. His hands were almost too small to do it properly, but he had been quite skilled at adapting his hand position to accommodate it. He flicked the thing, shooting it straight into a larger ring. Four of its marbles rolled free.

"Twelve points," he called, sticking his tongue into his lip as he stretched across the table to collect them.

Yaar's bulbous eyes twinkled with amusement. "Very good," he said. Then he positioned his marble in front of him.

Hanu jumped. "I forgot to tell you – we went to the movies for my birthday last week. I told you there'd be a surprise!"

"And which one did you see?" said Yaar. "You've been fond of *Duck Hannigan*, but *Haliburt's Heroics* was recently released." He flicked his marble with precision, sending all nine marbles from a smaller ring.

"Good one!" said Hanu. A thrill rolled around in his stomach, making him giggle uncontrollably. "I'm trying that move next!" He scanned the table, looking for his own shooting marble and found it parked right in front of him. He placed it into position, cradling it. Then he paused to look up. "I chose *Haliburt,* cause they give you a cool mask if you watch it. Mom says since I'm turning double-digits next year, I get to watch two movies if I want." Then he took his shot, sending seven marbles rolling sharply from the farthest ring.

"Thirty-five points," Yaar announced. "Your hard work seems to be paying off."

Hanu reached to collect his marbles from the table. "What do we play this game so much for?" he asked.

"Training," said Yaar. "It builds mental focus and acuity."

"How does it help me kick the Ancient Ones butt, though?" said Hanu. He dropped the marbles into his collection bowl with a loud clinking sound. "They're not scared of marbles, are they?"

Yaar's shoulders bounced as he rang an infectious laughter into the room. Hanu laughed along with him. Then, when they had composed themselves well enough, Yaar sighed. His eyes became serious. "It's not just about kicking their butt," he said. "It's about evolving to become something more." Then he steadied his hand over his marble and aimed for a larger ring. He flicked, then captured the four marbles that rolled free.

"Well, it's taking a real long time, isn't it?" Hanu said, positioning his marble to aim at a larger ring. "When are we gonna be evolved enough? I wanna play games for fun, not training."

"It will take quite a long time," said Yaar. "Another century or so, by the Intergalactic Council's count."

"How long is a century?" asked Hanu.

Yaar tilted his head, silent. It made Hanu look up from his marble. The Nergal smiled against heavy eyes. "Far too long to put off having fun," he said.

Hanu frowned at him. He crossed his arms stubbornly over his chest. "Why don't we just do that genetic upgrade thing you talked about? You know, assisted evolution or whatever."

Yaar looked away from him, focusing on his bowl of marbles instead. It was a great deal fuller than Hanu's. "The Intergalactic Council forbade it."

"So we have to suffer for another century?" said Hanu. He bent to find a good angle for his marble, sliding it slightly to the right. "Is that like twenty years? Thirty? I'll be way too old for fun by then."

"You must understand that humanity is a unique and powerful race," he said firmly. "Among your talents are a great aptitude for kindness, compassion and a capacity to love."

Hanu nodded. "Like how I love my mom."

"Right."

"And my teacher."

"Right."

Hanu beamed. "And you."

Then Yaar's eyes did something Hanu had never seen before. They glossed, then welled at the bottom with thick, brown tears. His lids laid heavy over them as his face contorted. Hanu watched the Nergal, alarmed, thinking perhaps he said something wrong. But the creature quickly recovered.

"Right," he said, smiling at him. "Your genetic composition is unfolding in perfection, according to your destiny."

"So I don't need the upgrade?"

Yaar's face was suddenly stern. Then he leaned into the table, much further in than you might expect for a creature so small. His face was close enough that Hanu could see the tears reabsorbing into the lining of his eyes. He opened his mouth, and it seemed he was calculating every word.

"Very soon, you will be made to forget our visits," he said. His voice was low, almost a whisper. "You will be made to forget that you are destined for more. But opportunity is always available to those who are proactive."

Hanu nodded. He stared into the creature's eyes, stricken by their intensity. "I'll never forget you, Yaar," he said, hoping to console the Nergal. "And I'll never forget our training. I'll help fight the Ancient Ones, no matter what."

The Nergal's eyes darted the room, though Hanu knew there was nobody else to be found. Then he drew in a sharp breath and spoke quickly. "To accelerate the shifting of your DNA – to give you a better chance at doing what martyrs before you couldn't – would require sacrifice." He hesitated, then his brows furrowed. "The process isn't pleasant. It would... hurt."

It was suddenly hard to swallow. Hanu's mouth had gone dry. "So are you saying you could do it?"

"I shouldn't do it," Yaar said. Then he nodded meaningfully. "But I would."

Hanu stared at the Nergal for a length of time before saying anything. A buzz of anxious excitement tingled all over him. Then he dipped his chin and took a ragged breath. "You should do it," he said.

Yaar squeezed his lips together, saying nothing for a moment. Then he stood, beckoning for Hanu to do the same.

Hanu scrambled to his feet, noticing how numb his hands and feet had gotten. His tongue was thick in his mouth, too. He took a steadying breath. He'd experienced pain before. Like when he fell off his scooter and scraped up half his leg. He had a knot on his knee for three days after that. And when his mother pulled out the little tooth in the front of his mouth because she thought it was ready to come out. She ended up having to yank it three times before it tore loose. He would be able to handle whatever pain Yaar would need to put him through.

Yaar stepped around the table, his eyes soft and remorseful. He placed a hand along the floor in front of Hanu and pulled the material upward until it stretched into a narrow console that stood between them. He touched the top of it and a compartment door slid open, revealing a beautiful green liquid jewel. It rolled around in the otherwise empty compartment, swiveling and folding and twisting upon itself.

"I share a sacred bond with this consciousness," said Yaar. "We have what you would call a symbiotic relationship."

Hanu squished up his face, but he didn't interject.

"It will assist in accelerating your DNA shift."

Hanu nodded. "Okay," he said. "What do I have to do?"

Yaar's nostrils flared. Then he squeezed his brows together in a pained grimace. "You must only touch it," he said.

With a slight hesitation, Hanu stretched an index finger toward the thing. It recoiled, moving away from him as best it could. But he persisted, shoving his finger right into the compartment with it. The thing chittered, then it shot a series of brilliantly green beams into his hand.

Pain immediately captured him.

Icy knives slithered down his body, cutting across every inch of his flesh. Then it pierced into him, tearing away at his insides. He clutched his stomach, then fell to the floor screaming. Hanu searched the room wildly. He needed his mother. He reached out to Yaar, but then the room suddenly went dark. He was being pulled from the memory. He allowed himself to leave quickly, relieved to have the pain end.

Hanu heaved and gasped, clutching the squishy foliage with both hands. Somehow he had moved several feet from Yaar and was hunched over on his knees. He coughed, then spit.

Yaar watched him quietly, apprehension tinting his face.

"You didn't believe I could do it on my own," he said, fighting to keep his breath even.

Yaar sprung from the grass and crossed over to the boy. "I believe you would evolve beautifully, in perfect timing according to your destiny," he said, stretching an arm out to him. "And it turns out love can make one quite selfish."

"I don't get it."

"One day you will," said Yaar.

"And the green thing?" said Hanu. He rubbed his chest. The pain had gone, but he was still quite jarred. "That was a Genesis Key, wasn't it?"

"It is mine, yes."

Hanu's eyes darted. There were a myriad of questions that were fighting for his attention. He stammered, then sucked in a steadying breath. "So you altered me," he said. "I remember most of that memory. I remember playing with you that day. Why don't I remember the Genesis Key part?"

Yaar's voice was thin. "You were distraught," he said. "Terribly so." He bent to sit next to Hanu, then watched him through wary eyes. "I offered to remove the memory of it from you until you were ready, and you agreed."

Hanu nodded, but he wasn't quite sure how he felt. He was relieved, he supposed, that his worst suspicions were proven to be untrue. Yaar wasn't evil, nor did he perform any kind of mind control on him. And he was curious. Did Yaar know he would eventually be imprisoned in the holding facility where the Builder conducted his experiments? Did he know Hanu would choose to defy Adam Lilley's orders and try to close the portal himself? He also felt a small pang of guilt, that the Nergal had faced serious consequences for it all.

He twisted into a sitting position, then tilted his head at Yaar. "That grumpy Nergal, Meni. She said what you did affected them all. Did everyone get punished? Is that why she was always so mad?"

"In a sense," said Yaar. He smiled sheepishly. "Our destiny was to assist humanity in its natural evolution until you reached a certain collective threshold. In return, we would learn from you. That was our duty to one another as a result of our initial intervention on your planet."

Hanu tittered a disbelieving laugh. "What could you possibly learn from humanity?"

Yaar's expression became very serious. "We've harvested quite a deep understanding of love," he said. Then he sighed. "And this is why the Intergalactic Council is furious with me. By accelerating your genetic evolution, I brought humanity beyond the collective threshold. I robbed everyone of what precious time they had left with their own charges."

A wave of anger rolled through Hanu, collecting at his face in a flash of heat. "So everyone let this war go on so you could learn about love?"

Yaar gazed calmly at him. "Not at all," he said reassuringly. "It was Cosmic Law that stopped us from interfering. And since I used unnatural means to accelerate your growth, I..." The Nergal allowed his voice to trail off as he gestured toward the beach with the sweep of a hand.

"So does that mean you're stuck here?"

The Nergal nodded feebly. "For a time. Until my destiny takes me elsewhere."

Hanu glanced around the beach, at the wall of constricting fog. An uneasy feeling washed over him. His voice was suddenly rather shaky. "Does it mean you're, you know..."

Yaar raised both brows, saying nothing to the boy.

"You sacrificed your life to help me."

The Nergal stretched his arms out in front of him, groaning leisurely. "You would have been quite old when humanity finally overcame the Ancient Ones," he said. "Far too old for fun."

Hanu's stomach sank. "And since I'm here, does that mean I..." He couldn't bring himself to say it. An incredible heaviness dropped into his stomach. "I won't be able to have nearly as much fun now," he whispered. "I'm sorry Yaar. I turned out to be a martyr after all."

Yaar beamed at the boy. "I don't have a choice in staying here," he said. "But as it turns out, you do. You can go back. Would you like to?"

Hanu looked into the Nergal's eyes. They shined, glossy with a hint of brown tears. He was suddenly aware of his heart beating fast. But he didn't answer right away. He breathed in the salty air for a few quiet moments. The waves crashed and broke over the mountainside. He licked his lips, moistening them. "I think it depends," he said. "Did the Living Library work?"

"Would it be so bad if it didn't?"

"I don't know." Hanu stood, allowing the grass to once again tickle between his toes. Yaar joined him. "It was a long shot, but I guess we still have the biomolecular cascade to fall back on."

"And would you find that solution agreeable?" asked Yaar.

"No, not really," said Hanu. "River said it would make it impossible to rehabilitate the environment afterward."

Yaar studied Hanu for a while, his wispy whiskers blowing gently in the breeze. "Then it might be up to you to help ensure there is an agreeable solution."

"I guess you're right," said Hanu. "Besides, I promised Ester."

Yaar smiled. "Then it is settled."

Then, before Hanu could say anything else – before he could find words for a teary goodbye or give the little creature so much as a handshake, the edges of his consciousness drew in, pulling him into darkness, certainly for the last time. Hanu fought against it, stammering, attempting to provide Yaar with a final word of gratitude. Then he relinquished control, knowing deeply that the Nergal knew exactly how Hanu felt.

A moment later, Hanu was being dragged from a transport pad. His knees buckled as he tried to right himself.

"Keep moving," a soldier barked, ushering him along.

He stumbled forward, gasping for air. He coughed through incredibly tender lungs, then remembered he had breathed in a large amount of hot, toxic air when Donna harvested the energy from the bomb. His eyes darted upward. He shielded them from the harsh afternoon light and, with a pang of guilt, he searched for Donna. The distortion was still there, looming menacingly over the city, but the bomb was nowhere to be seen. There was something new in the sky, though – an enormous, pulsing ball of light. At first glance, Hanu thought it was the sun. He squinted at the thing. It hung in the lower atmosphere, shining brightly as luminous waves rippled outward from it. He squinted, scanning the rest of the sky, but there was no sign of Garion's ship. He would have to worry about her later, then.

A quick scan of the area told him they were on a lawn just west of the palace, near the row of medical tents. He looked back to the transport pad to see that a steady stream of citizens were being transported in and were being ushered off the platform. There was weapons fire in the distance, along with the whining and whirring of aggressive craft movement. He wasn't sure what he expected, but he knew the Living Library should have changed something by now.

Perhaps something was wrong.

"Hanu, over here!" A familiar voice came through the crowd. He whipped around, trying to find its source. A mixture of relief and excitement and longing threatened to overtake him. It took a moment to spot her through the throng of terrified faces, but then he saw her. It was Vanessa.

She fought the crowd to get to him. He grabbed her through the throng and pulled her closer and she wrapped her arms around him. He hugged her close for quite a long time, then girded his stomach. It wasn't the time to slow down. "You're safe," he said to her.

"Where am I supposed to go?" she asked. Her eyes were wide and distressed. "I got separated from the Salcedos."

His eyes shot to the far side of the palace. She would be safe enough in a holding pattern there. But he was selfish. He didn't want to be separated from her again just yet – not after being apart for so long. He grabbed her hand. "Stay with me," he said, pulling her along. "We'll go to Headquarters. I need to figure out what's happening."

A minute later, they were climbing the palace stairs. Ester met them at the top, shock and grief melting from her tear-stained face. She grabbed Hanu by the shoulders, inspecting his raggedy uniform. "How did you end up here?" she asked. "I saw the missile explode. I thought you were dead." But she didn't bother waiting for an answer. She wrapped both arms around Vanessa in a long, tight hug before pulling the two of them further into the building.

Hanu filled the girls in on what happened with the bomb as they squeezed past scrambling soldiers. They made a beeline toward the tactical station. "I just don't understand why we're still fighting," he said, wrestling with a growing sense of unease. "Did the Living Library not do anything at all?"

Ester hesitated, pausing them. Her face was wearing an apology. "It seems not," she said. "Donna absorbed the blast, but that's about it. The Living Library's just hanging up there in the sky." She bit her lip, double-checking her watch. "The Hierarchy erected a new barrier a few minutes ago, and they'll be ready to launch the biomolecular cascade soon."

"That can't be," Hanu said feebly. Then he started toward the tactical station again. "They have to wait. It's up there doing something, right? Maybe they need to give it more time."

A moment later, he found a very stressed Adam Lilley. He followed the man as he scrambled between two consoles, doling out orders. "The Living Library's gonna work," said Hanu. "The nuke is neutralized, so they can't let Command in for now. Give it a chance."

Adam Lilley paused reluctantly, stealing a glance through the hole in the palace wall. The anomaly pulsed intensely in the distance. "It was an innovative plan, to say the least," he said.

Chapter Twenty-Three

"You tried. But I have to act swiftly to bring this thing to an end."

Hanu gritted his teeth. But he knew he would regret it if he wasn't persistent. "We've got nothing to lose by waiting just a few more minutes," he said. Vanessa and Ester looked at each other nervously.

Just then, River arrived. She leaned in on one of the consoles, catching her breath. Her eyes grew round at the sight of Hanu, but she didn't have time to address her surprise. "Mr. Lilley, there are already several environmental fluctuations that indicate the Living Library's working," she said. "Check your sensors."

Mr. Lilley ignored both of them. Instead, he beckoned to one of the security personnel. "Get them out of here," he said.

The soldier grabbed Hanu by the shoulder, and was just about to secure River when Paula appeared. "Don't bother," she told him. "He's just gonna come right back in."

The soldier raised an eyebrow at Mr. Lilley, who conceded with a reluctant nod. He let go of them.

"The cascade's going to interact with whatever's going on up there," she said, pointing through the hole in the wall. "There's no way to predict what the outcome might be."

Mr. Lilley's nostrils flared as he glowered at Hanu. Then he scanned his console, reading the data that was being produced by his various sensors. He closed his eyes. For a moment it looked like he would be violent, then he took a deep and steadying breath. "I'll hold off on the cascade for now," he said.

"But if nothing's happened in the next ten minutes, I'm launching it."

Paula nodded agreeably. Then Mr. Lilley began doling out new orders.

Ester turned on her heels and pushed her way through the scrambling soldiers, heading for the door. Vanessa followed closely in her wake. Hanu thanked Paula with a quick nod, then followed them.

They stopped short at the palace steps. Several people noticed the glowing orb by now, and had also stopped to stare at it. Hanu could tell something was, in fact, happening now because the light had begun to fade and the waves were now tearing from the thing in thick ribbons. The bystanders watched in awe.

"So what happened to Donna, anyway?" Hanu asked Ester. "Did she crash land somewhere?"

Ester's face bunched up. "Well," she said, her voice pitching with nerves. She grimaced at him. "That *is* Donna."

Vanessa's eyes popped open. Then she rounded on Ester with a question on her face.

Hanu's stomach grew rather hollow. "You mean the ship is *inside* of that thing?" he asked hopefully.

"Something like that," said Ester. She panted uncomfortably. "Garion's not gonna be very happy about that at all."

Hanu groaned. He paced the very limited strip of stairway, rubbing his temples. Then he dropped his hands. "Okay, we can't think about that right now," he said. "We'll have to deal with him later."

But Ester was wincing. She shook her head. "I don't think so," she said, watching something going on in the crowd below. "You'll probably have to deal with him now."

Hanu looked into the crowd as well, and noticed that Garion was making his way toward the palace. He parted through the refugees easily, as many of them scrambled to get out of his way. And not only because he was so much larger than them, but because his face was alarmingly bloodied and bruised, and he was swelling all over.

Hanu cowered behind the people in front of them. But Vanessa had already begun flagging him down. "Over here, Garion!" she yelled.

Hanu pulled her hands out of the air. "No, don't call him over here!" he hissed. He proceeded to hide behind Ester, but it was too late. A minute later, Garion was upon them.

"What's going on up there?" he asked breathlessly, gesturing toward the sky. But, thankfully, the conversation was cut short by a flash that swept over the horizon. Now everyone in the District was looking skyward as the Living Library flickered. Then, there was a squeezing sensation in Hanu's chest, and his heart had begun racing all of a sudden. The others felt it, too, and there was a collective moan that shivered throughout the courtyard.

Then something very interesting happened. Right above the Uninhabitable Zone, the sky began to twist and crumble. The thirsty atmosphere seemed to melt away, revealing a deep, azure blue that seemed to be hiding just underneath its surface all along, as if a barrier was suddenly disabled. It hurt Hanu's eyes to look at it. He started to turn away, but then he caught a glimpse of something else. As the wave crossed the sky to the west, a fleet of ships were made visible in the distance. They were small, hovering against the intensely blue sky over the Uninhabitable Zone. The crowd gasped, and there was a mild uproar as several people tried to run for cover.

"Oh, no," Vanessa groaned, squeezing Hanu's arm. One of the ships broke away and was approaching the District of Operations rather quickly. She squinted into the sky. "Is that Command?"

A tear escaped down Ester's cheek. "No," she said, smiling at Garion. "I've seen these ships before."

Before anyone could say anything else, she pulled Garion through the crowd and toward the clearing that was forming as the ship landed. Vanessa and Hanu labored to keep up, as people were less willing to get out of their way than Garion.

A number of brave souls gathered at the base of this ship, soldiers and civilians alike, so they had to squeeze through the crowd to get to the front. The thing was silver and mostly round, with knobby sensors and a myriad of antennae dotting the hull, giving the ship a unique texture. And, thankfully, it was far smaller than the Provenience; it nestled perfectly onto a stretch of road between the theatre and the remnants of the greenhouse.

A ramp rolled down the front side of the ship, allowing two aliens to emerge, causing pandemonium as the humans realized what was happening. The Ancient Ones descended the ramp, and approached Adam Lilley, who was now at the forefront of the mass. One of them was rather erect and proud; he had very few feathers, which bunched up in little tufts around his extremities and his scaled chest was luminous with a deep green glow. Hanu squinted at him, searching his memory. He'd never seen any of the Ancient ones *glowing* in all of his life. Then his eyes popped wide open.

These were the Deh.

Hanu's eyes searched the other one. He looked as though he was trying to make himself as small as possible. He bowed his head, looking at his own chest, which emanated a very dull green that was hardly even visible. Hanu squinted at him, realizing he was quite familiar. But how could it possibly be Agrigore?

Adam Lilley steeled his jaw. His hand flashed across his belt, finding his gun.

The first of the Ancient Ones raised a gentle hand. "No need to defend yourself, for we will not attack. I am Dharda, Ambassador to the Deh, and Primary Voice for this retrieval mission."

Mr. Lilley ignored his words, withdrawing his weapon anyway. He trained it toward the ground below him, holding it steady with both hands. He gestured over the District wall. "What's going on over there?" he asked. "What did you do?"

The extraterrestrial didn't bother looking over the wall. He continued to gaze warmly into Mr. Lilley's eyes. "We are not responsible for the transformation of your atmosphere at all," he said. "Cosmic Law has rendered your world unreachable for us, shrouded under a veil of distortion. Only now that *you* have lifted the veil are we able to interfere. And we are here to collect our counterparts."

"Too little, too late," Adam said firmly. He took a step forward, studying Agrigore's pitiful form. "We were perfectly ready to get rid of them ourselves."

"But you have," he said. Dharda drew back a massive, scaly leg and bent his knee, bowing deeply. Agrigore followed, bending even lower than his counterpart. "The Anuh have violated your planet for many centuries, and in unspeakable ways," he said. "We beg your forgiveness, and offer an assurance that you will not be coerced by our race again."

The muscles in Adam's jaw jumped. His eyes swept over the silent crowd and it was evident he was thinking hard about what he would say next. Hanu scanned the weary faces, too. Many of them were angry. Indignant. Filled with rage. Ester wasn't angry. Her lips quivered, her eyes soft and relieved. Vanessa wore a gratified smirk as she watched on. Silent tears traced the curves of her cheeks.

Mr. Lilley cleared his throat, ready to respond. "How could we do that?" he asked. He glared at the aliens. The red rings around his eyes were visible even from a distance. "How could we possibly forgive this? And look at you – " He gestured toward Agrigore, who re-doubled his efforts to lower his head.

"You're collecting them so they can just – what – walk free? Maybe do it again on some other planet?"

Several members of the crowd had begun to jeer, buzzing to life with a wave of anger. It quickly grew to a roar, but Dharda stood and raised his hand again. "We do not ask for your forgiveness for our sake," he said to the disgruntled crowd. And though he didn't raise his voice, almost the entire street heard him. There was a sudden hush. "We ask for your forgiveness so that your hearts may heal. We ask you to forgive what has happened, so that you do not carry a burden of resentment into your next phase of evolution. It will surely poison you long after we're gone."

Mr. Lilley stared at Agrigore with deadly focus. His nostrils flared. He shook his head silently, but he didn't retort.

"As for the Anuh," said Dharda, pulling Agrigore to his feet. "They will be taken back to our home world and rehabilitated. They will come peacefully, under Agrigore's guidance." Then the extraterrestrial looked over the crowd, searching. "We have but to collect one more individual – a descendant."

Garion shuffled dazedly from the crowd, with Ester's help. She nudged him forward, forcing him toward the clearing. He allowed her to do so, squeezing his lips together nervously. Vanessa and Hanu straggled closely behind.

Dharda beamed at him. "You have carried the hopes of your people," he said. Garion said nothing, stopping just short of where they were standing and allowing Dharda to study him through soft and longing eyes. Then he was on a knee again, this time bowing to Garion. "You are our highest hero."

Garion was taken aback, suddenly rigid. He glanced awkwardly at Hanu, who offered a confused chuckle. Then Adam Lilley moved, taking a knee as well, grinning at Garion. And since Hanu thought it was a fitting gesture, he took a knee, too. Many others followed suit, creating a wave as they lowered themselves to the ground.

Garion shook his head. He opened his mouth, then closed it again. Thick tears splashed from his eyes. He wiped his face with a torn sleeve, but it was proving useless. The tears continued to spill from his eyes and over his swollen cheeks. He turned in a small circle, acknowledging his friends with a nod. Then he swallowed hard and found his voice. "I can't leave without Donna," he said in a feeble whisper. His eyes swept over the grounds. "Where's my ship?"

Hanu looked away. His chest was tight as hot tears squeezed from his own eyes. He would have to tell Garion that he wouldn't be leaving with her, and that it was all his fault. He took a deep breath and forced himself to step forward, but Dharda was faster than he was.

"Her consciousness has already returned to us," he said simply.

Garion tilted his head suspiciously; his eyebrows furrowed. "Great," he said. "I was beginning to worry. Where is she?"

Hanu winced, shaking his head. He took another step after him. "She's up there, Garion."

Garion followed Hanu's gaze as he pointed into the sky. For

a while, his face was puzzled as he searched for her, but then it melted into a terrible grimace as he realized what Hanu was saying. "You mean she's – ?"

Hanu smiled apologetically. "I'm so sorry."

Garion whipped back around, searching for an answer from the Deh. He confirmed Hanu's claim with a swift nod. It made his shoulders drop. He went silent. Dharda watched him patiently, allowing him to grieve. Then a small and pitiful smile painted Garion's face. "I was always afraid she'd leave me here alone," he said. "But I guess I'm not really alone anymore, am I?"

Hanu's eyes darted over the horizon, his eyes stinging. "No," he said. "You're not."

Dharda made for Garion, grasping him firmly by the shoulders. He clicked his beak several times. Then he turned to Hanu. "No need for guilt," he said. He gazed toward the Living Library. "It was Donna's highest hope to carry humanity to this point. She has reached her fruition."

Then Paula, who had been watching from the crowd, stepped forward. "So will you be able to come and go as you please, now that the veil is lifted?"

"No," said the Deh. He gestured to Agrigore, urging him back up the ship's ramp. Two aliens silently descended to collect him. They secured him gently by the elbows, then they disappeared into the ship. "Earth is not meant to become part of the galactic community just yet. But you will be ready soon." Then he offered one more bow to Mr. Lilley and beckoned for

Garion.

Garion followed, but hesitated. His face was pained, painted with desperate confusion as he searched for one last glimpse of his friends. Vanessa was the first to move. She ran right up to him, squeezing him tightly around the middle without his permission. Ester followed, wrapping herself around the two. Hanu staggered toward them, but he couldn't bring himself to hug Garion. He shook his head, fighting down a protest. He glanced over at Sadie, who was wiping silent tears from her eyes. Her nostrils flared as though she were angry for being made to cry.

Dharda tilted his head, watching all of it unfold. He took a step toward the bunch, assessing them. "This planet has been your home," he said. "Yes, I see that now. Of course you know no other life, and you aren't sure that you want to."

Garion clenched his jaw. His eyes darted the crowd.

"I will not take you against your will," said Dharda. He dipped his chin, studying Garion with a kindness in his eyes that was far too unfamiliar. "You, Garion, may choose."

Garion nodded feebly. And for a while he said nothing. Then he smiled a wry smile. "I was just getting to the good part," he whispered. "I think I'll stay."

Epilogue:
The End of the Beginning

Hanu trudged through the quiet grounds of the cemetery. A gentle breeze accompanied him, encouraging him toward his destination. He resisted. He was in no rush to get to where he was going. He wound his way toward the plot, gazing over Capital City with heavy eyes. It had grown quite still over the last three years. After the wave of anger roared through the cities, there was fear. Then there was sadness. The masses were unsure of what to believe in anymore, and it showed.

But Hanu had his companions to believe in. They had all gone through the thing together, from the very beginning. And they held each other up in times of the most uncertainty. Not everyone was as lucky. And so the transition into knowing was a very difficult one for humanity. The disillusionment of not being as alone in the universe as they thought, while on the other hand being completely alone, sovereign, in constructing their own destiny was a curious juxtaposition. This was the next obstacle humanity would face.

A huddle of mourners marked a grave just up ahead. Hanu slowed his pace, unaware that he had come this far across the grounds already. He took slow and even breaths. The funeral marked the end of an era. This event would close a very important chapter in his life, and because of it, he would no longer be the same. So he indulged in these last few precious moments.

He stopped and admired a small tree that was growing alongside a thick headstone. He smiled, realizing that he'd never seen a sapling in Capital City before. The Earth had begun to replenish itself, with shy greenery arriving in unexpected places. Sidewalks began to crumble and break, allowing different forms of foliage to peek out from underneath. The Uninhabitable Zone still wasn't quite habitable yet, but in the radiation's absence, the ground softened and had become quite forgiving. Or, at least, it allowed what was already there to begin to thrive in patchy tufts of greens and reds.

Then there was a gentle hand, grasping Hanu's. He was pulled out of his reverie. He looked up to find Vanessa's smile. Her cheeks were rosy, kissed by the morning's cold. "It's starting soon," she said. "I'll help you."

He allowed her to pull him toward the front, where many of his friends were already seated in fold-out chairs. Reggie and Andy gave a solemn nod as he arrived, and Ester smiled gently as she wrestled with a particularly stubborn lock of Akesh's disheveled hair. Mrs. Salcedo busied herself as well, focusing way too hard on making sure Daniel's bowtie was straight. Daniel allowed this, staring off into the distance with a pitifully quivering lip.

Hanu allowed Vanessa to guide him into the chair next to hers. She rested her head on his shoulder. He brushed her hair smooth and planted a very soft kiss on it, thankful for her gentleness. Then he gasped as somebody right behind her fell to the ground. They all turned, alarmed.

It was Sadie.

"Damn it," she yelled loudly, pulling herself from the grass. Many of the onlookers gasped, and some of them moved to help her. But she nodded them away politely. She adjusted her dress, which was grossly frilled, and jammed her foot back into a high-heeled shoe. She smiled apologetically at the guests, trying to look as dignified as she could while she did this, then she slunk her way into the seat on the other side of Hanu.

"I fell three times on the way over here," she said to him, rubbing a small scrape on her elbow that had started to bleed. "I don't know why girls even bother with this stuff."

Vanessa chuckled, leaning in on her. "You could've worn flats," she said, wiggling her feet for Sadie to see her soft slippers.

Sadie rolled her eyes, grinning. "Well, I figured if I was gonna look like an idiot, I'd go all the way."

Suddenly James cleared his throat, bringing everyone's attention toward the enormous casket in the center of the gathering. He waited patiently in front of it as the mourners fell silent. The last of the stragglers took their seats as a soft, ethereal song played through a speaker. Hanu forced himself to look into the casket. He would not turn away from Garion at his last goodbye.

The intuit began. "It is with great honor that we gather here today," he said. "To celebrate the life of a dear friend."

Hanu sobbed, realizing he'd been holding his breath,

squeezing down an ache that was churning in the center of his chest. The start of the service had given him permission to cry, though, so took a shallow breath and allowed the pain to well up. It spilled out of him in the form of heavy, stinging tears. He cried into his hands, allowing Vanessa to cradle him. He was so consumed by grief, he could no longer hear what the intuit was saying.

A time later, when his sobbing had subdued, after he and Sadie and Ester and Akesh and Vanessa had all taken turns comforting one another, he realized the Intuit had been replaced by a different speaker. It was Cherry, actually. He scowled at her, confused by her presence. She stood there, behind the casket, wearing a lacey green dress. Her hands were clasped behind her back in a dignified way as she addressed the funeral. A few moment's orientation told him she was giving a speech.

He crossed his arms, then allowed them to unfold slowly as he drank in her words. She spoke of his passion and bravery. Of his gentleness and endless patience. And a regret that she allowed her own pain to drive her away from their friendship. Then, toward the end of her speech, she kissed her hand gently and set it gently on the lapel of Garion's suit.

Mr. Salcedo was the next to speak. He shuffled to the front, his face ragged and worn. He placed a small bouquet of handpicked flowers into the casket, then cleared his throat. Then he did his best to deliver Garion's eulogy.

When the sun rose considerably over the plot, and the service was over, he forced himself from his seat. He joined Ester, who had made her way to the front of the casket and was stroking Garion's ringlets.

"What are we supposed to do now?" he asked her.

She sniffled. "Not sure," she said. She looked at Hanu through tired, groggy eyes. "Live our best lives, I guess. That's what he fought for, isn't it?" But she didn't sound very convincing.

Hanu offered her a weak smile. Then he jumped, reaching into the pocket of his slacks. He pulled out a round, shiny button and held it to the light.

"What is that?" she said.

"It's a communication device," said Hanu. "A long time ago, I used it to call Garion. It's no good now, but I found it in his apartment two weeks ago." He slipped the button into the front pocket of Garion's blazer. "I want you to have it back," he said to him. "So you always remember our friendship; how we'll always be connected even if we can't see each other."

Ester leaned over the casket and kissed Garion's forehead. Then she smiled at Hanu and walked briskly away.

"I know what I'm gonna do," said Paula, who had been listening from the foot of the casket. "I'm gonna finally retire in peace, now that I don't have to keep you morons out of trouble."

Hanu smiled. "I thought you liked getting involved in our shenanigans."

Paula's face melted into a mischievous grin. She pulled Hanu into a tight embrace, hiding the tears that fell from her eyes. Then she sniffled, holding him at arm's length. "You've done well," she said. "You've all grown so much. I don't have to worry about you anymore."

Hanu nodded, allowing her to walk away. And as she left, he noticed someone else had been watching.

Kara Manel was standing at the edge of the plot, out of the way of the throngs of mourners that huddled together in groups. She smiled as Hanu made his way to where she was. He stopped right in front of her, still unsure if a hug would be appropriate. It had been a very hard reunion for the both of them. He settled with giving her a smile.

"You didn't have to come, mom."

She nodded gently. "I know he was a good friend."

For a while, Hanu couldn't think of anything to say. He stood there, watching a nearby huddle of people who were whispering pitifully amongst themselves. "So, where's Kait?"

"She was too afraid to come," said Kara. "She's never seen a... you know."

"I get it."

Kara rubbed her hands together as if warming them, then she drew in a sharp breath. "Would you like to come over for dinner on Tuesday night? I can make all of your favorites."

Hanu watched her fiddle with the buttons on her overcoat. She smiled at him, then cast her eyes downward.

"Yeah," he said. "That would be nice. And I guess I... I'll bring my girlfriend so you can meet her."

Her eyes lit up, lifting at the corners from a smile. "Okay," she said, nodding at him. "Then it's settled. I'll see you Tuesday."

Hanu was unsure of what to do next. He took a step closer and gave her a quick and tepid hug. Then he walked away. He allowed his feet to move quickly across the plot, though he was sure he wasn't ready to leave the funeral. Then someone called his name, stopping him. It was Vanessa.

"Dinner with mom again?" she teased, clasping his hand into hers. She allowed him to pull her along, walking leisurely toward where Ester stood with Akesh. "Lucky you."

"And lucky you." He smiled. "You have to come this time."

Vanessa stopped, forcing him to whip around to look at her. "Actually, I wouldn't mind that," she said.

Her smile crinkled her eyes at the corners. She was entirely too happy. Hanu exhaled, and he noticed that it was just a bit easier to breathe now. His chest wasn't quite so tight anymore, though the ache was still there. But it had subsided; taken a small break, as it sometimes did just long enough to allow him to appreciate the little things. He sighed. "I guess I'll be the only one struggling to survive it, then," he said.

Vanessa barked a laugh. "We've been through a lot worse," she said, pulling him onward. "I know we'll make it through dinner with your family."

❈·≺ ❈·≺ ❈·≺

"No problem can be solved from the same level of
consciousness that created it."
- Albert Einstein

❈·≺ ❈·≺ ❈·≺

About the Author

As a child in foster care, fiction stories offered Sasha the gifts of travel, perspective, and adventure. She graduated from Texas State University with a Bachelor of Science in Applied Sociology in 2012. An author and a social skills teacher, she currently lives in Texas.